OBSCURE

GHOSTMAKER BOOK 1

Krista Walsh

Raven's Quill Press

Ottawa, ON

Cover Design © John Wenzel/Chris Reddie
Model: Melysa Parent

Obscure / WALSH -- 1st ed.
Paperback ISBN: 978-1-9994923-6-6

To my friends in the Canadian public service.
Thank you for inspiring me and providing me the
tools to write my very own memo.

TOP SECRET

*To be included in and updated for the transitional departmental
material for all newly elected Prime Ministers of Canada*

To: The Prime Minister of Canada

From: The Minister of Supernatural, Magical and Occult Affairs

Subject: Transitional material for all branches within Supernatural,
Magical and Occult Affairs Canada

Established in 1867, Supernatural, Magical and Occult
Affairs Canada (SMOAC) is a self-governing federal department
that oversees eight supernatural branches running parallel
to departments and central agencies within the mundane
(non-supernatural) government structure (complete list included
below).

The Minister of Supernatural, Magical and Occult Affairs
serves as the head and ultimate authority of the department,
second only to the Prime Minister, with signing authority on
all projects and programs under [agreed-upon financial limit].
The Minister also serves as liaison to the Prime Minister's
Office (PMO) and coordinates communication across all
branches within the department and with Meril, queen beyond
the unseen wall (information on Meril, the unseen wall, supernatural beings and abilities, the perception filter and the realm
attached as **Appendix A** through **E**).

Per the *Supernatural and Mundane Leaders Accord (1867)* (**Appendix F**), the following departmental parameters are perpetual and non-negotiable:

- A budget, to be adjusted annually based on inflation and departmental necessity, for the maintenance, running and creation of supernatural programs and projects;

- Requirement of approval from the Minister of Supernatural, Magical and Occult Affairs for all mundane social programs and projects to ensure the preservation of secrecy and security of the Canadian supernatural population;

- Guaranteed and sufficient space for secret and secure supernatural resources, including hospitals, housing, government and military training;

- Cover to be provided under the mainstream department title of Domestic Affairs and Trade Canada; and,

- Limited communication between officers of SMOAC and PMO. Knowledge of SMOAC and the existence of supernatural beings to be classified as Top Secret on a need-to-know basis in order to ensure the safety of a vulnerable population.

Please be advised that all employees of SMOAC, and all those aware of the existence of SMOAC, are considered to be permanently bound to secrecy and will be in contravention of the *Security of Information Act* if they communicate any information about the supernatural realm to mundane society.

ENCL (**Appendix G** through **N**): Transitional material on active branch files involving:

- Domestic & International Trade
- Finance
- Policy
- Health
- Supernatural Special Forces & Security
- Research & Development
- Infrastructure
- Communications

Chapter 1

Jet

Anticipation buzzed through my blood like a hit of cocaine.

I couldn't sit still. Years of work were about to come to a head as my team of task force soldiers took on the Death's Head Syndicate, Canada's biggest supernatural crime organization. The feds versus the mob. Billions of dollars in drugs, smuggling, theft, who knew what other pies they had their fingers in, and we were about to take them down.

Soon. Another few minutes and it would be time to march, and I'd have to hold myself back from running in, abilities blazing, to put an end to every single one of the sons of bitches who had lurked so long in the shadows, rotting my city at its core.

Focus and strategy were what we needed today. I had to keep a level head. Lead my team. After, once we kicked their asses, we could let loose.

A hand rested on my shoulder, and I jumped, too absorbed in my thoughts to notice anyone entering the tactical van behind me. When I looked up, I found my lieutenant, Eric Sampson, standing beside me, his head and shoulders stooped against the low ceiling.

"Breathe, Cap. We've got this. No need to waste a good cup of coffee."

I scowled. "What are you talking about? I'm fine."

His gaze flicked to the space beside my head, and I turned to find three takeout coffee cups hovering over the table, the air molecules around them dense and vibrating. I gave myself a shake, and the cups settled without a drop spilled.

"All right," I said, spinning my chair around to face him, "maybe I'm a little wired."

"This is the day we've been planning for, Jet. I'd be worried if you weren't. I'm ready to run in there myself if we don't get started." He pressed his palms against the roof of the van, his blue eyes burning with eagerness. "First round's on you tonight, right?"

I laughed. "You guys better wow me if I'm racking up that much of a tab."

After all our years of working together, training together, climbing the ranks together, most of our thoughts could go unsaid. Like my absolute faith in the team we had handpicked and trained from recruitment.

"So what do you say?" Eric asked. "Are we ready to do this?"

I turned back to the pair of monitors on the table, one showing a collection of security feeds, the other set up to view body cam footage once the camera was switched on. "Have we seen them go in?"

"Jason spotted them about three minutes ago. A dozen heavy hitters. Some of O'Malley's toughs to protect the goods, probably. He didn't spot O'Malley, but that doesn't mean he's not here."

"We get him or not, it doesn't matter," I said, scanning the security footage. "All we need is for one of them to talk. Grab Zeke and Laura, and I'll meet you outside. Let's run through this one more time, then go rough up some bad guys."

Eric closed the door behind him as he left, and I took a moment to breathe in the silence.

This was it. As soon as I stepped outside, the play started and there would be no chance to hit pause.

Ready as I was to move in, I'd learned to appreciate the quiet before the storm, the opportunity to gather my thoughts, run through the plan, and imagine the victory. O'Malley's people rounded up like cattle with their hands all over the evidence, thrown behind bars with no defence to hide behind. Their one bargaining chip would be to deliver O'Malley to the department on a silver platter.

I smiled and relaxed in my chair. We had this. Now to make it happen.

I rose to my feet in the cramped space of the van and pulled a Kevlar vest over my black T-shirt and fatigues. The narrow patch on the left side of my chest read *Dawson*, the patch on my back read *SMOAC*, the letters of both peeling and faded. It was the downside of working for a government department only a small percentage of the population knew about. Supernatural, Magical and Occult Affairs Canada was not a subject of discussion across mundane news sources, and the lack of popularity meant a pathetically tiny budget for equipment. Two weeks ago, we'd upgraded the tech in our detainment centre for the first time in a decade, and I appreciated the timing. All the better to show these bastards the full SMOAC hospitality.

On my right shoulder was a custom patch: a wolf wearing a jetpack. Mandy, one of my newer recruits, had designed the logo last year to represent our squad. My wolves—my pack—and today they would make me proud.

Kitted up, I pulled my shoulder-length brown hair into a messy bun, patted the service revolver at one hip and my curved knife at the other, and puffed out one last breath. "All right, Dawson. Go time."

I stepped outside to find Eric waiting with two of my longest-serving troops. Zeke stood almost six-and-a-half feet tall, thick and square-jawed. A metal baton sat at his hip, and he tapped his fingers against it in a familiar rhythm. Beside him stood Laura, a tiny woman easy to underestimate—an appearance she used to her advantage.

"How are we feeling?" I asked.

Zeke grinned. "In the mood to pound some syndicate scum into the concrete."

"And haul in enough powder to put the entire ghost industry out of business," Laura said.

Zeke shrugged. "Yeah, that, too."

"Both sound like a win to me," said Eric, and I couldn't disagree.

Named after its fine white consistency and high mortality rate, ghost was the latest trend in supernaturally touched pharmaceuticals. A pinch was enough to do the trick, a few milligrams the difference between a great trip and a short life. Popular among mundanes who wanted to peer behind the veil and liven up their boring nine-to-five existence and supernaturals who wanted to tap into their full strength, even if only for a few minutes.

And they got it, all right. That flash of life. They learned just how terrifying the world could be right before their lungs shut down and they choked to death on nothing but air. We'd already had over a thousand ODs this year, and it was only June.

To have the syndicate crushed and the country's favourite street drug squashed in a single afternoon? It would be the win of the decade—not to mention of my career.

"Okay," I said, "run me through our morning."

Zeke pulled his shoulders back, and his smile faded as he slipped into mission mode. "Laura and I lead the squad into the building, me through the garage."

"Me through the service entrance at the back," Laura said.

"We have eyes on twelve of O'Malley's lackeys heading down the stairwell to the subbasement," Eric interjected, "so we know they're right where we want them."

Laura nodded and continued, "We head down the stairs at both entrances, penning them in."

"You and I bring up the rear," Eric said, "wrangling the troops and redirecting any muns who try to pass through the lobby."

I knew he was disappointed not to lead the mission. His supernaturally perfect aim had turned him into a cowboy over the years, and he loved nothing more than playing hero, but today I wanted him at my side. For one thing, I suspected the greater threat would come from the rats who tried to scatter out of the meeting when my guys busted in. For another, the last thing we needed was a bunch of mundanes poking their noses into our business. I needed someone with me who wouldn't cower if Mrs. Hoity-Toity from the penthouse got in their face.

"Once you give the signal," Zeke went on, "we enter the subbasement. A one-two wave with snake formation, flash-bang to stir them up, fan out around the room, close in."

"I go in high, McNeil goes in low," Laura said as she jerked her chin over my shoulder. I turned to find Jared, our water-shifter, doing a few warm-up stretches behind the van, turning his foot into a puddle and solidifying it again.

"While I lead the ground forces to round the bastards up,"

Zeke finished.

"As soon as we've nailed them to the floor," said Eric, "we take them out through the service entrance at the back and load them into the paddy wagon to take them for processing."

I nodded as he wrapped up the steps we'd spent months putting together. It sounded so simple. So straightforward. Just the way I liked it. "Let's get moving and make it happen."

We broke up, and Zeke whistled between his teeth, summoning the rest of our twenty-soldier unit. With barely a word, they broke into their assigned teams, Zeke leading one set of six, Laura the other.

Left with me were my remaining five troops. Eric, Sara, and Xander would stick with me to monitor the lobby, Katie and Adam would remain in the van to watch the security cameras and reroute the footage to our private SMOAC servers, ensuring no evidence of our mission fell into the wrong hands. Jason was already stationed on a nearby rooftop, sniper rifle in hand, ready to stop anyone who made it past our defences.

Every base covered.

"All right, Katie, Adam, show me what we're dealing with."

I followed them back into the van, and Katie took over the console, bringing up the six security cameras across a single screen. I crouched over Katie's shoulder to better see the tiny images.

"This footage is from twenty minutes ago," she said as she scrolled through the feed. "You can see O'Malley's men coming in through the back door here." She pointed at the screen. They came in by twos and threes, with the occasional solo guy dragging his feet. As though they were independently visiting residents in the building. Each batch paused at the intercom, waited to be buzzed in, then passed through to the lobby, but instead of heading left to the elevators, they continued straight across and entered the stairwell.

"The stairwell feed is over here," Adam said, and pointed to the square in the top right corner of the screen. "You can watch them go down… down… down… and disappear. Based on our earlier check, the security cameras stop at the parking lot. The subbasement is a blackout zone."

"Of course it is," I said. I suspected the owners of the building didn't realize the space existed—it was standard practice for supernatural architects to add an addition to a completed design as a safeguard. The city was riddled with underground storerooms and passages like this one. Anything to give supernaturals a place to hide if the world shifted and the mundanes came after us.

With Zeke's report confirmed—not that I didn't trust him, but I always preferred to see things for myself—my last pieces fell into place.

"You guys keep your eyes on those screens," I said. "Anyone else shows up, or you notice anything wonky with the connection, you let me know. I don't trust O'Malley not to play some last-minute trick, redirect the feed himself to keep his people from being found out."

"Yes, ma'am," Adam said, and scooched around me to pull out the second chair in front of the monitors. "Anyone moves a foot towards those doors, we'll let you know."

"We'll keep eyes on the lobby, too," Katie said. "No one will come close without you getting a heads-up."

I patted them both on the shoulder and left them to it.

"Hughes," I spoke into the comms system, "you in place?"

"Getting bored up here, PL," Jason said into my ear. PL. Packleader. Their nickname for me when they felt like being nice. "We ready to get this show on the road?"

"All goes well, you're going to stay bored until we're clear."

"Long as we bring these assholes down, I'll grin and bear it."

I smiled and tilted my head back to suck in the cool morning air. My lungs full, my heart racing, I walked towards the condo building. Eric fell into step behind me with Sara and Xander, and together we entered the foyer. I rested my hand on the door handle and pulled, but the door stayed put.

"Give me a moment," Katie said in my ear. "And… there."

The lock buzzed, and a moment later we were in the polished main lobby. My boots squeaked against the marble, and my face reflected in every surface of the high-polished room. It felt more like a museum than a residence. I half-expected to see *Do not touch* signs on everything within reach.

"Status?" I asked.

"In position," Zeke said.

"In position," said Laura.

We crossed the lobby and caught up with the back of Zeke's team. He caught my eye, I nodded, and he opened the door to the stairs.

"Move in," I said to Laura.

"Roger that," she replied, and in a smooth motion, Zeke started down the stairs.

His team zigzagged left to right like a wriggling snake as they headed towards the basement. It was probably an unnecessary precaution in the tight stairwell, but I wasn't taking chances. O'Malley had proved more than once that he was able to pivot in response to SMOAC's attempts to bind him, and I didn't want my guys taking more of a hit than they had to.

Sara and Xander tacked on to the end of his team but would stay near the service door, and Eric and I held firm where we were, maintaining a solid view of the lobby and the hallway leading to the back entrance.

While we waited, Eric pulled a small handheld monitor out of his chest pocket. He switched the power on, and Zeke's body cam footage came into view. Together, we watched his progress, past the point where the mundanes believed the stairwell ended to the closed door at the bottom that led to a room roughly twenty feet by thirty according to our earlier reconnaissance. The room would have been intended as a waiting space, somewhere for supernaturals to hide while the mundane heat died down, or to gather before they evacuated through the rear entrance.

Sometimes, it turned out, the room was used for less legitimate purposes. How many other subbasements across the city had O'Malley claimed as his own? How many seemingly innocent spaces had been used to hand off ghost or other smuggled goods?

Red flared in my vision as the hand of rage gripped me, but I did my best to breathe through it. The son of a bitch ruined everything he touched, a cancer in our city. I couldn't wait to throw him into a cell and close the door behind him. My greatest struggle would be not wrapping my hands around his throat before I did.

As the last of Zeke's team disappeared down the stairs, I stepped closer and brushed my fingers over the faint ridges that marked the centre of my forehead. My third eye, my secondary ability to read the recent past of whatever I came in contact with, stirred and opened.

The security footage confirmed Zeke's report that twelve people had gone downstairs, but I wanted to take a closer look now that I was here in person. Was O'Malley among the twelve? Could we be that lucky?

The possibility sent a vibration through my veins. If that were the case, if we were able to bring him down without making any deals, then Eric was damn right the first round at the bar would be on me. He'd stand a good chance of talking me into covering the entire night.

With my physical eyes closed, I replayed the past few minutes in the lobby, watching the shadowy figures of Zeke's half of the team head down the stairs. Back further, a few strangers wandering the lobby. One of them going into the stairwell. Further still. Further. Further, the visions fading as more time passed. The night-shift security guard doing his rounds.

I frowned. That wasn't right.

I moved forward in time, scanned every face that passed me by, the details growing clearer the more recent they were.

No sign of the people I'd seen on the security footage.

A stone formed in the pit of my stomach. Their presence on the footage ruled out any invisibility cover, so where the hell were they?

"We've reached B position," Laura said through my earpiece, her voice low. "I hear voices."

Voices had to mean there were people inside even if I couldn't detect them. So why was the rock in my gut getting heavier?

Through the body cam, I watched Zeke pull the metal baton from his belt and hold it out in front of him. It stretched and twisted into a strong, thin shield that covered him from head to knee. His ability to manipulate metal made him the perfect lead—any metal inside the room and he would be able to bind the dealers to the walls before they had time to attack. No matter what awaited us on the other side, we could handle it.

I hesitated only a moment longer before I gave the order. "Move."

Zeke pushed the door open on his end, and I imagined Laura following suit on the other, lifting off the floor as she drifted towards the ceiling, ready to fly overhead and catch her prey off guard from above. McNeil would slither in, the unseen puddle underfoot.

Inside, O'Malley's lackeys had gathered in the centre of a brightly lit space that had been turned into a sort of boardroom. Large table, a dozen chairs. Beige walls, abstract art, faded red carpet.

My mind stuttered. Our recon had reported an empty room. Nothing but concrete.

What the fuck is going on here?

Zeke threw in the flash-bang, and the view on the monitor blurred as smoke filled the enclosed space.

Through the fog, the truth revealed itself. The room should have been obscured behind the smoke, hidden from the camera.

Instead, the people, the conference table, the artwork stood out as clear as ever, unaffected by the noise or choking fog. A room of illusions.

I started down the stairs before I could second-guess myself.

"Stand down!" I ordered, but the command was buried under bursts of sound in the subbasement.

Who did O'Malley have on his team that could carry off an illusion this massive?

"Jet!" Eric called out behind me, but I didn't stop. Whatever was happening in that room, my team was in danger, and I wasn't about to let them face it on their own.

I heard Zeke through my earpiece shouting the order to get on the ground. Repeating the command when no one complied.

Sara and Xander stared at me as I passed them, then fell into step behind me.

"Illusions," I said. "The *fuckers.*"

There must have been signs on the security footage, but I hadn't seen them. Had only seen what I'd wanted to see—what O'Malley knew we wanted to see: the syndicate walking into my hands.

I rounded another flight of stairs, passed the basement.

The son of a bitch had played us.

I reached the subbasement door, which was still standing open behind half my team, and burst into the smoky space.

But I was too late to warn them that the illusions weren't the threat. Zeke rushed in, using his metal shield as a battering ram. One illusion burst out of its skin, transforming into a thick-hided worm that slithered towards him. Still others charged, teeth bared, claws at the ready.

Luvy drew a ball of fire between her palms and launched it at the worm.

Sara moved to my side, lightning charged between her fingers, and Xander was mid-change, thick blue scales covering half his face. Eric took his place on my right with his service weapon drawn.

He fired, and with his supernatural aim, the bullet struck the closest illusion between the eyes. The man vanished.

"What the fuck…" Eric said.

"They're not real!" I shouted, trying to be heard over the noise, but only the three around me held their fire.

One by one, as my team's blows struck, the illusions disappeared until only one person remained, huddled in the corner. I recognized him as one of O'Malley's low-ranking thugs.

Alone in the room, facing my team of seventeen, he straightened from his crouch.

And smiled.

The triumphant gleam in his eyes, the sly upturn of his lips, turned my blood to ice.

He should have been horrified his gambit had failed. Embarrassed at the very least. Had he and O'Malley planned this? Was he the lamb thrown to the wolves so O'Malley could escape our hold? Was that why, even though we'd caged him, he looked as pleased as if he'd won?

I stepped forward and called to him over the heads of my team, who were still adjusting to the changing face of the battle. "What do you say, Weldon? Are you going to come quietly?"

His grin widened, and a voice filled the air. Not Weldon's. An even greater taunt.

"Captain Dawson, nice to see you," O'Malley said, and I searched the ceiling for the camera, finally spotting it in the top corner above the door. "Sorry I couldn't be there, but I double-booked myself. I hope our gift makes up for it. It's what you were looking for, I think?"

He went quiet, and I scanned the room, wondering what the hell he was talking about. There was nothing but us and his thug. What gift?

As I met his lackey's eye, Weldon nodded at me and touched his fingers to his brow in a mock salute.

And then, as though someone flicked a switch, he disappeared, along with the conference table and chairs, the artwork, the ugly carpet. Instead of standing in a boardroom, I found myself near the doorway of an empty concrete space draped in plastic wrap. It covered the harsh fluorescents that hung from the ceiling and the vents near the floor.

In the pools of light, at home in the middle of the room and the only remaining touch of boardroom, was an office chair. A box three feet by four rested on the seat, filled with plastic pouches of white powder. Ghost. It had to be. A shit-ton of ghost.

Taped to what was very clearly a bomb.

"Get out," I ordered. "*Move!* Everyone out *now!*"

My team listened, not hesitating a moment to shift towards the doorways, but we weren't fast enough.

We never would have been fast enough.

The bomb went off. No noise. No earth-shattering vibration. Just a faint *snap* as the plastic bags burst and a puff of white cloud as the powder went airborne, the drug so fine it drifted through the air like particles of fairy dust.

My instincts took over. Stretching out my arms, I sank deep into my ability, connected every cell of my being to the pure oxygen molecules around me, and lashed them together in a dense weave that stretched the width and height of the room. I pushed harder, drawing the weave closer, tighter, creating a wall that separated me and everyone behind me from the madness on the other side.

Eric, Sara, and Xander were safe, but the others had been too close to the bomb for my shield to protect them. In front of me, as the powder filled the air, Saaqib's eyes rolled back in his head, and he collapsed to the ground in convulsions strong enough that blood leaked out of his mouth, his nose, his ears. Ellison's eyes flew wide, and his skin thickened into rough hide in time to deflect a blow from Renée, whose fingernails had extended into knife-sharp claws ready to tear him apart. Laura lost control of her flight and slammed into the plastic-covered concrete. Blood oozed from her skull as she slumped to the ground and fell into convulsions. She soon lay still.

Forced to watch as my team either succumbed to the drug or had their systems superpowered before their brains over-loaded, I fought to maintain the wall.

The air strained against my control, each atom want-ing space, but I exerted my will to hold it steady. My muscles screamed with the effort, joints locking until I was sure they'd snap. Still I held on. I had to. If this was all the help I could give, I wouldn't release my grip until the ghost either settled or killed me.

My heart raced, my pulse throbbed in my ears. I felt as though I were trapped in a time loop, doomed to replay the last few minutes a dozen times a second as I held the wall in place. At every repeat, I thought of something I could have done differently, every possibility branching into thousands of alternate outcomes. All of them as useless as the exit behind me.

I couldn't escape. I couldn't let the drug leave the room. There were too many people in the building. If the ghost reached the ventilation system, there would be no stopping it. So many more people, mundane and supernatural, would die.

I shoved my arms forward, forcing the wall back and containing the little flecks of white powder that danced and fluttered, so eager to reach me and everyone behind me, to crawl inside us and play jump rope with our brain chemistry.

"Jason, come in," Eric yelled behind me, and I did my best to hold on to my concentration through his rigid panic.

"Ready," Jason said through my earpiece.

"Call HQ," Eric ordered. "We're going to need people stat. Bomb squad, medics, containment, PR. *Everybody*. Have our liaison team reach out to the mun cops to clear the area. Push the perimeter back five blocks, close the roads."

"Roger." The line went quiet except for some muffled voices in my ear, and less than a minute later, Jason came back.

"What reason do we give?"

Eric's pause before he answered, as though he were hunting for the right words to describe the impossibility we faced, hit me like a punch to the gut. "O'Malley strapped a few kilos of ghost to a bomb. There was no meeting. Just a room full of powder, and it's mobile."

A moment of silence. "Shit."

Then Jason was gone, and my attention returned to the ghost as it tried to work its way around my hold.

Ellison had fallen. Renée. Zeke. Tina. Court and Rak fought each other, Court's demon venom spewing out while Rak's super speed kept him one step ahead. Until Rak stumbled, his throat growing taut, bursting with purple veins as his airways closed. His face turned red, his eyes bloodshot, and he collapsed to the ground. Court spat out a wad of venom that hit Rak in the face and burned through his cheek, but then Court was down as well, gasping for air.

I made myself watch it all, unable to help, unable to stop them, and too soon I lost track of who was who. Some bodies were sprawled across the floor, unmoving or trapped in convulsions, their faces so bloated I couldn't recognize them. From those still standing, shots rang out, knives flashed, abilities raged. For them, until they fell, there was nothing but treachery in every corner, accompanied by magic so heightened they had never been so powerful—until their brains gave out.

"Jet, come on," Eric said in my ear. "You need to back

away. We need to get out of here."

"You go. I need to stay here—hold this back—keep the air clear until the perimeter's moved. The colonel's on his way, he'll know what to do out there. Help Jason. Evacuate the building."

"Jet, I—"

"Go, Eric," I said, needing him to believe he wasn't abandoning me if he left. He wanted to follow our training, but none of our training had prepared us for this.

Still he paused. I wished I could turn to look at him, see his reaction, his face, in case I never had another chance. But I had to stay focused. I couldn't lose control for a moment or we would be as dead as the others.

Finally, though, he stepped away from me and turned to Sara and Xander. "You heard the captain. Get word out—we need to clear these apartments and empty the area."

Soon I was alone behind my invisible shield. The only survivor in the room as the others fought to their deaths. Their only witness. Their useless captain.

I clenched my teeth until the muscles in my jaw popped. Sweat beaded on my brow, but I held my stance and kept the air steady in front of me. The screams of my remaining team continued, rising in agony and despair as they came closer to their end.

I wanted to close my eyes and block them out, but to do so would be to abandon them at the last, and I couldn't do that. Not when being here with them was all I had to give. I couldn't help them. No matter how much I wanted to push this wall forward until I reached them. I couldn't control the ghost if my concentration slipped, and if I ran ahead to pull a single person free, the drug would not only get me but would be free to drift through the building. This was my post.

Even if it meant I had to watch every last one of my troops fall.

My muscles tightened and trembled, my bones straining and my joints on fire, and I drowned in my defeat. O'Malley had been ready for us. All our efforts had been a waste.

As Mandy, my last soldier, crumpled to the ground, leaving me alone with the powder dancing in the air, one thought looped through my mind.

Although I had no proof, I felt the truth deep in my pulsing blood: we'd been set up to die.

Chapter 2

Madison

I STARED ACROSS the table at the six men and single woman sitting in the sunlight that streamed through the glass windows of the twenty-fifth-floor boardroom.

My three team members flanked me. We were the power team. The best negotiators Supernatural, Magical and Occult Affairs Canada had to offer.

And we were being taken for a ride.

"I told you, Ms. Prince, none of your options are satisfactory. We're able to get a better deal trading with Germany than we are with our own country. The Canadian government needs to step up and recognize you're not our biggest customer. Not anymore."

Rising frustration threatened to add a flush to my cheeks, but I siphoned the cortisol out of my system, took a breath, and scanned the room. Somewhere, in one of these seven people, there had to be an emotional weakness, a hint of doubt or worry I could use to shatter their bluff. My ability to detect those weaknesses was what made me so good at this job. Today, there was nothing. Only a wall of confidence. No cracks for me to dig my fingers into.

How?

I shouldn't have even been here. I'd delegated my trade responsibilities a year ago when I'd taken a position as the minister's chief of staff, but after a string of deals gone bad, Minister Bastien had asked me to step in and help. I had the experience, the skills, and the ability to navigate where others couldn't… and I was failing.

I *needed* to make this work. Obscuglas was the only Canadian manufacturer of supernaturally touched windows, the glass designed to obscure reality, like a built-in blur effect. Although healthy mundane minds naturally blocked out any evidence of the supernatural—the wonders of the psychological perception filter—that cognitive mask didn't extend to reflections. All across the city, if the mundane paid enough attention, they would notice an entirely different world mirrored in storefront windows. Buildings they wouldn't see if they stared directly at them, supernatural quirks on otherwise human faces, magical abilities being used in the streets. Obscuglas offered additional security in a world where ground-floor windows were everywhere and everyone had instant access to cameras and the internet.

Unfortunately, the product was expensive to produce and install, and would be even more so if we were forced to negotiate with an out-of-country distributor, so it was my job to make this contract a reality, at the same time creating good jobs for the supernatural community.

I had dug deep into the company's public records and finances; I had monitored all other deals they'd made with organizations far smaller than the federal government. I had worked out dozens of proposals and believed I'd only need to hit the second or third before we landed on a deal that benefited both parties.

Somehow, the CEO of Obscuglas, Mr. Roy Desmond, had knocked down every one of them within fifteen minutes.

I tapped into his mind and analyzed his brain chemistry for any sign of guilt or malicious intent. Had he somehow gained information from someone in the minister's office? Considering how closely I kept the details of my work, it would have been a challenge for anyone to leak anything so crucial, but what alternatives were there? Especially since this was the third major deal to go bust in the last six months.

My mind zipped along his synapses, picking up every shift in his hormones. His smugness was strong, with a faint streak of uncertainty, as though he wondered if I had a final plan up my sleeve—at the moment, I didn't; I had given him my best offer—but nothing to suggest he was cheating me.

I was tempted to dig deeper into his brain and manipulate the chemicals travelling along their neural pathways. Each emotion sang at me with an almost physical texture, and it would be a simple task to force him to agree to the deal. With a little nudge, a surge of dopamine to get him excited or an elevation of serotonin to bring on some afternoon lethargy, I could easily persuade him. I could reduce him to a sobbing wreck here at the table if I wanted to.

I released his mind.

Discouraging though this meeting had been, I'd built my reputation on my skills, not by forcing people's actions.

"That's unfortunate, Mr. Desmond," I said. "Perhaps you'll give my team an extra two days to put together something you feel is more acceptable?"

"I wish I could, Ms. Prince, but we have another meeting this afternoon with a much more promising client. If you can get something to me within the next hour, maybe we can discuss it. Otherwise, I'm afraid we're allotting our resources elsewhere."

I sensed a hint of regret floating off him, but not enough to use. Desmond was a Canadian citizen who wanted to do right by his country, but he was a businessman first.

I stood up and extended my hand. "Thank you for your time."

Keeping my anger in check until I left the boardroom, I stormed back to my office, my thoughts so clouded I nearly slammed the door in the face of my senior team member.

"Oh, sorry, Mel."

Melissa smiled and brushed her red hair behind her ear. "I was calling you from down the hallway." Her smile faded. "What do you think happened in there?"

I pinched the bridge of my nose and went to my desk. "Either I'm getting predictable or more companies are hiring mind readers to sit in on negotiations." I looked her in the eye. "Or someone is leaking information."

Surprise sparked her neural circuits, but no discomfort or guilt accompanied it. "You don't really think so, do you?"

"First the failed meeting with SuperPharm for ready access to those antibiotics, remember? Then that social services group that refused to take on an increased client base. Now this. These are big losses. Resources our people need. When did government contracts stop being considered the ultimate win? Guaranteed work, jobs, money. We used to have to beat people away with sticks."

I raised the door of my overhead bin and grabbed the bottle of bourbon tucked behind a collection of notebooks. Melissa collected two glasses from my filing cabinet, and I poured a healthy dose into each.

"Cheers," I said, raising my glass. She clinked hers against mine, and we both drank deeply. After that meeting, I needed something to take the edge off my disappointment. Negotiating with Desmond had been as much fun as slamming my head against a stone wall, and I couldn't shake the feeling something was wrong. Did he know something I didn't? Something that had made him lose faith in the department?

"So what's next?" Melissa asked.

I dropped into my chair and brushed my dark hair over my shoulder. "You and the others have half an hour to come up with a new offer. If you have nothing by then, you have forty-five minutes to draft a report for the minister explaining why it's a better option to contract out-of-country for our windows."

Melissa bobbed her head and set her glass on the filing cabinet. "You got it." She paused at the office door. "Don't beat yourself up over this too much, Madison. It's been a rough couple of weeks."

"Thirty minutes," I said.

She nodded again and closed the door, leaving me in the blissful silence of my office. I set my glass aside and bowed my forehead against my desk, appreciating that the only feelings in the room were my own. I was able to guard myself against most heightened emotions, but the effort it took to keep my barriers up left me drained.

Especially when it came on the back of a total negotiation collapse.

A groan escaped the back of my throat, and I rolled my head back and forth on the cool surface, massaging the centre of my forehead. Jet was right—this did feel good.

A vibration on my desk pulled me out of my self-soothing,

and I sat up to look at my phone. A smile immediately loosened the muscles in my face, and a rush of anticipation eased my frustration.

STILL ON FOR TONIGHT? the text read.

Malcolm Bishop. One of the few people in the world who could have made me smile this morning. Although he was a mundane, Colm was the sort of person I'd dreamt about since my hormones kicked in. An ex-military surgeon at thirty-five years old, he now worked across the street as a clerk at Veteran's Affairs. Three dates in, and I was still on cloud nine… except for the nagging fact that we could never be more than a casual item unless I were honest with him about being a supernatural, which I was nowhere near ready to be.

Even so, after the day I'd had, I was all right with casual. At least it was something to look forward to.

ON AND IN DIRE NEED OF A GOOD MEAL AND A STRONG DRINK, I replied.

HAPPILY BOTH CAN BE ACCOMMODATED :) SEE YOU AT 7.

I set my phone aside and leaned back in my chair, my head much clearer than it had been a minute ago. Which was perfect, because I didn't have time to be foggy. I had to plan my next steps, find out how Desmond had known what my terms would be, and make sure my next meeting didn't crash and burn quite so magnificently.

The thought of Desmond drained some of the sunshine Colm's text had spilled into my day, and I took another deep swallow of my drink. Unfortunately, the alcohol did nothing to help the shakiness in my stomach. I shifted in my seat, kicked off my shoes, and curled my bare toes into the carpet.

This job was a bitch sometimes. Every day I came to work hoping to make some positive change for the Canadian supernatural population, and some days I succeeded—but the battle was uphill. Counting the supernaturals who blended into the mundane world, and the many more who were too big or too small to be included in the official census, we dealt with upwards of forty-five million members of society whose genetics meant their needs couldn't be met by mundane laws, norms, or care. How were the thousands of giants—so large their legs were taken for tree trunks—supposed to take advantage of the health care system when they got sick? Or what about the millions of sprites and brownies, so tiny they were usually seen as forest debris or dust bunnies in that corner of the kitchen a mundane always cursed themselves for missing?

A big part of my job was to monitor the resources that existed to help these beings thrive—and remain hidden. It didn't take a psychic to predict how the mundanes would react if they learned they shared the world with us. There would be war.

That was why SMOAC had been created in the first place. A diplomatic move by a few supernaturals at the dawn of a new nation. One of those supernaturals was my great-grandmother, Clarissa, whose portrait stared down at me from my office wall as a reminder of everything I fought for.

Everything I'd *been* fighting for since I joined the department ten years ago, working my way up, first as an analyst in foreign and domestic trade, then as SMOAC's chief negotiator, and now as the minister's chief of staff. It was exhausting, laborious, disheartening work, but worth it. Without this job, I would have no purpose, no choice but to return to what the mundane called Faerie and what people in the know called the realm, a layer of the world accessible only through a few crossing points when the right words were spoken. A place where all supernaturals were welcome as long as they upheld Queen Meril's law.

A queen who happened to be my great-great-grandmother, and who very much wanted me to return to court, something I'd only narrowly avoided over the years by being of greater use to the department than I would have been to her.

Maybe that was why my stomach refused to settle. The bourbon sloshed around my insides, and I worried it would try to make its way back up.

Unable to find a comfortable position in my chair, I gave up and crossed the room to the kettle sitting on the filing cabinet. While I waited for the water to boil, I leaned against the wall and stared out the window.

Stretched in front of me was the core of Canadian government—the collection of buildings and businesses that pumped the bureaucratic lifeblood through the country. The Peace Tower, flanked by the copper roofs and beautiful Gothic

Revival architecture of Centre Block, caught the afternoon sun, the flag at its pinnacle flapping in the warm summer breeze. The lawn in front of the building was covered in blankets and towels of people stopping for a midday snooze or yoga practice, tour groups, and quiet sit-ins. A regular summer day in the capital.

A knock at the door made me jump, and I turned as it opened. Minister Jean-Luc Bastien, a handsome man in his mid-fifties with a full dark beard and cat-yellow eyes, stood in the open doorway, taking up most of the space with his wide, muscular frame.

"Minister," I greeted, recognizing from his expression that this was not a social visit.

"You have a minute?" he asked, his Quebecois-accented voice gruff with fatigue.

I glanced at the kettle, but to my disappointment, it had barely started to bubble, removing my excuse to delay the inevitable. "Of course."

I returned to my desk and cleared off the papers I'd strewn about, while the minister made himself comfortable in the seat across from me. He crossed one leg over the other and smoothed the crisp line of his trousers.

He raised an eyebrow at the bourbon bottle still sitting in plain view. "Indulging already?"

"If you'd been in that boardroom, you would be, too."

I grabbed a clean glass from the overhead bin, and he hesitated only a moment before holding his thumb and index finger an inch apart.

"*Un petit peu,*" he said, and I did the honour of pouring. He took a sip and closed his eyes with a contented sigh as he swallowed, but when he looked at me again, his gaze was sharp. "What went on in there today, Madison?"

Crisp expression, crisp suit. That was our minister.

Fortunately, I knew better than to take it personally. Jean-Luc had led his department through more than one upheaval during his time in government. He was calm, forthright, as honest as a politician could be, and he maintained a good balance between keeping the prime minister in the know and handling supernatural affairs the way he thought best.

He was also a long-time family friend, a regular at all kinds of life functions and, back in Winnipeg, a frequent evening visitor, he and my father drinking scotch and exchanging government war stories, which was why I knew I was the best person to deliver the bad news.

"They knew our game," I said. "I presented our best offer, but they'd already doubled down."

"Did something leak?"

I searched his mind for any trace of anger, but there was none. Nothing but the spikiness of irritation and, worse, the cool dampness of disappointment.

With a breath, my energy evaporated. "I honestly don't know. I don't see how it could have, but this makes three times in the last few months we've lost a solid deal. Five in the past year. It's too often to be a coincidence."

If Jean-Luc's skull were transparent, I would have seen the mechanisms ticking with his calculations. As it was, his face gave nothing away, and he offered only a slight drop of his chin. I read him again, but the only change to his emotional state was heightened disappointment. I quickly pulled away. I had enough negative emotions of my own to deal with.

"You trust your team?" he asked.

"I do. Melissa and Abigail have both been with me for three years, and their work never ceases to impress. Bruce has only been here eight months, but he put thirty hours of overtime into this Obscuglas deal. If he's the leak, he's a dedicated one."

The minister's eyes narrowed, the pupils shrinking to vertical slits as he nodded. "You're too good at this job to risk it by being careless. I'll have Phyllis look into it. If someone in the office is betraying us, no one will sniff it out faster."

No doubt that was true, the old bat. Phyllis had been Jean-Luc's executive assistant since before I started here, and I'd never liked her. Her nose twitched whenever I walked by, accompanied by a sticky contempt. Rumour had it she believed I'd gained my position through bloodline rather than merit, and over the years, she'd never bothered to change her mind.

Jean-Luc appreciated her police dog mentality, though, which meant as long as he remained in government, Phyllis would be at his side and I would have to make the best of it.

"What do you intend to do?" he asked.

"Melissa and the team are working on another offer. They have—" I glanced at my watch "—fifteen minutes to get something on my desk."

"Think they can do it?"

"I think they'll try their best, but I don't believe it'll make a difference. Desmond seemed determined not to do business with us."

Jean-Luc frowned, his eyes flashing, and I sensed the first burn of white-hot anger, though I suspected it wasn't directed at me. Roy Desmond would need to be careful stepping foot in this building again if he didn't want his insides winding up on his outsides.

The minister stood up, brushed a non-existent wrinkle from his trousers, and tugged on his jacket. "You'll let me know the results of your team's analysis?"

"You'll hear when I do."

He nodded and walked out, closing the door softly behind him.

My kettle clicked.

I returned to the filing cabinet and opened a blue ceramic container decorated with painted lilies and lavender. The herbal scents of my grandmother's tea blend—a mix of lavender, lemongrass, and a few other herbs you wouldn't find on this side of the wall—wafted into the room, and I closed my eyes to sink into the calm. My blood sang in response, my nerves unwinding in anticipation.

I spooned the herbs into the infuser, poured the hot water into my cup, and returned to the window while the tea steeped.

Emergency vehicles raced down Wellington Street, breaking up the serenity of a few moments ago, and traffic was backed up all the way to the parliament buildings. Another day, another tragedy tearing someone's life apart.

I collected my tea, dumped the used herbs into the trash, and took it back to my desk. Lemony steam swirled over the lip of the mug and tickled my nose. The first sip danced on my taste buds with a burst of flavour and comfort. It was the joy of my grandmother's special tea: a complete emotional reset.

At least, that's what it was supposed to do.

Despite my tried-and-true method for finding my calm, my stomach wouldn't stop flip-flopping. Uneasiness spread through me, and I curled my fingers around my mug. The heat seeped into my bones but did nothing to touch the sudden chill that spiked in my core. It was as though a dark shadow had passed over the sunny day.

The screams of more sirens reached me from the street, and once again I rose to stare out the window.

Something's wrong.

I knew it as deeply as I knew Melissa, Abigail, and Bruce would fail to find a solution to the Obscuglas fiasco, and when my cellphone rang, I left my mug on the window ledge and hurried to answer it.

Jet Dawson's name glowed on the screen over a picture of her sticking her tongue out. I'd taken that photo almost ten years ago, before either of us had been weighed down by coffee shop addictions and too much responsibility.

"Are you all right?" I greeted her.

"Fine," she said, but I barely made her out, her voice drowning under sirens and shouts, so many people talking at once she might have been standing next to a beehive. What I did hear, though, turned my legs to jelly, and I braced myself on my desk. She sounded numb, stony, as though her emotions had shrivelled and blown away on the wind.

Before I could ask what had happened, Melissa stormed into my office without knocking.

"Have you seen this?" she asked as she grabbed the remote control from my desk. She turned up the volume on my small corner television that was always set to the news. The current coverage showed a familiar area of downtown, only a few blocks from the office. Where all the emergency vehicles were headed.

The woman on screen was sombre as she spoke into her microphone.

"… reported gas leak at the downtown de Lauer Estates. Maintenance crews were in the building when a fire started near the burst line, resulting in a blast that residents say they felt up to four blocks away. Police have evacuated a six-block radius, and emergency vehicles are on site. The number of casualties is as yet unknown."

"Jet," I said, my tongue unwieldy around my teeth. Casualties? *Jet's all right. She's on the phone. She's all right.* "I don't—what gas leak? What happened?"

"No gas leak," she said, and I might as well have been talking to a robot. There was no trace of my best friend in her emptiness. "Bomb. Ghostbomb. It was a setup. My team…"

The sour taste of vomit oozed up the back of my throat as my stomach roiled. Her team? My brain couldn't process most of what she'd said. All I knew was that I was here and she was there, and I wouldn't feel calm in my skin until I saw her with my own eyes.

"I'll be right there."

"No," Jet said, and for the first time I detected some inflection in her speech. "There's no point. Michael's here. I just wanted to tell you I made it out. I have to go."

The line went dead, the silence less empty than her voice had been.

"Madison?" Melissa said, bringing me back into the room. "What do we do?"

I pressed my lips together, biting down to break through my shock, and did my best to rally. "You stay focused on the contract. Jean-Luc won't care about windows in the face of whatever went on in that condo building, but once the dust settles, we better have answers."

Retain a sense of normalcy. It was the only thing I could

think to do.

Melissa left the room, and I rounded my desk, sank into my chair, and bowed my head into my shaking hands. Ghostbomb? It was so absurd that even though I couldn't have misheard, I also couldn't believe it was true. It would have taken hundreds of thousands of dollars of ghost to turn it into an effective bomb. And why?

I kept my eye on the news, desperate for more information. Something the mundanes wouldn't pick up on, the truth hidden somewhere between the lines, but the reporter added nothing of use. Finally, I spotted Jet stepping into the afternoon sun—her lieutenant, Eric Sampson, on one side of her; her commander, Colonel Michael Torrence, on the other.

I remained glued to the television, all thought of Obscuglas, Melissa, and my promise to Jean-Luc slipping away as I tried to tally what we'd lost.

And how much more we stood to lose once the queen found out.

Chapter 3

Jet

I SAT ON the curb in front of the evacuated building and let my phone drop into the grass beside me.

Although the safe zone for the public had been pushed back to a six-block radius, the crowd moving past me, around me, was too busy. Too loud. Everyone was shouting, calling out orders, reporting updates, securing the scene—and I sat by and watched. People spoke to me, and I didn't bother trying to understand what they said. Everything was chaos, a mishmash of activity I couldn't process.

Didn't *want* to process.

Processing would mean accepting what I'd seen and heard. I couldn't do it. Not yet.

And yet, there was Eric, standing with Michael, running through his version of events. His eyes were wild, bloodshot, but somehow he was able to say the words I couldn't form.

The rest of my team—the lucky few—stood dumbly near the tactical van. Xander held a coffee cup, but I hadn't seen him take a sip. Sara leaned against the side of the van with her arms crossed and her eyes closed. One might have believed she was unaffected by what had happened if it weren't for the occasional uncontrolled spark between her fingers and the wobble of her bottom lip.

The only members of the pack who showed any outward signs of emotion were Adam and Katie, who clung to one another at the back of the van. I was glad they had each other. Other than myself, they were the only ones who'd had front-row seats to the entire execution, trapped in the tactical van, watching and unable to help.

"Dawson," Michael said, coming up to me. I hadn't noticed him walking away from Eric, but my lieutenant was now suiting up to go back inside, leaving the colonel with me.

He knelt down and bundled me into a hug so tight I could barely breathe, and that's how I knew I was a mess. Since the day I'd started basic training, Michael had proved he wasn't a sentimental, touchy-feely guy, so for him to fuss over me like a mother hen—checking my eyes, my skin, my fingernails for any sign the ghost had reached me—I must have looked a wreck. "How are you holding up?"

I knew I should put on a brave face, get to my feet, do what needed to be done. The voice in the back of my head—the one that had been with me since I enlisted, always pushing me to do better—shouted at me to be professional, be tough.

My body wouldn't listen. The de Lauer building could have exploded right then, and I wouldn't have found the strength to flee the flames.

With a sigh, my commander settled on the curb beside me. "Do you need to go to the hospital?"

"No," I said, and the sound of my voice came as a shock. It was so distant. My brief conversation with Madison had been hard enough, and she'd been a disembodied echo on the phone. Speaking to Michael, hearing his unfamiliar sympathy, was an even greater struggle. "I have to stay here. I have to know—" *how many I lost.*

"I get it," he said. "Do you want anything? Coffee? Glass of water?"

Deep within me, buried under the numbness, I bristled. "No, I'm fine."

"What about one of those shock blankets? Something to warm you up while you wait."

Did I look like a child? Some sad little creature that needed to be coddled? I clenched my teeth to keep from lashing out and didn't bother to respond. This wasn't Michael. This wasn't my strict commander who called out every weakness until we faced it and defeated it.

He glanced at me sidelong. "Right, well, if you're good here, we're going to go in and see what we can find. All trace of ghost has been cleared from the lobby, but we're taking precautions with the basement where the ventilation's not as good. Sampson's rigged up to the body cam if you want to hang out in the van and watch."

I cringed. I didn't want to watch through any more cameras. The sense of helplessness, the uselessness…

Michael cleared his throat. "It'll probably take us a couple hours to get through it all, so if—"

"I'm going in with you."

His grey eyes widened. "You most certainly are not. Be satisfied I'm willing to let you stay on site."

"I can't sit here and do nothing," I said, and only when I got the words out did I appreciate how true they were. "I need to go in. I need to see for myself."

"Dawson, think about this. You pushed yourself to the breaking point in there. If one of your troops did what you did, would you let them turn around and go back in?"

Of course not. "If they felt strongly enough about it, yes. But that doesn't matter. I'm their captain. They need to see me on my feet."

Michael eyed me, his hesitation obvious.

"Either give me an official order to stand down or help me get a suit," I said.

My stomach twisted. I'd already vomited up the coffee I'd drunk this morning, but something in my insides refused to accept I was empty. I drew in a slow, deep breath, and on the exhale, as Michael nodded his agreement, my nausea settled.

He got to his feet, and I ignored his offered hand. I sensed my team's eyes on me as I crossed to the SMOAC emergency vehicles, but other than a quick nod in their direction, I kept my focus straight ahead. Until I knew more, until I faced this, I couldn't speak to them. As it stood, I had nothing to give but apologies.

As I went around the back of the tactical van, Jason approached me. His gaze cut to the crowd, to Michael, to something in his hands. I couldn't avoid him, so I waited for him to reach me, and when he stopped at my side, turning his back to block anyone's view, my attention landed on a scrap of paper between his fingers.

Without explanation, he handed it to me, and I scanned it over through blurred vision. Then I started at the beginning to take in what I'd read.

- Time for silence over

- Time to strike against the powers that promise us safety and security and fail us daily: SMOAC, unseen wall

- name names. Top SMOAC brass: Bastien, Gagnon, dig website. Meril, anyone associated with her

- We demand change, justice or we <u>destroy the wall</u>

- Meril sacrificing her own people for immortality

- Bastien supplying the sacrifices

- repeat: change, justice, or <u>the wall is next</u>. Reveal to world super-natural exists

- Today's message the beginning. Smarten up or anyone with links to

SMOAC/Meril is next

My hands trembled so badly that by the time I reached the end of the scribbles, I barely made out the last words. What the hell was I reading? Sacrifices? Destruction of the wall?

"Where did you find this, Master Corporal?" I asked through numb lips.

He nodded to the other side of the parking lot, where the original barricade for the street closure had stood. "It was lying on the ground. Like maybe someone dropped it on their way out?"

My head swam as I considered what would have happened if a mundane had found the paper instead of one of my team. The perception filter hid a lot of our reality, but a message this overt would have stood out.

They wouldn't have seen. Wouldn't have understood. Most of it is bullshit anyway. I tried to convince myself, but in truth, this tiny scrap of paper could have been catastrophic. A disaster we didn't need so close on the heels of the one we'd been dealt. Worse than that was the warning it contained. Today's message the beginning. If this bomb was the beginning, did we have to ready ourselves for more?

Anyone with links to SMOAC/Meril. What about someone with links to both? Was Madison in danger?

For her to be connected in any way to this insanity turned my blood to ice.

"Good find, Jason," I said, impressed my voice sounded so

level. "I'll take it from here. Stand down. Take a walk."

"Captain," he said, and stepped away, looking relieved to have passed the message on.

Now it burned my fingers, in itself a potential time bomb if it fell into the wrong hands or didn't make it into the right ones before whoever wrote it had time to act. My fingers tingled with the urgency, and I clutched the scrap tighter to avoid dropping it.

"Dawson?" Michael asked as he approached me with a suit.

"Hughes found this on the ground by the barricade," I said as I handed it to him, as relieved to pass it off as Jason had been.

Michael read the scribbles, and his jaw worked as he clenched his teeth, his eyes hard.

"Left by the person who delivered the bomb, do you think?" I asked. "It reads like… I don't even know. Like some kind of conspiracy theory. Sacrifices? Do you think whoever wrote this plans to publish it somewhere? Blog? Website? Is it syndicate, do you think? To what end?"

"Whoever wrote this won't get a chance to publish it. We'll make sure of that. Sacrifices, my ass. And naming names? Whoever wrote this is a coward who wants to discredit the department but won't put his name on the byline." He snorted in disgust. "Suit up if you plan to go in, Captain. I'll make a call and set comms branch on this. If O'Malley is looking to stir up shit by posting these lies for the world to see, he's in for a hell of a shock." He shook his head. "All we need is one nutjob conspiracy mun to grab hold of this, and the entire internet will flood with the crap. Why would he take the chance?"

I swallowed hard and tried to add this note to what had happened in the basement. Was the message an idle threat to stir up trouble, or were we really in for some kind of revolution?

Was it possible today's attack wasn't a one-time hit?

Gods forbid.

While Michael got on the phone with the department's communications branch, I obeyed his orders and suited up, fitting the respirator and face cover in place to protect me from any ghost lingering in the air. I felt like a marshmallow wading through sludge, but at least I'd be safe.

Unlike…

I didn't let myself finish the thought.

Whatever the person who'd set up the bomb and dropped the paper had intended, they hadn't succeeded. Not fully. I'd stopped the ghost, and we'd found the draft of the letter—blog post—whatever the hell it was. They'd only won a partial victory, and like hell if we would give them a chance to celebrate.

Madison.

The possible threat to her sat like a weight in my gut. Should I text her? Warn her?

Only make her worry.

I hated the way my brain worked sometimes, but it was true. If I texted her to say the syndicate was out to get her, she'd want to know more. She would dig, maybe even leave to come find out what I knew. Right now, she was safe at the office. The minister and her team would keep an eye on her. Later I would talk to her, reassure her I had her back. If she was a potential target for whatever the syndicate aimed to do, I would stand in their way.

For now, while I was sure she was out of danger, my team was my priority.

I refocused on the horror waiting for me and plodded towards the front doors.

The lobby carried a sense of abandon when I went inside. As though the last hour had sucked a hundred years out of the marble and leather. Everything had been sprayed down to get rid of the airborne ghost, so the polished sheen of the floor was covered in slurry and the couches were blotched with powder, water, and dirt.

Michael caught up with me, suited and masked, and together we found Eric waiting by the basement door. He started when he recognized me and squeezed my gloved hand as we passed into the stairwell.

"Joel took the bomb away," he said, his voice echoing and distorted through his mask. "Ed and Yasmeen are working on the plastic wrap. Yasmeen believes it was put up yesterday, which is why nothing showed on the security footage."

I thought of the illusions passing in front of the camera, the one living person waiting for us in the room who had winked out of view as soon as the truth had become clear. Weldon's vanishing act had no doubt been another illusion, letting him slip by us unseen. Had he dropped the letter on his way out, stuck being the syndicate's lackey?

Unfortunate for him it would mean a nasty end once we tracked him down.

We reached the bottom of the stairs, and I held my breath as Michael opened the door. The memory of Zeke walking through here not so long ago gripped my lungs, and it took me a moment to remember how to breathe.

I shouldn't have bothered. The air left my body a moment later anyway when the full impact of the scene hit me.

The room was a bloodbath. Spray across the walls and ceiling, pools of it on the floor. My suit kept out the stench— kept out the ghost particles floating through the air—kept out everything but the icy hand of grief that squeezed my chest.

I cast it off, knowing how easily it could root me to the floor if I let it, and turned my mind to the work ahead. The fallen had to be organized, identified, removed. They deserved every respect I could provide. This was my final duty to them, and I wouldn't fail. Not again.

Eric and I worked together, and with every lost soldier we shifted, I imprinted their name on my memory. I wouldn't forget, and I wouldn't let this go.

"Captain," Ed said, and I turned to face him. He was crouched next to a hulking figure with a metal shield, dinged and blood-spattered, lying beside him. Zeke. "He's alive."

Chapter 4

Madison

THE NEXT HOUR passed in a blur.

Within ten minutes of Jet's call, the minister was out of his office and rounding up anyone who had information to share. Rumours abounded. *The syndicate had struck. A new big bad was in town. Inside job. Five people dead. Ten. The entire team.* But very few facts trickled down the line.

When Melissa, Abigail, and Bruce came into my office to report their failure, I barely registered their frustration. The news replayed the same information, my phone remained infuriatingly silent, and, as far as I was concerned, Roy Desmond could go swim with the mermaids.

A few windows were the least of our worries right now.

The clock struck noon, and it was my turn to be summoned to Jean-Luc's conference room.

Most of the team was already there—Deputy Minister

Lucien Gagnon, two security officers, a full public relations team, and Phyllis. She gave me a sour look as I walked in, her grey hair pulled tightly back from her face, her powder-blue cardigan an inappropriate contrast to the sombreness of the meeting.

I ignored her and took a seat at the table opposite the minister. As his chief of staff, I had every right to be here.

My personal reasons for joining the meeting were no one's business. I had to know what Jet had suffered.

Surreptitiously, I slid my phone onto the desk beside my notepad in case she checked in again.

"What have we confirmed so far?" Jean-Luc asked, calling the meeting to order.

Patrick McClennan, head of security, shuffled his papers. "We're still waiting to tally the final numbers," he said, "but we suspect at least half the team involved in the raid is dead. According to the most recent report, the recovery team pulled a few survivors from the basement. Six that we're aware of have been taken to the Peaview."

The Peaview was the only supernatural hospital in the national capital region, located in the second subbasement of this very building. I hoped that meant Jet would be here soon, safe and able to report in.

McClennan cleared his throat and pulled his tablet out from under his papers. "We've also received the body cam footage from the raid. It follows everything from the moment Captain

Dawson gave her order to the moment the camera went dead. I warn you… it's graphic. I suggest you don't watch unless you absolutely must."

I was one of the few in the room who had no obligation to stare at the screen as McClennan hit play, but I couldn't look away.

Jet would have watched the same scene: her sergeant leading the way, extending his shield, pushing through the door.

Everyone around the table leaned forward to get a closer look as the fight broke out then cut short, the illusions disappearing, the remaining syndicate trash vanishing in the corner, and, finally, the shift in the room from boardroom to plastic-wrapped nightmare. We watched the chair in the centre of the floor, a banal piece of office furniture until Zeke spun it around to reveal the ticking clock attached to the packets of ghost.

My stomach twisted with the shaking footage as everyone scrambled to get away, so few of them making it to the door before the bomb went off. The puff of white that obscured the camera, then settled and filled the room in a light haze.

The chaos as soldier fell on soldier.

The camera collapsed to the ground with Jet's sergeant, but the angle on it allowed us to see what came next.

Vines shot out from one woman's hands and tightened around the throat of a man who returned the attack by throwing himself at her, his long fangs oozing venom as they plunged into her neck.

Another wielded six blades in her six hands, spinning and slashing with such speed I couldn't keep track. Blood sprayed around her, coating the walls, the droplets mixing with the powder in the air. A pool of water rose behind her, took on a human shape, and wrapped itself around her head. She flailed against it, slowed, her eyes going bloodshot as she gasped for breath and sucked in water, then collapsed—drowned on dry land.

Nightmare after nightmare played out on the screen, and my only source of gratitude was that McClennan had left the sound off.

Poor Jet. I tried to imagine how she must have felt as she watched this tragedy play out, but the sense of loss was too deep. The jaggedness of my grief from trying to put myself in her boots brought tears to my eyes.

I glanced at my phone. Still nothing.

She wouldn't be handling this well. No doubt she was blaming herself, beating herself up.

Michael is with her. He'll keep her level.

I hoped.

I had known Jet Dawson for ten years. We'd met during one of those orientation team-building sessions where various branches are thrown together for a day. It had taken ten minutes to discover our shared loyalty for SMOAC and our shared loathing of team-building events, and we'd spent the rest of the day hitting up the snack table chatting about our jobs, our motivations, our goals. From colleagues, we'd become friends, and now she was the only person who knew every secret of my life. Jet was one of the few people able to block her emotions from me, and one of the few where it didn't matter. I could read her as easily as I could a mirror.

"Thank you, Officer McClennan," Jean-Luc said, and his words were stilted, the hue around his lips a pale green.

The security officer nodded and set his tablet aside. His partner, Aveen, leaned forward with a small stack of papers that she handed out to each of us. "This came in a half-hour ago, so we haven't had much time to do anything with it beyond making copies for your office, Minister. According to the report, one of Dawson's troops found it at the scene. Our best guess is it came from whoever set the bomb, possibly from the man you saw in the footage, but unfortunately, none of the security cameras show that area of the parking lot to help us identify them."

"So we don't know if only one of O'Malley's gang was there, or if the entire syndicate was hiding in the crowd," Lucien said.

"I'm sorry, sir, but no," McClennan said. "Captain Dawson says no one else went downstairs, which supports the idea that it must have been this guy Weldon, but we're looking into it."

"We're pulling security footage from a few surrounding storefronts and condos, so hopefully we can catch the same view from another angle," Aveen added.

I scanned the paper in my hand, a print-out of a photo taken with a phone camera.

The point-form notes were written in a barely legible scrawl, some words underlined, others scribbled out and rewritten. The words themselves… I didn't know what to think, even though half the people around the table were mentioned by name. As was the queen. And, by association, me.

My heart raced, my palms went clammy, and I reached for my glass of water.

"We think the Death's Head is behind this attack?" Lucien asked, his brow scrunched in a deep frown.

"With O'Malley's people on the scene, who else could it be?" asked Jean-Luc. "Who else would take such a risk?" He shook his head. "Who else has enough money to throw around that much ghost?"

I rested my clasped hands on my notepad. "And we're sure that's what it was? Lab tests have confirmed?"

"The samples only arrived as we came upstairs," McClennan said, "but I trust our people on the ground. They know what they're looking at."

I cleared my disapproving expression before it settled in place. The minister wasn't the type of man who took information on someone's word. He needed facts. Evidence. Yes, ghost had some pretty specific effects, but they weren't unique. It was also possible I wanted McClennan to be wrong because of the repercussions if he were right.

"Could someone else have stepped into the game?" I asked. "Someone who wants us to think it's the syndicate? If it's not ghost, there's no guarantee O'Malley is responsible for the bomb. Even if he's involved, this kind of offensive manoeuvre is out of character. Too out in the open."

"There are no other players in the city, Madison," Lucien said. "And this note…" He shook the copy in his hand. "It *is* something they would do. If they publish this message somewhere, it will create pandemonium. We know they've been trying for years to gain a greater foothold in the city—what better way to do it than to stir up panic? Get people to turn against us for these *sacrifices* or whatever they're claiming, and use the fear to spread their own 'cure.'"

He wrapped his fingers around the word in air quotations, then flicked the paper away in disgust.

"I know you said you haven't had much time to work this angle," Jean-Luc said, "but has any risk assessment been done? What are the odds the threats mentioned here are real? Should we expect more bombs?"

Aveen tapped her fingers against her copy of the note. "Our best team is working on that right now, Minister. As it stands, they feel the risk is low. The cost of the ghost—if that's indeed what it was," she added, acknowledging my earlier question with a nod, "would prohibit mass production even if O'Malley ordered the attack. There are cheaper, easier ways to get attention than blasting ability-altering drugs into the air."

"I see," Jean-Luc said. "I want a draft of that assessment on my desk within the hour."

"Yes, Minister," McClennan said.

"In the meantime, what is our plan to prevent the note from getting out?" Jean-Luc asked, turning to his PR team, and from there the meeting switched to planning.

I took notes and offered input, but my thoughts were split between how I could help them and what I could do for Jet. Half her team dead, the few survivors in critical condition. She would need support.

And this conspiracy note…

Although the conversation had shifted away from what it might mean, I couldn't stop staring at the underlined portion. The threat to destroy the wall.

Everyone else in the room seemed to take the message as a syndicate ploy to cause trouble, but I couldn't swallow that assumption so easily. A threat to the wall was a threat to Meril. If she heard about this letter, how would *she* take it? It wasn't a subject of conversation for the PR team or even the security officers, but at some point soon, Jean-Luc and I would have to sit down and talk about what we would do if the queen of the unseen realm saw the need to take action to prevent the threat from being carried out.

In the hours that followed, minute after minute piling on with endless discussion about media lines and internal response, I did my best to stay focused on the business at hand. The prime minister was called and debriefed, more reports came in—confirming ghost, confirming nine dead and five hospitalized, confirming no fingerprints or identifying features on the scribbled note—and strategy was laid out for how to explain the blast to the supernatural public.

Throughout it all, however, emotions grew taut. Stress, fear, frustration gathered together in a suffocating cloud that slipped down my throat and choked me. I'd had no further word from Jet, and the air in the cramped conference room was thick and rank without the possibility of opening a window.

Another hour, more emotions. The patterns in the carpet were making me dizzy, and my colleagues' rising fear and worry filled my nose with their ripe stench. The reek of it, the skin-crawling oiliness of it, wriggled through my closely held guard. Another ten minutes and I would drown in it.

A phone or watch dinged to mark the time, and Jean-Luc shook himself out of his concentrated hunch to glance at the clock on the wall.

"Four hours," he said, rubbing his eyes. "I think we all need a break. Phyllis, would you mind going downstairs and grabbing us some coffees?"

"I'll go," I jumped in before she answered. Anything to get out and stretch my legs, find some grounding.

"Madison, we need you—" Jean-Luc started, but he must have seen the desperation on my face, because the argument in his eyes faded to understanding. "We need you to have a clear head to help us this afternoon. Please, yes, take a walk."

I nodded my thanks, rose from the table, and all but fled the conference room. Phyllis's gaze shot daggers at me as I passed her.

As soon as I was in the hallway, I dragged off my jacket to give myself some space, detoured to my office to grab my wallet and drop the jacket on my chair, and headed to the elevator bay. As I navigated my way through the people pacing the floor, their anger, worry, and excitement buffeted my mind, triggering similar reactions in my own brain chemistry—one frequency shifting to match another. I fought against it, doing my best to remain calm and maintain the same neutrality I'd shown in my meeting with Obscuglas. It was the only way I would get through this without breaking down.

Four hours had felt like thirty, and there was still the rest of my night to go. I could have borne it without complaint, relieved to have a role to play, if only Jet would get in touch. The silence from her was worse than the emotions pouring in from everyone else.

At this hour of the day, closing in on five o'clock, the lobby was close to empty, which meant the line at Tim's was short. Normally, I would have rejoiced, but tonight a wait out the door would have given me a longer reprieve from the conference room.

I ordered a full box of coffee and debated grabbing doughnuts as well, but the thought of sprinkles clashed too badly with city-destroying-bomb-made-of-drugs, so I left them behind. The caffeine would be good enough.

Too soon, the order was filled, and I turned around to go back upstairs. On my way to the elevator, however, my feet turned to lead, and I came to a standstill in the middle of the lobby.

Upstairs meant locked in meetings for who knew how long. It meant more waiting, more processing details as they came in, each one more horrifying than the last. Or, worse, an end to the details. What would we do when the information stopped and we could only work with what little we had?

Already, most of the information coming in was a repeat of what we knew. So far the contents of the note had made no online appearance, but no one was relaxing their guard. Jean-Luc had ordered the entire communications branch to monitor the web, radio, and televised news sources to ensure it never reached the public.

I couldn't help but notice that most of the discussion had revolved around preventing word from getting out instead of the fallout of the attack. As though the response team was afraid a misstep might trigger the writer of the note to act on their threat.

To a point, I understood and agreed with their concern. Most of us lived with the worry that one day the truth would come out that magic was real and monsters did live under the bed, and playing chicken with someone wanting to make it happen was not something to take lightly. It was bad enough that today's events crossed both mundane and supernatural media, raising questions we would have preferred to handle internally. This sort of crime—a mass murder aimed at our kind—hadn't occurred in decades. It would rattle the stability of our world, and the minister would need to stay ahead of the rumours to quell the panic.

At the same time, the department couldn't afford to do nothing, not without letting O'Malley walk away unpunished.

"Madison?"

The deep voice vibrated through my thoughts, jolting me out of the darkness, and I cradled the box of coffee against my chest to avoid spilling it all over the tiled floor as I turned around.

In front of me stood a man taller than me by about a head. His white dress shirt, contrasting beautifully with his dark skin, was undone at the collar and rolled to the elbows in his attempt to beat the heat. The material stretched across his broad shoulders and clung to the planes of his stomach. Despite my headache and queasiness, a quiet voice in my head appreciated how perfectly Malcolm Bishop matched the fantasy of him that lived in my memory.

On any other day, the sight of him would have calmed my nerves and brought me a sense of peace, but all I felt was a tide of guilt and regret.

"Colm, hi," I said.

"Is everything all right?" His brow furrowed. "What's wrong?"

My throat closed, and I drew in a slow breath through my nose to keep from crying. All afternoon in Jean-Luc's office, I'd been able to keep my emotions at bay. My horror at the body cam footage, worry for my friend, grief at what we'd lost… but here, away from people I felt the need to impress with my professionalism, faced with concern from someone I regarded so highly, I felt myself breaking down.

Not yet. Still so much to do.

I cleared my throat. "We had a bit of an emergency, actually. Something blew up in our faces."

The phrasing pained me, as though I were making light of the attack. Really, I just didn't have any other way to be honest with him. He had no idea what I did, beyond being a high-level chief of staff within the made-up Domestic Affairs and Trade Canada, and I was in no place or state of mind to enlighten him.

Supernatural ability was more of a twentieth-date conversation, after all the other flaws and embarrassing childhood stories were out in the open.

"I'm sorry," he said, and not only did he sound like he meant it, but by the gentleness in his dark eyes, I could almost believe he read through my vague explanation to the deeper emotional turmoil underneath. "I guess this means a rain check for tonight?"

I bowed my head to blink away the stinging in my eyes.

"For the best. I'm really upset about it, though. I could have used a night out."

"Hey," he said, and brushed his fingers along my arm towards my hand to bring my gaze to his. "We do what we have to, right? A rain check doesn't mean a month from now. Or we don't have to do a full dinner. Let me know when you're free, and we'll plan something, okay?"

I nodded, too overwhelmed by his understanding to speak. And I felt directly how genuine it was. His compassion melted off him like a soothing balm that wrapped around me in a tight hug.

"Thank you."

"Just promise me you'll get some rest," he said, his gaze dropping to the box of coffee. "Take it from a former surgeon and a veteran, coffee's not a sleep replacement."

Despite everything, I laughed, and he flashed me a smile that made my knees weak.

"We'll be in touch," he said, and scanned the lobby before leaning in and giving me a quick kiss on the cheek. Then he was gone, leaving me in a warm bubble as I took my coffee through the security gate and rode the elevator to the twenty-fifth floor.

The bubble burst when I stepped out of the elevator and found Jean-Luc waiting for me.

"Do you have a minute?" he asked.

"Of course," I said, confused. "Are we not going back to the conference room?"

He waved his hand in dismissal. "I'm tired of talking in circles. There's nothing new to learn until the security team finishes their analysis of that note or we track down O'Malley, so I sent everyone home. There's no need for all of us to be exhausted."

We reached my office. He followed me in and closed the door behind him. I set the box of coffee on my desk, poured some into two paper cups, added sugar to one and milk to both, and slid one over to him.

"We may as well make the most of the caffeine hit, then," I said.

"Oh, don't worry. I'll drain it myself before the night is through." He took a sip and closed his eyes as he breathed out, and I allowed him the moment of silence.

Sitting this close to him, I picked up every stress hormone flooding his system. Anger, confusion, and grief oozed like an oil spill, each new chemical release making the situation in his mind a million times worse.

Gently, I reached my mind out to his and did my best to soothe the tempest. The lines around his mouth relaxed.

"Thank you," he said, easing deeper into his chair as he opened his eyes.

"We can't have our fearless leader losing his head."

Jean-Luc smiled, but despite my efforts, his expression remained tinged with sadness. "I confess I don't know what to do. I've never had anything like this happen during my term, and I was only a director at the time of the Magic Riots in '93. An outright attack on our people…" He shook his head and raised his cat-like eyes to meet mine. "If your father can't be with me during this, I'm grateful you are. You tell me I can't lose my head, but let's be honest—if anyone in this building can hold themselves together in a time of crisis, it's you. We're going to need you."

"And you'll have me," I said. Where else would I be? My family had helped found this department. I had poured my life-blood into its day-to-day running for over a decade. I wouldn't stand by while some greedy crime boss destroyed it.

"Have you heard from her?" he asked, and I didn't need to ask who he meant.

"There's been no word from the queen or the Shadow Council. Either the incident wasn't big enough to catch her attention, or…"

"Or she's watching to see what we'll do," Jean-Luc finished, voicing what I wished we could leave unsaid. He arched an eyebrow. "Are you concerned?"

"Always," I said. There was no point in lying. "I'm the fourth generation in our family to choose the department over the court, and my uncle's made it clear she's looking to call me back. The only reason she's left me alone this long is because she sees the advantage of keeping the department strong."

"And tied to her," he said.

"Exactly. But if she smells trouble, if she thinks the department's control on this side of the wall might slip, or some madman with a blog and access to bombs is going to come after the barrier, she'll act."

His eyes narrowed. "She wouldn't shut us down. The repercussions on both sides would be catastrophic."

"You're taking a lot on faith. You know what she's capable of. For a hundred and fifty years, she's allowed us to split control of our people. She's done it gracefully and with little complaint. But if security around the wall is threatened?" I swallowed the bitter taste at the back of my throat. "Hopefully I'm looking at worst-case scenarios, but even if you're right and she doesn't kill the department, I wouldn't put it past her to chisel its foundations. Summon me back, along with anyone else she has a claim to, strip SMOAC of its lynchpins, make people lose confidence in us so they turn to her for help. Eventually, they'd have only one choice—return over the wall or end up stranded here. Anything to protect the realm."

Jean-Luc rubbed his fingers over his brow. "Let's hope it doesn't come to that. Merde. What were they hoping to do with that note?" He rested the crook of his forefinger over his top lip. "Is there any way we can hold her off?"

"Find out who's behind this before they act on their threats."

He pushed himself to his feet with what appeared to be extra effort. "Then I suppose I'd better stop hiding and get back to giving orders." His shoulders slumped. "After that, I'm going to get the hell out of here and give my kids a hug. Thanks for the refresh." He tapped the side of his head. "*Bonne soirée*, Prince. I hope you have more of that bourbon at home."

He took the box of coffee with him and closed my office door tightly, sealing me in. Usually I would have appreciated the gesture, but tonight it left me feeling distanced. Isolated.

I checked my phone again. It had been hours since I'd heard from Jet. She couldn't still be downtown.

For Meril's sake, Jet, I silently shouted into the ether. *Call me.*

And as though she finally heard me, the screen lit up with an incoming message.

THS SUCCKS.

I frowned. If Jet was misspelling texts that badly, she'd already hit the bottle somewhere.

WHERE ARE YOU? I asked, though I had a pretty good idea. I shut down my computer and cleared my desk.

ISHOLD HAVE DONEMKRE. I COULD HAVEDON. I LET THEM ALL DOWN.

The worry I'd felt over her silence abated. If she was talking, she wasn't doing anything too stupid. As long as I got to her first, she'd be all right. No, maybe not all right, not after everything she'd seen today, but she'd survive. I'd make sure of that.

IM GOINGA QUIT. GON TO MVE TO SASKATCHEWAN.

The woman couldn't string a full sentence together, yet somehow managed to spell Saskatchewan correctly.

I'll be there in ten minutes. Next round you order, make it two. I rethought my statement and added, Save one for me.

I locked all my drawers, grabbed my purse and jacket, and headed out. Despite the hour, the hallways were full of people running from cubicle to cubicle, from cubicle to photocopier, and I had to sidestep the storm as I passed through to the elevator bay. Guilt pinched my conscience for walking out when I could be doing something to help, but I buried it.

My friend was in pain, and the best way for me to help the department, and therefore myself, was to make sure she didn't spiral out of control.

Chapter 5

Jet

I RESTED MY forehead on the bartop, then rethought that decision when I landed on something sticky and sat up, sending the room into a spin. Round and round, each loop brought fresh memories of the past eight hours.

Me giving orders. Me going into the building. Me doing fuck-all when I sensed something was off.

A groan escaped the back of my throat, and I pulled my phone towards me.

My FAULT, I typed to Madison. I SHOULD HAVE STOPPED THEM. SHOULDN'T HAVE LET THEM OPEN THAT DOOR.

My fingers moved automatically across the touchscreen, but I suspected they weren't doing what my brain wanted them to do. Whatever. Madison would know what I meant. Madison always knew.

I set my phone aside, and a minute later picked it up and

started typing again. For hours I'd kept my emotions strapped in, but now that I was here on my own, whiskey bottle close at hand, I was falling apart. A house crumbling. A knitted sweater coming undone one stitch at a time. Texting Madison was the only thing stopping me from curling into a ball under the bar, and it was only because I knew she'd get it. She would understand. And then she could explain it to me.

Who better to know what might have gone through the minds of my troops in their final moments? I wanted to know. Needed to know. Maybe then I wouldn't be haunted by what-ifs.

Shit.

Ghost.

A drug that let you see all the mysteries of the goddamned universe before it stopped your heart. Ten minutes of having your eyes opened to the truth—of experiencing the greatest power that's ever run through your veins—before your brain started leaking out your ears.

Like what happened to half my squad.

Half my fucking squad.

I took another drink to swallow the branding iron searing the back of my throat.

How the fuck was I supposed to live with this?

More memories crowded out the others. Michael arriving in the middle of the chaos like an oasis of calm. As smoothly as if he'd been through something like this a dozen times. Him taking over the scene, getting the mundane cops on his side, helping to keep the media and crowds away.

Jason handing over that piece of paper covered in lies that threatened more death and destruction.

Me moving through the subbasement, shifting corpses. Holding Zeke's hand as the medics bundled him onto the stretcher, finding Mandy, Marc-André, Luvy, and Ray—the only other survivors in the room. Standing blankly in the corner watching the crime scene crew take down each piece of plastic wrap, careful not to stir up the resting white powder or leak blood onto the floor.

It had to have been the easiest crime scene cleanup the team had ever come across. A sick joke by whoever set us up. Because it had to have been a setup. Even in my drunken haze, I saw that much. The illusions had been designed to lure us in and make us think our intel was solid. They'd known we were watching. Adam and Katie had gone through the security footage while the rest of us were arranging the dead, and they hadn't seen anything new. Only Weldon leading his illusions downstairs. But no box, no plastic wrap, no ghostbomb in his hands. They'd gone back as far as they could, but the feed reset at midnight, which meant whoever had set the bomb and decorated the room had been there long before we arrived.

To make things worse, Katie had also checked out the camera I'd spotted in the corner of the room. Where O'Malley had watched my people die. The source of the feed was a dead end, but it was enough to know he'd been behind the camera.

More than once I wondered why he'd taken the risk of speaking, of letting us know he was behind the attack to come, and more than once in my drunken haze, I accepted he hadn't meant for any of us to get out of that room alive.

At the thought of his smug face, a deep heat stirred in my belly, and I squeezed my hand around my tumbler, willing myself not to snap.

Pressure built from the soles of my feet, up my legs, then spread through my core to flow down my arms and into my skull. I had to let go or start screaming, and either would draw unwanted attention. Behind the bar, the bottles rattled, and a few exclamations erupted around me as people braced themselves against the scarred cherrywood bartop. No doubt they suspected an earthquake instead of the human-looking woman who sat stooped over her whiskey glass, holding on as if it were a life preserver.

At least his smugness couldn't have lasted long. I hoped he'd still been watching as I pushed his ghost back. Enough of us had survived to know who to hunt down, and gods help me if I didn't drive my fist through the side of his head.

A hand rested on my shoulder, and I jumped. The jolt caused the pressure inside me to pop, and the bottle of whiskey at my elbow went flying across the bartop and smashed into a gazillion pieces on the floor.

More shrieks pierced my eardrums as the muns whirled around to find the cause of the accident, but the bartender,

Simon, shot me an unimpressed look. I stared back at him, ready to accept my eviction, but he must have seen this was the safest place for me because he rolled his eyes and went to fetch the broom.

It was all right. I would make it up to him later with a big fat tip.

I didn't bother turning around to see who had touched me. There was no point. Only one person would dare, and it was hard to miss the faint smoothing of my emotional hard edges. Not enough to wipe them out, but enough to make them a bit more identifiable.

It wasn't an improvement.

"How'd you know where I was?" I asked Madison.

She dropped her purse on the bar where the bottle had been and hauled herself onto the stool beside mine. "Where else would you be?"

I grunted in response. Mooney's Pub was the bar of choice for lots of government employees, supernatural and mundane alike. Both were welcome here, even if only one group knew it. Simon was half demon—the half that knew how to deal with nasty drunks—and the owner, Alyssa Mooney, a witch of impressive lineage, was an old friend to the community and to Madison and me personally.

It was why I knew if I broke a few bottles tonight, I'd still be allowed back tomorrow.

"I see you didn't order me that drink," Madison said.

I shrugged. "You said to grab yours on my next round. I hadn't finished my first one yet." I pointed toward the broken bottle. "So I guess your timing's perfect. Simon," I called, and he peered up at me from where he was sweeping glass off the floor. "Another bottle when you can, 'kay?"

He looked at Madison, who nodded. "It's been that kind of day. We'll share it."

I grunted again, having agreed to no such thing, but wasn't about to argue. I doubted he'd bring another one over just for me.

He finished cleaning up and disappeared to throw out the trash, leaving our tiny corner of the bar quiet. Dangerously quiet. I waited for Madison to break the ice, not ready to take the first step myself. I was glad she'd found me, but her steady presence, her comforting silence, proved everything I'd gone through was real.

On a normal day, she would have bitched about work. Maybe she would have had a run-in with her crush at the coffee shop, or maybe she had some juicy gossip to share about her boss.

Anything would have been better than this quiet compassion.

My throat started to tighten, my eyes to sting, and I threw back what was left in my glass. I wouldn't cry in front of these people, and I wasn't ready to talk.

Another wave of comfort washed over me, and the air stuck in my lungs threatened to choke me. Madison was wearing down the shell I'd spent all afternoon building, and I wished she wouldn't.

"Where are the others?" she finally asked.

My first reaction was to bite my tongue to stop myself from screaming that they were dead. They were most likely having their fluids drained and their organs weighed as we sat here.

I made myself relax. She meant the survivors. The people I had to stay focused on now.

"They were here for a while," I said, amazed I could get any sound out at all. "Eric, Jason, Sara… They stuck around for a few beers, but one by one they drifted off. I work with a bunch of lone wolves. They all want to lick their wounds in private."

My JetPack. Half the pack dead and the other half grieving. Me at the centre unable to help any of them.

Simon returned with a fresh bottle, set it down between us, and added two clean glasses beside it before whisking my old one away. He said nothing, which I appreciated. The man knew how to read a room.

Madison opened the bottle and poured a few healthy shots into each glass, slid one towards me, and wrapped her long fingers around the other. For a moment, I stared at the way her perfect French-manicured nails contrasted with the amber liquid in the glass. She was too damned classy for a place like this. Me, with my chewed fingernails and messy ponytail, I fit right in.

She spun on her stool to face me and crossed one leg over

the other. She sported a fitted navy pantsuit, the pink blouse giving her honeyed skin a golden glow. The woman hadn't even gone home before coming out to babysit my sorry ass. The worst part was, she didn't look upset about it.

My stomach sank further when I remembered she wasn't supposed to have gone home today.

"Your date," I said. Her coffee shop crush. She should have been lip-locked with him right now, not here with me.

"We rescheduled," she said. "He understood. Now talk to me."

That was the end of her request. No pity in her voice, no easy gentleness. It was an order. The pain in her hazel eyes told me she didn't want to hear it any more than I wanted to say it, but it had to be done. She hadn't worked with my guys—didn't know most of them—but they were part of the department she loved with blood and bone, and she had a right to know.

So I started at the beginning. I walked her through the information we'd received, the strategy Michael, Eric, and I had developed, the illusions walking past the security cameras, the unease I'd felt in the lobby when my third eye had come up empty, and the moment I'd realized my world had changed.

I told her everything, hoping it would stop the frantic loop playing in my head. The steady stream of images on that portable monitor. Eric had stayed so calm through it all. Calmer than I had. I knew inside he was just as wrecked—he'd helped me recruit every member of our team—but he'd appeared almost cold in his processing. Completely shut down to what had happened and focused only on what needed to be done. My inability to keep up made me feel like even more of a failure than I already did. I always swore I thrived under pressure, that I could keep my head in a crisis. Today made me doubt myself. I should have said something earlier, should have moved faster and done more to help. Should have stayed stronger.

"I let them down," I said, and it nearly broke me to admit it out loud. "Keeping the air clear, giving people time to get away—it was too much. And then to go back in there. To put on that suit and touch the bodies of people I laughed with this morning. Covered in blood, torn apart by their best friends. All I could do was beg the universe to let me find one who'd made it."

"And you did," Madison said, her voice soft.

"Five." The word came out strangled. "Zeke—he was first in. Got the full blast, but his damned shield—" I shook my head and wiped the back of my hand across my nose "—the damned shield saved his life. I don't know how he survived it. But Ellison—Ellie with his four-month-old baby waiting for him at home. Tina, with her mother's surgery coming up. Laura, Saaqib—"

I couldn't go on. Their names, everything they'd left behind, swept over me in a wave, and I squeezed my lips shut, my throat on fire with the strain of holding back my cries. Refusing to think, I poured more whiskey into my glass and threw it back.

It was the only alternative to vomiting all over the bar, and so far throwing up hadn't helped.

Madison rested her hand on my shoulder, and a wave of ease washed over me, soothing the fierceness of the ache without removing any of the pain.

This time when I rested my forehead on the bartop, I didn't care about the ick factor. The warmth of my friend's hand and the coolness of the counter were the most relief I'd experienced in hours.

The pressure in my chest ebbed, and in a moment my breaths came more easily, as though I weren't drowning in grief.

"We were set up, Madi," I said, my voice echoing back at me against the wood. "It had to have been a bad lead." I rolled my head back and forth. "I don't understand—it was a good source. A trusted source."

"Do you know that for sure?"

A spark of anger nudged me towards sobriety, but it slipped away with another sip of my drink. "Michael wouldn't have sent us in there if he hadn't checked. How else could it go?" That didn't sound right. "What else could have happened?" Close enough. "None of our informants would be stupid enough to lie. They know we'd find out. They wouldn't survive the week. And they've all been around so long. It had to have been wrong. Bad."

Words weren't working for me, so I pressed my lips together and shut up.

Madison propped her elbow on the bartop and spun her glass in a slow circle, making the whiskey dance. "So what do you think? That one of O'Malley's people weaseled out one of our very protected informants and fed them a few lies they were stupid enough to believe? Why? So the syndicate could blast the department with a bomb that easily cost them a few weeks of income?"

"I don't know," I said, and it came out as a whine. "Who else? It couldn't have just *happened*. They couldn't have just *guessed* we would be there on that day at that time. There has to have been a chain of events. Someone who pushed the intel."

A hiccup interrupted me, but I'd grabbed on to the thought and couldn't let it go. "The syndicate had to have known. They've been quiet for weeks. Long enough that I was starting to believe the Kingston bullshit. And if they knew, someone must have told them. And that's not all. The note. Spreading lies." I sat up with a jerk and swallowed bile. "You shouldn't be here, Madi. They're coming for you next. The note said so."

I had to find Weldon. I pictured the man huddled in the corner of the fake boardroom, the shit-eating grin on his face as he'd risen out of his cower and disappeared before the ghost had hit the fan. The need to slam his face into a curb a few times made my fingers twitch, and I curled my hands around my glass to keep them still.

His address was in the department's files. Not too much of a challenge to track him down. I'd butted heads with the guy before, and he'd always given me the impression that with a bit more heavy-handedness, he'd spill whatever I wanted to hear. If I got my hands on him, I could find out who'd spread the intel and get proof O'Malley was behind this. Because, drunk as I was, I knew a voice over a speaker wouldn't be evidence enough to throw that man's ass in jail. First, I needed something concrete. I needed to know why he'd struck a blow against SMOAC, why he'd killed my team. Then I would beat the shit out of him and throw him to what was left of my pack for them to finish the job. All I needed was proof, and I would take this right to his fucking door.

Getting to the source of the threat was the only way my friend would be safe. My friend, the wall, the department.

"I read the note," Madison said, and she sounded so calm. "Leading theory is O'Malley's people dropped it on purpose to stir up trouble. The lies are too absurd, and there would be no obvious benefit to the syndicate to release it. But comms is monitoring the situation."

"You need to be careful."

"I will be," she said, but I didn't know if she meant it or if she was indulging my drunkenness. "I'm sure we'll find whoever's responsible before we need to worry. Jean-Luc is on this. They'll route it back to O'Malley and bring him in."

Had she read my mind? I wouldn't put it past her.

"Not fast enough," I said. "Paperwork, red tape."

"You live by red tape. For as long as I've known you, red

tape has been your guiding arrow on the floor to help you be the best at your job. You turn your nose up at rogues. What about all those lectures you've given Eric over the years?"

"Look what good they've done me. Going by the book, giving responsible orders, and now my team is dead. There's no room for red tape right now. There's a sea and an ocean—" I stumbled, confused, then pressed on "—between knowing the syndicate is behind the blast and locking up O'Malley for the rest of his life. If we wait for all the bureaucratic shit, we could miss our chance. I want to find Weldon tonight."

"You won't find anyone in the state you're in. What you need is sleep. Security will probably have found him by tomorrow."

"So they get to work while I go home, curl up in my nice cozy bed, and get some shut-eye? What if they don't find him? Or what if they do, but he gets away? If I'm there, I could—"

"Get in the way?"

"Help, Madi," I said, and my throat closed again. "Help the way I couldn't in that basement. I shouldn't have hesitated. I should have run through his illusions and tackled him the moment I saw him, and I didn't. I have to make up for that."

Madison touched her fingers to mine. "You don't have to make up for anything. You did everything you could, and you'll continue to be there for your team. But you need to accept that you'll be more useful to them once you've rested. Give security tonight to hunt the man down, and then you can have your way with him before they ship him to Moongrave."

I grunted. The supernatural prison up in the Northwest Territories was too good for Weldon. Or anyone else who'd helped set this trap.

"I see that look in your eyes. What would you do if you found him? Kill him?"

"Not right away," I said, and it came out more sulkily than I would have liked. I knocked back my drink and swivelled on my barstool to face her. "I'd question him. Ask him who sent him there, who made the bomb, what O'Malley's endgame is."

Madison raised an eyebrow. "You believe you're better trained to do this than our security team? That's their job, Jet, and you know they're as eager to wrap this up as you are. No one from SMOAC is sleeping tonight."

"Oh, I believe they can find him and question him, sure. But if he's able to stand on his own two feet by the time they're through with him, I won't be satisfied. He killed my team. He, or someone he knows, has threatened *you*. You think that's going to matter to security?"

Madison's gaze bored into mine. "Do motivations really matter here? I thought the goal was to prevent any more damage from happening."

I shrugged. "I guess I'm not as big as other people in the department. My friends and family matter more to me than the rest of the world does."

"What about the law?" Madison asked, her voice so infuriatingly level. "You remember laws, right? The same laws you've spent your career upholding and enforcing? Your team doesn't want to visit you in jail because you broke them. I know you're hurting, but be smart."

My shoulders slumped, and I hunched over the bar. I didn't want her to be right, but she was. Tearing Weldon to pieces would still be me losing my head. Strong meant calm. Smart.

"Fine. If I find him first, I'll call it in. Before I break anything fatal, okay? But I need to know, Madi. I need answers for my team. And I need O'Malley to know he should be very afraid right now, because I'm coming for him, and I won't stop until he's buried under so many charges he'll never see the sun again."

Madison folded her hands on the bartop. I felt like I was in a therapy session. At least there was more alcohol to see me through. "I think you should go home. You're an emotional wreck and not in a good place to be running into trouble."

Again she was right, and denying it would only make her dig her heels in.

"Why don't we go for a walk first?" she said. "Give you a chance to sober up and clear your head. How long have you been here?"

I glanced at the clock and shook my head. I'd lost track of the hours.

"Exactly. Come on. Let's get out of here."

I knew there was only so far I could argue with her. She might look fragile and official, but the woman was as solid as the wall she worked so hard to protect.

"Fine. A short one." Then I'd go to the office and grab Weldon's address. I could be at his place before morning, maybe surprise him out of his sweet, sweet slumber. Give him nightmares for the rest of his life, just as he'd done to me.

I slid Madison's purse towards her, and when I looked up, my attention landed on a man sitting on the other side of the bar. At the sight of him, lightning seemed to fill the room, every molecule charging and landing as sparks on my skin.

It's impossible, popped into my head at the same time I swore to myself, *That is Gideon Leigh*, and neither part of me knew what was real.

Although he was a good ten metres away, I felt his dark hair under my fingers, hair that looked like it should crunch under the pressure but was soft as down, the hard muscles of his arms, the intensity of his brown eyes.

Under that imagined gaze, the sparks absorbed into my flesh and turned to ice water in my veins. It couldn't be him. The universe wouldn't be so cruel as to send Gideon to Ottawa today of all days.

He's in New York. He can't be here. He'd have told me he was coming. He wouldn't dare come. It's all in my head.

The thoughts ping-ponged back and forth, a whirling dervish of shock, horror, and—goddammit it—hope that pulled me under and, for one blissful moment, made me forget everything else.

A gentle hand resting on mine once more jerked me back to the present, and I sucked in a breath. For a second, I worried I'd forgotten how to breathe.

"Jet?" Madison asked, fresh concern in her eyes. I realized she must have been talking when I zoned out. I'd missed every word she'd said. "Are you all right? You look like you've seen a ghost."

Reluctantly, I shifted my gaze back across the bar, and my heart lurched on finding the seat empty. I couldn't say what was stronger: my relief or my disappointment.

I pushed my drink aside and rose unsteadily to my feet. "That's the problem. Tonight is full of ghosts."

Chapter 6

Gideon

Particle by particle, I pulled myself into corporeal form, the mist I'd become solidifying into flesh, blood, and synthetic fibres. As soon as my body and clothing were whole again, I peered around the wall where I'd hidden myself.

Like a coward.

But even as I stared and watched Jet grab her jacket and walk out—walk being a generous term for the way she stumbled across the floor—I knew I'd made the right call.

Just my luck that in a city made of bars, my contact chose this one.

I couldn't decide whether that luck was good or bad.

Jet tripped in the doorway. Instinct made me step forward to help her, but before I got far, her friend in the pantsuit caught her around the waist and steadied her balance as they went outside.

The moment the door closed behind them, I sagged against the wall and kicked myself for even thinking about going over to say hi. I wasn't supposed to be here. I was breaking a whack-ton of federal laws by being here. To announce my visit to a fed would be asking to get my ass kicked and sent home, especially when she looked like she'd had her ass kicked herself. Considering how we'd parted ways two years ago, probably the last thing she wanted if she was feeling vulnerable was to see me.

Though I couldn't help but wonder what was wrong. I'd seen Jet Dawson angry—furious—nuclear. I would have sworn I'd seen her at her most broken. Tonight she looked well past broken. More like shattered. I hoped she was all right.

Common sense told me to forget her, and I was grateful she'd already left, taking temptation with her.

Let it go.

It was best for both of us if she didn't know I was in town. At least not until I'd gotten the information I'd come for.

I tried to put her out of my mind and returned to my contact at the bar. Not for the first time, I had to search my memory for the guy's name. Davis, I thought, though it didn't really matter. I wouldn't remember in another hour, anyway. The man blended in with any bar he called home. Literally blended. Like a chameleon on steroids. Most people would have looked right past him as though he were part of the decor. It wouldn't have surprised me to learn people regularly tried to sit on him, not realizing a living being occupied his stool. Beige cargo jacket over a white-and-red plaid work shirt, salt-and-pepper hair flattened by a black cap with *Eh?* written in friendly red letters across the front, jeans, and sneakers. Your average Joe. Just ignore the red-lined eyes and the hint of fangs when he smiled. A sloth demon down on his luck. Or maybe too damned lazy to do anything other than sit and work up his tab.

He stared at me with a raised eyebrow as I sat down beside him, but I pretended not to notice.

"You were saying?" I said. Casual. As though I'd gone to take a piss and not simply vanished from my seat into a cloud of mist to avoid my one-time partner.

My contact rolled his eyes and took a sip of beer. My kind of guy. No questions.

"I was saying I don't know why you wasted your time coming all the way up here. Don't you work for some kind of private security firm stateside? I thought you people had oodles of cash to track people down."

"Budget cuts," I said. "How about you tell me what you know."

He gave a drawn-out shrug. "Anyone with an ear to the rumour mill knows the bulk of the horde shipped out to Kingston a month ago. The syndicate's out. Ottawa got too hot for 'em." He snorted. "Or too boring."

As someone who'd kept both ears to the rumour mill, the information landed with a dull *whump*. "You're sure? But the club—"

Davis waved his hand in dismissal. "O'Malley still owns The Afterlife, sure. Why would he give up a sweet side hustle like that? But it's not his headquarters anymore. I'm tellin' ya, they vamoosed."

I usually tried not to assume anything on a mission, but the ones I had formed before coming up here had just made an ass out of me.

I didn't get it.

I'd come to Ottawa on good information. Or, at least, what I'd thought was good information. It should have been good information. My people had snooped into Jet's private intel—not that I would ever, *ever* tell her that—and according to everything she had on file, Mark O'Malley was still right here in the capital running the Death's Head Syndicate out of The Afterlife. If Davis was right, how could she not know he'd moved on?

Had she messed with her files? Let them fall out of date in case people like me poked around?

It was something I would do, but I didn't see Jet taking a messy strategy like that. She was too by-the-book. Everything according to the rules.

I knew I could have called her and asked for help. Maybe I should have. It would have felt less slimy than pawing through her secret-level files to get the information myself. I'd almost done it, too, right before I'd booked my plane ticket north. Had the phone in my hand and everything. A quick conversation to let her know my people at SilverGuard had heard the syndicate was making moves to push ghost across the border, an expansion of their business we had so far prevented.

My bosses wanted me to come up here in person—quick and quiet, authorized to gather intelligence and reveal my presence to as few people as possible—but if Jet had been willing to work with me, I might have avoided the trip.

In the end, I couldn't take the chance she wouldn't cooperate. Not only would she have cut off my line of inquiry, but she would have been alerted to my interest. She might have even made it a pain in the ass for me to cross the border.

Not impossible, of course—not for someone with my ability to mist my way past security—but more of a challenge.

So I'd come and had so far succeeded in keeping my head down while I went behind Jet's back and dug up whatever I could on the syndicate's spreading roots. Not an easy choice, but nothing about my job was easy. It was ruthless, demanding, and made sure I never forgot work came first, no matter who I had to hurt to get it done.

And as shitty as I felt about it, I knew on some level Jet would understand. Deep down. Beneath the betrayal. After all, she was as committed to SMOAC as I was to SilverGuard. It was the nature of the job that we did what we had to do.

"Anything else you want from me, or are you good if I turn back to my game while you scry the future out of the bartop?"

Whatshisname's voice pulled me back to the bar, the noise

of the crowd breaking through the filter of my thoughts.

"So you're saying Kingston?" I asked.

"Yessir."

If that was true, my bosses did have something to worry about. The supernatural border didn't quite line up with the mundane Canada-U.S. line, which meant depending on the avenues O'Malley intended to take, he could have an easy time slipping past mundane security into New York. As great as Border Services was, they weren't quite up to snuff when it came to supernatural smuggling. All kinds of magic could cover up what wasn't meant to be found.

"Thanks for your help."

He tipped his glass my way. "Thank you for the drink."

And just like that, he may as well have disappeared. I *knew* he was sitting beside me, but my brain skipped over him as he became more blank space than mass of flesh in my peripheral vision. Just like a sloth demon to slink away once the work was done, though I guessed I was lucky he'd agreed to talk to me at all.

Having gathered what I could, I threw some funny-coloured money on the counter. As I shoved my wallet into my pocket, I glanced at the television screen above the bar hoping to catch the score, but someone had switched the channel to the local news.

I was about to turn away when the crowd standing behind the reporter caught my attention, dozens of people—at least half of them visibly supes—jostling for a better view of what looked like a standard high-rise. The footage was from earlier today. The sun was still high—I likely hadn't arrived in town yet. A city street, not far from here by the look of it, filled with people and lined with police barricades. Our kind usually didn't like to gather unless it was in private or for something important. The more of us there were, the more strain it put on the perception filter to keep us hidden. Whatever had happened downtown had caused Ottawa's supernaturals to throw caution to the wind.

I dropped my gaze to the strip of words rolling along the bottom of the screen. *Nine confirmed dead in fatal gas leak. Street closed until further notice.*

Why should I care? It was sad, sure, but this wasn't my town. These weren't my people.

But I couldn't get Jet out of my head. The lost look on her face, the way she'd stumbled out the door as though the foundation of her universe had crumbled. My heart raced as I tried to guess how the two might be connected, because deep in my bones, I knew they were. Supernaturals in the crowd, nine dead, Jet devastated. Had she been there? Had she tried to prevent whatever had happened?

I curled my fingers around the phone in my back pocket, once more fighting the temptation to make sure she was okay. She didn't have to know I was close—just that I was thinking about her, that I was here if she needed to talk.

Because that would really brighten her day. The punch of reality made me pull my hand out of my pocket.

I searched the TV screen, hoping for more information. Something that might slip between the lines of what the mundane public was being told and the truth, but the story changed to a four-car pileup on the 417.

She has someone with her, I reminded myself, and did my best to hang on to that. My history with Jet had been a short, sweet firestorm, but I knew enough to suspect she wouldn't let anyone stick close to her for long if she felt weak.

I walked out of the bar, leaving behind the laughter and light inside.

A few people stood smoking on the sidewalk, and my body reacted to the smell of burning tobacco and nicotine, longing to join them and indulge in the vice that would take me out of my head for a minute.

I managed to hold back and walked past the group with a nod of regret before heading down the dark street. Stopping would risk opening myself up to conversation, and it was better for everyone that my presence go unnoticed.

As I walked towards the university and my shady accommodations, I let my thoughts wander. Kingston. Gas leak. Jet. Although I couldn't see the lines, the connection had to be there. The only jobs Jet worked these days were high profile, and from everything I'd learned, the Death's Head was the highest it got—a pulsing, spreading sickness that threatened to infect everything it touched. My mission in Ottawa was to make sure the plague didn't spread across the border, but that didn't mean I wasn't worried about the death toll up north.

As I tried to work it all out, three questions kept popping up to push everything else away. Questions I couldn't answer. Questions I didn't want to ask aloud.

What had really happened in that high-rise?

If it was connected to the Death's Head, how far would Jet go to stop them?

And the biggest question of all: how badly would she hurt me if SilverGuard got there first?

Chapter 7

Jet

THE HUMIDITY WRAPPED around me as soon as I left the sweet air conditioning in the bar. It clogged my pores and soaked my hair and clothes, suffocating me right out in the open. I tried to push it away, rearranging the air molecules to give me space, but I was too drunk and too exhausted to keep it up for long, and the air snapped back like an elastic band.

I staggered on my feet, and it was only because Madison was holding me steady that I made it to the corner. There had already been one embarrassing moment in the bar when I'd almost fallen on my face, and if she hadn't caught me, I'd probably still be lying on the floor.

"Which way did you want to go?" she asked as we turned onto the main street. "We might find a coffee shop still open, or I could help you home."

A bus sped by, the lights and billboards a flash of colour

that drew my eye, and the swift movement brought on a bout of dizziness. My stomach churned, and I sucked in a deep breath to stop myself from bringing up an entire night of whiskey.

"I don't want more people and I don't want to go home," I said once the nausea settled. "What's for me at home?"

"Your bed? A hot shower? A cup of tea?"

"Nice try, Madi, but you're not changing my mind that easily." I laughed with the classiest of snorts, and Madison rolled her eyes skyward. I didn't know why she was pushing it. She had to know that if I did go home, I would drink myself into oblivion. Not my usual coping strategy, but today was beyond punching bags and meditation. Tea. Right.

"So what's the plan, then?" she asked.

I don't know if it was her easy willingness to waste her night with a heartbroken drunk or the lingering illusion of Gideon's face across the bar—and the old wounds the thought of him had opened up—but I had to get away. Be alone.

Knowing Madison wouldn't let me out of her sight if she thought I was about to stumble into oncoming traffic, I worked to push through my alcoholic wobble and latch on to the glimmer of sobriety waiting for me beyond it. Just enough to form a few coherent sentences.

"I think I'm okay on my own," I said, and carefully pulled my arm out of her grip.

Her brow creased, and she didn't need to speak for me to hear her disapproval.

"I'll be fine," I said. Did my words slur? I paused, cleared my throat, and tried again. "Seriously. I need to cry, maybe scream a little. I don't need witnesses for that."

I hoped that would be enough to convince her. If I'd been sober, I would have known better.

"Forget your mental state for a second," she said. "You held an entire cloud of ghost in place today. You have to be feeling it. Why don't I get you home and stick around while you take a bath? We don't need to talk—I'll stay out of your way. You know how you'll feel tomorrow if you don't."

Impatience and a growing sense of claustrophobia squeezed the back of my neck. I didn't need to be managed, I needed space. I needed to find out where Weldon was, how to keep Madison safe.

My muscles and joints felt fine, loose and limber. All a bath would do was give me a place to stew—mentally and physically.

"Once I sober up, I'll take a bath." I tried not to sound as irritated as I felt, but by the faint flinch in Madison's expression, I guessed I'd failed. I counted to ten to calm myself down and lowered the guard around my emotions to give her a full blast of them. Anything to convince her I wasn't about to start a fight with a stranger or jump off a bridge the moment she walked away. "I'll be okay. I need some time to myself."

Madison frowned, her gaze moving across my face, but finally she let out a little huff and set her hands on her hips. "Fine. But promise me you'll take a walk before you hunt down that guy. Give it some serious thought. Serious, sober thought."

My shoulders relaxed. "Thanks, Madi. I promise." I hesitated, then added, "I'm glad you came to find me. I needed you, and you were there."

"Always," she said.

I held out my arms, and she stepped into them, gathering me into a tight hug.

"Call me if you need anything, okay?" she said. "I don't care about the time. If you get home and you're sitting in the dark and you feel like you want to punch a hole through your wall, pick up the phone instead. And if you do go after him, call me first. You shouldn't go on your own."

My throat tightened, grief, gratitude, and a spike of fear over being left alone with my thoughts giving me a moment's urge to change my mind and take Madison up on her offer to stay with me. I steadied my resolve and said, "I will."

I hoped her concerns were unfounded. Right now, I felt more stable than I had in hours. No less heartbroken, but less unravelled. As soon as more alcohol left my system, I would concentrate on strategy. When the grief returned, as I was sure it would, I would bury myself in tactics and logic. Work had always saved me in the past, so I would put it to use tonight.

"As for you, go straight home, all right? I don't know if there's anything else to worry about right now, but don't take any chances. If you sense anyone or anything around that shouldn't be, call me."

"I promise." She let me go and walked away, shooting me a last look over her shoulder before she crossed the street and headed home.

I didn't know what I'd done to deserve her friendship, but I'd never been more grateful for her. Without her, I would probably still be at the bar, drinking until Simon cut me off, imagining even more impossible faces in the crowd.

The woman was a saint.

There was nothing I wouldn't do for her. Jump in front of a moving vehicle, take a bullet—whatever. Everything I should have done for my team and hadn't.

A sharp pain squeezed my chest and cut off my airways. I reached for the side of a building and prayed the dark spots in my vision didn't mean I was about to pass out.

With effort, I sucked in one breath, then another, and as the spots receded, I sank to the ground and pressed my back into the brick wall. The pain spread, tightening my stomach, my shoulders.

What was happening? Why did it feel like my insides were pulling apart at the seams?

A scream built deep within me and tears pricked the corners of my eyes, and it was only when the first sob burst out of me that I realized Madison had taken her beautiful mood-balancing power with her. My grief and shock and brokenness had returned in a crashing wave, and now that I was alone, I wished I hadn't left the bar. Or at least that I'd taken the bottle of whiskey with me.

I fought to get myself under control. This pain would pass. The inability to breathe, the tightness in my chest—it was all in my head. I would survive this. I had to survive this. My squad needed me to.

Walking. Walking would help.

Slowly, using the wall to inch myself up, I rose to my feet. My balance was shaky, but soon enough I found it and put one foot in front of the other down the street.

To my horror, the alcohol-induced haze was lifting, so I picked up my pace. If I couldn't be drunk and I couldn't control my emotions, I would sweat it out. Keep my muscles moving until only the physical pain remained.

Deep as my longing was to go after Weldon immediately, I'd made Madison a promise, and even in my current state, I recognized it was a smart one to keep. Finding him while I was drunk meant I wouldn't be at my best. He could slip away... or wind up dead before I could stop myself. So first, keep my promise and sober up, then go to the office to get his address.

Working on the assumption that the faster I moved, the faster I would sweat out the booze, I took a roundabout way to work, following the streetlights, turning left and right at random. Downtown Ottawa was made of one-way streets, organized little blocks that kept anyone—even the most inebriated— from getting too lost. I navigated my way past my apartment building and ended up along the canal.

In the winter, this place was a hub of tourist activity. One of the longest skating rinks in the world, peppered with hot chocolate and fried pastry stands.

In the summer, it was a murky body of water that cyclists and joggers got to smell as they commuted across town.

At night, it was even less to look at.

I paused against the railing and stared into the dark depths, the water lit only by the streetlights that lined the bicycle path. The pools of light caught the wriggle of mer hair along the surface—the mass of green tresses most mundanes took for seaweed. The merfolk were probably waiting for some drunk to teeter in so they could enjoy a late-night snack, and I shoved away from the railing and continued down the path to make sure it wasn't me.

Walking had worn down the sharp edges of my grief, but the dark beast prowled close to the surface of my mind, waiting for me to slow down so it could pounce and devour me. The air pulsed with an energy I could almost taste. It buzzed over my skin and set my bones vibrating. I had to move. As long as my legs kept taking me from one street to another, offering my mind new sights and smells to stay distracted, I could keep the monster at bay. My boots hit the pavement with a steady beat, and I focused on the sound to drown out the screams lingering in my ears.

Despite my efforts, my footsteps morphed into the drop of bodies on a plastic-wrapped floor. My breaths became the heavy pants of friend fighting friend in a dimly lit room obscured by drifting white powder.

Rage built in my gut, bubbled up the back of my throat, and flooded down my arms and into my hands, curling my fingers into fists that flew out and struck the drywall of a construction barrier. Dust clouded in my face, choking me, and I set off at a run. Hopefully no taxpayer had witnessed my wilful destruction of property.

I wished I could have torn down the entire wall.

I ran until my lungs burned, and by the time I slowed, I had made my way back downtown. Alcohol still coursed through my veins, but my head was clearer and the desire to drive Weldon's face into the floor was as strong as ever, so I checked off my promise to Madison as complete and entered the office building.

I dug my pass out of my jacket pocket, punched in my after-hours code, and pushed my way through the rotating doors into the lobby. The rubber soles of my boots squeaked against the tile, drawing the attention of the two commissionaires behind the counter.

I flashed them my pass, swiped it over the security panel, and when the gates opened, forced myself to walk into the elevator bay. The space was too cramped, too closed in, and the air only got denser as I stepped into the elevator and saw the button for the second subbasement. The Peaview Hospital. Where the surviving members of my team would have been admitted.

My heart thrummed, winding my nerves tight.

Stay focused. Weldon first. Answers first.

But how could I avoid my team and still call myself their captain? They had risked their lives for a mission I could have stopped, and by some miracle had made it through. They deserved whatever support I could offer.

Before I changed my mind, I hit the button for the hospital—an option that would never appear to anyone who didn't know to see it—and closed my eyes as the door slid shut. As the elevator dropped, I couldn't shake my terror of what I would find when I got downstairs. What if more of them had died since being admitted? What if they were alive but lifeless, plugged into machines that would keep their hearts beating even though they would never laugh at each other's stupid jokes again?

My joints were starting to ache, the muscles in my shoulders seizing up. In the centre of my brow, my third eye shrieked, catching the details of every small thing I touched and the movements of people throughout the building. On most days, I could filter it out and narrow in on what I wanted to see. Tonight, I picked up traces of the thousands who had used this elevator today. Rough jabs at the buttons, distracted brushes. Cotton, polyester, wool. A spilled coffee. A make-out session. Stomping feet. A dropped cellphone.

Every second felt like hours, stretching my sanity, and when the doors finally opened, I jumped at the cheerful *ping*.

I stepped into the empty hallway of the subbasement. The fluorescent lights hummed in the ceiling, a high-pitched whine that normally would have made my nerves jump out of my skin but tonight served to drown out my third eye.

Compared to the emptiness of the lobby, the hospital was a madhouse. Nurses and doctors, porters and aides scurried here and there. Beds were moved, orders were called. The sound system announced a code purple in room 132, and one begrudging janitor sighed and grabbed his bucket.

I walked down the hallway towards the information desk, where a woman in blue scrubs sat with her forehead resting in her hands, a cascade of charts lined up in front of her. Speckles of grey touched her dark hair and a few fine lines creased the corners of her mouth. Tonight was no doubt busier than she'd seen it in a while.

"Good evening," I said. My voice barely made it through the cacophony, and I had to repeat myself before Miriam— according to her name tag—looked up. The silver gaze that met mine showed the telltale weariness of someone who had worked here far longer and seen more than most people could endure. She was probably worried I was going to dump more work on her plate.

"I'm Captain Jet Dawson." I swallowed hard. "A few members of my squad were brought in this afternoon. The gas leak incident."

Apparently I'd spoken the magic words, because Miriam's

demeanour shifted. Her shoulders straightened, her mouth went soft, and her eyes melted into pools of sympathy. I clenched my teeth and held myself rigid, certain that if I gave her a chance, she would hug me. I didn't need her pity. Didn't want it. I wanted my team.

"Of course," she said. "Colonel Torrence mentioned you might stop by tonight. Follow me, I'll take you to them."

I wanted to tell her not to bother. All I needed was the room number and I could find my own way, but she rushed around the counter with such motherly eagerness, I didn't have it in me to shoo her away.

It touched my heart even as I shied away from the kindness. It was so much harder to stay strong when people were nice.

Miriam led me away from the chaos to a large room at the end of the ward. Six beds were arranged around the space, two per wall. Five of them were occupied. Here, the noise of the hospital was dulled, and only the steady beep of heart monitors filled the silence.

A chill ran down my back at the stillness in the room. Too still for my lively pack.

"How are they?" I asked, stepping towards Zeke. According to the machines, everything was stable, but he was hooked up to a ventilator and showed no reaction when I looped my fingers through his.

"Dr. MacDonald won't know until the test results come in, but there's been no change since this afternoon, so he's hoping for the best." She adjusted Mandy's pillow and straightened her sheet. "Ghost isn't a friendly drug, as I'm sure you know. Even if they wake up, we don't know what state they'll be in."

I understood what she was too polite to say: that given the alternatives, it might be better if they didn't wake up.

Miriam rested a soft hand on my shoulder. "I'll give you some time. There's no rush."

"Thank you," I said, and wished I could tell her how grateful I was that she didn't insist on staying with me.

She left the room, and though she left the door open, me and my team might as well have been the only six people on the floor.

I couldn't decide what to do first. At least with Miriam here, I'd had some grounding. Some idea of how I was supposed to behave. Alone, I felt unanchored. I moved from bed to bed, hoping to get some response from one of them but receiving only a series of reassuring beeps. Zeke, Marc-André, Mandy, Luvy, Ray. All of them with lives and families, dreams and ambitions.

"You'll get through this," I said to them. "You'll all be at home in no time. Mandy, you have that stained glass thing to finish for my grandmother's birthday, remember? And Ray, that bike is going to rust if you don't take it for a ride."

After I made the tour, I started for the door, ready to begin my search for Weldon, but as though my feet had a mind of their own, I shuffled back to Zeke's bedside and pulled up a chair. The steady in-out of the ventilator left me on edge. I leaned back and took in his face: the long lashes that settled on his sallow skin, the shaved brown hair that left a faint stubble along his scalp. He had been with me for ten years and was as much my rock as Eric. As I sat there, staring at his slack face, I didn't know what I would do if he didn't pull through.

"Stay strong for me, you hear?" I said. "That's an order."

I half-expected his shoulders to straighten as he snapped to attention, but there was only the automated rise and fall of his chest.

I sank deeper into my chair and stretched my legs out in front of me. Now that my initial fears had faded, I was glad I'd come. I hoped in some strange way they knew I was here and that my visit would give them the strength to fight whatever chemicals were pulling them towards oblivion.

And now that I'd put my mind at ease about these five, I felt I owed it to the rest of my squad to reassure them as well. Time was ticking towards dawn and my deadline to leave the Weldon search to security, but even so, I pulled out my phone and opened the JetPack group chat. Adam and Katie had started it as a joke over a year ago—we spent so much time together, it was ridiculous for us to stay in touch during our off-hours—and it had remained active ever since. Family photos, memes, and jokes flooded the feed day in, day out, and it pained me that the last message had come from Ellie over twelve hours ago. Ellie, who now lay dead in the morgue.

I ground my teeth and set my thumbs to the keyboard.

At the hospital, I wrote. Our guys are stable. Doc is waiting for test results. Someone make a note to mock Ray's hair when he wakes up. Verging on Flock of Seagulls territory right now.

Anything to give them some good news and maybe a bit of a smile. Though considering the hour, I hoped most of them wouldn't see the message until tomorrow. They needed the sleep.

The thought of closing my eyes and taking a rest triggered a thousand images as my day cycled through its millionth repetition. I felt like I'd been stuck in the same loop since the dawn of time. Had I ever not been standing outside a stairwell debating whether to call off the mission? Not been listening to my squad tear each other and themselves to pieces and choking on their own blood? Not been caught in a plastic-wrapped room using every ounce of strength I possessed to hold back a cloud of toxic powder that could have wiped out an entire block if it got past me?

The memory continued into the bar, me drinking with Jason and the others until their families and friends had lured them away to gentler comforts. It continued past the time I nearly drank myself unconscious and after Madison had arrived.

It stumbled over the familiar face across the bar.

In the silence of the hospital room, I latched on to that moment, searching for assurance that Gideon Leigh hadn't actually been there. That it had been some random guy with brown hair and a rugged jaw line. My brain had planted Gideon's face on him because my subconscious was a bitch.

In a twisted way, it made sense he would pop into my head today. After all, he'd held the starring role the last time my life had blown up. I tried to push the memories away, but they slammed against my skull. New York City two years ago. Brooklyn. A case I'd consulted on with the FBI. A handsome agent who'd won me over with his wit and willingness to do whatever it took to get the job done. Anything. Even lie to me.

Gideon had needed help gaining access to a smuggling ring that was sneaking unprocessed supernaturals into Canada. He'd made me laugh, impressed me with his dedication to the job, and, after a week, his skills off the job. Goddamn, he was perfect. Lean muscle, eyes that melted into pools of chocolate when he saw something he wanted, and a smile that tightened my stomach and sent shocks of pleasure through my body.

And he hadn't been an agent at all. Just a goddamn private security officer. Nothing more than a spy who had used me to get information.

I still remembered his expression when he'd told me the truth. Three weeks into the operation. We'd shut down the smugglers and were celebrating with a quick fuck in what he'd told me was his "undercover apartment" in Brooklyn. Bullshit. It had been his tiny, dirty place all along. As much of a lie as everything else he'd told me. And he'd confessed the truth like it was no big deal. Like I would *understand.* The shock had come as a physical blow. After everything I'd trusted him with, after I'd let my guard drop, and he'd paid me back with lies.

Even now, two years later, the memory made me want to punch him in the face. Then kiss him until I ran out of breath. Then punch him in the face again.

Anger simmered deep within me, and I tore my thoughts away. For good this time, I told myself. What was the point of hanging on to a ghost when I had the living to focus on?

But the truth was, I should have known better. I should have seen through Gideon's charms from the start. Just as I should have called a stop to this mission at the first twinge of my third eye. Some part of me had known, and I hadn't acted. And now I was here, and my team was…

I dug the heels of my palms into my eyes and swallowed a scream. The effort of holding it back set fire to my chest, and the pain was sweet. Deserved. What right did I have to be here safe and well when my team lay dead and others possibly in danger?

How is that going to help them?

Upstairs I would find Weldon's address, and once I tracked him down, I would make him tell me everything I needed to nail O'Malley. That was how I would help my team. That was what Madison hadn't understood about why I couldn't hand him off to the security team so easily.

On unsteady legs, I rose to my feet and tested my balance

by leaning over to lay my hand on Zeke's shoulder. "Get some rest, bud. I'll be back to check on you guys soon."

The steady beep of his heart monitor followed me out the door and echoed in my ears all the way to my office.

My floor, one above the hospital, was busy when I arrived, but almost entirely with security officers on the other side of the building. Our task force units wouldn't be called in until there were doors to break down. Arrests and questioning were done by people with skills beyond smashing skulls.

Which benefited me, because it meant there was no one to ask me what I was doing digging through Michael's filing cabinet at one o'clock in the morning.

I pulled the file marked *Death's Head* and splayed it across his desk. It was a massive file, one of several, with every detail we'd collected over the years. Including, thankfully, the addresses of some of O'Malley's minions. Not that the information had ever helped us much—they never took their business home and kept their heads low enough that we rarely had reason to knock on their doors—but tonight the info hoarding would pay off.

I hoped.

Mike Weldon's information was near the bottom of the list. He was far from a syndicate heavy hitter, but annoying enough to have caught our attention.

I scribbled his address on a scrap piece of paper—by chance, he lived only a half-hour walk away—then quickly scanned the rest of his file. Other than his ability to create and maintain mass illusions, he was nothing special. No mention of bomb making, which meant someone else was involved, and I was going to find out who and stop them before they made another one.

I tidied Michael's office, made sure the filing cabinet was locked, and left the building.

Again the humidity hit me as I stepped outside, but I ignored it and set off at a comfortable jog towards the bridge that would take me into Vanier, one of Ottawa's rougher neighbourhoods. Weldon's address echoed in my head with every slap of my boots against the pavement.

A few voices reached me from house parties along the way, but I kept to myself until I stopped in front of a tidy ranch-style bungalow. Opening my third eye, I took in the property, wanting a better idea of what to expect before I approached. Silvery shadows moved around me. *Weldon returning home no more than three hours ago. Three more shadows heading towards the front door within the last hour.*

Shit.

Security team?

It was possible I'd missed my shot… but something about the way the shadows moved didn't look right for one of our teams. They weren't covering the exits or each other. Almost as though they knew Weldon would have no issue with them being here.

I pushed forward in time, and soon the shadows appeared

again, leaving the house only shortly before I'd arrived. Recently enough that I could make out three men. Large, striding confidently towards a sleek muscle car parked on the street in front of the house.

I dipped into a half-crouch to avoid being in full view of the picture window and crept towards the front door. My stomach dropped on finding the door unlocked, and as I pushed it open and stepped into the house, I gave up trying to be discreet.

The place reeked of blood.

Phone in hand, I turned on the flashlight and made my way into the living room, careful not to step on anything security might need to process.

Because there, lying on the floor with his nose broken and his neck snapped, was Mike Weldon.

O'Malley had beat me to him.

Chapter 8

Madison

I CRAWLED INTO bed, emotionally drained, psychologically fractured. How had my life tilted so much in such a brief span of time? Barely registering one change before another hit me over the head.

Today's events had me reeling, and as I pulled up my comforter, making sure I left enough room for my tabby cat Persephone to get comfortable beside me, I was ready for sleep to elude me.

When I opened my eyes and found myself in a forest fully in bloom with flowers that weren't in season, I wished I'd tried harder to stay awake. I opened my mind to take in my surroundings, and although I sensed no one, I knew I wasn't alone.

Even if this hadn't been a dream state, I wouldn't have sensed her. The one person in the world who could block off her energy so completely, I didn't even detect her as a void.

Meril.

"Your Majesty," I said to the sunflowers dancing on an imaginary breeze. Their cheerful yellow petals were bright and vibrant, as full of life and happiness as the waking world was of death and heartbreak.

"Hello, granddaughter," her soft voice spoke behind me. I wasn't fooled. Beneath the feathery gentleness were barbs sharp enough to pierce my soul if I wasn't careful.

I didn't want to turn around and face her, but knew her illusion of softness would give way if I didn't. It was one thing to strive to remain out of her sights, but a whole other problem to disrespect her.

Steeling myself, I turned.

The queen sat on a stone bench among the flowers, looking nothing like how I knew her to be in person. Gone were the gowns and trappings of court she usually wore, and in their place was a figure-clinging dress of the palest blue lace. She might have been formed from the sky, a shard of the universe, an eternal.

For all I knew, that's exactly what she was. Just because I was related to her didn't mean I had any clue about her origins. Goddess? Demon? All of the above? My abilities, my blood, descended from her, but were part of the same mystery that made up most supernatural heritage, and I did my best not to dwell on it.

A far more immediate concern weighed on me—why were

we here? That it had something to do with the attack and threat on my life was a given, but what new nightmare had I awoken into?

"You have news to share with me?" she asked, and I swallowed a laugh. Asking me as if she didn't have all the details already.

"I'm sure your people have a better idea of what happened than I do, Your Majesty," I said. "The attack on the building today came as a surprise to the department, and everyone involved is seeking answers."

"I'm pleased to hear such a threat is receiving the minister's full attention within his limited means."

I pressed my palms flat against my thighs to keep them from curling into fists. "His means are not so limited, Your Majesty. He has the resources of the entire department at his disposal."

"And yet you've not caught the man who waged the attack."

I raised my chin in a show of confidence. "No, Your Majesty. Not that I've heard."

"Come," she said, and gestured to the space beside her. "Sit."

I didn't want to get any closer to her. Dream state or not, I didn't trust that she wouldn't grab me and drag me over the wall. I also couldn't ignore a direct command, so I perched myself at the far end of the stone, leaving as much of a gap between us as possible.

"You understand what will happen if the guilty are not caught and punished."

"Yes, Your Majesty."

"I cannot allow any threat to the realm."

"I know, Your Majesty."

I kept my focus on the flowers in front of us that danced so trouble-free in the false breeze, but I felt her stare burning a hole into my head. Was she trying to dig out secrets? She was welcome to them if it helped get me out of this place sooner.

"If Jean-Luc is unable to track them down and the threat rises, I want you on my council, Madison. You have done remarkable work maintaining the stability of the department on your side of the wall, but I will not allow my blood to stand in the path of danger when she could be serving at my side."

I slid my tongue around the bitterness spilling from the back of my throat. This wasn't about keeping me safe; she wanted to be sure she could use me. Meril forbid the queen lose a pawn.

"I have faith the situation won't come to that, Your Majesty. There are many people on this side of the wall who would ensure my protection if my life were indeed in danger."

Jet had already made that clear, and while some of her motivation might be that she didn't want to lose her best friend, I also trusted that she wanted to keep me safe for my own sake.

"If the guilty party attacks again, if our secret gets out, if the wall is threatened, your personal safety is no longer my priority."

"Yes, Your Majesty."

"I will do whatever is necessary to protect the realm."

In a dream within a dream, the scene in front of me melted away into a world of fire and ash. Lava flowed in rivers between high-rises that hadn't been there a second ago. Flames reached out from upper windows, screams rang in my ears, and in the distance an army marched, supernaturals of all kinds with Meril at its head. Not the queen who sat beside me, but the behemoth she could become if provoked. Giant wings made of night sky and shadow stretched behind her to cloak the country in her power. Her eyes flashed with lightning, and thunder rumbled from her mouth.

The threat of her omnipotence was something neither side of the realm had ever experienced, but the myth of her had ensured her position since the dawn of time.

I did not want to be around if the myth stepped into reality.

As the darkness brightened into day, the storm calmed, and the meadow returned, I bowed my head. "Yes, Your Majesty."

"Warn your minister. Inform him of the consequences should he not resolve this situation speedily and discreetly."

"I will, Your Majesty."

The world around me faded, my audience coming to an end now that Meril had achieved her purpose, and the queen and I were all that remained in a space of pure white. She took my hand in hers. Her fingers were marble, cold and firm, but she pressed mine gently as a silent, inscrutable message.

Then she was gone, her melodic tones replaced by Persephone's angry yowls as I lurched up in a cold sweat.

My room was dark and still, silent except for the ticking clock in the living room.

I let out a breath and dropped my chin to my chest. I did not look forward to speaking with Jean-Luc in the morning.

Chapter 9

Jet

THE SECURITY OFFICERS took twenty minutes to arrive at Weldon's home. I waited on the front step for the pair to look around and used the time to hammer out an explanation for why I was here.

This wasn't my job.

My job was to kick down doors and make arrests of people and groups the security team deemed high-risk. They identified the threat, I dealt with it.

So showing up at the house of the man I'd seen in the de Lauer subbasement went against every regulation, and that wasn't me. Madison had been right in what she'd said at the bar—I followed the rules. I liked rules. Rules made it easy to keep things black and white, which in my job was essential. I didn't have time to make a million judgement calls when I walked onto a scene. Good, bad, victim, threat. That's all there was to it. Try to make sure no one got killed, lock away the people who deserved it.

That way of thinking had earned me promotions while Eric lagged behind. The only reason he stood as my lieutenant now was because I'd pushed him to take every test, to second-guess every instinct he possessed to run wildly into any situation.

Now here I was, breaking all my own rules, all the department's rules, and hoping I'd escape without a serious slap on the wrist.

When the officers emerged, I rose from the step to meet them.

"What were you doing here, Captain?" asked the one named Lesser, according to her badge.

"Staking out the property," I said. It was as good a reason as any. "I've had run-ins with Weldon in the past and knew where he lived, so I thought I'd sit on his house for a while. Not like I would have slept much tonight, anyway."

"Mmhmm," she said, and I ignored her skepticism as her partner, Dyer, made a note in his little notebook. "What made you go into the house?"

"I saw three people leaving about an hour ago, but the house was too dark, too quiet. Just struck me as odd for someone who'd had guests over. So on a whim I tried the door and found it unlocked."

Dyer made another note. "Could you identify any of the people you saw leaving?"

I wished I could, and for the second time today cursed the limitations of my third eye. How easy it would be if I could link Weldon's visitors to O'Malley.

Because one of the realizations I'd had while I sat on the porch was that Weldon's death had screwed us. He'd been our only known connection to the Death's Head Syndicate. The only one who could have corroborated my report that I'd heard the voice over the camera system in that plastic-wrapped room.

So yes, I wished I could have recognized faces. Sent the security team to question O'Malley's goons while the rest of my team gathered up to take them down. A backhanded approach to destroy the syndicate, as much a revenge mission as a legal one, and take O'Malley and his ghost down for good.

Instead, all I could offer was, "Not in this light, no. Just shadows. Big guys, though."

"Right, well," Lesser said, and Dyer tucked his notebook away. "You're lucky it looks like he's been dead for a while, otherwise your being here so soon after what he did to your people wouldn't look so good on your record."

I blanched. Were they seriously suggesting I'd killed him?

I crossed my fingers I'd still been with Madison at the bar when he was killed.

"We'll take it from here," Dyer said. "Keep your phone on in case we have more questions, but you're free to go."

I opened my mouth to ask if I could stay. A few minutes in Weldon's house and maybe I'd find the evidence I needed, but the pair was already walking away, and I opted to get out while I could.

Though where the hell was I supposed to go?

The rush of finding Weldon, of accepting that O'Malley had been a step ahead of us once more, had erased the last of my alcoholic haze, leaving me sad and exhausted. With Weldon's death went my only course of action. The aim I'd latched on to like a life raft. Without him, without any other tie to the syndicate, I was floating again, stuck with the option of going home, crawling into bed, and lying in the dark thinking about my fallen team.

I groaned and kicked an empty beer can lying in the street. To hell with that. I wanted to be alone, but I needed someone to be alone with who understood why. Really understood it. Not Madison's gentle empathy or not Zeke's silent company.

With no other place to go, I turned my feet towards Eric's apartment.

The lights on the second floor of the Victorian walk-up were on, but I wouldn't have left even if they weren't. Eric had lived through the day at my side and cared as much as I did about the troops we'd lost—and the ones we might still lose.

I rang the doorbell and propped myself against the wall as I waited.

What time was it? After last call, anyway. The bars had been emptying as I'd walked up Bank Street, and I regretted my missed opportunity to grab another drink for the road.

Footsteps sounded from inside as Eric came downstairs, and the door opened. He stood there in white-and-black boxers and a white T-shirt, cradling a half-finished bottle of scotch at his side. His eyes were red-lined, his face pale. At the sight of me, he opened his mouth to speak, but I shook my head. I didn't want to hear it.

I jerked my chin towards the bottle. "You drinking without me?"

I reached for it, and he let go without a fuss, his gaze following me as I took a swig. The alcohol burned down the back of my throat and settled in my stomach, bringing me part of the way back to where I'd been when I'd left Mooney's.

Good.

"You have any better ideas?" he asked.

I took another drink and quirked my eyebrow as I returned the bottle. He stood aside to let me in and led the way upstairs. The grey carpet crunched under my boots with years of salt and dirt, the cracked walls and broken window adding to the grunge—a shame for a beautiful old home. But when Eric opened the door to the second-floor apartment, I stepped into the tidiness of his living space. The broadloom carpet was clean and uncluttered in the entryway, a vast change from my own apartment, and every item on every surface had its proper place.

"Need a glass, or do you want to keep things simple?" He waggled the bottle in front of me, and I shrugged.

"Booze is booze. Anything sounds good to me."

I kicked off my boots and took the scotch from him, taking it into the bedroom.

"Jet…" he said, following me.

Despite the state of him, I didn't hear any drunken slur in his words. How had he spent his night, then, if not doing his best to hide at the bottom of a bottle? How else had he been coping?

I hit the light switch, and a small bedside table lamp turned on, casting its soft glow over the tall queen-size bed with its navy-blue duvet and white sheets.

Without waiting, I took off my jacket and threw it at a chair in the corner. It missed the seat and slid to the floor.

Eric leaned his shoulder against the door frame. "You talk to Madison?"

I nodded. "She talked. I listened. She said nothing I hadn't already thought of myself. Didn't help. Weldon's dead."

"What?" I don't think I could have shocked him more.

"I went to his place, hoped to talk to him, get him to rat out O'Malley, but the boss's guys beat me there by half an hour. Smashed Weldon's face into the floor."

I wandered the empty space in his room, unable to keep still. A photo of him, Zeke, Laura, and Ellie sat on his dresser. The four had their arms around each other's shoulders and wore wide grins, their faces and uniform tees spattered in mud. I had taken the photo six years ago at the end of a training weekend in British Columbia. All of them thick with muscle, hair slick with sweat, proud of their bruises. Now, of the four, one of them lay in a coma and two were dead.

Another swig of scotch numbed the tearing pain in my chest, and for a moment I couldn't move.

Eric closed the distance between us. He didn't touch me, but the air tingled against my bare arm.

"I'm sorry, Jet," he said. "I know that was our best lead."

"Our only lead," I said, talking to the photo instead of him. "I doubt O'Malley's going to go all 'aw shucks, you got me' when we ask him about it." My disappointment hurt almost as much as my grief. Answers would have helped us heal. An arrest would have helped us find closure. Instead, I was left with the weight of my guilt and no reprieve from the pain. "I should have stopped them. The second I caught the blip with the illusions, I should have pulled them back."

"You couldn't have known, Jet." His voice was husky, intense. I couldn't look at him, not trusting myself not to cry. "You followed protocol. You did what you were supposed to do."

"And look where it got me. I should have listened to your ideas during planning. You wanted to break the rules and wait for them to come out. If I'd listened to you, this wouldn't have happened."

Eric's strong fingers slipped between mine, his skin cool despite the weather. With a gentle pressure, he turned me towards him. "Even if we'd waited, no one would have come out," he said, his blue eyes bright with conviction and unshed tears. "Eventually we would have gone in, and who knows how it would have turned out. The shadows in the lobby might have been too old for you to notice anything was wrong, so you wouldn't have been on your guard. You wouldn't have been so quick to raise the wall. You followed the rules and saved lives. Remember that, or you'll go crazy."

Fourteen years this man had been there for me, both of us raising the other up, pushing and dragging each other towards the next goal.

"I'm glad you didn't rush ahead of me," I said. "I'm glad I ordered you to stay behind."

He said nothing, just brushed my hair behind my ear. His touch, so familiar, raised goosebumps along the back of my neck, and I leaned into him to soak up his heat. His body shifted to meet mine, and my goosebumps spread down my arms and across my stomach. Warmth grew under my skin, blood rushing through my veins in a steady pulse—as steady as Zeke's heart monitor across town.

I'd come here to form a plan of action, but now I wanted to lose myself. Forget how all the pieces were supposed to fit— the painful truth that they'd never fit the same way again. I would need to create a new picture, but to do that, I'd have to erase the old one.

I took two gulps from the bottle before I set it on the dresser, the glass obscuring the photograph behind it. The alcohol brought its sweet detachment, and I barely felt my fingers as I pulled my T-shirt over my head, giving it a tug when it caught on my ponytail, and tossed it across the room to rest with my jacket.

"Hey," Eric said, pulling me to him, "what's going on in that head of yours?"

He ducked to catch my eye, but I didn't want to see my pain staring back at me. Instead, I turned my attention to the lines of his neck as they travelled under the collar of his T-shirt and brushed my lips along the soft curve of his skin, inhaling the faint headiness of alcohol and a whiff of leather that lingered from his favourite jacket.

Our ranks had stopped meaning anything to either of us about five years back, and we'd taken to scratching each other's itches when the need arose. Tonight, the itch was unbearable.

"Jet," he said, and though he tensed beneath my touch, his voice was rough with want. "Come on, why don't we get something to eat? The Diner's open."

I didn't want him to stop me. Didn't want responsible or gentle or honourable. My temper flared, and on the other side of the room, the lamp rattled. "Do you really want to grab something to fucking eat, Eric?"

His attention slid to the lamp and back to me without any

trace of surprise. Just acceptance and an ever-increasing desire, the blue of his eyes deepening into a rich indigo. I could almost hear the debate in his head about whether he should be a good man and sober me up, give us a chance to talk, or whether he should give in and take me the way we both wanted him to.

I had no such dilemma.

For the last fourteen hours, I'd been too lost in possibilities and what-ifs. I was caught in a tornado, unable to see straight and with no way of getting my feet on the ground. All I needed was time with my troops, but Eric was one of the few I had left. The two of us in a room full of corpses. I needed to remind myself I hadn't died with them. That I could still feel. Breathe. Fuck. Whatever it took to find the spark that kept me going— the spark that, right now, was on the brink of going out.

A low growl rumbled from the back of his throat as he decided, and I curled my arm around his neck to bring his lips to mine. His large hands settled on my hips, his fingers curling into my waist to pull me closer. I slid my hands under his T-shirt and pulled it over his head to reveal the planes of his chest. A scar ran from sternum to belly button, a souvenir from his fight with a wizard, and I traced the ridges, enjoying the way my touch set off a wave of shivers under his skin.

In one smooth motion, he unhooked my bra and threw it across the room. Though his attention had already turned to my chest, his lips curving around my nipple in a way that left me gasping, my bra landed in the centre of the chair—Eric with his perfect aim. Mr. Bullseye himself.

His tongue danced and swirled, and any ability I had to hold myself up evaporated. He grabbed my ass and lifted me up. I wrapped my legs around his waist as he carried me to the bed, and I kept him with me as he laid me down, grinding myself against him, wanting more.

He trailed his lips down my stomach and unsnapped the button of my jeans as he went, tugging them over my thighs, my calves. He tossed my clothes to join my bra on the chair.

Then he was on top of me, his weight and warmth a comfort to all the fractured pieces of my heart. His ragged breath matched mine, and I drank in the heat, the passion, the *life* that came from his kiss. His hands were everywhere, exploring and teasing, removing the last barriers that divided us. On another night, I might have drawn out every sensation, savoured every wave of pleasure, but desire left me aching, and I needed release—that perfect moment where time stopped and nothing else existed.

Twisting my legs through his, I flipped Eric onto his back. His hands slipped upwards, cupping my breasts as I positioned myself over him, and he growled again, the sound mixing with my gasp as I took him in. For a moment, I stayed completely still, adjusting my focus from need to satisfaction, but when the feel of him inside me stopped being enough, I fell into a rolling rhythm that made him arch his back and dig his fingers into the thick of my hips.

My skin flushed with rising heat, and my breath grew quick and shallow. The deeper I followed my most primal instinct, the further I moved from any conscious thought, until there was nothing left but me, Eric, and the tide rising within us. When the wave finally crested, I rode it as long and as far as it would take me, and wished I never had to come back.

When our need finally subsided, our bodies and minds emptied of anything but each other, Eric passed out at my side, the blue duvet cover wrapped around our legs.

I watched him sleep for a while, taking in the way his eyelashes fluttered as he dreamed, the light twitches of his arms and legs. His breathing grew deep and even, and, to look at him, I'd never have guessed he'd walked through hell today.

But the longer I lay there, stripped of noise or distraction, the clearer my memories became, and I found myself back in my team's hospital room, each beep of the machines a grating accusation of how I'd messed up. Without the heat of the alcohol or Eric's body moving against mine, the coldness of my pain returned. It crept up my calves, my groin, into my stomach. From there it shot through my veins like ice water, and I shivered despite the warmth of the early morning.

I couldn't stay here. Grief prowled the outskirts of my mind, ready to pummel me, and now that I'd indulged in my final distraction, I wanted to go home and lick my wounds in private. I couldn't talk it out with Eric. Sharing my body was one thing. Sharing my vulnerabilities was something else entirely.

No matter what existed between us, I was still his captain. He needed me to be strong.

Moving slowly so as not to wake him, I slid out of bed and into my clothes. With a last look over my shoulder to appreciate that at least in sleep my friend could escape the worst of what we'd seen, I let myself out and headed home.

A piercing scream woke me a few hours later, and it took a minute for rational thought to sink through the images of blood and gore that had chased me through the night. I was in my bed. The scream was my ringing cellphone.

Who the hell was calling me this early in the morning?

I reached for my phone and knocked over my alarm clock. It hit the floor and turned on, filling my bedroom with the irritating voice of a morning show host giving a rundown of the local news.

"… multiple deaths following an explosion caused by a gas leak in a downtown high-rise. Residents are saying they suspected something was wrong with the gas lines, some even say they smelled a strange odour as early as last week, but no immediate move was made to inspect for damage. Commu-Tech Properties has—"

"Shut up," I said to the radio, and threw my pillow over it. They had no idea what they were talking about.

The phone had gone silent, but now started again. I found it sticking out from under my bed. Rolling onto my back, I squinted into the bright glare of the screen. An absurd number of missed calls and text messages demanded my attention, but I ignored them.

Madison's name showed on the display, along with a picture of her with her eyes squeezed shut and her tongue sticking out, and even with her I hesitated to answer. She would ask how I was, make sure I hadn't done anything stupid, and I didn't want to discuss either of those things. But she was my best friend. She'd hauled my ass out of the bar last night. No one else would have done that. The least I owed her was to reassure her I was alive.

"Hey," I said. Or I tried to. It came out more than a little garbled.

On the other end of the line, Madison sighed. "How many bottles did you drink last night? Are you a shrivelled prune this morning, or did you remember to down at least one glass of water?"

I grunted in response and smacked my tongue against the roof of my mouth to work some moisture into my cheeks. There was definitely a bit of the mummy about me this morning, but as memories of yesterday returned, all I wanted was another bottle of whiskey.

"Did you go after Weldon?" she asked

"Yeah."

Silence.

"Didn't do anything. Was dead when I got there."

"What?" Her tone, almost identical to Eric's the night before, might have made me laugh if I didn't feel so much like throwing up. "You need to get out of bed."

"Why?"

"Because the longer you stay there lying in the dark, the worse you're going to feel. Besides, I've learned a few things while you've been snoring, and I thought you might want to hear my idea before I take it to the security team to track down."

I snatched the pillow off the clock on the floor and squinted at the LED display, working to make sense of all the double lines.

"C'mon, Madi, it's not even eight o'clock. What are you doing at work?"

"I couldn't sleep, but that's a whole other thing. Do you want to hear my idea or not?"

"Yes," I grumbled.

"Then get up and get dressed. I want to hear you putting on pants while I talk, or I won't say anything."

I muttered a few choice words under my breath, but followed her instructions. Not because I thought she'd know if I lied to her, but because she was right. Again.

I grabbed my jeans from the day before but stopped short of pulling them on. The thought of having anything from yesterday against my skin was more than I could handle. I tossed them into the garbage can in the corner of the room along with my dirty T-shirt and made a note to burn them later. In my underwear, I walked into the bathroom, and set the phone on the counter.

"I'm brushing my teeth," I said, putting the call on speaker.

"Thank goodness. I'd hate to be within a kilometre of you right now. Maybe shower while you're at it."

"Bitch," I mumbled through a mouthful of foaming toothpaste.

"Call me when you're done?"

When she'd first called, I hadn't wanted to answer the phone, but now I found I didn't want to hang up. The silence of my apartment was too heavy. So I spat into the sink and said, "Nah, you talk while I wash. Better than listening to the shit on the news."

While Madison walked me through the paperwork she'd explored this morning—me trying to take in what she was saying but my fried brain only able to make sense of the occasional sentence—I stripped down and stepped into the steam of a hot shower. The water bit into my shoulders, working its way deep into my muscles and relaxing the tension I'd been too drunk and then too hungover to notice. Once I really sobered up, I'd be in a shit-ton more pain, physically and emotionally. At least both problems could be solved by more alcohol.

"Are you listening?" Madison asked, her voice rising above the hiss of the shower.

"Mmhmm." I massaged shampoo into my scalp.

"As I'm sure you know, because I'm well aware how much attention you pay during departmental briefings, we require all our informants to provide as detailed a trail as possible about where they get their information. We want to know who, what, where, when, and how. Then the security officers overlay the answers and see if there are any common factors. If everyone is getting their information from the same place, we dig deeper, which makes sense. Is it one group trying to feed us false information, or is one guy's mouth too big?"

I could have interrupted her to tell her I knew all this, but her no-nonsense tone was soothing, and I was in no rush to get out from under the water.

"On the other hand," she continued, "some overlap gives credence, because it means everyone is saying the same thing."

"Where do we fall in this case?"

"Everything about the tip looks legitimate, but I think we should get security to take a second pass. It strikes me that somewhere along the line, maybe one of the informants slipped, sharing intel with someone they shouldn't have or getting it from someone they didn't tell us about. I'm going to keep reading to make sure I'm not making something out of nothing, but what do you think?"

"Makes sense to me." I frowned. "Why the change of heart? Last night you wanted to leave everything to security. Why are you digging?"

There was a hesitation on the line, and then she said, "These guys were your friends. If I can help in any way… Make things easier for Jean-Luc, clear the threat… Anyway, I want to do my part."

I knew there was more, but accepted I'd have to see her in person to get it out of her. All the more reason to get my butt out of the shower.

"Well, I think it's worth looking into," I said. In fact, the more I thought about it, the more I liked it. The paper-pushers dealt more closely with the informants than I or my troops did. They took the details and wrote the reports; we broke down the doors. It was a system that had worked for over a century. Somehow that system had collapsed, and I needed to know why.

"Are you going to come in?" Madison asked.

"Hmm?" Now that I was clean, warm, and clearer-headed, guilt started creeping in that I hadn't given her my full attention.

"So we can go over this together. I want your opinion on what I've gathered before I take it to the security office. Unless you want to wallow at home all day."

The last thing I wanted was to return to the office. Not only because it risked someone questioning me about Weldon, but also because, unlike last night, there would be people there today. I imagined hundreds of pairs of eyes staring at me as I walked across the floor, everyone knowing about the attack. Would they blame me? Worse, would they pity me? How was I supposed to face them so soon after so much had gone wrong?

But Madison's theory echoed in my ear. One of our informants might know something, which meant they had a better idea than I did why my squad was dead. And if one of them knew something, there was no fire I wouldn't walk through to learn it, too. Forget the security office. If Madison had discovered anything in that paperwork, I would take it from her and run with it myself.

"I'll be there in thirty."

Chapter 10

Gideon

I STOOD IN the park next to a museum that looked like some sort of small castle. The parking lot was full of kids arriving for the morning tour, and I tucked myself deeper behind the trees to avoid being seen. Kids paid way more attention to their surroundings than adults did, and the last thing I needed was for some nosy child to come up and ask what I was doing.

Because what would I say?

There was no good reason for me to be here. I knew I shouldn't be. Yet three hours ago I'd called a cab and headed to Jet's apartment building in Centretown. I knew her address as well as I knew my own, having looked it up more than once since she'd shouted her way out my door. My fingers had been itching to text her ever since to see how she was doing. I'd even come close to sending some sort of apology for what I'd done. Despite my best intentions, I'd never been able to do it.

It had never felt like the right time to have my guts torn out and handed to me by a pissed-off and more than capable woman.

But seeing her last night—not just the shock of seeing her, but the state of her—had stayed with me. I hadn't been able to sleep, and more than once I'd dialled the first few digits of her number only to hang up, figuring if she was upset, I was the last person in the world she'd want to talk to.

So instead, apparently, I'd taken to stalking.

I won't say it was one of my smarter, classier decisions, but with my particular skill set and supernatural ability, I could at least say I was good at it. I'd marked when she'd gotten up, about thirty minutes ago, and watched her pace her apartment, disappear for a while, and return for another round of pacing, fully dressed for the day. Ten minutes ago, she'd started a pot of coffee, which meant my creepy staring had come to an end. Wherever she was going, she was getting ready to leave, and I had to grab my opportunity to talk to her.

I tossed the butt of my sixth cigarette onto the ground—an awful, disgusting habit, but I was in no mental state to worry about littering—and crossed the street towards her building.

If my only reason for coming had been to make sure Jet wasn't in trouble, I don't think I could have brought myself to go in. When it came to emotions, I was a snivelling coward. Fortunately, my chief priority for bothering her didn't allow for fear. Or consideration of her feelings, for that matter. I'd come to Ottawa to get information—information Jet had. I'd learned all I could from my contacts about the Death's Head Syndicate and the movement of ghost, but I believed there was more to learn before I made my report to SilverGuard.

My decision to stick around the Great White North had nothing to do with the fact that my handler had called this morning and told me what had really happened in the basement of that high-rise, that a ghostbomb had detonated and wiped nine people off the face of the earth in the time it had taken me to smoke my first cigarette of the day. It certainly had nothing to do with the fact that, with half Jet's team dead, there was a possibility she could also be in danger.

No, siree. My number one priority was gathering intel and stopping the bad guy, same as it always was.

I watched a woman drag an overgrown bullmastiff out of the building, waited until she was out of sight and no one else was around, then stepped into the foyer. The list of apartments was on the wall next to the intercom, and I gave it a quick scan to double-check Jet's number. According to my information, she was apartment 403, and sure enough next to the number was the name *OFF, F.* Sounded about right.

I glanced around to confirm my first observation that there were no security cameras and checked over my shoulder to make sure no one was coming in behind me. Confident there were no witnesses, I turned my thoughts to the atoms that made up my physical form and allowed the molecules to dissolve, morphing into a barely visible mist.

It was a strange feeling, letting my molecular makeup melt away, stretching out my awareness to include my clothes and anything I carried on me. It had taken years to get this good. The first time I'd dissolved, they'd found me naked. True, I'd been a toddler so naked wasn't unusual, but when that toddler was you and a moment ago you'd been wearing clothes, it threw your world into a spin. More challenging than taking clothes with me was maintaining a level of consciousness when my entire body was smoke. I didn't know if I could bring myself back if I didn't, and I'd never been tempted to try.

I drifted towards the second set of doors that would take me into the building proper and spread myself against the glass, searching for the tiniest cracks that would let me through. Eventually I sensed the gap along the floor and travelled through it until I was sure all of me was safely on the other side.

Atom by atom, I pulled myself together, and a few moments later I was standing in front of the mailboxes near the bottom of the staircase. I debated misting upstairs to escape any curious eyes along the way, but the building was quiet, so I decided to risk it and go on foot. I wasn't in that much of a rush to face Jet's reaction to my being here, and when it did come, I wanted to make sure I had a full tank of energy to respond.

When I finally made it to the fourth floor, I stood outside 403 for a full minute, my hand raised, half the voices in my head shouting at me to run away, the other half goading me to knock, leaving me paralyzed with indecision.

The quiet voice telling me to get this over with won in the end, and I brought my knuckles down against the door.

I pictured Jet stiffening at the sound. I imagined her debating whether she should answer, not wanting to deal with anyone but wondering if maybe, just maybe, it might be someone with news.

While she made up her mind, I took the time to smack a smile on my face and summon the pretense of easy arrogance. I hated having to play the role of cocky asshole, but it was a persona that came naturally to me, and right now it was the only way I could think of to keep some distance between us. I remembered all too well the power this woman had over the walls I kept around me, and I couldn't let myself get pulled back into that emotional riptide.

The job had to come first, even if right now I would have preferred to give it all up rather than risk hurting her when she had to be going through hell. Too bad for both of us that SilverGuard was the only thing in my life I had going for me. I couldn't afford to do less than my best.

Floorboards creaked as she crossed the apartment, and I stepped out of view, not wanting to influence her decision to open the door by giving myself away too soon.

I imagined her second debate: if she couldn't see who was knocking, should she ignore the summons? I bet myself she would give in to her curiosity.

I won.

The door opened, and if I'd been a crueller person, the

expression on Jet's face would have made my week. Her face paled, her lips parted, and a sound escaped the back of her throat that was little more than a croak. The muscles of her left arm tightened as she squeezed the door handle, and there was a noticeable wobble in her legs.

I had time to take in all these little details but no more before she slammed the door in my face.

Frankly, I was relieved. I thought my glimpses of her at the bar and through her window had been enough to brace me for meeting her again. I already had the upper hand because she'd had no idea I'd crossed the border.

"Idiot," I whispered to myself, and rolled my gaze towards the ceiling.

In truth, I was undone. All my intentions, my motivations, my courage, had flown out the window at the end of the hall-way the moment I'd looked into her eyes. I was ready to forget why I'd come and hurry home. If my legs had cooperated, I might have done exactly that, but they stayed locked, leaving me trapped and at Jet's mercy.

Her distress, obvious by the cursing coming through the door, just about equalled mine, and hearing her had the strange effect of putting me at ease. The string of creative words coming out of her mouth were the same I'd heard two years ago. Even though her repertoire had grown, the familiarity of it reassured me that at least I knew where I stood with her.

The stream of swearing died off, and I regained my composure, crossing my arms and repositioning my cocky smile. I had to control myself and not let pity or sympathy get in the way of why I was here.

When the door opened again, though, my reaction was almost as strong as the first time.

The woman was beautiful. Even with the bloodshot eyes ringed with sleepless bruises, even in a pair of ratty jeans and a plain black T-shirt. Not beautiful in any Hollywood sense. She had the same brown eyes and brown hair tied up in a messy ponytail you'd pass a hundred times on the street, but with a presence and confidence that struck you from ten feet away. Part of that vibe could have been because she had the ability to throw me across the room with a thought, but most of it came from her deep sense of self. This was a woman who knew her place in the world, and, even now, when that place had been shaken to its core, she held steady.

My entire body responded to her. I wanted to take her in my arms and kiss her until we both got dizzy. I wanted to ask for forgiveness, though I doubted I'd get it. I wanted to tell her how sorry I was that her world had turned upside down. I wanted to do all that and more but did nothing, knowing full well her only reaction would be to inflict some serious pain on my person.

So I held on to my stupid fake smile and hoped she couldn't read through it.

"Hey," I said. It had sounded smoother in my head.

Her eyes narrowed into a glare I remembered well. "I knew I saw you at the bar. Should have known my imagination couldn't be twisted enough to conjure you up out of nowhere. What do you want?"

I hadn't expected a warm greeting, but so far this was going better than I'd hoped. More quietly, anyway. Less physical pain.

"I was in town and thought I'd swing by and say hi."

"You've said it. Now what?"

There was no way to get to the point kindly, so I jumped in, damn the consequences.

"Now I thought we could talk about the recent spike in ghost sales."

Her body tensed at the mention of the drug, and her nostrils flared as she took a sharp breath. I'd taken her by surprise, all right, but her shock lasted only long enough for my words to sink in, and then she stepped forward, the air between us vibrating, her gaze lethal.

"You came all the way here for that when an email would have saved us both the time and trouble?"

I glanced down the hallway towards the neighbour's door, a silent indication that what I had to say was not for sensitive ears.

She followed my gaze, huffed, and jerked the door open. "Come in, but don't make yourself comfortable."

It felt a bit like stepping into the lion's den as I crossed the threshold into her apartment, and what I found was not what I had pictured.

"Wow," I said before I could stop myself.

"What?" she asked, with about as much genuine curiosity as a wall. That was the trouble with automatic responses—you spit them out even when you didn't care about the answer.

"Nothing," I said, which was stupid because clearly it was something. People rarely said *wow* for the hell of it. "It's just… simpler than I would have expected. Smaller. You've been living here a while, haven't you?"

Jet dropped onto a stool at her kitchen island and drew her coffee mug closer. "Hey, we can't all have your luck and rent a shit heap in Brooklyn."

Memories, not my proudest, rose, and I shifted my attention to an empty corner of the room to escape her glower. My apartment had been the primary base of operations during the case we'd worked together and for the fleeting relationship we'd enjoyed. I'd told her it was a cover for the op, which was why it was so dingy and cramped, but no, it was just my apartment. To be fair, I'd never imagined I would let her far enough into my life that she would learn the truth.

Since she'd walked out, I'd kept my place spotless, a strange new phenomenon for me, attached to some foolish, lingering hope that she'd come back and see it again sometime.

Based on her attitude towards me so far, I could do away with that hope for good.

It was also nice to know how angry she still was about our history. It meant I'd have to tread carefully to avoid making things worse. And that the information I needed wouldn't be as easy to get as begging a favour or five.

The stress and awkwardness of the moment had my muscles clenching and my heartbeat racing, and without thinking, I reached for the pack of smokes tucked into my sleeve.

"You light one of those in here, you die," Jet said, her sharp eyes following my fingers. "You really want one that badly?"

"Can't say I do," I said, dropping my hands, which now felt empty and useless, by my sides.

To hide my discomfort, I approached the island and rested my palms on the wooden surface, tapping the pads of my fingers in a steady rhythm.

For a moment, we stared at each other. I had no idea what she was thinking. Yes, she wanted to throw me out the window, I could see that easily enough, but was that all there was, or did she feel the same confusion and uncertainty I did? I wished I could get a better handle on the situation before I pressed forward.

She didn't give me many options.

When it became clear she wasn't about to help the conversation along, I decided it would be best to throw myself right in. "SilverGuard's chasing down a rumour that ghost is being smuggled in higher quantities across the border and that the source is right here in Ottawa."

Her shoulders tensed, and I was glad the island was between us because it looked like she was ready to throw a punch.

"Where did you hear that?" she asked.

I shrugged, aiming to keep it casual. "I have my sources. I came up here for a risk assessment. Didn't think I'd wind up with a live demonstration of how a lethal party drug could be used as a terrorist weapon."

Shit. I'd gone too far with that last part. If I knew about the ghostbomb, I had to know who she'd lost in the blast, which made me the shittiest of shits who ever walked the earth.

I allowed my show of indifference to slip. "I'm sorry about your team."

It had to be said, but I didn't want to insult her by treating it with kid gloves. If there was anything Jet Dawson hated more than me, it was pity.

She appeared to have frozen into a solid, her lips barely moving as she said, "Tell me what you know."

I hesitated. I'd known before I knocked that I would need to give information in order to get any, but I was bound by strict rules and security clearance about sharing intelligence without having it first approved by my handler. Outside, I'd decided to keep my story to a minimum. I was already on SilverGuard's shit list because of how things had gone down with Jet in New York, and I needed to be careful to prove myself and not fuck things up further. But now that I was upstairs, staring into the eyes of a woman who'd lost so much, I had to offer something more than the bare facts she already had. I was asking her to break the rules and trust me with details—the least I could do was break a few of my own.

In the end, I opted to tell her everything. Everything except what SilverGuard would kill me for sharing with a foreign agent.

"I was at the bar last night to meet a contact. He told me O'Malley's up and left Ottawa, moved his operation to Kingston. He seemed surprised I'd bothered to waste my time here."

Jet worked her jaw, grinding her teeth hard enough that I heard it from across the island.

Risking my life and the safety of her molars, I asked, "Are you sure you didn't miss something?"

"Our security officers hunted down the Kingston rumour," she said, the words bursting out as though she'd suffered this conversation before. "They chased every lead that said the syndicate had moved out. Nothing came of it. All our informants say O'Malley's still here, working out of The Afterlife. Your guy is right about one thing, though—you did waste your time coming here. There's nothing you need to worry about. I'm on it. I'm going to find out who set off the ghostbomb, find out who's producing the ghost, and make them go away. You can go home and sleep well knowing you did your job. The risk has been assessed."

She'd risen to her feet as she talked and was halfway towards the door when she finished. I understood a dismissal when I saw one, so I pushed away from the island and approached her. There were so many things I wanted to say. Maybe even squeeze in an apology if the opportunity presented itself. But I didn't have time for anything before her phone rang.

She pulled it out of her pocket, and I caught the name *Madison* on the screen before looking away.

"Is that all?" she asked.

The goodbye was so final. I wanted to tell her it wasn't, not by a long shot, but the words shrivelled on my tongue. I attempted a smile instead. "It was an unexpected surprise, seeing you again."

Her gaze ran over my face, and she nodded. "It was," she said. "I didn't think hell would have frozen over so quickly."

She stepped aside to let me through, then closed the door on my ass.

Chapter 11

Madison

I PACED THE length of my office from window to door, pausing occasionally to glance at my phone and the papers on my desk.

The six separate piles of paperwork taunted me, daring me to keep reading through the drivel that could be true or could be complete dross for all I was able to confirm. Our security team hadn't wanted to give me the documentation at all, but when I'd pointed out that I'd had a hand in negotiating these contracts, they'd seen no harm in letting me get a glance at the final copies. I'd also had to call in a few big favours and take advantage of one file clerk's grief over a recent breakup, which made me feel more than a little like a pile of garbage.

Though I was starting to worry those favours had been wasted. The information was kept vague to protect our informants, and what we did have on file checked out. I hated to think I'd woken Jet up for nothing. She could probably pass out for a week and not have recovered the energy she'd spent yesterday—but I knew she wasn't the sort who did well with quiet contemplation. She needed action, and I needed help ending this threat. Even if she thought my idea was bunk, we would be closer to a true way forward. If we did find evidence of a leak, Jet could be with me when I took the information to our security team. She would be in the loop, the intel would be chased down, and hopefully Meril would stay off my back.

That was if Jet was still in a mind to help me. When I'd called her back to tell her I'd pulled more files, she'd sounded off, tense and holding back anger. I couldn't think what might have happened in the twenty minutes since my first call, but obviously something had.

I hoped it wasn't anything that would make her do something stupid or reckless.

I tried to tell myself Jet wouldn't do that. Her job came first, and she would never risk it out of anger. But I had never seen her the way she'd been last night. How could I have? Tragedies like yesterday messed up your brain function, changed hormones and habits, decreased rational thought. They caused people to act erratically, and Jet wasn't immune.

The news story playing on the TV in the background caught my attention. Protesters marched outside the de Lauer building, shouting for better property management regulations. It had been like this since the blast. Despite how it came across in the mundane news broadcasts, the supernatural community was in an uproar over the attack. On our side of the world, you had to read between the lines and spot the signs the mundanes couldn't see properly. The minister had worked to keep most of the details out of the press, but it had slipped out that ghost was involved, and any supernatural with an ounce of common sense understood the danger. Jean-Luc had his work cut out for him to quell their fear, and I hoped he came up with a solid public relations stance quickly.

The louder the supernatural community became, the more we risked Meril feeling her power slipping, and the sooner she would act.

I groaned and slid my shoes on. Staying up here in my office made it too easy to ruminate, and my grandmother's tea could only do so much. I needed some fresh air to clear my head.

What I didn't consider was that by nine o'clock in the morning, the lines at both coffee shops in the lobby were out the door. As a general rule, nothing increased stress levels more than a long line for coffee, so for the sake of my sanity, I opted out.

When I turned back to the elevators, I bumped into a wide, muscular frame. Large hands caught my shoulders, preventing me from stumbling backwards, and apologies spilled out on both sides. At the familiar voice, I looked up, and an embarrassed laugh bubbled past my lips, echoed by the man in front of me.

"Madison," Colm said. "Hi. Second time in two days. Lucky me."

My cheeks grew warm, and I couldn't hide my stupid grin.

A series of witty remarks spun through my mind, but my subconscious tagged them as far too cheesy to be uttered, so I ended up saying nothing.

What I really wanted to say was that his was the only face I was happy to see right now, and that if I had my way, I would whisk him off somewhere quiet where we could talk and forget the rest of the world for an hour or ten.

Unfortunately, talking would lead to questions, and so many of his questions needed answers I was either too much of a coward to give, terrified he'd run away or think I was crazy, or under strict regulation not to offer.

All of which meant that no matter how badly he made my heart race and my stomach spin, I would have to be happy with the minor distraction he provided, a bright point on a dark day.

"I'm more impressed you managed to escape your desk two days in a row," I said. "Did you have to wait for everyone in the office to look the other way?"

He leaned in close enough that I smelled the faint muskiness of his aftershave. "It's how I keep my military training honed. When the backs are turned, you duck, cover, and keep moving. Don't stop until you're at the elevators, and never look back." He looked at his watch. "I figure I have another three minutes and forty-two seconds before they notice I'm gone."

I chuckled and glanced at his empty hands. "Were you here to get coffee?"

"I was until I saw that line." He grimaced, then his dark gaze softened as looked me over. "How are things going with you? Still rough today?"

I ran my hand over my hair. "How can you tell? Do I look that bad?"

His eyes widened, and he raised his hands in defence. "Not at all. You just look—I mean, you seemed…" He fell silent when I lost the ability to hide my smile, and his grin grew to match mine. "You okay?"

"I am." I wished I could tell him the truth. I wanted to spill out the whole messy business and hear his thoughts on what I should do about Meril. He struck me as the kind of person who would tackle a problem with logic. Cut and dry, no messing around with things like emotions. He would have been trained for it.

One day, when revealing the truth wouldn't put him in danger—and when I found my nerve—I would find a way to open his eyes. Until then, awkward silences and frustrated evasions would have to do.

And I felt every strained second of this one. His three-and-a-half minutes were ticking by, and despite the crowds, he wanted his coffee. I saw it in the way his eyes flicked towards the shortening line, caught in the familiar internal debate about whether he could make it before the next wave of caffeine addicts hit. I didn't need to be an empath to understand that look. It was a common expression on the face of every public servant.

Fortunately, Jet chose that minute to walk through the door.

"I wish we didn't have to cut this short," I said, "but my meeting has shown up. I'll talk to you later?"

"I look forward to it," he said, and his smile was bright enough to chase away the lurking shadows of my thoughts.

With a pinch of regret, I left him and headed over to Jet, wishing I could have one part of my life that wasn't so damned confusing.

When I reached her, I had to do a double take. She'd obviously had a worse night than I'd realized. Either that, or that twenty-minute gap between phone calls had done her in. She'd pulled her damp hair into a messy ponytail, and now that it was drying, it had gone lumpy on top. No makeup except for some lingering raccoon eyes, and a bloodshot stare. Her black jeans were ripped at the knees, and her leather jacket was one I could have sworn I'd made her throw out years ago. The only tidy thing about her was her T-shirt, which was plain, black, and would have been difficult to ruin.

"You look…" I started, then trailed off.

"As good as I feel?" she asked, and fell into step with me as I walked towards the elevator bay. "I threw my jeans and jacket into the trash and then remembered I haven't gone shopping in six years."

"When you feel up to it, we'll rectify that," I said.

Jet shrugged, which was all the reaction I expected. This woman didn't shop. It had been a struggle to get her out for the work holiday party a few years ago, and it was an experience I hadn't bothered to repeat.

She hesitated before swiping her pass over the security panel, making her fall behind, but I waited in front of the elevator for her to catch up. I wanted to ask how she was feeling, how she'd slept, but she'd raised the guard around her emotions so high, I thought it best to leave the direction of the conversation to her. Fussing over her would only make her pull away, which would be more dangerous for her than letting her share her thoughts as she wished to.

At least she was here, showered, and dressed. Baby steps.

We maintained a steady silence up to the twenty-fifth floor, and when we stepped out of the elevator, that silence spread to anyone who saw us, confusion written across their faces as they took in Jet's appearance. It didn't surprise me they didn't know who she was. She was a soldier, and the twenty-fifth floor was home to the bureaucrats. Michael was a common enough face upstairs, but the toughs and the paper-pushers rarely mingled.

We reached my office, and Jet's shoulders relaxed when I closed the door behind us. She dropped into the chair across from my desk, and I sat down in front of the stacks of paper. For a moment, the silence continued, but when I made no move to dive into why I'd called her here, she leaned forward and angled one of the stacks towards her to scan the contents. "This is what you've put together?"

My hope that she'd reward my lack of questions with unprompted answers went out the window, and I resigned myself to getting straight to business.

"It's not much, but maybe you'll see something I don't."

"Who do we have?"

"Seven informants came forward with details of the sale. Sanderson's been with us eight years, Lafontaine twelve, Deorksen three—O'Malley's hairstylist, of all people. It's amazing what people let slip around the person trimming their hair. Ashley's been with us four years, McKee eight, Dougall three months, and Rourke—well, you know Rourke."

Jet frowned. "I do indeed. Worth talking to, but I think we can rule him out as a knowing leak, so that's something, anyway. What about New Guy? What's his story?"

I pulled Dougall's file forward. "He first came to us with details about a growing gang war between the witches and the vampires over in Old Ottawa South. We'd heard rumours, but he was the first person to bring us anything concrete. Our people checked it out and prevented what would have been a nasty battle." I shuddered. "I still have nightmares about the weeks we spent negotiating the terms of the ceasefire."

I didn't enjoy working with vampires. Being dead, they didn't give off any emotional auras. They were voids. Walking negative space. I didn't know where I stood with them, a rare enough occurrence that I couldn't wrap my head around it to get comfortable.

"Since then, he's worked pretty closely with a few of our agents to keep an eye on other shifting feuds, so when he came to us with news about the syndicate and the de Lauer Estates, we were ready to listen." I paused, not wanting to jettison my idea so quickly but needing to lay my cards on the table. "Frankly, it's what makes me worry I'm wasting our time with this. Yes, a leak through the grapevine is the simplest answer, but I just don't see how it's possible. The vetting is too thorough for something that major to slip past us."

"You really think the syndicate is so good they came up with a story our people couldn't see through?"

"No... I don't know. Maybe? Or maybe the intel was correct, but word leaked some other way that we were coming and they set their trap at the last minute."

"Or maybe the minister isn't willing to admit he let his department make such a huge mistake."

Jet's bitterness spilled around her guard in heavy waves, and no matter how hard I tried to respect her privacy by blocking it out, it soaked into my pores.

"Jean-Luc was here earlier than I was this morning, Jet," I said gently. "He wants answers as much as you do, but you know there isn't a single element of our informants' lives we don't delve into. If security had found anything suspicious, they wouldn't have accepted the tip."

"What if the syndicate bought one of them? It wouldn't be the first time we were double-crossed."

"Which is why we changed our protocol. These days, it would take too many greased palms to make it worthwhile. It's more likely the syndicate caught wind of our moves and cleared out." Jet narrowed her eyes, and I knew I was losing her. In another moment, she would be out the door and either back to bed or back to the bar, and I didn't want either of those things to happen. Not with Meril's shadow hanging over my shoulder. "That being said, maybe you should take a look. If you see anything we can take to the security office, I say we run with it."

"Sure," she said, with more grace and less reluctance to touch the files than I'd expected.

I frowned. "What's going on?"

"What do you mean?"

"That was too easy. It's paperwork. Why are you okay with this?"

"I think you're right," she said. "It's worth going through what we have. I also think you're right that we won't find anything worth taking to security."

"Then…" Dread kicked up a dance in my gut.

"I think I should talk to the informants myself."

There it was.

"That's not an option. What would you say? 'Hey, Rourke, you passing information to O'Malley these days?' Because that wouldn't jeopardize our position whatsoever. Or get me fired. Or hike up the threat."

Meril's words echoed in my head, and I wiped my sweaty palms on my thighs. Jet didn't understand, and I didn't want to make her worry by telling her about my midnight visitor. But if she flew into this with the same rashness she'd shown last night, I'd lose any bargaining chips I had to stay on this side of the wall.

"Come on, Madi, what other leads do we have?"

I pressed my lips together and dropped my gaze to the files. I didn't want to tell her about this morning's fruitless meeting where we'd discussed the security team's most recent report. There had been nothing at Weldon's house to connect him to O'Malley, and even though it was general knowledge he was a low-ranked syndicate thug, that wasn't enough to get us through the doors of The Afterlife to talk to his boss. Added to all that, the bomb had come back clear of prints, made with generic parts purchasable at any hardware store.

Basically, there were no other leads.

Unfortunately, my silence obviously said as much, because Jet leaned forward and rested her hand on the stack. "Exactly. And what do you think security would say if you brought them your idea based on what's here?"

Frustration drew a groan out of me as I bowed my head in my hands. "That going to speak to the informants officially would be a liability."

"Which suggests an unofficial visit would be better, don't you think?"

This was a horrible idea.

"We have the note," I said. "They haven't given up on finding something there yet."

Jet looked skeptical. "Was it written on some kind of fancy paper with super rare ink?"

"No, but—"

"Then the only option they have is to wait until someone acts on the bullshit lies. I'm suggesting we act before they do that."

"Comms branch has been on top of social media pages, blogs, known conspiracy theorist websites, the local news—if any part of that message makes its way out, they'll know about it and can use the information to trace the author to its source."

"Great, and in the meantime?"

I didn't have a reply. Meril said we needed to resolve this soon. Before any other attacks, before any further threat to the wall. Officially, our hands were tied, but that didn't mean I was ready to let Jet take over. If I'd had any suspicion this had been her plan when she'd arrived, I never would have shared what I knew. I'd been trying to help, and instead I'd given her a new target for her stubborn one-track mind.

"What am I supposed to do instead, Madi? Sit around and wait for O'Malley to come after you next? The department? The wall? If it means making sure the ghostbombs stop and you're safe, I'll do whatever it takes."

This wasn't like Jet. I narrowed my eyes and looked her over—the messy ponytail, the bruises under her eyes, the faint white lines on her brow that outlined a pupil staring from a narrowed eye. It looked like her, but grief had shaken something loose.

And there was something else. Something she was trying very hard to hide.

She held out her hand, and I crossed my arms over the files. "You're special forces, not security. You're not trained to do legwork."

"I don't plan to go out there with tactical gear and a squad," she said. Her throat bobbed as a wave of sorrow settled over her, and my heart squeezed. She cleared her throat and pressed on. "I'll keep it low-key. If it's nothing, it's nothing, and no one needs to know I poked around. I can't sit at home on bereavement leave. You know that. It's why you called me here in the first place. At least if I'm out there asking questions, I won't be haunted by the idea we overlooked whoever set that bomb. Or someone who might be planning something worse."

She twitched her extended fingers, again requesting the files.

I eyed her open hand and wished I had more time to consider my options and figure out the best course of action. I hated the idea of letting her run around on her own in her current state.

"You could get fired," I said.

"For getting my hair styled and grabbing a drink at The Afterlife? Not likely."

We both knew that wasn't true, but if the threat to her career wasn't enough, I had an ace up my sleeve. "I could get fired."

"Only if I told anyone where I got my information, which I wouldn't do."

Useless ace.

There was no point wasting my breath with more arguments if she wasn't going to hear them.

I also knew too well that if I continued to say no, she would sit there, hand outstretched, until I collapsed from dehydration, exhaustion, or a burst kidney. This was a woman who would happily stake out a target's house for three days waiting for them to get home. Patience and stubbornness, that was Jet Dawson.

Still, maybe I could talk her out of doing too much damage. "Fine, but only if you promise not to act on anything you discover. You stumble on the leak, you take it to the security office. No handling it yourself. I'm holding you to that."

Jet stared at me, her mouth open, hesitating, and I slid the stack away from her.

"I promise," she said, in a tone her own father wouldn't believe.

I slid the stack further. I was already breaking protocol by having this information out in the open in front of her. To hand it over would be a breach of need-to-know. My fear of Meril had pushed me this far, but I wasn't about to take any chances that Jet would mess up. Or worse, get killed.

"I said I promise." She raised her hand, the model of a responsible adult female who was absolutely not sure it was a promise she intended to keep.

We stared at each other, and I stretched my mind towards her guard to see what I could pick up. She was holding back, so it was only fair game. What I found was a dark sludge of confusion, grief, anger, and guilt that not even the strongest barrier could shield completely. Not exactly reassuring.

But then, even as the raging storm reached a peak, it calmed. I shifted my attention from her neural circuits to her body language. The lines around her eyes softened, her shoulders relaxed. Not by much, but enough to tell me she'd argued herself down from whatever ledge she was standing on.

"I know I'm going off the map with this," she said, "but I promise to veer back onto recognizable roads if I learn anything. I just want to help move things along. Find a lead for our investigators to follow. Otherwise we're sitting here twiddling our thumbs, and O'Malley has more time to dig his claws in." She met my eye squarely. "How will the queen react to that?"

She may as well have punched me in the gut. She couldn't know about Meril's late-night visit, which meant she was feeding on my worries. For the first time since I heard about the blast, despite the sadness I sensed emanating from her, I snapped.

"That's low. Even for you."

Jet held my gaze. "Tell me I'm wrong."

In classic Jet fashion, she'd wriggled her way free of my arguments and found a weakness to attack. It was why she was so successful at her job. It was why it was sometimes so difficult to be her friend.

I thought of my meeting with the queen, the threats clear in every word she uttered, not only to myself but to life on this side of the wall. Everything was at her discretion, including the lives of her people, and although for most supernaturals outside the realm she was out of sight, out of mind, for those closer to her circle, she was a looming reminder of what awaited if one disobeyed her edicts.

"She'll sit still for a thousand years if her will and whims are respected," my grandmother had once said, "but if given cause to rise, she will bring with her a storm so violent there won't be time to batten down the hatches before she razes the country to the ground."

I had to prevent her from getting involved, no matter the risk.

With strangled frustration, I gathered the seven slim contact files and held them out. "I hate it when you're right."

Jet huffed a laugh but didn't bother to explain it as she accepted the papers. The frustration that had surrounded her like a black cloud thinned, and her posture shifted.

"Thanks," she said. "I owe you."

I nodded but didn't answer. If she succeeded, I would be the one in her debt.

"And I'm sorry," she added. "I shouldn't have pulled the queen line. That wasn't fair."

I sensed her regret, and while it didn't make me feel better about the knife edge I stood on, I appreciated her acknowledgement that she was an asshole.

"All I can say is I hope we're wrong about this," I said. "I hope you find nothing. If the leak came from the informants, it means the entire departmental structure is cracking." I kicked off my shoes and leaned back in my chair. "If you are going to talk with these people, I'd feel a lot better if someone went with you. Someone you trust. Eric, maybe?"

Jet's brow furrowed, and she shook her head. "I can't. I'm taking a huge chance here, and I'm okay with that because if I do nothing while the threat is still out there… I can't. I've got to keep putting one foot in front of the other. But I know how badly this could go. If I convinced Eric or Jason or Sara to come with me, I would be risking their futures as well as mine. That includes you." She tapped the files. "If I get caught with these, I'll say I dug them up myself."

I read her again but didn't sense any increased anger at the mention of her lieutenant. Eric wasn't the cause of her strange temper, then. And suddenly I had to know what it was. If she was putting herself in danger, I needed to know she was heading into it with a clear head. Any lack of focus could wind up being the trigger that tipped her into the viper pit and me into the chains of Meril's court.

"There's something else going on, isn't there." Statement, not question.

Jet started. "What do you mean?"

"On the phone earlier today, and even now… Something else happened. You've got an extreme case of the angries, and I don't think they're related to the attack."

Confusion crossed her face, followed by a red flush in her cheeks as her eyes clouded over. Even without prodding her too deeply, I sensed her blood pressure skyrocketing.

"There you go again," I said.

Her fury lashed out at me, then veered before it landed. I didn't think I'd ever seen her this furious. Not her usual flash-fire rage but twisted, deep, lava-hot. Passionate.

"Gideon's in town," she said, and for a moment my grasp on her emotions went blank as I registered my own surprise.

"Gideon," I repeated. "SilverGuard Gideon? Jerkwad Gideon?"

"One and the same," she said, and everything about her mood finally made sense.

She crossed her arms and slouched into her chair. Through the window, the sun had reached the perfect angle to spill golden light across the office, blinding anyone unlucky enough to look at anything glossy. Where had the day gone?

"What's he doing north of the border?" I asked.

"He says he's doing a risk assessment. SilverGuard has concerns about ghost being smuggled into the States, and he wants to know if they should be worried. I told him no."

"That's a long trip to ask a simple question."

She snorted, a most elegant sound. "That's what I said. But whatever, it's not my money he's spending. Hopefully by now he's on a flight back to New York."

Gideon Leigh. I'd never seen Jet as torn up as when she'd come home from New York two years ago. And he was here. Now of all times. Fate really was a bitch sometimes.

"How do you feel about that?" I aimed to keep my tone casual, but even so, I felt another flash of anger directed towards me, an irritated invitation to read her mental state for myself. I ignored it and held her gaze.

Finally, she huffed out a breath. "I'm pissed off that a security firm with so much sway with the United States government thinks it's entitled to come onto our soil and poke around."

I picked at the seam on my armrest. "You don't think your feelings are a little more personal than that?"

She rolled her eyes and shifted in her seat. "Fine. I'm pissed off he's in my city. I'm pissed off he tracked me down and came to my apartment. The nerve of the son of a bitch."

I tried to keep my expression neutral, but concern—and more than a little curiosity—egged me on. "Is that all?"

"Of course that's all. Do you expect me to be happy he's here? Do you think I've been pining for him?"

My disobedient lips curled into a smile I worked to hide. "No, that's definitely not what I think." Something else fell into place, and I had no trouble wiping the smirk off my face. "Last night in the bar, was that him you thought you saw?"

She nodded. "Turns out it was. But I kicked him out. He's gone."

"Right," I said. "Yes. That's a good thing."

As far as I was concerned, it would be best if Gideon never showed his face again. He'd hurt my best friend and didn't deserve another second of her time. But now that he was here and had presented himself to Jet, would the thought of him distract her from the task that lay ahead? Maybe it would be better if someone locked them in a room to scream and yell and beat the crap out of each other so they could finally put their issues to rest.

Jet's confusion about the situation wasn't the least reassuring. Her thoughts and emotions were tangled up in him. I crossed my fingers she'd forget about him when the time came to focus on more pressing matters. More than ever, the thought of her going alone to speak with our informants filled me with uneasiness.

"Anyway," she said, tapping the files again as she stood up, "I guess I should get started on this. The sooner the better, right?"

Without giving myself time to think, I said, "Why don't I go with you?"

She froze, and by the way she swayed on her feet, first towards the door, then towards me, I knew she was tempted. Understandably so. I was a mild-mannered public servant by day, but if I let myself go, I was as powerful as any supernatural on Meril's council.

After a moment, however, she shook her head. "I told you, I won't risk your career any more than I have." She gave me a tight smile. "I also can't see you blending in very well at The Afterlife."

I held her gaze an extra beat, giving her a moment to change her mind and me a final chance to scan her thoughts. Nothing intrusive, just enough to feel better that I wasn't unleashing my doom by letting her walk out the door. Now that she'd spilled the truth about Gideon, though, the maelstrom around her aura had subsided and a far more familiar Jet stood before me. "Fine. Call me as often as you can to let me know how you're doing."

She winked at me and left my office, and I crossed my fingers she wasn't about to make my situation a million times worse.

Chapter 12

Gideon

I WALKED INTO the bathroom of my cramped room and started throwing my few personals into my carry-on.

I was done here. Goodbye ghost attacks, goodbye government town, goodbye Jet. My mission had been to follow the ghost, track down the source, and bring the information back to SilverGuard.

Check.

Even though there were a bunch of shadowy figures involved and gaps in the distribution chain, I had enough to call it a job well done. Jet would take care of the rest. O'Malley and his gang had gone after her team, and there was no way she wouldn't burn this city to the ground—legally and professionally, of course—to prove it and throw them in prison to rot.

From this point on, we could monitor the situation from our head office. No need for me to torture the woman, or myself, by sticking around.

My phone rang as I zipped my bag shut.

I dropped onto the side of the over-firm mattress. "Hello?"

"Nightwatch, report," an artificially deepened voice said.

My point of contact at SilverGuard when I was away on missions. Eight years I'd worked with this person, code name Dark Wire, and I had no idea what they looked like, how old they were, or what species they were. It was like talking to a void that talked back, gave orders, and accepted everything I learned as a meal for its endless hunger.

"Mission complete," I said. "I tracked down the Kingston rumour and determined the probability to sit around seventeen per cent." There were equations we were supposed to use for our official reports, but over the years I'd become pretty good at bullshitting the numbers. "There's a much higher chance the syndicate is still in Ottawa."

"And the ghost?"

"Moving, but no immediate plans to ship it across the border in quantity."

I hoped I was right about that. The attack on the condo building was definitely a red flag, but the warning remained unclear. Were they attempting to gain a firmer foothold in the city, or hoping to distract the authorities while they made their international push? Only someone higher up the syndicate food chain would know for sure, and I wasn't anywhere near that level of intel.

"What about the SMOAC captain?" Dark Wire asked, and the reference to Jet made my butt clench. I hated that they knew about her, let alone wanted to drag her into this.

"She's following their trail but doesn't know anything we don't. A dead resource."

It was true enough. She was so thrown by the loss of her troops, I doubted she was in the headspace to put together any other details she might know.

"Bullshit," they said. "You can't tell me the team leader doesn't know where to find her target. I understand the syndicate lackey who was at the condo when the bomb went off is dead, but there must be another connection to the syndicate."

I bit my tongue. I had to stay quiet. Anything else would turn their attention closer to Jet, and she was caught in enough nets. I'd done as much as I was willing to do to her. I'd dug through her secure files and barged in on her at home to badger her with questions. All this when she had no need to hear from me. When all I wanted to do was open a bottle of whiskey and share it with her. Help her get through the next couple of nights until she was able to see the dawn on her own.

"If she doesn't know how to trace the attack to O'Malley, she will soon," Dark Wire said, and I bowed my head.

"Will she?" I asked.

No, no, no. Please no. Order me home. Get me the hell out of here.

"You tell me. Based on the psychological profile we built off your report, she's a pit bull. Not likely to let go of a challenge once she gets started. Her team's been killed. Do you believe she'll drop this?"

I clenched my teeth and scraped my fingers through my hair, wondering how much luck I'd have keeping my job if I lied. If I told them yes, that she was too broken up, and then she went and solved this on her own, I'd be booted from Silver-Guard before my next pay cheque. They had no use for people who couldn't read their sources.

I don't want to do this. For fuck's sake, I don't want to do this.

But what choice did I have? The job came first.

"No."

"Then stay with her." The order squeezed my soul, dragging it into the darkest regions of hell. "If she talks to anyone, I want you there. Anything she learns, you learn. And when the opportunity presents itself, you will take control of the operation and bring it home for us to handle. I don't care how you do it. Until then, you will send us regular reports. Silence will not go unnoticed. Understood?"

Somehow I summoned myself up from the pit I'd fallen into. To do this, I would need to charm her, gain her trust. She would need to let me in. Again. And if she learned I was playing her, she'd kill me. Now more than ever, this betrayal would destroy her.

I could quit. Throw in the towel and walk away to save the feelings of a woman who had messed me up more than anyone else ever had. To do what? Sling burgers? Forget the job that had been the mainstay of my life since I was eighteen?

I couldn't do it. Not even for her.

I just had to pray she never found out.

"Understood."

Chapter 13

Jet

I GOT INTO the elevator with the files tucked under my arm like a talisman. I knew there was something Madison wasn't telling me about why she was indulging my madness, but right now, I didn't care. The moment she'd handed me the information, I'd felt my first rush of anticipation since I'd walked into the de Lauer building.

It lasted until I reached the lobby and bumped into Michael, the last person in the world I wanted to see, especially carrying files I had no business holding.

"Dawson?" he asked once he made sure his coffee was safe. "What the hell are you doing here? You look like crap."

"I was just—" What the hell was I supposed to tell him? I couldn't lie to my commander. The man who had trained me from a pup. I also couldn't tell him the truth. He'd have me under house arrest before I finished my explanation. I knew he'd understand, but he wouldn't agree. "I couldn't sleep. Figured I'd check in on my guys."

Sorry, Zeke.

He narrowed his eyes, then nodded towards the opening elevator. "Before you do that, come with me to the office. You eaten anything yet today?"

My stomach turned, and I shook my head. I'd had nothing but the coffee I'd wanted to spew out all over Gideon's shoes.

"That changes now," he said, raising his bag of food. "Come on."

My feet like lead, I shuffled into the elevator behind him and held back a sigh as he hit the button for the first subbasement, the floor above the hospital. My second home. Upstairs, everyone had looked at me as though I didn't belong, but down here, I was someone. Soldiers and officers of all ranks and specialties acknowledged me as I strode down the hallway, and I did my best to mirror their detached demeanour. I couldn't let them see me tremble.

As we approached Michael's office, his executive assistant, Aline, offered a sympathetic smile, which I returned with a grimace before escaping into the sanctity of the colonel's private space.

"Sit down." He pointed at the chair across his desk and tossed two of the sausage breakfast sandwiches my way. "Eat."

"I'm not—"

"Don't care."

I sat down and tucked the files between my thigh and the chair as he went around his desk, dropped into his seat, and tore into the remaining sandwich. While he ate, I took a moment to stare at the stranger sitting in front of me. His eyes were red and puffy with sleeplessness and there was scruff along his jaw. Had he not gone home last night?

Guilt pinched my last nerve. Here I was, sneaking into his office at night, going behind his back, making plans that would get me fired and him in serious trouble, while he was buried under his own stresses.

None of that changed my plans, but it was enough to make me think Madison had the right of it. Keep my head down, don't draw attention, take what I learned to security. I had to protect Michael as much as anyone else.

Obeying my commanding officer, I polished off the two sandwiches and greedily eyed his coffee as he wrapped up his breakfast. Normally I was a cup-a-day woman, but desperate times called for desperate amounts of caffeine.

Once he finished, he wadded the trash into a ball and tossed it into his garbage can. "All right," he said as he leaned forward on his desk, his stern index finger pointed at me. "Now that I'm sure you have something in your gut, I want you to turn right around and go home, Captain. I don't want to see your face for at least three days. In fact, if you dropped a request on my desk for a month off, I would approve two."

I added my trash to his, wiped my mouth with a napkin,

and shook my head. "You know that won't happen, Colonel. I need to stay in the loop. It's been twenty-four hours, have you heard anything?"

"Nada," he said, lying through his teeth.

"I'll find out eventually. You wouldn't prefer I hear it from you?"

"I would *prefer* you get out of this windowless cave and get some rest." He stood up and came around the desk. I thought he was going to hug me again, but he stopped a foot away and caught my eye. "What happened yesterday is not something you can afford to rush back from, Jet. Emotionally and physically, you need time to heal."

I gritted my teeth and refused to move. I knew this man, and I knew how to out-stubborn him.

He met my stare for a full thirty seconds before he relaxed and shook his head. "Three days, Jet. That's all I'm asking. You meet with Dr. Casselman, you go through the proper steps, and then I'll have you at a desk until you're cleared for active duty."

Horror cooled my blood. "Michael, you can't mean that."

"The sooner you book your appointment with the doc, the sooner you're back."

I shuddered. Desk work and doctors, my two least favourite things. But if he wouldn't let me in on the official investigation, maybe I could pull some information out of him that would help with mine.

"Can you at least give me an idea of what leads they're

following? Anything from the note?"

"Nothing," he said, and this time I knew he was telling the truth. For one thing, it matched what Madison had already told me.

"Have we set up a tip line?" I asked. "What about looking into whoever told us about the meet in the first place?"

He frowned. "The informants? But why—no. I'm not having this conversation. Get out of here, go see your guys, and go home. I'll check in with you later, and if you're not asleep, you're going to have to explain why."

I raised an eyebrow. "Wouldn't you calling wake me up?"

He pointed at the door. "Out."

"Fine." I held up my hands, used my feet to shove myself out of my chair, grabbed my files, and started for the door.

Michael called me back as I reached it. "This isn't a punishment, Dawson," he said, his voice gentle again. "I'm trying to look out for you. Just as you'd do for one of your own."

I limited myself to a nod, not trusting myself to speak, and left. On my way out the door, I kept my gaze straight ahead, avoiding any possible looks or words of sympathy, but on my way to the elevators, I passed the office I shared with Eric and couldn't help but go in.

I closed the door, sealed myself inside, and felt the muscles in my neck relax in the familiar surroundings. The room was full of mementos from our career. Awards, training certificates, photos. I collapsed into my chair, opened the files, and took pictures of each page with my phone, figuring it would be easier if I didn't have to cart around so much paper.

Once I finished and locked the files safely in my desk drawer, I sat back in my chair and stared at the group shot of our squad hanging on the wall. All twenty-one of us in uniform, polished and unsmiling. The better shot was on my dresser at home, taken three minutes later when the decorum had vanished.

These guys were my life. I understood Michael's position, but I couldn't pass off the hunt for their murderer to someone else. I owed them answers. I owed them for not listening to my gut.

And while I still believed it would be better for everyone if I tackled this by myself, Madison was right that I needed support—and that Eric was my best choice. No one else was as skilled at bending the rules without breaking them. Hopefully he'd have a few tips for me.

I pulled my phone out of my pocket and dialled his number. He answered after the third ring, sounding half-asleep, or maybe still drunk.

"Hey," I said.

"Hey yourself. Where'd you run off to last night?"

The last thing I wanted to do was be honest with him. Telling him I didn't want to stick around long enough for us to cry together would show a side of myself I wasn't ready to share, even with him.

"Couldn't sleep. Needed to walk."

"Where are you now?"

"At the office."

"Really?"

"I was here to see Madison about something, but the colonel brought me downstairs and fed me."

He grunted. "Food. Right. Should do that." A pause on the line. "You doing okay?"

I played with a loose thread sticking out from under the number pad of my keyboard. "All right. I wasn't, but I kind of took on an unofficial job."

"Oh?" Less sleepy now, more interested.

"Yeah…" I drew in a deep breath. There was no one I trusted more with my secret, but even so, it felt like a gamble to let anyone else in on my stupidity. But hey, if he was able to talk me down and offer another idea, I was all ears. "There's this lead, something the bigwigs aren't following up on because it's a long shot. I figured I'd look into it myself."

There was a shuffle of bedsheets and the thump of the headboard, and I pictured him sitting up in bed. "About who planted the bomb?"

"The bomb, the setup, whatever. Someone has to know something, right? I got the files for the informants who told us about the deal. Thought I'd go talk to them. Off the books, under the radar. See what they know."

"I'm coming with you."

Another shuffle as he threw the sheets back.

"No," I said, wanting to catch him before he jumped into his pants. "I don't think that's a good idea. Not yet, anyway. No one can know I'm looking into it. Not even the colonel. For my sake and the network's. No attention drawn."

Another pause, and then, "Right. Yeah. I guess that makes sense. You can't do this on your own, though."

"I'm only sniffing, seeing if I can catch a whiff of a trail. The moment I do, I'm taking it to security, and they can take it up the chain. But I wanted you to know. In case."

"Of course," he said. "You need backup, you need anything, I'm on it."

A chuckle bubbled up the back of my throat—nerves or relief, I wasn't sure. "I was worried you'd put up more of a fight."

His laugh echoed mine. "I won't say I'm not shocked that Rulebook Dawson is taking a step outside the box, but if anything, I'm proud of you. I wouldn't be able to sit on my ass, either. Now that I know one of our own is on this, I'll rest easier."

"You'll guide the team until I have something to give them?"

"You got it, Cap. I'll keep them shipshape." He cleared his throat. "Jolie's coming into the office today to get Ellie's stuff. You want to be there for that?"

My chest tightened, and I bowed my head. "I'll feel better seeing them all once I've done something to make up for— once I have something to tell them. You good to take it on?"

"Yeah, no worries. I'll give her your love. Take care of yourself, Jet. Be safe. We can't afford to lose you, too."

When I got to my team's hospital room, I found Katie sitting next to Luvy, their fingers entwined. At the sight of me, she let go and rose to her feet.

"Captain."

"At ease," I said. "Of course. We're not on duty today."

The woman wavered, sank into her chair, and reclaimed her partner's hand. "They're still asleep," she said as I made my tour of the room. "The doctor was here earlier. Says Mandy's colouring is better, and Marc-André is breathing on his own."

"That's great news," I said, and paused by Mandy's bed. She did look a closer to life than she had on my earlier visit.

Closer than Katie did at the moment.

"Have you slept?" I asked.

She wiped the tears from her eyes and shook her head. "I can't. Not when they have so much to say."

My blood chilled. On top of being a computer whiz, Katie was a powerful medium. One who could block ghosts out as easily as she could communicate with them. If she'd let them talk, I knew who "they" had to be.

"You found the team?" I asked.

"A few of them," she said, sniffling. "Laura's gone. Samuel.

Caro. But Ellison was still around. He asked me to look in on Jolie." Tears streamed down her cheeks. "Tina asked for help with her mom. But all of them—all of them—are afraid. Not for what happened, but what might happen. They suffered. Some went too quickly to feel it, but others…" She let out a strangled cry and lowered her head to Luvy's hand, holding her even tighter.

I crouched beside her and rested my hand on her shoulder. "You need to let them go. I know how hard that's going to be, but they're gone. Their suffering is over. You need to sleep. They'd want you to take care of yourself."

She lifted her haunted gaze to mine. "How can I, knowing whoever did this is still out there? That what happened to them might happen again? The way they describe it—like having their minds stretched and torn, knives slicing through their bodies. The agony of killing their best friends but unable to hold off the madness making them do it."

Her whole body was shaking now, and I put my arms around her to keep her from falling out of her chair.

"Do you want me to call your mom?" I asked. "She can come get you."

"No. She can't see me like this."

She could barely speak through her chattering teeth, and I reached for the call button. Katie needed to rest, and there was only so much I could do for her. This was delayed shock and exhaustion—no wonder, considering all she'd seen and heard.

The nurse arrived, not Miriam this time but a brusque young woman who grabbed a blanket and flung it around Katie's shoulders. "You come along with me, and we'll get you a cup of tea, okay? Dr. Murray will give you something to calm you down."

She nodded at me as she helped the sobbing Katie out of the room, and I staggered over to the side of Zeke's bed and collapsed in the chair with a heavy sigh.

"I promise I'm not sitting on my ass feeling sorry for myself," I said. "I'm working on something. You guys need closure, and the official streams won't move fast enough. Red tape, approvals, all that government bullshit. We're talking about the syndicate here. Any delay gives them time to clean up."

I strained to hear any constructive criticism from the beep of the heart monitor or the hiss and wheeze of the ventilator, but there was nothing.

To shake off my disappointment, I unlocked my phone and scrolled through the text messages and missed calls I'd ignored this morning. Service wasn't great down here, but at least I was able to scroll through the call log.

My father had called five times since yesterday afternoon, and I'd have to call him back soon if I didn't want him showing up at my door. The call from my brother was a surprise, and I guessed it had been at my father's urging. My grandmother had called once, and even without calling her back, I knew every-thing she was going to say: she was glad I was all right, I was strong enough to survive this, it wasn't my fault.

Not in the right state of mind to return their calls, I switched to my texts.

Some new messages from friends who'd spotted me on the news at the de Lauer Estates and wanted to check in, but there were fewer than a dozen. Over the past ten years, my social circle had shrunk to an embarrassing number. Madison was the closest friend I had who wasn't in uniform.

The rest of my circle was my squad, and most of them were now gone.

Out of habit, not really expecting anything, I opened the team's group chat. The message I'd sent last night had disappeared under a wave of chatter, and I scrolled up to see what I'd missed. My heart pinched at the photos they'd shared in the past few hours, most like the one on Eric's dresser—teammates bonding through sweat and tears.

THX FOR THE UPDATE, PL, Jason had replied to my message. PL. I hardly felt like I deserved the endearment. OMW THERE NOW.

STOPPED BY AN HOUR AGO, wrote Sara. ON TOP OF THE HAIR, LET'S MAKE SURE TO TELL RAY HIS BREATH STINKS. NO IMPROVE-MENTS.

That had been at four o'clock this morning.

A few hours of silence before the messages became more frequent, if short and lacking their usual ribbing.

Mostly they checked in on each other, encouraging one

another to get out of the house. A few of them who shared a place had gone for a run this morning and invited the rest of us to join them. I'd missed it but doubted I could have dragged myself out of bed.

It wasn't only commiseration between them, though. There was anger, too.

What do we know?

Who's on this? Anyone we can press for info?

The news is bullshit. Gas leak my ass. All these stupid rich idiots in their expensive condos with no idea what happened in there.

Fuckers are going to pay. Give me a name and that'll be the end of it.

And then, Anyone heard from PL since this morning? Sara had asked at ten o'clock.

Not a peep, Xander had replied. PL, you here?

No one had sent anything since. I hoped they weren't waiting for me to resurface. It was my job to keep their spirits up and help them stay focused, and I didn't feel up to the task.

But I couldn't let them think I'd disappeared. Even in grief, I was their leader. The one who was supposed to keep them together. How the hell I was going to do that, I had no idea, but letting them know I hadn't abandoned them was probably a good start.

At Peaview now. No punching heads until we get the okay.

I ignored the fact that Madison had given me the same advice half an hour ago and I was on the fence about taking it. She was my best friend. I was their boss.

I'M ON THIS. THE COLONEL'S ON THIS. NO ONE'S GETTING AWAY WITH ANYTHING. YOU THINK I'D LET THAT HAPPEN?

As I typed the words, a shudder of pent-up energy pulsed through me and the cables attached to Zeke's heart monitor rose off the floor. I jumped at the movement and rolled my neck to calm myself before I unplugged his machine.

A piercing alarm jerked my attention to the other side of the room, where Mandy was flailing against her pillows. I rushed over and hit the call button, but Miriam was already at my side, pulling me away from the bed.

"We'll have to ask you to leave, Captain," she said, her voice calm.

"But—"

"Please don't argue. We're going to try to help her."

More people rushed in with a cart full of equipment, and I had no chance to ask questions before I found myself in the hallway, the door closed in my face.

My heart raced, and I tasted blood at the back of my throat. I couldn't lose another one. Not when she'd been improving. She'd looked so healthy, moments away from waking up.

I pressed my ear against the door, heard muffled voices shouting orders, the beeps and alarms of various machines. After a few minutes of not being able to differentiate one sound from another, I left my post and tried pacing, hoping the steady movement would keep my head from rushing down darker paths.

The minutes inched closer to an hour, and eventually the room went silent. I stopped short and stared at the door, willing it to open and terrified of what I would learn when it did. My stomach twisted into knots, my head grew light, and I forced myself through a series a deep breaths.

The door opened.

Miriam stepped aside and made room for me to come in. Her expression told me everything I needed to know, but I refused to accept it until I reached the doctor standing at Mandy's bedside.

"I'm sorry," he said. "The damage to her heart was too great."

Numbness blanketed me. Grief lurked behind the veil of shock, but for now it stayed at a distance with a promise to catch up with me soon. With a foggy head and dry mouth, I looked down at Mandy. At what remained of her. Gone was the pink glow in her cheeks, gone were the signs of life returning.

"Ghost is a brutal drug," the doctor said. "Just when we think we have everything under control, it swings around for another hit. The sooner we get this stuff off the streets, the better I'll sleep at night." He rested his hand on my arm as he turned towards the door. "I'll have the nurses in soon to look after her. Should I inform Colonel Torrence?"

I thought about calling Michael myself. Calling Eric, the team, Mandy's family.

My heart throbbed, threatening to stop under the pressure of my sorrow.

Such a necessary duty—a responsibility that belonged to me—but I couldn't bring myself to do it.

Ashamed, heartbroken, I nodded. The doctor squeezed my arm, then he and the nurses left, giving me a moment to myself. As soon as the door closed behind them, I dropped into the chair by Mandy's side.

Another soldier lost. Another friend. And Michael expected me to sit by, grieve for them, and do nothing?

I would wait until the day he followed his own advice. When his wife passed away three years ago, it had taken an express order from the minister to get him to take bereavement leave. The man had become a complete workaholic, working eighteen hours a day to avoid going home to an empty bed.

As long as there was something I could do to bring myself closer to the truth, to see justice done for those we'd lost, I had to do it. It was the only way I would be able to rest easy.

I stared through my streaming tears at Mandy's slack face, her pink skin fading to a mottled grey.

The longer I watched death grab hold of her, the stronger my motivation grew to take action. For Zeke and Katie, for Jolie, for everyone else who needed to know what happened, to ease the fears of my lost team and assure them no one would suffer the way they had. To hell with protocol and rules and waiting. Someone out there had crossed the wrong pack, and I would make them pay for it.

"I promise I'll figure this out," I said to her. "One way or another, O'Malley will answer for what he's done."

I rested my hand on her shoulder in silent farewell, then left her to the nurses as they returned.

She was gone, but the next time I visited, I would have something to give my remaining team besides apologies.

I left the hospital, escaped into an empty stairwell, dropped onto a step, and sat in silence. After a minute, the awaiting grief wrapped itself around me, and I gave myself time to cry. Mandy deserved my tears, and for this sweet, precious moment, I had no one who needed me to be strong.

For twenty minutes, I sat huddled with my pain, my head in my hands, mourning her loss until the wave of sadness finally ebbed and exhaustion set in. Slowly, I sat up, wiped my eyes, and used the banister to haul myself to my feet.

The only way to push through my fatigue was to get started, and I couldn't do that in the stairwell. One of the people whose file I carried on my phone could know something about the ghostbomb. One of them could point us in the right direction.

While I didn't know the first thing about getting information out of people, what choice did I have? The alarm from Mandy's heart monitor rang in my ears, and Katie's horror over what our fallen wolves had told her haunted me. Offering a toast to the friends and family we'd lost would be a lovely gesture, but offering O'Malley's head would be a better one. To lay out the evidence and explain why we were toasting their memory instead of our success, to look O'Malley in the eye and tell him he'd lost.

How hard could it be to play detective? All I had to do was find these people, ask how they got their information, and either determine whether they were lying or see if there was anything they hadn't told us. If all went well, I'd have a solid lead to bring to security and could tell my pack progress was being made.

It was just after five o'clock, which put me right in the middle of rush hour. If I wanted to hit as many of these names today as possible, I'd have to move strategically. I scrolled through the files and perused the addresses. The informants were located across various parts of the city, with a few of them downtown and walkable from my place, one in South Keys, and another in Nepean. It made sense to start outwards and work in, winding up in Centretown at The Afterlife late in the evening when there was a better chance I'd find who I was looking for. And a better chance of a crowd. It was easier to go unnoticed when you were one among many.

I went down the rest of the stairs and entered the parking

garage, but as my Mustang came into view, I drew to a sudden stop.

Gideon was leaning against my trunk, one foot over the other, arms crossed. Heat pierced my heart at the sight of him, and I told myself there was only anger behind it.

"What the actual fuck?" I greeted. "Are you stalking me now?"

"Me? No, it's a coincidence," he said, his lips sliding into a sly smile. "I love parking garages. The sights, the smells. Best way to get to know a city. I take pictures and put them up on my wall."

"A vast improvement to the last time I saw your decorating style, I'm sure."

I crossed my arms to mirror his posture and scanned him over: the dark brown hair shaved on both sides and longer on top; the chocolate brown eyes that hinted at secrets whispered in the dark; the stubble along his jawline, a well-tended style choice. He wore a white T-shirt that hugged the muscles of his arms and chest in a way that would have made the old me look twice, a black vest, and black jeans that highlighted everything they were supposed to. The black leather bracelet around his left wrist was still there, a detail that had stayed with me in sharp definition for two years.

I took in the scar that cut through his right eyebrow and the one on his chin. He claimed he'd received both injuries in the line of duty, but what did I know when it came to this man?

He was a great actor. I didn't know what was real and what he'd told me to get into my secure briefcase.

Only partially a euphemism.

"What do you want, Gideon? You got what you came for." Suspicion snaked through my mind. "What you say you came for, anyway."

He pushed away from my car and closed the distance between us, stuffing his fingers in his pockets and hooking his thumbs through the belt loops. Even standing tall, he appeared to be slouching. If he was trying to appear relaxed, I didn't believe it. I knew from experience he was always ready to pounce. The pose set off a familiar tingle in the base of my stomach that travelled downwards, but I did my best to ignore it. The bastard didn't deserve it.

"You made such a quick exit this morning, I figured you'd learned something. I wanted to know if you needed backup."

I couldn't help but laugh in his face. "You've got to be kidding. Backup? You? I need to be able to trust my reinforcements, Gideon, and you lost that privilege."

Lost it, set it on fire, and flushed it down the toilet. I wasn't proud of the fact I'd let him get close enough to break my heart. Rule one of the job was never get emotionally attached to anyone. Even getting too close to your squad ran the risk of leaving you, well, like me in my current condition. Clearly I'd always been one to walk the edge of that particular guideline.

In a twisted way, I understood why he'd lied to me. He was

working the job, same as I would have done. But the fact that it had been me on the receiving end of his bullshit had done nothing for my ego or my faith in relationships. Not so much that he'd played me, but that I'd never suspected it.

I left him and made for my car.

"Come on, Jet," he said. "I know as well as you do you'd be fine on your own. But I also know you'd be safer and probably get the job done faster with a bit of extra heavy at your side."

I stopped in my tracks, turned around, and ground my teeth. From the way the corner of his mouth curled into that smug expression he loved to wear, he heard it.

He was right. The only reason I hadn't wanted Eric with me was to protect him from any fallout. Gideon didn't fall under that protection.

Taking him into my confidence, however, meant giving a certain amount of power to SilverGuard. He would have access to information that, under any other circumstances, I would never share. While Madison had been right—as usual—that my venting about SilverGuard's connection to the American government was a projection of the true source of my anger, the concern was real. It would mean working with a foreign entity that held a lot of sway, and if any of my superiors found out, I could kiss my job and security clearance goodbye.

On the other hand…

A mental groan echoed through my head.

On the other hand, I was technically on leave, working on

my own time, and my people didn't have to find out. While I was capable of working alone, thank you very much, with two people, we could play tactics. Trade off the chisel as we chipped away at the walls. Gideon was obviously playing some bigger game—he hadn't stuck around Ottawa just to help me—and had his own mission, his own goals. But if they aligned with mine, I could at least trust him not to fuck this up.

Jet, you're an idiot.

I knew it, but that didn't stop me from seeing the advantage of doing some using of my own. Gideon was a spy. He knew how to get information out of people, which, at the moment, was a skill I needed.

While I didn't trust him with my heart, I did trust him enough to have my back. He was an asshole, but he cared about getting the job done. There was another bonus as well: he wasn't my responsibility if things went south.

"Fine," I said. "But I'm taking point, and you'll withhold any reports to SilverGuard until you've run them by me. My country, my lead."

His smile grew wider. "I wouldn't have it any other way."

Chapter 14

Gideon

I CLIMBED INTO the passenger seat of Jet's car and closed my eyes as I leaned back against the headrest. Jet didn't seem to be in an overly chatty mood, so I thought it smart to sit here like a good boy and keep my mouth shut. Much as I didn't mind being target practice for her biting tongue, it would be better if she paced herself.

Aside from that, it was what Dark Wire had told me to do.

Unfortunately, sitting quietly gave me time to dwell on the fact that I was riding in Jet's car pretending my sole reason for being here was to help her out when, really, I was playing spy. Just like in New York. Maybe it was true you couldn't dump the past in a black hole and move on. That it stuck with you, influencing your every step. Your every bad decision.

Again I wished walking away from the job was an option.

The idea was tempting. I could tell Jet why I had actually

come back and ask if she would help me clear my last mission before I called it quits. Maybe I could settle down and find a job where my identity didn't change every other week and I didn't have to push away every single person who started to get close. There was something to be said for a bit of stability and openness.

For some people.

Even as I chewed on the thought of leaving it all behind, I knew I'd never be able to stick with stable.

I'd joined SilverGuard after years of having no one in my life except the lady who snuck me yesterday's rolls at the local bakery and the homeless guys in the alley outside the slum I called home. I'd been recruited by a guy who'd caught me misting into a bank vault to keep myself off the streets. Instead of hauling my ass to jail, he'd given me a job and put me on the straight and narrow-ish. It's what I'd been doing the last eighteen years. It was how I defined myself. If I left, what would I do except go back to robbing banks? Stay here and beg Jet to forgive me? Find a way to make myself useful in her world?

The stern set of her jaw, cold and familiar, sparked my desire to trail my tongue down her neck until she unclenched her teeth. If only she would open up, forgive me for being a shit, and listen to me without driving her knee into my sensitives, I would jump at the chance to make things right with her.

But as shitty as I felt for lying, she'd made her feelings clear. The job was my one sure thing, and I would do whatever was needed to keep it.

We continued in silence through some late-afternoon traffic, heading well out of downtown, past a shopping centre and a movie theatre. The parking lot was packed, and kids of all ages were running towards the restaurant. They were so young and clueless. Lucky bastards.

Jet drove past them and eventually turned into a residential area. Once there, she slowed down.

"Keep an eye out for one twenty-five," she said, the first words she'd spoken since we'd gotten into the car.

Wanting to prove I was an obedient second, I kept my eyes peeled as we rolled along, calling it out when it came into view.

"Nice place," I said, scanning the front yard. The grass looked like it hadn't been mowed since the end of the Cold War. The porch paint was peeling, and the screen door hung off its hinges. The rest of the houses in the area were clean and well put together, so I guessed this guy was less than popular at the annual block party.

"Who are we talking to?" I asked as Jet pulled into the driveway.

"Who *I'm* talking to," she said. "You're listening unless I ask, remember?"

I pulled a zipper across my lips and smiled. I refused to give her a chance to tell me I didn't keep my promises. Even if I didn't always tell the truth.

We got out of the car, and I followed Jet up the driveway

to the porch. She tried the first step, but her foot went straight through, so we opted to go around the side of the house, following a clear-cut path along the carport.

The backyard was in a marginally better state than the front, in that its concrete steps were only partly crumbled. Jet approached the back door and knocked, setting off what sounded like a very large dog.

A grating masculine voice yelled at it to shut up, and a moment later, the door opened, revealing a scruffy man in a white wife beater and navy-blue sweats. His eyes were bloodshot and his chin bristled with a five… maybe more like an eight o'clock shadow.

"What do you want?" he grumbled.

Jet pulled her ID out of her pocket and flashed it with all the confidence of someone who had a right to be here. "I'm with the SMOAC task force, Mr. Lafontaine. Can we speak with you for a moment?"

His gaze jumped from her to me, and I registered far more alertness in his hooded brown eyes than I would have guessed. "And who's this guy?"

"My partner," Jet said, though it sounded like it cost her to get the words out. "Is this a good time?"

Lafontaine grunted. "Sure. Not like I have anything better to do. Come on in. Watch the mess."

I did my best to keep my expression neutral as I stepped into the house and immediately crushed an old potato chip bag under my boot. Beer cans lay scattered across the floor and over the round table in the 70s-style kitchen. The vinyl-covered chairs were cracked and worn, and I didn't want to guess at how long it'd been since someone had scrubbed the stove. My housekeeping skills were far from impressive, but at least I could pride myself on not sharing my place with roaches.

"I'd offer you someplace to sit, but everything's covered in dog hair," Lafontaine said, and as he spoke, a grey-whiskered Rottweiler sauntered into the room, looking far less threatening than it sounded. It sank down at Lafontaine's feet, rolled onto its side, and released a loud huff, its brown eyes settling on me. As I looked away from the dog, I did a double-take when I spotted Lafontaine's notably canine feet sticking out from his sweatpants. The paws were wide and covered with thick brown fur that matched the stubble on his chin.

An adlet, then. Half-dog, half-human. Incredibly rare. I'd never met one in person, but the state of his house and his hermit-like appearance suddenly made a lot more sense.

"Gorgeous pup," Jet said.

"Mac. Big oaf. About as useful a guard dog as that beer can over there." He jerked his head to the series of cans sitting on top of the fridge. How was this man still alive?

Jet leaned her hip against the counter—intentionally or by luck avoiding an unidentifiable black smear by the sink.

"Mr. Lafontaine, I'm here because you came forward with information about a certain criminal organization setting up operations in the basement of the de Lauer Estates. Do you remember that?"

That was Jet, getting straight to the point with the smoothness of a thumbtack on a chair.

The lines around Lafontaine's mouth hardened, and he crossed his arms. "Of course I remember. What do you think I am? Some senile idiot?"

Having promised to stay out of Jet's way, I pressed my lips together, but I could see we were losing the guy. I got the sense he was ready enough to talk, but if she got him on full defensive, he'd dry up like the Sahara.

"Can you tell me where you first heard about the operation?" she asked, obviously not noticing the shift in his posture, or, if she noticed, not realizing what it meant for her interview. "Was it from someone in particular? Your file says you overheard something about it at The Afterlife."

Lafontaine snorted. "Then you're reading the wrong file, lady. Do I look like someone who squats at The Afterlife? Nah, I was *behind* the club, taking myself for a walk and seeing if I could scrounge up some dinner." I must have made a noise because he snarled at me, revealing an impressive set of teeth. "What? You never heard of an adlet going on an urban hunt?"

"Go on," Jet said, interrupting his growing hostility.

He shrugged. "I was behind the dumpster when the door opened and these two guys stepped out. One said, 'Everything ready for tomorrow?' and the other said, 'Yeah, de Lauer at eleven o'clock.' The first one ordered the other to prep the troops, then grabbed him by the shoulder and told him to do it right. They couldn't afford fuck-ups. The second guy went back inside, and the first headed down the alley to the parking lot. I got outta there."

"And went straight to the feds?" I asked, the question slipping out before I could stop it. Jet shot me a glare.

Lafontaine scratched the back of his neck. "I may not look like much, and maybe I'm not exactly a useful member of society, but I know when something doesn't sound right."

"So you were being a good citizen," I said, amused.

To a point, I believed his story. He didn't embellish, he didn't take credit for being a hero. But it sounded too easy. If informants with his timing were on every street corner, cold cases wouldn't exist.

"Listen, friend, I don't know who you are or what you think I'm holding back, but it happened the way it happened. I don't know who those people were. I certainly didn't know their plan was to plant a bomb and shut down an entire street corner. If I did, maybe I wouldn't have come forward, right? Maybe I would've kept my mouth shut and my head down. But I did, and you got your information."

Mac sat up in response to the man's increasing anger, and a low growl rumbled in the back of his throat.

Jet stepped between us, drawing Lafontaine's attention to her. "We appreciate your help, Mitchel," she said, her tone softer now, if not quite gentle. "We just wanted to confirm what you'd heard, maybe see if there was anything you remembered since you made your report. Something that might tell us more about who was talking."

I stepped back, letting her play good cop.

Lafontaine remained wary, throwing me some nasty side-eye, but the dog lay back down. "I don't know what more I can tell you. I didn't see them. I could only tell there were two people by the shadows and the sounds of their voices. I'm good with voices."

"Is there anything you can tell me about the voices, then? Were they rough? Smooth? Young? Old?"

He chewed on the inside of his cheek and raised one dog leg to scratch the back of the other. I watched, fascinated. Did he wear shoes or did he go out in public with his bare paws and have faith no one would notice, because who would believe it if they did?

I'd been part of this community all my life, and it still blew my mind how comfortable some supes were with hiding in plain sight.

"The first one, the one giving the orders, he sounded older. Like someone used to taking command and not putting up with bullshit. The second—well, he didn't sound like he enjoyed being the beta. A lot of push-back, like he was used to giving orders himself. He sounded a bit angrier, rougher, but well in control. They mumbled a lot, trying to keep quiet. I don't know that I'd recognize either of them again."

The corners of Jet's mouth twitched downwards, and I shared some of her disappointment. It would have been great if Lafontaine could have walked us right up to these jag-offs' doors. Still, it was something. We had an alpha out-alphaing an alpha. That could mean some internal conflicts in the syndicate, and if that were the case, there would be signs of it elsewhere. Maybe something we could follow. Some bitter feelings we could manipulate.

"Thanks, Mitchel," Jet said. "I appreciate your help."

He uncrossed his arms, and Mac rolled to his feet. "If you wouldn't mind, I'd rather not have the whole neighbourhood seeing you here. Now that I know these pricks mean business, I don't want anything more to do with them—or with you."

I eyed the dog as we let ourselves out, but it stayed at Lafontaine's side.

Jet said nothing as we returned to the car, then continued her silence as she backed out of the driveway and headed towards the main street.

I could almost hear the wheels in her head turning.

"What do you think?" I asked.

"I think when I ask you to keep your mouth shut, you should keep your mouth shut."

Irritation rippled through me as I sank deeper into my seat. I doubted she would have gotten as much out of the guy as she had if I hadn't pushed her out of her straight-to-business attitude, but if she thought otherwise, I wasn't about to argue with her.

And if she didn't want to talk about what Lafontaine had told us, then I wouldn't rush to offer my insights, either.

Had she noticed the guy looked scared shitless when we left? I suspected he and Mac wouldn't stick around town any longer than they had to.

Had it struck her how convenient it was that Lafontaine had been in the alley at exactly the right time to hear such a critical conversation?

Had she considered the possibility that the whole scene had been staged to increase the odds her team would be in the de Lauer basement when the ghostbomb went off?

I hoped I was wrong, that it was some power struggle within the syndicate, but as things stood, I didn't think we could take anything for granted.

Chapter 15

Jet

ANGER FIZZED UNDER my skin as I drove out of South Keys towards Nepean. I had told Gideon to stay quiet until asked, and he'd butted his nose into my interrogation anyway. And the worst part was, he'd proved how unprepared I was for this mission. I would never have softened up Lafontaine if it hadn't been for Mr. Hothead beside me goading him on, pushing me to rein him back.

I'd take it as a lesson learned. Detachment was great in a crisis but useless when trying to connect with people. A bit of compassion and empathy were far more helpful. Damn, Madison made this look so easy.

For it to be Gideon who showed me my error added insult to injury, but I did my best to put it behind me. The next interview would be smoother. I was grateful I'd started in South Keys with a good-natured adlet. Way better than if I'd started with the lutin. Hobgoblins were notorious shitheads.

I navigated our way through traffic without saying a word, wishing I'd gotten around to fixing the car radio. Yet the longer we drove, the more comfortable the silence became. It no longer felt like Gideon had something he wanted to say. Instead, he sat back and stared out the window as we sped along the 417, going opposite the afternoon commute.

I took the next exit and detoured the construction before finally winding up in a semi-modest part of town. The street was a mix of cozy bungalows from the 60s and modern mini-mansions that came off as impersonal and sterile.

Peter Dougall lived in one of the bungalows. Compared to Lafontaine's house, it was in magazine-worthy shape, with a glassed-in front porch against a whitewashed facade. The curtains were drawn across the row of windows looking over the porch, and I crossed my fingers we weren't walking into any surprises.

Gideon stayed a few feet behind me as I knocked on the door, and I stepped back to avoid crowding Dougall when he answered.

It took a second time knocking to bring him to the door, and nothing about him fit with his surroundings. Old, ratty running shoes and faded, baggy jeans that were torn at the knees. His grey T-shirt looked about three sizes too big, and he wore an unbuttoned plaid shirt over top, rolled to the elbows. His thick brown hair was pulled into a low knot at the back of his neck. A few loose strands had fallen free, and I wanted to take a pair of scissors to them.

His features were as plain as the rest of him, his blue eyes small, his nose long, and his lips thin.

Nothing about him stood out. Which, I guessed, was why he'd gotten away with overhearing as much as he had.

"Peter Dougall?" I asked, crossing my fingers I had the wrong person.

"Yes, ma'am?" His voice was soft, almost reedy.

Also, *ma'am*? I resisted the urge to grimace, pulled my ID out of my pocket, and introduced myself. Unlike Lafontaine, who'd acknowledged my presence as a matter of course, Dougall took a step back into the shadows of his home and hunched his shoulders. Defensive. Interesting.

"Can I help you?" He sounded civil, but less open than he had a moment ago. SMOAC agents had that effect on supernaturals, similar to a mundane's reaction when the cops showed up unannounced. A visit from either usually meant something terrible had happened or you were in a heap of trouble.

Pulling from the lessons I'd learned with Lafontaine, I performed a mental run-through of my strategy. Step one: put the informant at ease.

"You're not in any trouble," I said. "I wanted to follow up on the statement you made regarding the Death's Head Syndicate's connection to the de Lauer Estates."

Although he said nothing, Gideon went still behind me, and in the same breath, Dougall's expression shut down. What had I done wrong this time?

It took me longer than it should have to realize referring to a violent crime syndicate by name and mentioning how this guy had snitched on them was not the best way to make him feel safe.

Time to back pedal.

"They won't find out," I said.

"You did." His gaze darted down both sides of the street.

"Can we come in for a minute?" I kept my tone as gentle as I would with a spooked horse. "We won't be long."

"I don't think that's a good idea. The last couple days, I swear someone's been watching the house, and now you show up. How do I know you're not with them?"

"Because if I were, I wouldn't be asking, and because we take better care of our people than that." I did my best to hold on to my patience, but it was difficult. Give me a stakeout, and I could sit around for days waiting for someone to come home, but the moment they did, I was the first one to kick down the door and drag them back out. Once people were involved, I wasn't used to taking my time.

"What do you say, Dougall? Something you tell me could be what puts these guys away for the rest of their lives. I can't get them without your help."

His face paled, and I kicked myself for pushing too hard.

I am so bad at this.

The fear that I would crush any chance we had with him nudged me to look to Gideon for help, but I kept my attention firmly on Dougall. I'd planned to do this on my own, and Gideon would soon be gone. If I wanted to get to the bottom of the attack, I had to clean up my own messes.

"Peter, you came to us for a reason. You knew telling someone what you heard might save lives. There's a good chance speaking to us will prevent anyone else from being hurt."

There. The flash of uncertainty in his eyes, the desire to help and be a hero, if only in this one small way.

"Five minutes," I said.

He scanned the street again as he chewed his bottom lip, but after a moment, his mouth drawn tight and his brow furrowed with resentment, he stepped aside and opened the door wider.

"Come in or go away. I don't want you standing on the porch where everyone can see you." He kept an eye on the road as we stepped into the house and hurried to shut the door behind us.

Unlike Lafontaine's place, Dougall's living room was tidy. Nothing but an autumn-coloured velour couch topped with a crocheted afghan, a woven rug on a parquet floor, and a fireplace stuffed with boxes. More boxes sat piled in the corner, neatly stacked.

Based on the decor, the location, and the state of the place, I guessed he'd taken over the house from a dead relative. A grandmother, maybe, considering the old black-and-white baby photos on the wall.

Like Lafontaine, Dougall didn't offer us a seat, but unlike

the adlet, he didn't apologize for it. Instead, he remained standing in the middle of the living room, his arms wrapped around
his middle and his focus on the floor. When a car with a broken
muffler sped down the street, he jumped and shifted towards
the doorway to the kitchen, as though worried someone might
see him through the closed curtains.

"You don't need to worry," I said.

"Really?" he asked with a snort. "Do you know what the
syndicate is capable of?"

I bit my tongue and refrained from pointing out that half
my squad was dead because of the syndicate. The reminder
wasn't likely to relax him.

"I do," I said. "If you're concerned about staying here, I
can talk to people. We can find you somewhere safe to live until
this is dealt with."

He shook his head sharply. "I'm not going anywhere. I
shouldn't have gone to you in the first place. I don't know what
I was thinking."

"You've reported things before without trouble, isn't that
right?" Gideon asked, and this time I didn't react. I'd already
shown I was as graceful as an ogre handling a teacup, so if he
had an idea on how to get this guy to calm down, I'd give him
some wiggle room.

"Sure," Dougall said, shoving his hands deep in his pockets, "but not like this. Those were small things that had nothing
to do with the syndicate, for fuck's sake. That's big fish terri-

tory, and I'm a small fish kinda guy, you know? Petty crimes, that kinda thing."

"We're not asking you to do anything more than talk," I said, lowering my voice even more. "Just take us through what you've already told us and see if there's anything else you remember."

Lafontaine had described the voices of the people he'd heard. If Dougall could help put faces to those voices, we might have something solid to go on. Proof that at least one of them was O'Malley. Evidence we could use against him and whoever he was working with.

"This conversation is off the record, yeah? I don't want it coming out that I talked to you people again. This is it. After this, I'm done. You come here again, and I'll—I'll have you up on harassment or something."

Despite myself, I glanced at Gideon, who replied with a subtle shrug. It wasn't the ideal situation, and the intelligence branch might string me up for losing them a solid informant, but at the moment, I didn't care. If making this promise would get Dougall talking, I couldn't hesitate.

"This is it," I agreed. "No one from SMOAC knows I'm here, and no one will ever come to your house again."

I didn't know how I would explain it to Madison, but that was a problem for later.

Dougall visibly relaxed and rubbed his thumb across his nose. "It was just a passing conversation, you know? At The Afterlife. I work there, right? But I remember the night real well. Buddy of mine was in the band, The Wendigos, and I came out from the kitchens to check them out. Not really my type of music, but good energy. Anyway, this drunk sits down next to me, and I know I know him. He's one of those guys who stands out because of his illusions, you know? Whedon, Weylon. Whatever. Guy works some cool magic."

Weldon, the bastard. I clenched my teeth but stayed silent.

"Anyway, I remember he was involved in that robbery I told you guys about a few months ago. You remember—some couple storming convenience stores, her using her ability to switch off the power and another guy blowing out the back wall with his mind. This was the guy who'd tipped me off about that one. Made it look like there were six people there instead of two. I figure why not get him talking tonight, see what he's up to, if there's anything else I can get a handle on. I wanted the finder's fee, right?"

He shrugged. "So anyway, I ask him what he's doing these days, say I'm a friend of Manny's—Mr. Exploding Head. He tells me he's working this new job he's not allowed to talk about. I buy him another drink and ask if there's any money in it, that I could use a little top-up. He says there's no cash yet, but there's a promise of a big payout at the end if everything goes well. I ask him who I could see to get in, and he mentions Big Joe Murphy. Now, I've heard of Big Joe, and I'm not about to go talking to him out of the blue. So I tell this guy that, and he shakes his head. Tells me Big Joe's not in charge of this operation. That he's as small a fish as any of us compared to the top dogs. So bit by bit I get him talking about who else is wrapped up in it. He throws out names like Sammy G and Storms Anderson. These guys make my asshole clench shut, right? Because I know the kinds of things they're involved in and what their abilities are."

I struggled to keep up with him now that he was rolling, mentally noting names and details. If these people were part of the de Lauer trap, Dougall was right to be scared. Sammy's criminal history made him a legend in the department, and Storms haunted the dreams of more than one retired agent.

Dougall dropped his arms, shifted his weight from one foot to the other, clenched and unclenched his fingers, jittery with the energy he'd been holding back a few minutes ago. "At this point, I'm barely poking this guy for information. He's drinking, talking about the ghost changing hands. That's when I checked out."

My palms prickled with excitement. Would it be enough to get security to roll on O'Malley? The names were solid and the details lined up with what we knew. Weldon's name would clinch the connection. It had to. It was still hearsay, but at least this gave them somewhere to start.

"What about the Kingston rumour?" Gideon cut in, and I stood back and let him ask his questions. Dougall was on a roll, telling us more than we expected. If Gideon could guide his ramblings onto more specific details, I'd let him play.

To my surprise, however, Dougall hooted with laughter. "You're not telling me you believe that bullshit? From what I hear, O'Malley started the rumour himself. He knew you guys would run over there at the first whiff of movement, so he created a few hot spots, named names, made sure he was seen at some of the clubs, then as soon as you followed the trail, he came home and carried on business as usual."

As though he suddenly heard the words coming out of his mouth, Dougall clamped his lips shut, and his tiny eyes grew wide. After a moment's silence, he hunched his shoulders and wrapped his arms around his stomach again. "Shit, man, why'd you let me go off like that? You're going to find my corpse in a gutter somewhere, and all because I kept blabbing to you people."

"You helped us, Dougall. There's no need to be ashamed of that," I said.

He dug his toe into the rug. "I guess it doesn't matter if they get me or not. You hear all these things working in the kitchens, and you start to realize it's not worth it. We're talking about some really bad guys, and, by the sounds of it, nothing they're planning is going to do this city any good."

He ducked his head, closing in on himself, and I knew we were done. I tried to feel good that we'd nailed down a few new names—names we could follow up on and compare to Lafontaine's descriptions of the voices in the alley—but suspected there was a well of untapped information in this man we weren't going to access. And never would, thanks to the deal I'd made. Not unless his conscience got the better of him and he came to us, but I guessed that would only happen if he found himself in serious trouble.

"All right, Dougall." I pulled a business card out of my wallet with my cell number written on it. "If you need us for anything, give this number a call. Any time, day or night. If you change your mind about wanting a safe place to hide or need someone to drive by to make sure you're okay, you only need to ask."

He took the card and nodded his thanks, but didn't say anything else. I caught Gideon's eye, and he started towards the door, letting us out onto the porch. I made sure the door was closed, and, because of Dougall's paranoia or my own sixth sense, scanned the length of the street. I saw nothing, but that didn't mean Dougall was wrong about someone watching the house.

"You good?" Gideon asked.

"Yeah, let's go."

We got into the car, and Gideon stretched his long legs out in front of him. "So? You think he's legit?"

"I don't think he'd be so terrified if he wasn't. And I understand why he is. Working under their noses and passing along what he hears? That takes balls."

And here I was putting those balls under a guillotine for O'Malley to strike them off if he learned about it.

Should I have pushed Dougall harder? Would the ethical

move have been to walk away and let him go into hiding? I doubted O'Malley would care if he talked to us a million times—that first breach of confidence would be enough to take his head—but each new interaction increased the odds he'd find out.

I knew I should care I'd increased the risk for this guy, but I couldn't summon the guilt. Zeke's ashen face, Katie's tears— the need to make things right overpowered everything else.

Sorry, Dougall. You made your move, and now you're another unwilling pawn on the game board.

I gave myself a shake and started the car.

"He doesn't strike me as a guy with a lot of guts," Gideon said, and I was grateful for the distraction.

"His file says you're right. History of theft, mostly small jobs. Guy's nimble-fingered, but the pace of the kitchens keeps him too busy to pick pockets. He hasn't been much trouble in the past year or so."

I put the car in reverse and took a last look at the house. The curtains fluttered, and I imagined Dougall standing there, watching us, waiting for us to leave. "The names he mentioned, it checks out. Those guys are known members of the syndicate, and Weldon's already been killed for his part in the attack." I puffed out a breath. "But I don't know. I get the feeling there's more here."

"Keep the door open?"

I nodded. "No point closing anything yet. Hopefully we'll

luck out and someone can corroborate what Dougall told us."

"On to the next, then?"

"On to the next."

We spent the rest of the afternoon circling back towards downtown, knocking another three informants off the list. The hairstylist nearly had a heart attack when we walked through the door, and he refused to talk to us until we stepped into his tiny supply cupboard, which led to an uncomfortable—but lovely smelling—twenty minutes, during which we learned nothing new but at least confirmed his original story.

One refused to let us in until we threatened to shout our questions through the door. One had been eager to repeat what she'd already told us, as though she worried we would take back her finder's fee if she didn't.

As frustrating as it was to make so little progress, I appreciated how much worse it would have been if I'd tried to do this alone. With Gideon and me trading questions, each of us applying our own methods to get them talking, we managed to pry out twice as much information.

Our sixth contact was a dishwasher at The Afterlife, a ghoul who worked closely with Dougall, though I doubted either of them knew the other also worked for us. From the moment we arrived at his apartment, I smelled something funny.

"What I gave you wasn't enough?" he asked, a shaky smile on his face. "I take time out of my day and put my life on the line sharing what I hear, and you come back for more? Fine by me if you bring the cash."

He released a nervous giggle and danced from one foot to the other. Like Dougall on cocaine.

"We want to go through what you told us before," I said.

"I don't do seconds on anything I hand over," he said, shaking his head. "It gets less valuable with every telling, see? Better you read the file. It's all there."

At that, Gideon stepped forward. Compared to Dancy Pants, he was as steady and cool as an iceberg. He loomed over the other man, and his brown eyes bored into him. "You like to be the centre of attention, don't you?"

I stood back and let him take over, curious to see his angle and reluctant to tear my gaze away from the defined width of his shoulders.

"Me? Nah, man. I don't like drawing attention to myself. That's why I work dishes. I could be a cook. I could be a great one. But that's too much responsibility, you know? I like where I am." He tapped his temple. "You pick things up when no one notices you."

I scoffed. With his loud mouth and constant energy, this guy may as well have been dressed in neon. Either he possessed a complete lack of self-awareness or his level of denial would have given Freud wet dreams.

"Kitchens can be pretty loud, though, can't they?" Gideon asked. "And it's not like you can be away from your station for long without someone giving you shit."

"Well, no…" he said, wiping his hands on his chest. "But I still hear things."

Gideon moved in closer. "I don't think you did this time, though, did you? Not directly, anyway."

His voice was smooth, laced with the unspoken threat of what he did to bullshitters, and I felt the corner of my mouth quirk in an involuntary smile.

The guy was a lying son of a bitch, but damn, watching him work sent shock waves through my belly.

The ghoul's eyes darted towards me in a panic. "I did. I swear. I—well, okay, maybe not directly." An uncomfortable heat rose in my veins as anger crept through me, and I finally looked away from Gideon. "The rumours are everywhere. I picked it up and passed it along, is that so bad?" My rage simmered, growing to a boil. "There was some truth to it, wasn't there? Come on, guys, I needed the money."

Fury overwhelmed me, and I raised my hand and sent a blast of air at the ghoul strong enough to slam him against the paper-thin wall of his living room. He flailed his arms to get free, but I held him pinned as I stepped closer.

"Your bad intel led to the deaths of ten veteran troops," I growled. I wanted to tear off his head and stick it on a spike as a warning to anyone else who might be tempted to fuck with me. But I drew back, and he sagged to the ground. My hands trembled, and I clenched my fists and drew myself up. "Keep whatever money we gave you, asswipe. It's the last you'll get from us."

I turned on my heel and marched out before my restraint disappeared and I sent a good swing into the ghoul's face.

How had his tip made it down the line?

As I headed back to the car, I told myself it didn't matter. We still had the other five.

"Buck up," Gideon said as we drove into the heart of downtown. "We're ahead of where we were."

He was right, even if it was small comfort.

"And hey," he added, "you have to admit it's been fun, working together again. We still make a pretty great team."

I wasn't ready to admit any such thing out loud, so I shot him a glare and took the next turn with an emphasized jerk. The last thing I intended to do was inflate this man's already massive ego.

As though he read my thoughts and saw through them, he flashed me a cheeky grin, and I scowled and looked away. One day on the job with him, and already I felt the walls between us weakening. I refused to let them crumble. The sooner we found what we were looking for, the better it would be.

With only one lead left to follow, I pulled into the parking lot of The Afterlife.

Chapter 16

Gideon

THE AFTERLIFE WAS one of the few places in this city that catered exclusively to supernaturals. Any mundane walking down the street would see it as an empty warehouse.

It was also the kind of place that made you want to shower as soon as you walked through the door.

Not just because you knew it was dirty—the low lights weren't enough to hide the layers of grunge on the tables—but because the atmosphere was as thick and sticky as the floors. The bar was full of supernaturals swaggering around, ogling the burlesque dancers with their feather fans and sequined underwear, and trying to one-up each other's abilities. *In Corner A, we have a fire-breather who's the life of the party until he burns the place down, and in Corner B, a shape-changer who's gotten himself partially stuck as a bull.*

I rolled my eyes and walked past them, sticking close to Jet to avoid losing her in the crowd. My stomach growled, reminding me that both lunch and supper had gone by without a break, but I thought better of eating anything they served here. The last thing I wanted to catch was a case of arsenic.

Lack of food aside, I thought the day had gone well. We'd met some people, had some laughs, I was still breathing. In terms of the job, of course, all our trekking around had been a bust. Even the Kingston lead I'd gotten had been squashed. I had nothing to bring back to Dark Wire and, therefore, no excuse to say my farewells and go home.

But Jet hadn't given up. Dougall's intel had sparked her hope, and every failure had fuelled her to push harder. As I'd known it would. It was why I loved to watch her work. Why she was such a great leader.

Though I was surprised to find her stepping this far out of bounds. The Jet Dawson I'd known in New York, the one whose career I'd followed ever since through files I shouldn't have read, was a stickler for the rules. She followed orders, nothing more, nothing less. Tonight, she had broken over a dozen of them without flinching.

Either this side of her had existed all along and I hadn't noticed, or she'd lost her mind. As worried as I was that she would push too far, my blood warmed at the thought of where we might end up.

There was something she hoped to learn—something she hadn't found yet—and the night wasn't over. We had one more informant to question, and I wasn't going anywhere. I had to see how the rest played out. Her success would be mine, and after the way our day had gone, I wanted to enjoy the moment with her.

"I know it's a risk coming here," she'd said before we'd gotten out of the car, "but this is the best place to find him. Who knows, we could spot Big Joe or Storms while we wait. Maybe even O'Malley himself."

The edge of excitement in her voice, the hint of desire to tear O'Malley's nuts off and serve them to him on an After-life-stamped platter, had made my stomach clench with an unfamiliar, protective fear. "Would you go after him directly?" I'd asked in a tone I hoped sounded indifferent.

She'd shrugged. "Depends how I feel."

Not the answer I'd wanted.

Now that we were in the club, I was on high alert. The entire place was a potential powder keg hooked to blow, and I needed to find the off switch. If Jet called O'Malley out on his turf, things could get real messy real quick. He was a brutal piece of work. The type to leave heads on dining tables as a message, and who made people disappear as quickly as I inhaled a Snickers bar. At the same time, the thought of her going up against him was a pretty big turn-on. With the right advantage, I was sure she could come out on top. As she preferred to be.

We approached the bar, and Jet nudged a stool out of the way, preferring to stand beside it. I didn't blame her.

The bartender came over, and she ordered a round for both of us. I hid my surprise at her generosity. After how she'd been with me all day, I hadn't expected any show of camaraderie, but I accepted the gesture as standard practice between partners on the job.

While we waited for our drinks, I leaned my back against the bar and stared out over the growing crowd. Most of them had hit the dance floor, moving to music I could almost justify calling industrial. Everyone else lined the sides, standing at tables doing shots or risking who knew what skin conditions in low-slung chairs in deep, dark corners.

As the minutes passed, I sipped my beer and kept to myself. Jet was focused on the bar, waiting for her informant to show, so I watched the room, taking in the flow of movement, the possible escape routes. A few of the burlesque dancers made eyes at me, and I allowed myself to join the crowd of oglers, appreciating the wave of their fans and the skilled way they peeled off a glove here and a stocking there in time with the music.

"Come on," Jet said. "If I stay here glowering at every person who comes in, people are going to notice."

Her beer was already empty, and she was tapping her fingers against the bar, almost vibrating with restless energy. I set my drink down next to hers.

"What did you have in mind?"

She pushed out a sharp exhale. "Screw it, we're going to

dance. At least that way I can keep an eye on the door."

She could have told me she was going to pluck out her eyes and use them to play jacks and I wouldn't have been more surprised.

But she was already peeling off her jacket, revealing her plain black tee.

"You want to dance with me?" I asked.

She rolled her eyes, set her folded jacket on the bar, and grabbed my hand. "Don't read anything into it. It's a cover. Like most of your life."

I laughed, but only to hide the sting. I wished her accusation weren't so true. Despite the disappointments we'd faced, today was one of the most satisfying workdays I'd had in years. Riding with Jet had reminded me how much fun I could have when I teamed up with someone on my level, and I hated that I couldn't be honest with her. I wanted to talk things out, clear the air, but the fact that I was only here because of another mission I couldn't tell her about didn't do much to earn me the role of Stand-Up Guy.

All I could do was bear her sharp tongue and remind myself this was part of the job. We didn't form attachments. We didn't get into relationships. We did the work and finished the mission, keeping our countries safe from things like mind-opening drugs that killed mundanes and burned out supes.

It was all business.

So I tried to detach as we headed to the floor, and I told

myself it meant nothing when I slid my arm around her waist, drawing her to me. Her hips fit against mine, and my blood warmed at the press of her body. The energy of the crowd, the anticipation of what this informant might tell us, the possibility that O'Malley might walk in set my pulse racing. Beneath it was the drumming of a slow, driving beat.

Jet slid her hands up my chest, her fingers still tapping that impatient rhythm, and I squeezed her hip, reminding her she was supposed to at least look like she was having fun. If no one was fooled by her looking impatient at a bar, even fewer people would be fooled by her standing stiff as a board on the dance floor.

She huffed at being corrected, but reached up and pulled her ponytail free, sending her thick brown hair tumbling over her shoulders. It covered half her face and tickled her neck, and the temptation came over me to brush it out of the way and kiss her soft skin.

The music's getting to me, I told myself, but I didn't have time to tamp down my rising desire before she fell into a smooth, undulating rhythm. For a moment, a too-brief moment, we were back where we'd been in New York. Working together on more than one level, moving as one and heading towards the same goal. My body reacted to her closeness and the smell of her shampoo. Every cell sang with the longing to pull her closer, to leave the club and go someplace quiet where we could talk without words and share the only form of honesty available to us.

I licked my lips and swallowed hard. We were here to work, and that part of our lives was over. Finished. She didn't want it, and, frankly, neither did I. If I didn't have to hurt her again—or deal with my tangled feelings—I wouldn't.

As the song continued, Jet melted deeper into me, but when I glanced down, I found her attention was focused on the bar. I slid my arm tighter around her waist and concentrated on the other side of the room. The burlesque dancers had wrapped up their set and were taking a break, mingling with the crowd. The drunks hooted and hollered at them, with only a few being ignorant enough to try to cop a feel, but the dancers put them in their place quickly enough, preventing any potential violence.

It felt like a regular Friday night out, but any chance we had of pretending for a few hours that everything was fine vanished when Jet stiffened in my arms.

"Here we go," she said, seemingly more to herself than to me.

I followed her gaze to the bar, where a new arrival had grabbed a stool close to where we'd been standing. He was a dumpy-looking guy, but then, so were most of the people we'd talked to. During peak hours, The Afterlife brought in all kinds of folks looking to have a good time; the rest of their open hours were for people like him—the ones looking to escape at the bottom of a glass.

Jet pulled away—I refused to get my hopes up that I sensed a slight hesitation—and my skin cooled. I set aside the twinge of regret as I followed her to the bar.

"Hey there, Rourke," she said, coming up on the guy's left. He wore a hunting jacket over a red T-shirt, and his balding head reflected the glaring pot lights.

At the sight of her, he grunted and shifted on his stool to put his back to her. I filled up the space on his right, closing him in.

"You know this guy?" I asked.

"Sure," she said. "Rourke and I go way back to my training days. Had his heart set on being a soldier but couldn't reach the fitness standards. Right, Rourke?"

"Fuck off."

"Hey now, is that any way to talk to an old fellow recruit?"

Rourke didn't answer. He accepted his beer when the bartender set it down and tucked right in, as though Jet and I didn't exist.

"How are things going, Rourke?" Jet asked.

His only response was to hunch closer to his drink, but then he glanced across the bar and let out a mumbled, "Shit."

I followed his gaze and spotted four men coming towards us.

"Who are they?" Jet asked, keeping her voice low.

"Bad news," Rourke said.

They reached us, and I recognized the leader as the shape-changer from Corner B. He'd successfully returned to his human form, though a pair of horns still protruded from his brow. An intentional fashion trend? I wondered if anyone had told him he looked stupid.

"These two giving you trouble, Rourke?" he asked.

"No trouble here, Mike. Go on back to your beer."

Mike scanned us over. "How about you two get out of here and leave him alone?"

He directed the order to me, but it was Jet who answered, taking a step forward to close the space between them. "We're just trying to have a conversation. One that doesn't concern you. So how about you walk away and let us chat?"

Mike opened his mouth to speak, but she cut him off. "No, no, let me guess—Rourke here's your buddy, and you can't have your buddy being intimidated. You're a fine, upstanding citizen, and you need to step in when it looks like trouble. Is that it? How close am I?"

She took another step towards him, and although she only came up to his chest, no one could deny she was scary. Even from a few feet away, the radiating energy of her ability caused my hair to stand on end, and I didn't know how these four weren't running for the door. My heart was racing, though it wasn't from fear.

She cocked her head to the side. "I'm sure your interest has nothing to do with the fact that Rourke pays you money to leave him alone and you're worried we're moving in on your hustle, right?"

The shape-changer's gaze jumped to Rourke, but Jet shifted to block his view. "Don't look at him, he didn't say anything. I know your type, Mike, and believe me when I say I know how to deal with beasts like you."

Mike scowled, the furrow between his brows drawing his horns together. "You'd better stand down, little girl." His buddies snorted at what I took to be his attempt at cleverness. "You don't want to get on my bad side."

Jet frowned and stood on her tiptoes, checking out Mike's face from multiple angles. "Funny," she said. "Doesn't look like you have a good side."

At that, Mike's friends betrayed him by laughing out loud, and I didn't hesitate to join in.

Mike flushed a deep red as his anger overcame his smugness, and he reached out to grab Jet's arm. She was ready for him and closed her hand around his wrist, twisting his arm backwards. Mike jerked away and prepared to follow up with a full blow, but she ducked down and delivered a punch of her own into his gut.

He doubled over, out of breath, and one of his friends, a man who in the glow of the pot lights appeared to be made of rock, swept out his foot and took Jet's legs out from under her. She landed on her back with enough force to rattle the glasses on the bar, but when he moved forward to drive his foot into her side, she took hold of his ankle and pulled, taking him to the ground with her.

My blood boiled with the urge to jump into the fight, to taste some action after days of playing it cautious, so to hold myself back, I waved the bartender down and signed for two more drinks, then returned my attention to Jet.

Mike's other two friends, who were so generic with their black hair and black clothes I couldn't help but think of them as Thing One and Thing Two, had so far stayed back to let the others do the dirty work, but now that Rocky had been grounded, they stepped in to help. They didn't have time to land a single kick before Jet flipped onto her feet.

I tensed as Mike charged at her, but she caught him around the waist and spun him into Thing One, sending them both colliding into the bar. Thing Two grabbed a beer bottle and hurled it her way, but she dodged to the left, and the bottle struck a staggering Rocky in the head. Tiny pebbles and shards of glass clattered down the side of his face, and he growled as he grabbed Jet from behind. He wrapped his thick arm around her neck and squeezed.

She slammed on his instep and swung her elbow into his gut. Neither attack had any effect. She repeated the manoeuvre three more times, but the guy hung on. Jet's face had gone from pink to a dark red, almost purple.

My heart thundered, and I clung to the edge of the bartop to stop myself from getting involved. Jet could handle this. She wouldn't want me to step in.

At my side, Rourke grunted and ran a hand over his sweaty

brow. "Aren't you going to help her?"

The bartender arrived with our drinks, and I forced myself to laugh as I grabbed a bottle and settled my back against the bar, propping my elbows on the surface behind me. "Do I look as stupid as those guys?"

Despite my feigned nonchalance, I didn't take my eyes off her. I sipped my beer and watched as Mike wound up to strike her across the face. At the last minute, she slammed her head back, catching Rocky in the nose. Obviously her head was hard enough to crush stone, because he let her go, leaving himself open to receive Mike's backhanded fist.

By the look on Jet's face, she was done playing. The air around us vibrated as she stretched out her arms, and for a moment, all four men rose a few inches off the floor before she slammed them down onto their backs. Although they were breathing, none of them rushed to get back up and go for round two.

Sweat dripped along Jet's hairline, and she wobbled on unsteady legs. I felt a pinch of doubt and cursed myself. Rourke was right—I should have done something. She'd looked so self-assured out there, so ready for anything they might throw at her, that I'd forgotten everything she'd suffered in the past twenty-four hours. On a good day, that quick use of her ability wouldn't have affected her, but today it seemed to have drained every ounce of strength.

I liked to think I would have made a move if she'd shown

any obvious signs of distress, but was that true? She would have hidden her panic until the end, and by then it might have been too late. Even worse was the thought that she might feel I'd abandoned her, though I knew she'd never admit it.

I watched her closely as she staggered towards the bar and downed half her beer in a single go. When she set the bottle down with a shaking hand, she gave me a nod. "Thanks for the drink."

A wave of relief washed over me. My instincts had been right. She hadn't wanted me to step in. Despite the toll it had taken, she'd had this from the start.

Next time, though, I would pay closer attention, and I wouldn't hesitate. If whatever she was going through meant she wasn't up to the challenge, I could handle her bruised ego if it meant her survival.

Once Jet caught her breath, she tied her hair into its usual ponytail, pulled her jacket back on, and turned to Rourke. "What do you say now? You got time for a beer?"

Chapter 17

Madison

I SIPPED MY tea and ran my fingers through Persephone's fur. Her loud purrs vibrated against the top of my curled leg. A book sat open against the armrest—the long-awaited sequel in a thriller series I'd followed for years. Anyone outside looking in might have seen a woman at her most relaxed, but I hadn't turned the page in over half an hour, my tea was cold, and the only reason I wasn't pacing the length of my condo was the unbreakable rule that a comfortable cat cannot be moved.

I'd had no word from Jet, and Jean-Luc had passed by me this afternoon without any acknowledgement, too caught up in his growing worry and tension.

After hours of sitting around my office waiting for news and not hearing anything, I'd given up and come home. Now I had to wonder what the point had been—I wasn't any more at ease than I would have been at work.

At least here I was in pyjamas and far from any high-heeled shoes.

The clock on the wall lulled me deeper into my thoughts, my limbs growing heavy, my eyelids weighing down. Although my stress continued to rage against the sides of my skull, my subconscious pulled me closer to dreams. My living room faded, the ticking clock morphed into the tap of raindrops on leaves, and suddenly I wasn't in my apartment anymore but in the meadow. Rain on the flowers and stone, the colours bright and vivid despite the grey sky.

The touch of Meril on everything, a sharp reminder that time was passing, and she was not a patient queen.

A melodic ring jerked me back into my body, and a startled Persephone leapt off my lap and scurried under the dining table. Smacking my lips to work some moisture back into my mouth, I grabbed my phone as though it were a lifeline away from the unspoken threat.

I'd hoped it was Jet but was surprised to see my great-uncle's name instead. Surprise quickly spiked into fear. Sercario was in the upper echelon of the queen's council. If he was calling...

Was the trip to the meadow more than a reminder?

It had been barely twenty-four hours since she'd met with me. Was she really only giving me a day to corner someone the department had been hunting for years?

My heart in my throat, I answered the call. "Serc?"

"What have you learned?"

I swallowed hard. Straight to business, then. No *How are you*, no *Been a while*. My palms grew clammy, and I wiped my free hand across my thigh to dry it off. If he wanted to get right to the point, I would follow his lead.

Let's get this over with.

"We have no new information regarding the incident. We continue to follow the theory that it was a targeted attack on the department, but although we have a few leads, none of them has brought us anything."

It never occurred to me to lie. Serc, my grandmother's brother, was an empath like me, and he would have undoubtedly heard through it.

"What's being done?"

Now that the shock of his call was wearing off, it left room for other, more volatile emotions to creep in. "Is this an official call from the Shadow Council? If so, there are proper channels for that."

I was in no mood to give him shortcuts that both the minister and the queen could use against me.

A soft breath came down the line, and when he spoke again, some of his brusqueness was gone. "You're right, Madi, I'm sorry. This isn't an official call. The court is aware of the problem, but no orders have come down from the queen. Yet. I'm calling because I want to be ahead of things when she inevitably asks for an update. I think it's better it comes from me so she doesn't have to reach out to you, don't you agree?"

The tension drained out of me, and I melted into my chair. Persephone took my relaxed posture as a sign she was safe to come back and made herself comfortable in the crook of my curled legs.

This wasn't my summons. I still had time.

"She already did," I said.

"She what?"

"Last night. The meadow. And right before you called, a friendly reminder that she's waiting."

A drawn-out pause and then, "I had no idea. By her silence, I thought she was trusting—but that was foolish of me, obviously. What did you tell her?"

"The same thing I told you. That our teams are looking into what happened and how we can move forward in an offensive effort. Since she and I spoke, though, an unofficial investigation has started digging into the information that led us to the ambush in the first place. I'm waiting to hear the results."

There. A formal report he could take to Meril. At least she'd know I was holding up my end of the bargain. We were doing everything we could. She had to give me more time.

"Did she give you any idea of her intentions?" he asked.

"Nothing overt, lots implied. If we don't resolve this soon, she will act, and her response will be swift and brutal. No one on this side wants that to happen, Uncle."

"You might not believe me, but most over here don't want

it, either," he said. "What about with regard to you?"

I stroked Persephone's ears. "My recall to court was mentioned, though she hasn't made it official yet. I think she's giving me some rope to hang myself with."

"Would it truly be the worst thing?" His voice was soft, non-judgemental. "You would have a position here. Authority. Security."

I pinched the bridge of my nose. "Maybe if I'd been raised there, I could handle the pressure of having my life in her hands, but I can do more—become more—over here than I ever could under her micromanaging. At least on this side I have the freedom to make mistakes without worrying I'll lose my head because of it."

"I understand, and although I wonder if you wouldn't be protected here from everything happening on your side, I respect your decision."

Persephone mewed and looked up at me, and I realized my fingers had curled into her fur. I loosened my hold and made every attempt to sound confident. "Her Majesty has made it clear she wants answers yesterday, so if it were in your power to buy us—buy me—a few days, I would appreciate it."

"I'll do what I can, Madi. I promise. Your grandmother would kill me if I didn't try to put off your recall, and I don't need that earache right now. I can't guarantee the delay will be significant, however."

"Thank you, Uncle."

He hung up without farewell, and I set down my phone and closed my book.

There was no point pretending to relax tonight.

"Come on, Jet," I said, staring at my phone and willing it to ring. "What in Meril's name are you up to?"

Chapter 18

Jet

IT TOOK LONGER than it should have to catch my breath, and the beer I'd guzzled wasn't sitting well. Every joint and muscle ached, and when I broke down and dropped onto the bar stool, pain shot through my hips. Exhaustion tugged at my limbs, begging me to go home and crawl into bed. I was tempted to step outside to get some air until the nausea settled, but I refused to do anything that gave away my weakness.

I'd won. That was all that mattered. Despite the few close shaves, I was grateful Gideon had stayed out of it. After everything we'd done today, all the failures and frustrations, I would have been humiliated to have him play hero. Especially when, on any other day, I would have brought those guys down in less than a minute.

It should have been easy. Barely an effort. But I'd been off my game from the moment I'd left the dance floor. The driving beat of the music worked through my blood, and my pulse throbbed in time with the bass, taking me back to the press of the crowd, the smell of Gideon's skin and the hint of lingering soap. His closeness after so many years apart.

I couldn't dwell on it. I'd come here to speak with Rourke, not to play nostalgia with another life. And after protecting him from the playground bullies, I hoped my old acquaintance was ready to chat. He was a solid resource. Although I'd called him out for not making the squad, he could have offered a lot to the department if he'd been given a chance to stay on.

At least he'd agreed to have a drink with us.

The bartender swapped out our bottles, and I shifted my weight to stop the uneven stool from grinding into my ass cheeks.

"Look," Rourke started as soon as he had a few more sips in him. "I don't want to get involved in whatever you have with these guys, all right?" He kept his gruff voice low, but unlike Dougall's outward panic, he was cautious, not spooked. "The intel I bring to you guys, it's on my terms. It's how it's always been. Yeah, I didn't get to live my dream of being a soldier, but maybe that's for the best. I don't think I would have wanted to be in that high-rise yesterday when the bomb went off. My life might not be full of anything special, but it's mine and I like it, you know what I mean?"

Looking around at his crowded, filthy, vice-ridden home away from home, I wasn't sure I did. I also understood my lifestyle wasn't for everyone. There was always the chance that tomorrow I wouldn't come home.

It was why I didn't have any pets.

"Snitches might be looked down on, but in my own way I make a difference," he said.

"And you have, Rourke," I said. "I flipped through your file. You've been with us ever since you dropped out of training." I wasn't trying to butter him up, just telling it like it was. Over fifty solid tips in the last thirteen years. A high-stakes game and getting paid peanuts to do it. Country-wide security threats had been shut down thanks to this barfly, and because of the protections on our informants, he couldn't even receive the public accolades he deserved.

He snorted and shot me a dirty look. "And how did you get a look at my file, hmm?" He shook his head and drank his beer. "Never mind. Probably for the best I don't know. My point is, I can't have you coming here and pushing me for information. That's not how this works. When I have something—anything—I'll get in touch."

His objection wasn't unexpected. By coming here, we had compromised his position. Yes, he was a drunk who'd made The Afterlife his haunt long before he realized he could make money from passing along what he heard, but that was beside the point. He was a man whose goal had once been to keep his community safe, and he hadn't been able to achieve it. It wasn't hard to appreciate how those dashed dreams could mess a person up.

Unfortunately for him, we needed all the help we could get.

Doing my best to respect his situation, I lowered my voice until he could just hear me over the music. "We owe you, Rourke. Big time. For everything you've done. But my troops got taken down hard, and one of the reasons we were there at all was because of the information you provided."

Rourke tensed, and I caught Gideon's questioning stare, but I went on. "I'm not blaming you. Your information was as good as anyone else's, and we had no reason to doubt it. But somewhere along the way, the intel glitched. So if there is anything you can add to your statement, you've got to tell me. For the sake of the unit you once wanted to join."

Nothing could have prepared me for the tears that welled in his eyes. In that moment, I fully understood how deeply everything had hit him, and in a strange, twisted way, I was glad I'd pushed him. At least now he could be part of the solution and not just part of the problem.

He sipped his drink and cleared his throat, and when he straightened up, the tears were gone, though the haggard expression remained. "I knew at the time something was off. I debated long and hard about bringing forward what I heard— and for the record, if it's not in my file, I want it known I made a point of saying I was uneasy." He stabbed his finger against the bartop, emphasizing his point, then wrapped his hands around his bottle. "It struck me as odd that plans were being talked about out in the open. Normally these guys are pretty tight-lipped. I don't think anyone but O'Malley knows when some of his goons come into town. So what are they doing gabbing details in front of the bar, huh?"

He shook his head again and shifted in his seat. His gaze darted quickly around the room, but soon landed on his beer, as though he figured he'd draw less attention if he kept his eyes to himself.

I made sure to keep up with him on the drinking so we looked like nothing more than a few buddies catching up. On Rourke's other side, Gideon played with a paper coaster, peeling the layers apart at the corners. His bottle was empty, and when the bartender passed, he waved for another.

"It's been quiet the last couple months," Rourke said. "They've been talking about moving their operation to Kingston, and by the way faces have been changing around here, I thought they already had. The only news I've been able to report to you guys has been a few bits and pieces about ghost deliveries. Big Joe was flapping his lips about how production is ramping up, enough that he paid cash for his kid's private school, and Fire Fred was going on last week about how they've found buyers as far as Whistler and down into Seattle."

Gideon sat up straighter, his attention solidly on Rourke, and I wondered if he'd gotten his confirmation that the States did have cause for concern. I hoped he upheld his end of the agreement and didn't rush the information to SilverGuard. I needed time to sort everything out before the Americans swept in and set up operations at the border. Their involvement could send the syndicate scurrying into hiding and make SMOAC's job much more difficult.

I tried to catch his gaze, but his narrowed eyes left Rourke's face to bore into the bartop. I'd have to pull him aside later and ask what his plans were.

Beside me, Rourke pressed his fingers into the ridges over his eyebrows and squeezed his eyes shut. "Even at the time, I thought it was weird. I shouldn't have heard any of those conversations. In all my years, they've been good about keeping their business dealings to the back room. Sure, sometimes one of O'Malley's minions let something slip, but more often than not, I never saw that person again. I kept my head down and figured I'd become so much a part of the background they didn't notice I was here." He shrugged. "Anyway, nothing ever came of it. No one looked at me like they knew I'd heard them, and as far as I know, their plans went ahead despite the information I passed along. Then, a few days ago, I was sitting here as usual, probably about three beers in, and overheard a conversation going on just over there."

He jerked his chin past Gideon to a shadowed corner of the room, and I turned to check it out as though the shadowy figures would still be sitting there.

"I couldn't see who was talking," Rourke continued, "but it sounded like Big Joe and someone else, someone I didn't recognize. They were huddled next to the bar, like they were trying to keep their conversation private, but it was early enough in the day that the music was low and the crowds were small, so I heard everything. They talked about a ghost shipment, how they had a contact in the de Lauer building. They were going to pass it off in the subbasement for the contact to ship out west. No skin off their noses, no paper trail back to them."

He fell quiet, and his entire face scrunched up as though he were about to cry. Then he sniffed and took a swig of beer. "Fuck," he said as he set the bottle down hard enough to make the remaining contents spit out the top. "I took the information and ran with it. I never thought—it never even occurred to me I was meant to hear every word."

As soon as he said the words aloud, my blood ran cold. If he was right, then everything I feared was true. There had never been a shipment of ghost in that basement. There had only ever been a ghostbomb with SMOAC written all over it.

But the problem was so much bigger than that. If Rourke's suspicions were right, how long had the syndicate been feeding information into the department?

How long had we been eating right out of O'Malley's hand?

Chapter 19

Gideon

I STEPPED INTO the humid night air and stood back as a stunned Jet followed me out.

She hadn't said a word since Rourke had dropped his revelation other than to assure him she didn't blame him for coming forward. The guy looked broken, and I hoped he had someone to talk it out with besides his next bottle.

And that he wouldn't find himself in deeper shit now that he knew he was nothing more than a pawn. What would the syndicate do if they realized he was no longer useful?

"Think it would be smart to get him out of town?" I asked Jet.

She offered a vague nod. "I'll talk to Madison in the morning. He's not safe here." Her throat bobbed with a hard swallow. "If he's right, then none of the people who came forward are. The syndicate laid their trap right out in the open, and everyone fell into it. O'Malley must be laughing his ass off right now."

Her shock was wearing off, and in its place radiated an anger so thick and heady, I felt myself bracing for an assault.

I forced myself to relax and focus on the fact that Rourke's news hadn't shattered her. Anger was better than grief. Anger would keep her moving.

"What are you going to do?"

Her gaze sharpened as she looked at me. "The better question is what are *you* going to do? You got your confirmation about the ghost shipments. Even if it was all a trap, they mentioned the magic words about a delivery moving across the border. Are you going to run home and report to your people?"

I understood the note of concern, how my going home would be the last thing she'd want me to do. One word to SilverGuard, and they would form a full initiative to block the border and make sure that shit didn't cross into our world. American dealers were begging to get their hands on it for the street value, but no one else would benefit. Not the people who died from it, not the cops who had to deal with it, and not the Department of Supernaturals that worked so hard to keep the mundanes and supernaturals on opposite sides of the perception filter. Ghost led to a lot of eye-opening. It introduced questions that were difficult to explain and raised suspicions that were difficult to quash.

Personally, I felt the whole secrecy thing was a waste of time, money, and effort, but I wasn't the best judge. I could mist away if anyone tried to mess with me. Others of my kind weren't so lucky. It wasn't like the mundanes had shown themselves to be the most open-minded and accepting of people's differences.

But the fact remained that, in Jet's mind, her goals and mine no longer aligned. Unless her goal was to stop the syndicate from reaching the border.

Up here, the supernatural community was split between the prime minister and the queen, which meant sometimes splitting the costs as well. In my neck of the woods, everything went through the White House, and every penny had to be accounted for. A big expense like a border operation would mean a lot of explaining to a lot of people who weren't supposed to know the truth. If the Canadian government was ready to foot the bill instead of us, maybe Dark Wire would forgive me the delayed update.

SilverGuard would want the credit of ending the ghost threat, but as long as I got it for them, they wouldn't care how I did it.

"I have a job to finish," I said, "and that could mean going home, or it could mean helping you put an end to this. It's your call."

I knew the odds weren't in my favour for her agreeing. Accepting my help would mean getting even comfier in bed with a foreign agency. But it also meant she could keep an eye on me and make sure I played by her rules, which would be harder for her to resist.

A tiny voice in the back of my head acknowledged my real desire to stay—to have Jet's back if things went south—but I had to prepare for the very real possibility that she would give me the boot. If she did, I would have no choice but to go home and make my report. I would be hands-off going forward and could only hope that somewhere down the road I learned how everything worked out for her.

My thoughts spun in a million directions with no idea what was going through Jet's mind until she drew to a halt beside her car and fiddled with her keys, eying me. What was she looking for? Some sign that I was holding something back from her? Hell, if she could sniff out the truth, I wouldn't mind. It'd save me the trouble of hiding that I was here for more than a simple risk assessment. But for all her distrust of me, I didn't think she was clear-headed enough where I was concerned to be that perceptive. Too much anger and hurt about our history blinded her to the idea that I would be that much of an asshole a second time.

"No," she said at last, to my disappointment but lack of surprise. "I'm going to take the information to security and let them run with it from here. They'll know the operations we need to put in place to root out O'Malley. Either we have a mole in the department who let the syndicate know we were ready to move, or they guessed it and drew us in themselves. Either way, we have more weight now. The evidence that this was a setup should motivate a more focused investigation. Dougall gave us names, and Rourke confirmed one of them. It's a start."

This was the Jet I knew. The one who stopped shy of true professional independence and deferred to the higher ranks. The one who kept to her boundaries. Rourke's intelligence must have shocked her back to reason.

Great for her career, but not ideal for my next steps. A moment ago, I'd been ready to embrace the reality of going home and moving on with my life, but in the face of her refusal, I realized I wasn't ready to let go. I wanted to keep chasing, keep fighting. Although she hadn't thrown me a bone since our paths had crossed, I'd enjoyed working with her again, and I didn't want to give it up. As soon as she brought the department into it, the entire process would slow down. I would go home, report to Dark Wire, blockades would be set up at the border, the syndicate would run and hide, and there would be the feds, on both sides, dawdling over their paperwork and red tape. The turtle chasing the hare.

There was also the matter of the potential accolades I'd receive if I closed this case with no risk or security worries on our side.

With my hopes on the line, I said, "I hate to rain on your parade, but are you sure that's the tactic you want to take? If you have a mole, do you really want to run around screaming about it? Whoever it is will know to cover their tracks. You'll lose them. Right now, you have the upper hand. You could keep pressing buttons under the radar, keep turning over rocks to see what climbs out, then step on it before the problem gets any bigger."

I hated how easy it was to sound objective when my reasons were so personal. It left me with a slick, oily feeling in my gut—though not enough to make me back down.

But my attempts to manipulate only made Jet dig her heels in deeper.

"I'm not some half-cocked vigilante out for blood," she said, as though we hadn't spent the whole day coercing people into talking to us. Captain Dawson was definitely back in the driver's seat. "I want answers, not revenge, and I won't do anything that'll make SMOAC come off as an undisciplined shitshow. I respect my commander and my team too much for that. The team members I lost deserve proper justice. I did my part, now it's time to keep my promise and hand it over."

I opened my mouth to take another stab at convincing her, but she cut me off. "Thanks for your help, Gideon. I'm not ashamed to say I couldn't have gotten this far without you, but you can head home now. Make your report. Do what you have to do. We're done."

And just like that, she got into the car, started the engine, and sped off, leaving me alone in the parking lot.

Chapter 20

Jet

I'D SET AN alarm before going to bed so I could call the security office at an early hour. After wracking my brain trying to figure out how to relay what I'd learned without getting my or Madison's pay cheques cut off, I'd decided an anonymous tip was the way to go. I hoped I could also protect Rourke and the others for having spilled yet another serving of beans.

What I'd learned was far from definitive, but if I got someone with an ounce of sense on the phone, it was enough to get the official train moving.

The only part of yesterday that didn't sit well on my conscience was leaving Gideon in the club's parking lot. He'd helped me get people talking, and I couldn't deny it had been nice to know I wasn't alone if I ran into trouble. It had even been nice to work with someone who anticipated my next move and fell into step with me in a way that made the dance seamless. Eric was the only other person I'd worked with who came close to that level of collaboration, and even then, he always looked to me to lead. With Gideon, I worked with an equal, sharing the responsibility. It was a reminder of why my time in New York hadn't been *all* bad. The least I could have done was give him a lift somewhere.

The truth was I'd been too worried he'd convince me to keep poking around where I wasn't supposed to. The man was too persuasive for his own good.

But what did it matter in the end? He'd gotten what he'd come for and was no doubt heading home to make a full report. It meant SMOAC would need to rush through the usual bureaucracy and move in before the Americans took action and gave us away, but that would no longer be my problem.

Not officially, anyway. Now that my eyes were open, I wouldn't be closing them again. O'Malley could try to crawl back under his rock or make use of the darkest shadows, but I would know where he was.

All my best laid plans went to shit, however, when I was woken up before my alarm by my ringing cellphone and the furious tones of my commander saying, "Dawson, you have thirty minutes to get your ass in my office and tell me what the fuck you've been doing."

In an icy wave, my tentative optimism evaporated, and I lurched out of bed as though he'd barged into my bedroom.

"Colonel?"

What could he possibly know?

"We received a report last night that you were seen at The Afterlife asking questions. Is this true?"

A lot, it turned out.

"Colonel, I—"

"No, I don't want to hear your excuses over the phone. I told you to take time off, and instead you're running around the city playing Nancy Drew. I can't believe you brought Sampson in on this with you."

Confusion left me speechless until the answer clued in. Whoever had ratted me out had seen a man with me. They didn't know about Gideon. Thank whatever small mercies were out there. I didn't bother to correct him.

"Get to the office sharpish," he said. "The deputy minister wants an explanation, and then we'll decide what to do about you. If you even have a job after this. For fuck's sake, Dawson."

He hung up, and I dropped onto the bed, the dead phone in my hand and my heart in my throat.

Here I was thinking we'd been so careful. Had my fight with Mike drawn more eyes than we'd realized?

Shit.

I shoved my hands through my hair and started getting ready, speeding through a shower and racing out the door within ten minutes, letting me walk into Michael's office with five minutes to spare.

Aline kept her eyes down as I approached, grabbed a stack

of papers, and hurried off as Michael came out. "Any sign of—there you are," he said when he saw me. "Come on. You can give me the rundown in the elevator on our way up. I better like what I hear."

My mouth was dry as we got into the elevator together, and he punched in a code to ensure it made no other stop on our way up to the twenty-fifth floor. He carried himself well, his shoulders back and his chin raised, daring anyone to cross him the wrong way, but the dark circles under his eyes gave away his restless midnight hours.

"Talk," he said as soon as the doors closed.

I'd prepared my statement on the drive over, but even still it came out stumbling as I did my best to justify my actions. "I saw there was a lead being ignored with the informants. I wanted to ask a few questions to find out if there was anything to it before I delivered my suspicions to security. That's all."

"'That's all,' she says. As if you didn't risk tossing our entire op in the trash. The informants aren't a lead, Jet. You put them in danger for nothing."

My cheeks flushed, and the air in the elevator grew thin as I reined in my anger. "With respect, sir, it wasn't nothing. One tip proved to be second hand, and I have reason to believe more than one person received their information intentionally."

Michael narrowed his eyes and jabbed the button to stop the elevator somewhere near the twenty-second floor. "What do you mean?"

"I mean O'Malley screwed with the intel. About de Lauer and who knows what else."

"You have proof?"

"No," I admitted, "but from what I heard yesterday, it sure looks like it. That's what I was going to take to security this morning."

He pressed his lips together and hit the button for the elevator to continue. "When we get up there, you take your cue from me and don't speak unless I tell you, understood?"

The doors opened, and I rushed to keep up with him as he marched onto the floor. "What? Why?"

I'd already braced myself for the lecture and the slap on the wrist that would come from this meeting. I'd broken protocol by talking with the informants. A few days' suspension and a black spot on my record were consequences I was willing to accept.

"Don't question me, Dawson," he said, dropping his voice so I had to strain to hear him as we crossed towards the deputy's office. "There's only so much he can do to me, but if he's in a mood to find a scapegoat to throw to the media vultures, he may very well choose you. Rash task force captain who failed to do her due diligence suspended for putting more people at risk in her efforts to cover up her incompetence."

My stomach twisted. I hadn't thought of it like that. Would Gagnon really throw me under the bus after what I'd learned?

"If we play it like it was my idea, like you were following

orders, he has no leg to stand on. So everything you did was by my say-so, got it?"

"Yes, sir," I said through stiff lips. "Thank you, sir."

Michael's posture softened, and he dropped his chin in a slight nod. "No thanks needed. Your team needs you. They can't afford to lose you and the rest of their squad in the same week."

My heart pinched, but all I could do was nod in return. Where would I be without him at my back, helping me see things I missed? All I could hope was that I did my best to live up to his high opinion of me.

The deputy minister reached his reception area at the same time we did. He looked harried, his tie crooked and his jacket partially tucked into the back of his pants. In any other situation, Lucien Gagnon was a tidy, well-put-together man in his fifties, with well-tended grey hair and green eyes that gave the impression he was staring into your soul. Which, in a way, he was. It was no secret in the department that he possessed an uncanny bullshit meter. Literally. One of his particular genetic quirks—inherited from some angelic ancestor, maybe—was his ability to assess whether a person was lying to him. He did not deal well with liars. Fortunately for me, I was coming here with cold hard facts, even if he didn't want to hear them.

"*Michel, capitaine,*" he greeted in his thick Franco-Ontarian accent. "Let's do this quickly, shall we? I meet with the minister in twenty minutes."

We followed him into his office, and Michael closed the door, trapping us inside. My pulse hammered in my wrists, my throat, my chest, but I did my best to appear confident. I might be in trouble, but I had a trump card.

"Now, is someone going to tell me why I was woken up first thing this morning with reports of an unauthorized investigation being carried out on what is essentially enemy soil? You do realize we're trying *not* to show our hand to Mark O'Malley or his syndicate, do you not, Captain Dawson?"

I pulled my shoulders back, but obeyed Michael's orders and said nothing.

"The investigation was not unauthorized," Michael said. "I thought it best she ask around."

Gagnon's eyebrows shot upwards. "You?"

"After what happened at the de Lauer building, I knew my remaining troops wouldn't be happy to hand the investigation over to security. Not completely. So I gave Dawson some leeway. Turns out it was a smart move. Something here stinks, Lucien, and I don't just mean the attack."

Gagnon's shoulders dropped, and some of the heat left his face. "Of course, and forgive me for not immediately offering *mes condoléances* for your loss, Captain. I can't imagine what a blow that must have been. Please, sit."

I shot Michael a look and followed his lead as he made himself comfortable in a red upholstered chair. Once seated, which did nothing to remove the closed-in feeling of being stuck in a room with these two, I eyed the deputy, watching for any sign that he knew Michael had stretched the truth, but there was nothing except the same corporate sympathy and a glimmer of curiosity.

"Jet, why don't you tell Lucien what you learned."

I cleared my throat and started with my visit to Lafontaine, leaving out where I'd gotten the informants' addresses. By the time I finished a quick summary of the highlights, Gagnon was sitting back in his chair, his expression pinched with concern.

"You walk a fine line allowing this kind of operation, *Michel.*"

Michael nodded. "That's why Dawson was the best person for the task. She was there. She knew the right questions, the red flags to watch for. She's also not some fed in a suit, so not as quick to give us away."

None of this was untrue, which was probably why Michael looked so relaxed spinning his tale.

Gagnon didn't look impressed. "Next time, any ops like that go through me. This situation is too fragile to make mistakes."

"Understood," Michael said.

The deputy minister shifted in his seat and steepled his fingers together on the desk, pursing his lips as though carrying out some internal debate. The furrow on his brow had grown deeper throughout my summary, and I worried if the trend continued, his entire face would curl in on itself.

Finally, he leaned forward and clasped his hands. "While

you were asking your questions, our people have been posing a few of our own, and although I don't have any official reports yet—so this information does not leave this office—what I've heard so far confirms what you say."

He passed a hand over his face and his shoulders sagged. "I don't want this to come down to a blaming game, because once all the evidence is in front of us, I'm sure it will prove mistakes were made at every turn. But I will say, on the surface, it looks like this tragedy was caused by an overeagerness to close in on the syndicate. The information came in, it was corroborated, and the minister signed off. Maybe he signed off too quickly. The branch responsible for vetting the intelligence never finished their checks. Not as thoroughly as usual, anyway. I advised Minister Bastien to wait, but the information told us O'Malley was making his move, so protocols were… rushed."

Michael's hands clenched into fists in his lap, and his face turned a startling shade of red. The air grew thick, the molecules slowing, and my arms grew too heavy to lift, all kinetic energy suspended. I'd never experienced my commander losing control of his ability before, so could only imagine the extent of his rage. "Are you telling me my troops died because of unverified information? We went in believing the raid had been cleared at all levels. The minister knew it was a dangerous mission, even if the intel *had* been confirmed."

"*Je sais, Michel,*" the deputy minister said, his voice measured and calm, if full of remorse.

But Michael pushed himself to his feet and paced the room. The air around me grew closer, hotter. I pushed back, exerting my own ability to gain some breathing room, but the effort of maintaining it was exhausting. "We planned a full raid, a complete operation, based on unfounded *rumour*? We lost ten people. Ten *good* people."

I wanted to tell him to calm down, that nothing useful would come of his pissing off the powers that be, but even if I'd been able to speak, I knew it wouldn't make things better. Especially since, while I understood the sensitive political undercurrents at play, I was too pissed off myself. Any attempt to convince Michael to sit down could very easily turn into tearing Gagnon a new one for his shoddy work. Michael might get away with his outburst thanks to his years and experience. I doubted I would be so lucky.

After a moment, the pressure in the room lifted, and he sat down without my intervention. Sweat beaded his brow, leaving the line of his white hair damp. "I want to know what you're going to do about this. You've had your suspicions confirmed thanks to what Jet found for you. What's next?"

"We won't let it end here," Gagnon said. "We'll use every resource available to track down the source of the misinformation, and justice will be served. I promise you. I don't need to tell you that our security team is composed of some highly dedicated and competent people. They will get to the bottom of this."

It was only when he fell silent that I realized how badly I'd tensed while he was speaking. After his confession of such a major fuck-up, I'd expected more than the official line. *Please know we're taking your matter seriously. We'll be sure to inform you once the situation has been resolved.*

He sounded like an automated message, lacking any personal touch.

Fair, he couldn't come clean with us about everything. That's not how the hierarchy worked in government. And probably for good reason. Even less would get done if they had to debate and discuss every small matter with every single person at every single level. But this was my squad. These were Michael's troops. Someone should have been tearing through the paperwork to find out how much intel hadn't been vetted. The informants should have been called in, re-questioned, protected.

I did my best to unclench my jaw and relax the muscles along my spine. It wasn't easy. I found myself waiting for Michael to get angry again. I wanted to rile him up. I wanted him to order me to gather my remaining team and bring in as many of O'Malley's people as we could track down. A mass raid. A hard crackdown on any syndicate activity, and let us deal with evidence and due process later. I wanted the deputy to assure me that no one would rest until we had the justice he promised. No vacation, no breaks, until every last one of the sons of bitches who'd let this happen had been held accountable.

Instead, all I had were politics and bureaucracy and a boss who had the experience to face both with heroic stoicism. It wasn't enough. Not nearly.

"Thank you, Lucien," Michael said, standing up. By his tone, I guessed it was my turn to do the same. We'd shared what we'd come to share, and the deputy had made his decision. As far as protocol went, we were done here. "We appreciate everything you're doing. Let us know if we can help in any way."

"You'll be the first one I call," Gagnon swore.

"The informants," I said, daring Michael's anger and Gagnon's offence at my speaking out of turn. "I don't think they're safe in Ottawa anymore. They should have protection details put on them until we can get them out of town."

"Of course," the deputy minister said. "I'll put in the order immediately. Now go home and get some sleep, both of you. It won't be long before you're needed."

He stood up, showed us to the door, and then it was as if we weren't there. He turned his back to us to speak with his assistant, and we headed towards the elevators.

I was shaking, my racing pulse making my fingers tremble. I didn't want to lose my shit in front of Michael, who, I was sure, was just as unsatisfied.

That was it? That was the end? Now I could go home and rest easy with the promise that everything would be taken care of? I'd gone to bed feeling so hopeful, but when I tried to picture giving this update to my troops, I couldn't do it.

As soon as the elevator doors closed, I said, "I'm going to keep going on this myself."

Michael's eyes widened and his nostrils flared. "Excuse me?"

I squared my shoulders to steel my nerve. "I've already got a head start on it. I have connections I can use, and I know how to be discreet. It might not be part of my job, but I don't trust politicians. I can't leave this in the deputy's hands. Not when he's only giving us vague promises that he'll put his best on it."

"I know the meeting didn't go the way you wanted," he said as the elevator started down, "and I hope you know this isn't the end for me, either. Gagnon's in a tricky position where he has to backpedal a decision the minister made, and do it in a way that won't blow up his career. It's bullshit, but that's politics for you. I'll stay on top of him."

"I know," I said, and felt myself deflating. Michael cared as much as I did, but that didn't make it any easier to walk away.

"You're angry and impatient, and let me tell you, Dawson, so am I, but you need to leave this alone."

"But—"

"Not only are you not trained to take this on, but your career path is on too steady a climb to mess things up by running in headfirst. You may hate politics, but politics is exactly what could keep you at captain for the rest of your life instead of giving you the freedom you need to work your way up. You don't want to gamble everything on stubbornness."

I pressed my lips together, wanting to argue that I didn't care. Promotions meant nothing if it came at the cost of unfulfilled justice for my team. But I knew he'd have another argument ready for me.

"Listen," he said, all militaristic stiffness gone and his tone softened to that of a concerned parent, "the deputy might act like he's dragging his feet when it comes to paperwork, but it's in his best interests to find the truth. The supernatural community has taken notice, or haven't you seen the news? If he wants to avoid riots in the streets, he'll find out who set us up. You need to have some faith. If not in him, then in the department."

I clung to silence, unable to think of a single thing to say that didn't sound sulky. I'd devoted my life to SMOAC. To call the department's values and priorities into question would be an act of hypocrisy.

"What you *should* focus on is rallying your troops," he continued. "They need you. They need to be ready for when we find these assholes—through the appropriate channels. You haven't reached out to your team other than Sampson with these ideas of yours, have you?"

"No."

He let out a breath of relief. "Good. The fewer people I need to talk down, the better. I'd hate to have to let go of my entire crack squad because of some misguided attempt at heroism."

I bit my tongue. Never had I been more relieved I'd left my

pack out of this. I'd been right, the stakes for them were too high. If there was risk to bear, I'd carry it on my own shoulders.

But his suggesting that I hadn't been doing a good job of keeping them together hit me like a slap. I'd never stopped thinking about them, of course, but how long had it been since I'd checked in? Not since yesterday afternoon.

"What about your family?" he asked. "Have you talked to them?"

I made a face. "I left a message with my dad. They know I'm alive. You'd think my nearly dying would be enough to get my mother to talk to me, but nope, not yet."

Michael opened his mouth, no doubt to express sympathy, then slammed it shut and said instead, "Lucien is right about one thing. You need to sleep. Have you done any of that in the last forty-eight?"

"A few hours here and there," I said. "I can't stay down long enough for it to make a difference."

The elevator hit the subbasement and opened onto the Peaview lobby. I stared in confusion at our destination, but before I could ask, Michael stuck his hand out to keep the doors from closing. "Here's what you're going to do—you're going to talk to Dr. Casselman, then you're going to go home, pour yourself a drink, and put on the most boring black-and-white movie you can find. You're going to sit there and watch it until your brain decides it would rather black out than watch another minute."

I chuckled at the image he presented. "Isn't that how you spend every Friday?"

"Hey now, don't mock your elders," he said. "Seriously, you good?"

Concern creased the corners of his eyes, and I nodded, not wanting to do anything to add to his stress. This man had been there for me since the beginning, encouraging me not only to succeed, but to surpass expectation. I didn't know what I'd done to deserve his support, but I valued it more than I could ever express.

"I'm good," I said. "I can't guarantee I'll sleep, but I'll follow your orders as far as the going home and drinking are concerned."

He smiled, but the worry remained. "Good. For now. But first, go get yourself checked out by our counsellors. That's non-negotiable."

And standard protocol, as I well knew.

"Got it, sir."

"Then get."

He released the elevator doors and disappeared as they closed between us.

Chapter 21

Madison

I CHECKED THE stove clock. Eight forty-three in the morning. I checked my phone. Still no messages.

It had been almost a full day since Jet had walked out of my office with that list of informants. For all I knew, she was lying in a ditch somewhere, or she'd run the whole system into the mud. Maybe I was being impatient, but after my conversation with Serc, all I could think about were the trillion reasons I needed a quick turnaround on this lead. The floor was eggshells, and we were wearing steel-toed boots. One heavy step could send us plummeting into hell.

The TV in the living room filled my apartment with the latest updates of protests happening on Parliament Hill. Minor affairs, angry people calling for change. Change the mundane population would hear as either tax reform or a shift to clean energy but the supernatural community would hear as a cry for protection. The attack in the de Lauer Estates had shaken the city, and I was sure Ottawa wouldn't be the only region feeling the aftershocks.

Not wanting to hear any more, I switched off the TV, grabbed Persephone, and made myself comfortable at the kitchen table.

I sipped my coffee and stared out the window over the downtown core. My high-rise condo had once offered the most beautiful view of the Gatineau Hills across the river, nothing but rolling trees reflecting the best of each season. Last year, another high-rise had gone up that was even taller than mine, and now all I had was a full view of my across-the-way-neighbours' living room and a hint of downtown around the corner.

This morning, Ross and Rachel—as I'd named them— were screaming at each other. He kept trying to walk away, and she followed. Hands flapping, fingers pointing. Even though I had no idea what they were fighting about, I wanted to yell at them to shut up, sit down, and be grateful their world was carrying on as usual.

My phone pinged, and I unlocked it to find an email from Jean-Luc. My heart stopped as I prepared for bad news, and though no new tragedy had occurred, my blood pressure rose as I read.

JUST HAD WORD THAT OBSCUGLAS SIGNED A CONTRACT WITH GLOBALCOMM. TERMS WERE LEAKED, AND THEY EDGED US OUT BY A HAIR. ANY WORD ON YOUR TEAM'S REPORT? I KNOW THE DEPART-

MENT IS IN CHAOS AND EMOTIONS ARE HIGH, BUT THAT'S ALL THE MORE REASON TO PRESENT A STRONG, UNITED FRONT. WE SHOULD SPEAK TOMORROW MORNING IF POSSIBLE AND DECIDE HOW YOU WANT TO MOVE FORWARD. WE CAN'T AFFORD TO LOSE ANOTHER MAJOR DEAL.

JL.

I read his email a second time, then a third. GlobalComm was a property developer for most of the business parks in Alberta. Successful, but nowhere near as secure as the federal government. How had they negotiated well enough to overtake us? It was beyond frustrating—it was humiliating.

Jean-Luc was right. Trade had to remain strong. With everything else in shambles, it was the only way to maintain credibility as a department. Stability, if nothing else. A successful negotiation was also the best way to prove my necessity on this side of the wall.

I started to draft a reply assuring him I would be ready with a plan tomorrow morning when my phone lit up with Jet sticking her tongue out at me.

"Where the hell have you been?" I asked as I answered.

"Good morning to you, too," she said, and her defeated tone did nothing to make me feel better. "Sorry. I should have called you when I got in, but figured you wouldn't want to be woken up at three o'clock with bad news."

"Always, Jet. Always call me with bad news. I'm sure anything you have to tell me is better than what's been going through my head."

"O'Malley's been leading the department by the nose for who knows how long, and de Lauer was the result."

I slumped in my chair, speechless.

"Told you."

"But—" I leaned forward, and Persephone jumped onto the table and began grooming. "That's impossible. Our information is vetted. It would have been triple-checked."

"Gagnon confirmed this morning there may have been some… lacking in the vetting stages on this one."

I bowed my head and curled my fingers into my hair. "Gagnon?"

"He knows."

"Meril have mercy," I sighed. "What the hell, Jet?"

"I'm sorry! I don't know what happened. Michael called me at the ass-crack of dawn to say someone saw me at The Afterlife. Don't worry, I left your name out of it."

"Thanks for that, at least." I rubbed my eyes before reaching for my coffee, then put Jet on speaker and set the phone on the table so I had both hands free to panic if I needed to. "What else did Lucien say?"

"That his best people were on this and my intel wouldn't go to waste."

She sounded bitter, and I couldn't blame her. Standard government line.

"He does mean it."

"I know."

I also knew that didn't count for much.

"Where are you now?" I asked.

"Sitting in my car at the office trying to figure out what the hell comes next. I did what I set out to do. I was going to hand things over to security this morning, but I guess I don't need to do that anymore. So what now? Take Michael's suggestion, go home, and put my feet up? That's what the shrink thinks I should do."

"You had your appointment?"

"Oh yeah. An hour of sitting in a cold office with a white noise machine filling my head with static, being told it's perfectly normal to feel the way I do, but I shouldn't beat myself up about it." She adopted an exaggerated gentle tone, and I couldn't help but smile. Jet would have hated that.

"I don't know," she continued. "Pretty sure I sounded sane enough that no one's concerned for my general well-being, but not enough to put me back to work. Michael says desk job until I'm cleared."

"I'm sorry."

"So give me something to do."

I sat up straight in my chair. "Excuse me?"

"You gave me the tip about the informants. Madison Prince would never enable me to go off the books unless helping me break the rules was a lesser evil than something else. I didn't pry the other day, but now I'm asking."

I shook myself out of my surprise and spun my coffee mug around in a circle. If I'd known Jet was in a mental place to be so perceptive yesterday, I might have been more careful.

"Meril met me in a dream the other night. She knows about the attack."

"Shit," she said, drawing the word out in a groan.

"I don't know what her deadline is, but she was pretty clear. Either we clean up ASAP without any further mess, or she's crossing the wall, and I get my summons to court."

"Goddamn it. All right, so what can we do? If we hand everything over to the department, that deadline could fly right by without giving us a real chance to meet it. Have you picked up anything else I can follow? I promise I'll do better at keeping my head down this time."

I chewed on my lip and thought about everything I'd overheard in the office the other day. The note was still a dead end—at this point, I suspected its only purpose was to waste our resources—and most of the executives were more concerned about the growing protests than the attack.

"I don't," I said, but as I said it, an idea popped into my mind. "Wait, you said the syndicate's been manipulating us for a while?"

"That's Rourke's guess. At least a few months, but who knows."

I frowned and considered Jean-Luc's email. If O'Malley's people were feeding us information, was it possible they'd meddled with the department in other ways? Spread rumours to deter people from working with us? Made outright threats? I doubted asking Desmond directly would net me any results, but maybe there was a more roundabout, silent way of testing my theory.

"There's something I can follow on my end to see how far back their interference goes, but as for you, do you think you could prod any of the informants a second time?"

It was a bad idea, I knew it, but the clock on the wall kept ticking, and I had to make the most of my time before it stopped.

"Possibly," Jet said, sounding uncertain. I wished she were close enough for me to pick up what was going through her mind. "The new guy. Dougall. He might have been holding back. I'm the last person he wants to see, and it's more likely he'll bar the door against me, but it could be worth a shot."

"Want me to come with you?" I asked. "I can try to smooth the way, help shake things loose."

"You are exactly who I need with me, but I don't think it's a good idea. I've already been outed once, so you should stay far away to avoid getting burned. I'll update you as soon as I can."

I wished her luck, hung up, and bowed my head in my hands. Leaks, tainted intel, possible coercion. Already this was bigger than I'd thought when I sent Jet out with those names. How much bigger would it get before we untangled this mess?

Worry and frustration ate at me and were only slightly dampened when my phone rang again and my grandmother's name came up on the screen.

"*Sina,*" I greeted, falling easily into her mother tongue, a language that predated most others spoken in this country. The language spoken beyond the wall.

Nan had tried to teach my mother with little success, and my brother and sisters had never bothered, but I'd been fascinated by the realm as a child and devoured as much knowledge as possible. It was part of what had helped me reach my post in government. And part of why I'd caught the queen's interest. A double-edged sword.

"*Sina, chailene,*" she replied in her warm, gentle voice. *Hello, my dove.* "*Mun fyre?*" *Are you well?*

"Of course," I replied in English. "Why wouldn't I be?"

"We've all seen the news," she said. "We know what happened the other day. We've been waiting for you to call."

We. I pictured her sitting around the table in my parents' breakfast nook in their Winnipeg home, fussing over me from afar. Had my older sister joined them, her two kids balanced on her hips as she worried? Guilt tugged at my conscience for not putting them at ease sooner, but I shooed it away. "I know, I'm sorry. Things have been… busy."

"You were always one for understatements," Nan said with a trace of humour. "Tell me."

I filled her in on what I could, leaving out the classified bits and the parts I knew would make her worry more. "And now the protests have started."

"I know," she said. "Here, too. Nothing to draw attention beyond the local news, but they're happening. Cries for increased security, concerns about twisted priorities. A few accusations that authority from the realm is becoming more of a liability than a benefit."

I groaned. "I'm sure Meril will love that. If we don't answer their questions and do something to calm them down, I can only imagine how much worse it'll get."

"The people are afraid," Nan said, "and they have reason to be. This ghost drug has the potential to destroy the filters that protect us, if it doesn't kill us first. I like our prime minister, and I think the governments are doing a fine job of balancing progress with safety, but from the public perspective, it does look like they're hesitant to help the supernatural community if it doesn't help the mundanes at the same time. We're always lower on their priority list."

I wished I could argue otherwise, but she wasn't wrong.

"We'll do what we can to fix this."

"I know, *chailene*, of that I have no doubt."

I just hope it's in time.

The words went unsaid on both ends of the line, but I knew we were thinking it.

"Serc called," I said.

"He told me. He called you stubborn and foolish for not considering the benefits of crossing over. I reminded him he'd stayed on the queen's council at a time when doing so might have branded him a traitor to his people. That should keep him quiet for a while."

"Thank you. What do you think?"

"I agree with Serc that Meril won't rush to act. Stepping in too soon would cause as many issues as waiting too long. She knows that. But you know patience is not her strength. If she feels not enough is being done, she will take a stand."

"Where do you think she'd start?" If I had a better idea of Meril's strategy, I could be on the lookout. Have some warning before she closed in if she chose to keep me in the dark.

"By deploying her Eyes. Calling back those she believes are loyal to the court. If the protests get too loud against her, she might take fiercer action to silence them and remind those involved who their true ruler is. Maybe by summoning everyone back, maybe by sending her private security to have words with them. If the situation becomes too widespread, she'll come through herself with an army. You know how the border of the realm lies. Once she makes that decision, we'll be pulling part of the United States into the fight."

I spun the chain around my neck. The border around the queen's territory lay close enough to the mundane Canadian border to avoid any legislative confusion with the American government, but dipped south enough in a few places that she would technically straddle both countries if she officially passed onto this side of the wall.

A diplomatic nightmare in so many ways.

"And you know what that means, *chailene*. If she summons the Shadow Council, you will be called."

I couldn't prevent the groan that snuck out from between my lips, and Nan offered a faint, sympathetic chuckle. "I know you're concerned, and I won't say you don't have reason to be, but your life wouldn't end if you were recalled. It would only change. At least you'd be safe. You'd be able to help her face this fight from a position of power."

"I've built my life here, Nan. I have friends, a home, a job." *The dream of a relationship with Colm.* "I'm making a difference. Sure, I could do Meril's bidding on the other side, but it would only maintain the status quo for our kind, not move things forward. My dream is for the supernatural and mundane to walk side by side as equals, whether or not everyone knows it. We're getting there, but the movement needs a driving force to keep things going."

"Meril has sat on her throne for so long, I think she's forgotten the concept of forward momentum. But such a move benefits her as well. Perhaps you would be the voice she needs to show her the way."

"But I'm—"

"You're not ready, and that's all right."

I brushed my hair behind my ear and leaned back in my chair. "So what do I do? I feel like everything is slipping away, and the more I try to hold on, the harder it is to keep my grip."

"You need to keep your eyes open and watch your back,"

she said, and a thread of steel now edged her voice. "You remember everything I taught you, and if the situation gets too bad, you do whatever it takes to stay ahead of it. If these protests tell us anything, it's that the stability we've taken for granted is as fragile now as it's ever been. If the ground beneath your feet begins to crack, you need to be ready to jump."

As she spoke, her strength slid down the line and into my bones. I felt myself growing taller, my instincts growing sharper. Nan had always been my guiding light. She taught me how to develop my ability, hone it, control it. She taught me everything I knew about the court, the wall, and all the dynamics involved. I trusted her wisdom—and never more than when it came to my place in the world. If she suspected I would soon be put to the test, I knew better than to ignore her.

She fell silent except for a soft breath in my ear. "Trust yourself, *chailene*. You'll know what to do. Hopefully it won't come to it, but if the time comes, I hope you'll know who to trust and who to let go."

It had been the first lesson she'd ever taught me: everyone was disposable.

I hoped she was right and things wouldn't escalate that far, but if they did, regardless of whether or not I returned to court, I needed to be ready to turn my back on everything— including, and maybe especially, the people I cared for most.

Sometimes that was the cost of survival.

Chapter 22

Jet

As soon as I ended my call with Madison, I wondered if I'd made a mistake by asking for her input. Not only did it put her at the heart of my rule-breaking for a second time, but it also meant I had no choice but to go against Michael's orders and continue down this path.

I wasn't so clueless to my own wishes to know I'd called her for exactly that reason. For permission. But even so, my future forked into two paths: one path dutiful soldier and the other relentless vigilante. I'd already started in one direction and been pulled back. How many more chances would I get before I passed the point of no return?

Did it matter?

My motivations might not have been enough to push me towards hunting down Dougall, but Meril's visit to Madison complicated things. The day Madison told me she was ready to join the Shadow Council, I would do my best to support her. Until then, there was no way I would let some crowned tyrant manhandle her over the wall.

"Sorry, Michael," I said to my steering wheel. "Sisters before… sir-sters."

Michael was right about one thing, however. I needed to check in with my team. While I refused to give them the same bullshit party line Gagnon had used on me, I could at least let them know moves were being made.

With no clear idea what to say, I grabbed my phone, opened the group chat, and crossed my fingers inspiration would hit me once I fell into their flow of conversation.

Very quickly, I appreciated how disconnected I'd become from them in such a short amount of time.

JANE'S WIFE CAME BY TODAY, Jason had written yesterday. SHE DOESN'T KNOW WHAT TO DO WITH HERSELF. I SUGGESTED SOME OF US GO OUT AND DRINK. ANYONE IN?

Sara and Adam had been quick to say yes, and I was glad to see them getting involved. Adam especially was the sort to isolate.

Yesterday evening, Renée had said, MOM WON'T GET OFF THE PHONE WITH ME, BEGGING ME TO QUIT. SHE DOESN'T GET I'M EVEN MORE DETERMINED TO FIGHT, and the message made my blood sing.

At least they weren't broken. Shaken and scarred, but still my pack. The little wolf emoji reactions confirmed that at least five others agreed.

Then this morning at three o'clock, about the time I was walking out of The Afterlife, Xander had written, ANYONE AROUND TO CHAT? CAN'T SLEEP. JUST FINISHED A BOTTLE OF GIN. HOLED UP IN THE BASEMENT. WIFE'S ASLEEP UPSTAIRS, AND I DON'T WANNA WAKE HER UP.

YEAH, MAN, Jason had replied. I'M IN THE SAME BOAT. MINUS THE GIN. WHAT ARE YOU DOING—THAT STUFF IS SHIT. I WENT STRAIGHT FOR THE COGNAC WE'VE BEEN SAVING FOR A SPECIAL OCCASION. IF I'M GOING TO DRINK MYSELF INTO OBLIVION, I WANT TO DO IT IN STYLE.

PUT DOWN THE BOTTLES AND GO TO SLEEP, Eric had replied. The sight of his name made my throat tighten, and I heard his voice as clearly as if he were sitting in the car with me. THE LAST THING I WANT TO SEE IS BEER GUTS ON THE TASK FORCE'S BEST TEAM. TOMORROW MORNING, 0700, MEET ME AT THE GYM. YOU WANT TO SLEEP? HELL, I'LL RUN YOU UNTIL YOU'RE TOO TIRED TO RAISE AN EYELID. JUST AS OUR PL WOULD EXPECT FROM US.

My heart clenched. He'd stepped in when I couldn't, ready to steer them in the right direction. Just what they needed.

ANYONE HEARD FROM OUR BELOVED CAPTAIN? Jason had asked.

NO WORD ON MY END, said Eric. I'M SURE SHE'S FINE.

SOMEONE SHOULD CHECK ON HER.

LET'S GIVE HER A FEW DAYS. CAN'T SAY I BLAME HER FOR NEEDING SOME TIME AWAY FROM HER PHONE.

I appreciated Eric making excuses, but raising them up was my responsibility, and a fraction of everything I owed them.

Still here, wolves, I wrote. Paperwork's a bitch, but I'm not letting it win. Not when someone out there needs a boot up the ass. Until we know who, listen sharp to your lieutenant. Can't have you oafs out of shape and boozed up when the order comes to march. You give me ten kms a day and minimum two hours at the gym until I tell you otherwise.

It was the best I could do for now. Keep them moving, let them know I was here and ready to take charge. That I was strong enough to handle this. At least they had Eric in the meantime.

As though he read my mind—or more likely he saw my message—my phone rang.

"You all right?" he asked, and something in his voice told me he wasn't speaking of generics.

"Yeah, why?"

"The colonel called me this morning. Asked what I was doing with you at The Afterlife."

"Dammit." I rested my head in my hand. "I'm sorry, Eric. I should have given you a heads-up. Someone saw me there last night. They thought you were with me. Did you tell him?"

"That it wasn't me? Not a word."

"Thank you."

"Though now I have to wonder who it was." Was that jealousy I heard?

"Someone whose career I didn't have to worry about. Next time I'll do better to keep your name out of it."

"Next time?"

I groaned. "I know. I'd only planned on the once, but things have come up. I need to take another stab at prying information out of these guys."

"Jet…" He sighed. "Are you sure? Michael told me what Gagnon said. It sounds like they're on this. I don't want you to get slammed for crossing lines for no reason."

I blinked in surprise. "Is this Eric Sampson telling me to step back?"

"This is your lieutenant telling his captain to be smart. I can handle the team, but they need you. Not suspended, not fired, not with citations that will affect your ability to lead them. I know you want to do this for them, I get it, but take a sec to think about your priorities here."

I clapped my mouth shut and breathed heavily through my nose until my throat relaxed. His words struck a chord deep in my conscience, and I knew he was right. Michael was right. I needed to be there for my team. I also needed to be there for Madison.

"I will," I said. "I promise."

One more conversation with Dougall, and then I was done.

"Talk soon?"

"You bet."

I set my phone down and stared out the windshield. I knew I should get moving, but I needed a moment to get out of my head and give my subconscious time to work things out. And since I didn't want to be stuck alone with my dark thoughts, I decided to visit the reason I was so determined to press forward.

A nurse hailed me as I stepped back onto the floor of the Peaview. "Captain Dawson?"

My heart stopped. "Yes?"

She approached, and I searched her eyes for sympathy, for any kind of warning that she was about to drop more bad news on my shoulders.

"I don't know if the doctor reached you this morning, but three of your soldiers have woken up. We moved them to a separate room if you'd like to follow me."

Relief—almost giddiness—left me speechless, and I could only nod as I followed her down the hallway to a room a few doors away from where Zeke still slept. I paused outside the door, surprised to find myself afraid to go in. My joy was measureless, but beneath it was a dark cloud of uncertainty. How would they react when they saw me? They were here because of me. Their friends were dead because of me.

I swallowed around the ball that lodged in my throat.

Suck it up, Dawson. You've earned whatever they throw at you.

Trembling with nerves, I walked in to find two of the three awake and alert.

"Hey, PL," Marc-André greeted me. "Nice of you to stop by." His face was pale, the heavy bruises under his eyes standing out as though he'd been clobbered, but considering yesterday he'd been on a ventilator, he looked fantastic.

"You look awful," Luvy said, as smiling as ever, even if her glee was blurred by an expression of lingering pain. Her thick hair was pulled into a tight braid, revealing every line of exhaustion around her eyes.

"You guys look great." I pulled a chair to the middle of the room where I could see them all. Ray lay snoring in the corner. "How are you feeling?"

"Like we've been hit by a snowplow, churned up, and spat out the back end in more or less full pieces," Marc-André said in little more than a hoarse whisper.

Luvy nodded. "The docs say for one reason or another, the ghost didn't hit us as hard or metabolize as quickly." She frowned. "I know we're lucky. I know that compared—" She stopped, swallowed, and her gaze fell. "But it's hard to feel it right now."

"I don't know how anyone could do this to themselves voluntarily," Marc said in a strained attempt to lighten the mood. "I'd hate for this to be a regular Saturday morning."

He chuckled and Luvy smirked, and I wished they didn't feel the need to be strong in front of me. As though they worried I would judge them for showing fear that they'd come so close to meeting the same end as their friends.

"Captain?" Luvy called me out of my thoughts. "You okay?"

I smoothed out my hair and smiled. "Relieved as all hell to see you three getting better. Especially since now I can tell you to your faces that I met with the colonel this morning, and he has everyone on this case. So you'd better rest up and get yourselves in a good place to join us once we have an address."

I cringed inwardly at the lie, but it was worth it to watch the light rise in their eyes. If I didn't know how to hold their hands, at least I could motivate them, give them a solid reason to carry on and push themselves to fight any lingering effects of the ghost.

I'd tell them the same thing tomorrow if I had to, and if I could get Dougall to talk, maybe it would soon be true.

"No names yet?" Ray asked, and the sound of his gruff voice took me by surprise. I hadn't noticed his snoring had stopped.

"Not yet," I admitted. "Or at least, none confirmed. But we'll get them."

"Any theories?" Marc asked.

"A few," I said, and though I didn't think they were ready for the full details of my investigation, I knew they wouldn't let me get away with saying nothing. "We know O'Malley is behind it, but there's no evidence to prove it yet. It looks like he has something bigger planned, and he wanted to cause some damage, slow us down."

Ray's eyes narrowed. "Someone needs to string that fucker up by his ballsac."

"What kind of plan?" Luvy asked.

A waiting silence settled on the room, wrapped around me, and made it difficult to think. Bringing up the attack had been a mistake. My troops needed support and encouragement, not suspicions that their department was taking on water.

In a weak attempt to shake off the mood, I said, "Knowing him, it could be anything. Whatever it is, we'll stop him, but there's no point focusing on what-ifs."

"What-ifs are the difference between preparation and improvisation," Marc said, quoting one of my often-used lines.

"Sure," I said. "And when you're back on your feet, we can throw around as many as you want. Until then, trust that I'll update you on anything important. Your priority is rehab. Understood?"

Marc-André nodded as Luvy voiced her agreement. Ray was asleep again.

I pushed myself out of the chair. "Get some rest, but I'll let the others know they should come and say hi. I won't tell them you're awake—let that be a surprise. It'll make their day."

I would have suggested they surprise them in the group chat, but the last thing these three needed was to scroll through that mess of heartbreak and struggle.

As I pulled my chair back into the corner, Luvy's deep brown eyes caught mine.

"You sure everything is all right, PL?" she asked, and I wished she hadn't. The question, the emotion behind it, the situation surrounding it, made me force a certainty I didn't feel.

"The only thing you need to worry about is getting your ass out of bed. Everything else is under control."

Although I didn't feel I'd been convincing, Luvy must have been too exhausted to doubt me, because she relaxed into the hospital pillows and was asleep before I closed the door behind me.

For a moment, all I could do was lean against the wall and take a few deep breaths, and only once I settled my nerves did I seek out Zeke. He still hadn't woken up, but he was off the ventilator, which by itself made him look more alive.

"Your colour looks better today." I smoothed out a crease in his hospital gown. "The others are awake, so they're under orders to give you shit for being a slugabed."

I settled in the chair beside him and watched the lines of his heart monitor blip across the screen. After a few minutes of silence, I already felt steadier in my skin. Even unconscious, Zeke was a grounding force.

"It was weird talking to the others today," I confessed. "I know it shouldn't have been, but I went in there expecting at least one of them to call me out on fucking up. To blame me for what happened. But there was so much... trust. It almost made everything worse. I made the call that led you in there—where is the anger? I fucked up, so why aren't they turning their backs on me? I feel like it's more than I deserve."

Getting my thoughts off my chest didn't make me feel any lighter, but there was a sense of relief in saying it out loud, the thoughts no longer looping through my head in silence.

Maybe next time I'd have the guts to say it to someone who could look me in the eye.

"I'm doing what I can to set things right. Eric thinks I should follow orders—shocking, right? He's usually the first one to play rogue and see how far he can push the line, but this time…" I shrugged. "I get it. This is big. Way bigger than some war game or cat and mouse with an ogre trying to avoid being sent over the wall. This is a career-breaker. An international disaster, possibly, but a national disaster at the very least. To keep pushing without permission, without resources, without knowing all the details is so incredibly *stupid.*"

I knew it.

I didn't need the colonel to tell me, or my lieutenant. I'd figured it out all on my own.

"But the thought of dumping this in some politician's hands feels like shirking responsibility, and I can't abandon Mad—my friends." Even here, I didn't want to risk drawing her into this. I leaned forward, resting my hands on my knees. "The others asked if we have any theories, and now it has me thinking. The syndicate spent a lot of money trying to wipe out the task force's A-team. They had to think it was worth it. That standing whole we were too big of a threat."

I rubbed my hands over my face and wished I'd taken time to eat before coming into the office.

"Were we getting too close to something, or are they planning something large-scale enough that they need us out of the way? Inflict maximum damage to scatter the people who might stop them. All these rumours about them trying to reach the States. If they did that, they could leave the Canadian market behind. And if that's the case, they'll want to take advantage of the chaos they created when they think no one's watching them. Everyone is so focused on the PR fiasco."

Zeke's heart monitor beeped in response, and I watched his chest rise and fall. What would he have said if he were awake?

Probably nothing. He would trust me to lead in that stoic way he had and let me figure the rest out myself. He was as loyal to me and the pack as I was to the department. A department that was now under attack. A department I had sworn to protect, whatever the cost.

I also had to protect Madison from the queen, and my team deserved all my effort in bringing O'Malley and the syndicate to their knees.

"Thanks, Zeke," I said, patting him on the shoulder. "You helped me out, as you always do."

His fingers twitched, and I held my breath, hoping he would open his eyes. A minute passed with no change. Still, he was close. I felt it in my bones. He was a stubborn son of a bitch, and when he wanted to wake up, he would.

I left his room and walked the length of the hospital floor, revved up and ready to return to Dougall.

The twenty-minute drive to Nepean gave me a wide enough window to second-guess my plan, but by the time I pulled up in front of the bungalow, I was determined to go through with it.

But after I stopped the engine, I found myself sitting in the car, unable to get out.

Something was wrong.

Slowly, I pulled the handle and pushed the door open. As I stepped out, the hairs on the back of my neck danced. Without taking my eyes off the house, I bent down, grabbed my hooked blade from where I usually stored it beside the driver's seat, and took a few steps up the drive.

Shadows swarmed me where I stood. Three of them, heading towards the bungalow. By the faded image, I guessed whoever it was had come by early this morning or last night.

Fuck.

It was Weldon's place all over again.

Chapter 23

❦

Jet

I SAT IN the car staring through the windshield at the quiet house. There had been no movement inside for the last five minutes, and I didn't want to think about what that meant for poor Dougall.

The only thing holding me back from going in was knowing I should stay far away from this mess. I should call security like I had with Weldon and let them deal with it. I'd already gotten myself into enough shit with Michael and Gagnon. One more ding on my name, and I would be lucky to get a suspension.

But how would I justify being here again? What if I was wrong about the situation and ratted myself out for nothing? Would it be better to go in, check on the state of things, and call security if there was anything to report?

I wouldn't have hesitated, except I'd seen three shadows go into the house and hadn't seen them leave. Were O'Malley's thugs still inside? If they were, I couldn't face them by myself. It pained me to admit my weakness, but it was true. The brawl at The Afterlife had proved that. My muscles and joints still ached from exerting my ability as hard and as often as I had, and I didn't think I had it in me to hold my own against three trained professionals.

Which left me with another problem.

I couldn't call Eric for help. Not when I'd just promised him I was done. And the rest of my squad was out because of the danger involved. My career, my risk. I was their captain, and the possibility that they would feel obliged to do something out of a sense of loyalty was not a good enough excuse to put their lives in jeopardy.

That left me with one option, and having left him in a parking lot in the small hours of the morning, there was no way this wouldn't be awkward.

"Did hell freeze over a second time this week, because I doubt you missed me," Gideon said on answering his phone, and I wished he were here so I could punch him. A good partner he might be, but his ego was infuriating. I knew my request would fan the flames of his high self-opinion, but at least he understood what was at stake.

I also had to wonder if part of me wasn't calling so I could see him again.

I forced the thought away, buried my pride, and said, "I'm at Dougall's and could use someone to watch my six."

I prepared myself for a few clever comments about not being able to go a day without his help, but all he said was, "You sure he'll talk to us? You promised no more visits."

"Yeah, well, I'm breaking a lot of promises today. Things have changed, and I wanted to try to dig up whatever he was holding back. Now I think I might be too late."

Was that a flutter in one of the bedroom curtains? I stared at it and saw the flutter again, but the consistency of the movement made me think it might be from a draft, not a signal.

"I'll be there in twenty," Gideon said.

His quick agreement left me speechless. Not a single quip? No attempt at negotiation? Why? A familiar distrust wriggled uncomfortably in my gut, but it found no footing. Why would he dick around with me when his life and career would be just as much at risk as mine were? And anyway, did it matter what his reasons were if I'd gotten what I wanted?

He hung up, and I turned off my phone. If Eric or Michael tried to get in touch with me this afternoon, I didn't want to have to lie about where I was. Better to be unreachable and not get my head ripped off.

I kept my eye on the house while I waited, and nothing broke the stillness of the property until my passenger door opened and Gideon slipped into the seat beside me.

"Anything happening?"

"Nothing at all, which is what worries me."

He leaned forward to get a better view through the windshield. "Could be he's at work."

I frowned. "If so, he might have some unwanted guests waiting for him when he gets home."

"You want to check it out?"

"No," I said, letting myself be honest for a moment. "But let's do it anyway. I don't suppose you're armed?"

In a smooth move, Gideon slid up the leg of his jeans, reached for his boot, and came back with a knife, the blade as long as his palm. "Didn't I mention I was a boy scout?"

I curled my fingers around the hilt of my own knife, and together we got out of the car.

"Want me to go in first and take a look?" he asked. His fingers turned to mist before my eyes.

The offer was tempting. He could get in and survey the place without being seen, which would be great if anyone was inside. But we were dealing with the syndicate. Any number of unpleasant surprises could lie beyond that door, and if I was going to put anyone's life on the line, it would be mine.

"I'll take point, you stay close." I sheathed my blade and jogged up the long driveway, ducking my head under the windows as I climbed the steps to the enclosed porch. Gideon followed on my tail, the steel of his blade reflecting the after-noon sun as he angled it into a defensive position.

"Do you feel that?" I asked, and he shook his head. "The energy around this place. It's… different."

I had a creeping sensation that the windows were watching

us. The air around the house was so tight it was almost vibrating, ready to unleash. I closed my physical eyes and opened my third, stretching my awareness as far as it would reach. From this distance, the details were murky, but there was tension, anticipation. Almost eagerness. What had happened here since yesterday?

My third eye throbbed as I placed my hand on the siding, and images flashed through my head of three people climbing these stairs. The shadows were clearer now that I was making physical contact, but still not enough for me to identify them.

A lump formed in my chest, trickling dread down into my gut. I opened my eyes, crept forward, and pushed the front door open. A sweep of the house with my third eye didn't reveal anyone lurking, but I kept my hands raised, ready to fight, as I stepped into the living room.

The place was in shambles. The boxes that had been so tidily stacked had toppled, the contents—broken glassware, blankets, DVDs—strewn across the floor. A chair had been knocked over, a lamp smashed.

"Whatever happened here, it looks like Dougall tried to fight back," Gideon said, kicking aside a fireplace poker.

Four shadows going out the back door.

"I think the house is empty. Three in, four out."

"Think they took him?"

My stomach tightened. "Wouldn't that make my day. Dougall?" I projected my voice to reach far into the house, and although I expected no response, I was disappointed by the silence. "All right, first we clear the house, then we poke around. If there's anything to give away who was here and where they might have gone, I want to find it."

Gideon nodded and moved to my left, poking his head into the kitchen while I headed down the hallway to check the bedrooms.

The vibrating anticipation I'd sensed outside grew worse, and it took me a minute to realize it was my own racing heart-beat. I paused and closed my eyes. *Shadows running towards the room at the end of the hall. Boxes being moved.* What would I find when I got there? A dead body or three? I hoped it wouldn't be Dougall. I didn't want to have to live with a dead civilian on my conscience, too.

Despite what I'd seen, I put off checking that last room. The bathroom was clear, as was the first bedroom. Halfway down the hall, more visions slammed my third eye. *The three figures from the porch pushing their way down the narrow passage, following Dougall.* Unlike my previous vision, their movements were slower, revealing no rush or obvious anger. *More boxes being moved. Dougall looking over his shoulder as he entered the room.* Their steadiness was even more unnerving than the rampage it had first appeared to be.

I pressed my hand to my head to steady myself. Nothing made sense. Was I actually seeing the same three people, or had exhaustion jumbled the scenes from other events in the house?

Dougall's moving day, maybe? I was too tired to think it through, and without being able to interpret anything, my third eye was useless.

There was nothing left but to see for myself.

The door loomed ahead of me, and I didn't want to open it. Why should I? Gideon and I could walk out right now. I could call in a tip to security and pass off the search. It didn't have to be me. The repercussions would be bad enough considering I wasn't supposed to be here, so why should I have to face whatever waited behind the door?

But even as I came up with a string of reasons not to go ahead, I rested my fingers on the door handle and turned it.

At the slight pressure, the door fell off its hinges and crashed to the floor. A queen-size bed was tucked into the corner of the room with a brown-and-white striped comforter, and an old wooden desk sat against the back wall, scarred and worn. A standing fan had been placed in the corner beside the window, the blades whipping through their silent rotation to blow cool air towards the door. And in the middle of the room was a chair with a plastic bag of white powder attached to a timer that was set to go off in ten… nine… eight…

"*Gideon*," I shouted as I ran back the way I'd come. He was closer than I'd thought, and I bumped into him on my retreat. I grabbed him by the arm and shoved him ahead of me. "Move—*move!*"

The timer pinged, the plastic bag exploded with a snap, and

a cloud of white powder blew down the hallway, sped along by the lazy breeze of the fan.

The weight of what I had to do dragged me down, and it took more effort than it should have to force Gideon through the front door.

I spun around and raised my hands in front of me. The air molecules resisted my first attempts to grab hold of them, and my joints screamed as I exerted more control. The powder reached the living room, and I only just caught it before it hit me.

With a growl, I pushed it back, creating more space between me and the flecks of white dust that could kill me in a few agonizing minutes. The air trembled.

Every single thought was focused on holding the ghost in place, and I slid one foot backwards, then the other, inching towards the front door.

My arms shook, my hold slipped, and a small burst of powder broke through the invisible wall I'd raised. I reached for it, blocked it, but in my distraction, another patch opened.

I can't do this.

It was too much too soon after containing the bigger burst at the de Lauer building. I didn't have the strength to do it again.

"Come on, Jet," Gideon called from the doorway. "A few more steps. You're almost there."

Dammit, why hadn't he run? What was he still doing so

close to the blast? With a scream, I threw more effort into my wall, and the blowing powder struck against it as though it were made of glass.

If he was too stupid to leave, I had to protect him. He was here because of me. I couldn't let him get hurt.

If we made it out alive, I would kick his ass from here to Alberta for being such an idiot.

Renewed vigour filled my muscles, and I curved the air around the edges of the white cloud, attempting to mould it into a more controllable shape. Sweat dripped from my brow, and a metallic-tasting droplet landed on my lip from my bloody nose.

Another step backwards towards the door.

Once I was out of here, the threat would be contained. A few more seconds, and we would be safe. The door would be closed, and the windows…

Shit. Windows.

I cast my memory to the rooms I'd checked. Had any of the windows been open? Had it just been the fan controlling the powder's spread, or were flecks of ghost floating into the neighbourhood?

My foot hit the porch, and Gideon reached around me to grab the door handle. As soon as I was outside, he jerked the door shut, and we tore to the end of the porch. I jammed the second door closed, and only when I was sure the ghost couldn't make it through the cracks did I drop my hold on the air and sag to the ground.

Gideon dropped to one knee, his hand on my back, and as I wiped the blood off my face with the back of my hand, I looked into his eyes to make sure he was all right.

His pupils were dilated, his breath coming quick, and it took me a second to be sure he was reacting to the adrenaline rush, not a ghost hit. My body was in a similar state. My heart thundered, and my skin under Gideon's touch grew warm.

He was so close, I felt his heat radiating off him, saw the tremble in his arms and the tightness in his jaw.

The sharp desire to lean in and trail my lips along his jawline sent shocks through my lower belly, and I couldn't fight it off. Again, I'd almost died. If my hold on the ghost had slipped, we both would have been consumed by it. But here we were, together, alive—something the rush of blood in my ears wouldn't let me forget.

His tongue flicked over his bottom lip and his eyes darkened, a familiar sight that shot electric pulses under my skin.

I shifted my weight, ready to lean in, but before I had a chance, a loud, furious voice cut through my haze of adrenaline-induced longing.

"Dawson!"

Michael.

"Shit," I mumbled, and bowed my head, the fire in my blood evaporating, leaving me iced over.

I used the wall of the porch enclosure to rise to my feet, waving away Gideon's offer of help, and shuffled to the driveway. Three unmarked cars were parked on the street, blocking the house from anyone driving by. Michael stood next to one of them, Eric at his side.

Double shit.

"What the fuck is going on here?" Michael hissed as I approached. His face was red, his eyes wild with anger. "We've been trying to call you for over an hour only to reach your voicemail, and now we find you here?"

At the mention of my phone, I pulled it out of my pocket and turned it on. When it finished its reboot, I saw I'd missed over a dozen calls from him and Eric, and I didn't look forward to going through my messages later.

Gideon stood behind me, saying nothing, and I wished more than anything I'd had time to get him out of sight before anyone saw him. Explaining my presence was going to be hard enough, but justifying his would be a whole other problem. I would be lucky not to get brought up on charges.

Fuck.

Michael took hold of my arm to bring me closer and, in a volume meant for my ears alone, repeated, "What the fuck are you doing here, Jet?"

I drew in a breath to steady my shaking legs and wavering vision. There would be time later to recover. For now, it was better to get my confession over with. Putting it off wouldn't make it easier.

I glanced at Eric and wished I hadn't. He was staring at me

with a look of such disappointment that shame flooded my gut. I should have told him my plan. He might not have agreed with me, but at least he would have known. For the first time in our career, I'd kept a secret from him, and I felt like a garbage pile.

"I came here to talk to Dougall," I said. "I think he had more to tell me about O'Malley's dealings, and I wanted to see if I could get it out of him."

Michael scowled, his grey eyes raging. "And now we've lost any chance of using him. Are you proud of yourself? Dougall called *us* this morning saying he needed protection in exchange for information. Is he in there?"

I shook my head. "No. I think someone took him. Shadows." Confusion muddled my thoughts, and I glanced over my shoulder. The sections of window not blocked by curtain were thick with white dust. "There was a ghostbomb."

Michael backed off, his face going slack. "What?"

His gaze jumped to the house and back to me, as though hoping he'd misheard.

I wished he had, especially as the implications of that powder-laced chair hit me with its full significance. Again O'Malley had known someone was coming. The visions my third eye had picked up wove into a story I understood. The shadows had broken into the house, and the boxes they were moving had been to set up the bomb. But from what I'd seen, Dougall had been helping them.

Right now, that didn't matter. I turned back to Michael, and the shame I'd felt a moment ago was gone. If I hadn't shown up before the others, they would all be dead or dying right now. "I didn't mess this up, sir. You wouldn't have found anyone even if you'd arrived first. They were gone before I got here, and there was a bomb strapped to a chair, just like in the de Lauer basement. The house is full of ghost, and we need to tent the property before it gets out. We could lose the entire street if it's not contained."

"Jesus H—Carstairs, get over here," Michael shouted to a brawny soldier with stupid facial hair standing next to the second car. He lumbered over, his wide jaw set. I'd never seen the man before and watched him closely as Michael barked out his orders. "Get on the phone with the minister's office. We need a full cleanup crew, and we need it now. Don't spread panic, but point out that if we lose any muns to loose ghost, it's going to be on the minister to explain it to the PM, got it?"

Carstairs nodded and pulled his phone out of his pocket, marching over to a quiet spot to relay the colonel's message.

"Who's he?" I asked once he was out of earshot.

"Hmm?" Michael glanced from me to him. "Oh. New recruit. We had to start replacing the fallen."

My heart stopped. My team? He was replacing my team, and I hadn't been included?

Michael must have read my expression, because his lip curled with impatience. "We can discuss it later. Right now, we have bigger issues to deal with."

Although I knew he was right, I felt like he'd swept the ground out from under me, and while Michael ran through logistics with the rest of his team, my sanity slowly unravelled. What was going on? New recruits? Dougall calling the department after I'd given him my private number and promise of help? And what did it mean that he'd helped cart boxes into his bedroom? Was he involved?

If he wasn't involved, then he was in no small amount of trouble, if he wasn't already dead. If he *was* involved, then we had to question everything he'd told us. It meant the Kingston rumour was back on the table. It meant for the last three months we might have been chasing air, and they'd been laughing at us while they set up a brand new operation in a brand new city with no one to get in their way.

O'Malley had been a step ahead this entire time, guessing SMOAC's moves and acting before anyone caught up, keeping the truth buried from even the best investigators in the department.

I felt like I was going to be sick.

All this time and money trying to run him down, all these people dead, and all for no progress whatsoever.

How could the syndicate be this smart and this smooth? They were crime bosses, drug dealers, and they were manipulating some of the smartest minds in the country's supernatural community. It didn't seem possible. For months we thought we'd been playing cat and mouse, when really it was a game of cat and shadow, and now they'd vanished altogether.

The only way I could understand O'Malley's success was if everyone who could have done something had been living with their eyes squeezed shut.

No, this goes beyond laziness. The lack of vetting information, that could be chalked up to someone not paying attention, but letting people act on that unconfirmed information? Not chasing down the Kingston rumour to a certainty? Giving O'Malley chance after chance to outrun us? Sure, the department was forced to swim through a sea of bureaucracy, but for every single manoeuvre against the syndicate to have failed screamed incompetence on a broad scale.

Or a mole.

My strength flagged under the weight of my suspicions. I limped over to the maple tree at the edge of the yard and leaned against the trunk so I didn't fall on my ass. Gideon kept close on one side, while Eric followed me on the other.

"Jet, what the hell is going on?" he asked, shifting so his back was to Gideon and he stood between us. "Why didn't you call me? Why did you come without backup? Without orders?"

I noted his dismissal of Gideon and didn't bother to correct him. The less attention I drew to him, the better for everyone.

"Because I didn't want Michael to come down on you, too," I said, squinting through lowered lashes into his blue eyes. "I would have told you if I'd found anything, but I knew you wouldn't want me to come."

His shoulders sagged. "You all right?"

"I need a shot of whiskey, three shots of espresso, and six days of sleep, but yeah, I'll be fine."

Finally, as though remembering Gideon was there, he looked over his shoulder. Gideon quirked an eyebrow, daring him to ask questions, but Eric turned away again, stepping back to give me some personal space.

As we stood there awaiting Michael's orders, the two men stared at each other, appraising, silently questioning who the other was, and I didn't bother with introductions.

Asking Gideon to come had been a mistake.

Oh, hindsight, my old friend.

My head throbbed, and I closed my eyes, my third eye drifting over the scene in front of me. I understood that sense of anticipation now. Whoever had set up the bomb—Dougall or the three shadows going after him—had arranged everything. Either Dougall had called the department of his own volition or he'd been made to call, but they knew someone would come to pick him up, which meant it was likely the person or people behind this were nearby. They'd want to see how it played out. Tally the body count.

Would they care their plan had failed, or would they celebrate the further distraction?

A shadow fell over me, and I looked up to find Michael had returned. I waited for the lecture and scrambled to figure out what to say in my defence, but all he said was, "We'll talk about this later, Dawson. I want you to head to the office and get yourself checked out while you wait for me. You're not to talk to anyone or do anything until you've been cleared by the medical officer and made your official report, is that clear?"

I pushed away from the tree and stood up straight. "Yes, sir."

Gideon nudged me with his elbow, but I ignored him. What more did he want from me? To stand and fight with my commanding officer after my second time caught disobeying orders?

There was a time and place for rebellion, and in the face of a pissed-off colonel was not one of them. Even if I wanted to, I was too tired to fight. It was easier to let fourteen years' worth of training take over. There would be time for words later.

Before I could walk to my car, three more vehicles pulled up. The minister stepped out of the middle car, followed closely by Deputy Minister Gagnon and Madison.

Madison's gaze fell on me and widened in shock. Apparently the news hadn't gotten around yet that I was involved. I gave it another ten minutes before everyone knew a task force captain had gone against protocol. Someone would be calling for my job by end of day.

Michael rested his hand on my shoulder—not gently—and steered me towards the new arrivals at the side of the road.

"Minister, Deputy," he greeted. "Ms. Prince."

"What happened here?" Minister Bastien asked, his yellow eyes narrow, his voice gruff.

"We received a request for assistance from one of our informants, arrived to pick him up, and found a ghostbomb instead. Captain Dawson successfully contained the blast, but we'll need to clear the area before we go inside."

His fingers squeezed my shoulder, and I stiffened under his grip. *I'm not ratting you out*, his gesture said, *but don't think this is over.* I was as grateful as I was resigned. Whatever his reasons were for protecting me, it wouldn't prevent him from flaying me alive when we got back to his office.

"Orders have been given?" the minister asked.

"Yes, sir."

"Good." Bastien shook his head and glared at the house. "What a mess. The syndicate is too good at what they do. They know exactly how we'll respond, so they know exactly how to set the scene. If we had ignored the informant's request, they would have set a backup plan in motion, I'm sure. Somehow they always know."

His frustration validated my earlier suspicions. Something about this situation didn't smell right.

The minister's attention shifted over my right shoulder, and his brow furrowed. I followed his gaze to Gideon, and my shoulders crept a little closer to my ears.

"The SilverGuard officer. How are you involved in this?" Bastien demanded.

Surprised, I turned from Gideon to the minister.

"Not at all, Minister. I came up here to gather information, and my path led to Dougall," Gideon said, as calmly as though he'd expected the question. My embarrassment deepened. Of course the minister had heard SilverGuard was in the country. I couldn't even try to pretend Gideon was an old family friend. The full extent of my stupidity was in the open for everyone to see.

Bastien stepped forward, tightening the circle, and dropped his voice so no one beyond the seven of us could hear him.

"If I find out you helped this son of a bitch disappear, there won't be a corner in hell you'll be able to hide in. I ask again, how are you involved?"

My mouth went dry. A cloudy dread swept through the bottom of my stomach and crept up to wrap around my lungs as I shifted on my feet to keep both men in view.

"I was not involved with Dougall beyond what Captain Dawson can corroborate," Gideon said.

There was an edge to his voice, as though the minister were pushing his luck by asking twice and if he went for a third, the response wouldn't be so civil.

The dread had reached the edges of my brain, closing in and turning everything around me to fog. What was I not seeing? I caught Madison's eye, but she gave a subtle shake of her head. She had no more idea than I did.

"My people say you've been here three days," Bastien said, "poking into affairs that don't concern you."

The deputy minister nodded. "I can confirm. We've spoken

to many contacts who told us of an American asking questions about the syndicate. Lucky for us we found you here—we were ready to track you down to ask what SilverGuard thinks they're doing. Is it a coincidence, I wonder, that the same week you pay us a visit, we have to deal with two syndicate attacks?"

He waved his hand towards the house, which was now roped off with police tape. The area over the bedroom was hidden under a thick white tent, and, with an incredible response time, a crew dressed in haz-mat suits was working to stretch the structure over the rest of the house.

"We're not accusing you of being involved in the explosion," Bastien said, casting the deputy a sharp look, "but you certainly haven't made the clean-up any easier by asking questions and spreading worry. Why did SilverGuard send you?"

"I was tasked with finding and taking down the source of the ghost," Gideon said without apology, and my already tense muscles turned to stone. "It's been getting more and more obvious that your local teams aren't up to the job as distribution moves closer to the border."

Eric grunted, his cheeks flushed pink at the insult. I, on the other hand, was too numb to feel the sting.

How was I still standing? Gideon had told me he was here to do a risk assessment. A simple survey to see how worried his people should be, not that he intended to take the operation out of my hands. What would he have done if we hadn't been caught? Left me in the dark and gone home to shoulder

SMOAC out of the way so he could take credit for shutting down the syndicate? He'd lied to me. I'd trusted him, and he'd lied to me *again*.

The ground lurched under my feet, and I clenched my fists at my sides to hold myself steady.

When will you learn, Jet? First Dougall might have played me for a fool, and now it turned out Gideon had as well.

My entire life, I'd prided myself on my ability to read people. How could I have been so wrong?

One of the clean-up crew took advantage of the pause in conversation to approach us. "Minister, could we borrow you? There's some paperwork we need you to sign."

"Of course." Bastien nodded to Gagnon, then jerked his head towards Gideon. "You'll take care of this situation?"

He walked away, and Gagnon stepped forward to take his place, waving Carstairs and another unfamiliar face over. "Take this man into custody and begin the process to send him back to the United States."

Gideon squared his shoulders and said nothing. He looked at me, but I focused straight ahead. I couldn't meet his eye. I didn't trust myself not to spit on him. Anger and disappointment, shame and regret choked me, threatening my self-control. I wanted to grab hold of the air molecules around the maple tree and heave the whole thing out of the ground. I wanted to bring the houses down. The only way to hold myself back was to put every ounce of strength I had into staying still, unmoving.

If Gideon Leigh expected me to step in and say something on his behalf, he'd misjudged me as badly as I had him. He'd made his choice.

Let him live with the consequences.

Chapter 24

Madison

I FELT LIKE I'd been caught in some kind of crime drama. The police tape, the milling agents, the roadblocks and camera crews. Only the disorienting emotions swirling through the air grounded me in the horrible reality.

A reality I wasn't entirely sure why I was a part of. I'd gone into the office as Jean-Luc had requested, and the next thing I'd known, we were getting into his car and driving out to Nepean.

I had my suspicions. With emotions running as high as they were, I wondered if he wanted me to level them off enough to let people discuss the situation with clear heads. I would certainly do my best, but not until asked. With this many people and moods running tense, it would not be a simple feat.

Though I wished I could do *something* to find neutral ground to stand on. Lucien had given his orders to take Gideon into custody, and by the gleam in one of the soldiers' eyes, he was more than ready to wrestle him into the car. Eric buried his feelings better, but he couldn't hide his anger or jealousy. Not from me, anyway, who could see through his well-trained stoicism.

As it was, there was nothing I could do but stare as they closed in on Gideon.

Gideon Leigh. Jet's Gideon. Gideon the Jerkwad, in the flesh. He was just as attractive as Jet had described, with his lean, muscular form, firm jaw, and creases in the corners of his eyes that gave away the easiness of his smile. Though right now, he showed none of the charm she said he was capable of. If anything, he looked cold, unconcerned about the fact he'd been found out—not only by a foreign government but also by the woman he'd promised to help.

Anger prickled under my skin, and it was a relief to experience an emotion of my own instead of filtering somebody else's. How dare he look so indifferent? He should have been begging Jet to forgive him, not trying to catch her eye to see if she'd help him before the soldiers escorted him away.

After everything he'd done, he obviously hadn't learned anything.

I felt for Jet. To have put her trust in someone who didn't deserve it only to have their betrayal revealed right after almost dying, and by the people who could end her career… I was amazed she appeared as calm as she did.

Her only visible tell was how hard she was working not to look at him. Her gaze stayed focused on her feet, on the house, on Eric. Anywhere but on the person who had hurt her. Even with three people between us, I felt the sharpness of her pain.

The electricity of it spurred my anger further—until a different emotion caught my attention. Fear. Regret.

I followed it as I would a strong odour, and for a brief moment, as the rough soldier jerked him towards the car, my eye met Gideon's. They bustled him into the backseat and slammed the door, cutting me off from whatever he felt.

But it had been enough. Jet was right—the man was an expert liar. Even now, with the threat of deportation hanging over him, he looked as relaxed as a cat lounging in the grass. Everything a smokescreen for feelings as strong and deep as the roots of the maple tree.

Did Jet suspect, or did she buy his act?

Her refusal to say anything on his behalf was a pretty good answer, but the way she watched the car now that Gideon couldn't see her sent a whole different message. The only time I'd ever seen her so intense was when she was on the job.

In the shuffle, I made my way to her side and nudged her in the ribs, hoping to wake her up. Yes, he'd lied. Yes, he was a jerk. But did she really want him to get lost in SMOAC's subbasements without giving security a reason to go easy on him?

I wanted her to say something, worried she would regret it if she didn't. Despite everything this man had done, he meant something to her. I didn't have to read her to know it. The way she spoke about him, even when she was furious.

She ignored my attempt to get her attention, and the opportunity vanished as Jean-Luc returned to us, his expression stormy. If he was trying to contain his displeasure, he needn't have bothered. I read his simmering anger easily enough, and Jet had to know he wasn't thrilled with the situation.

"Now for the two of you," he started, and I froze. I'd hardly expected to be a target for his fury. I felt like a child under the eyes of a disappointed parent, as though it were my father standing in front of me instead of his best friend.

"It has come to my attention that Madison provided you information about the people who came forward about de Lauer."

A flare of panic passed through me, and I did my best to wrangle it. Someone who'd helped me must have given me up.

You knew it was a possibility. Suck it up and accept the consequences.

It explained why the minister had asked me to drive here with him. He hadn't needed my help with crowd control—he'd wanted to lecture both of us at once.

"Under the circumstances," he continued, "seeing as how your involvement uncovered a second bomb and prevented further casualties, I'm willing to overlook the breach in protocol. But—" the corner of his mouth twitched as his restraint slipped "—it ends here. The only reason I feel generous is because no one was in the house. I will not have representatives of our department breaching security and standing in the way of authorized action. As of this moment, this case is off limits to both of you, and if I catch wind of either of your names being associated with anyone involved with the syndicate or any of these informants, I will have your jobs. Do I make myself absolutely clear?"

By now, most of the people nearby were staring at us, drawn by Jean-Luc's rising voice, and it was a challenge for me to maintain a neutral expression. I hated being called out. I'd always been the goody-goody who followed orders and never got into trouble. I was the type in high school who cried when a teacher expressed disappointment in my behaviour. Even now, I felt the familiar burn in the back of my throat, along with the desire to apologize and justify my actions. I swallowed it. For one thing, the minister was in no mood to hear excuses, and, for another, I didn't feel sorry. We'd done what we thought was necessary to keep the queen off my back and uncover some buried intel.

If I had any regrets, it was that my information had nearly gotten Jet killed by another ghostbomb. If she hadn't been so quick to prevent the powder from taking over the house, her name would have been added to the long list of the fallen.

So instead of arguing, or crying, or asking for forgiveness, I simply said, "Yes, sir."

"Yes, sir," Jet repeated, and she was impossible to read. She'd blocked herself from me, and her expression was inscrutable, her shoulders back and spine straight. She was a soldier responding to a reprimand and nothing more. It made me worry about what was actually going on inside her head.

"Good," he said. "As for the issue of this SilverGuard agent being found with you, I will leave the matter with Colonel Torrence. Perhaps current… emotional factors need to be taken into consideration." He cleared his throat and shifted on his feet, as though the mention of Jet's fragile state was more than he wanted to discuss. Then the lines around his eyes hardened. "Though I hope it goes without saying that all contact with Mr. Leigh stops here."

"Yes, sir," came the same robotic reply.

"Excellent. Now go. It's Sunday, and I would like to spend at least some of it with my family. Michael, come talk to me. I want to hear what your plan is."

Michael moved to follow him, but when Jean-Luc's attention was grabbed by more paperwork that needed signing, he stopped and draped his arm around Jet's shoulders, more gently than he had when he'd escorted her to the minister earlier. He turned her so both their backs faced the road, and I glanced over his shoulder at the news cameras trying to decide whether they were people of interest before following the minister.

"Why don't you take some time off like I told you to?" Michael suggested. "You've been through hell over the last couple days, and you haven't taken any time to rest. You're driving yourself crazy, and you're not in a place to make smart decisions. SilverGuard, Dawson? Really?"

Jet only stared ahead, like she was drunk or drugged. There

was no response in her eyes, no awareness. She had more attention for the tree than for her commander.

"Hey," he said, and nudged her shoulder with his. "You hearing me, kid?"

I looked between them, wrapping the compassion and care coming off Michael around me like a protective blanket. His affection and respect for her was clear, as much a fatherly concern as that of a superior officer, and the warmth of it stood out in sharp contrast to the coldness of the rest of the scene. He could have ripped her apart, taken her stripes, had her thrown in the car behind Gideon's, but he saw through her recklessness to the root cause. Jet must have realized how lucky she was, because she gave herself a shake and rose out of her stupor.

"Yeah," she said. "I'm hearing you. I'll leave my report on your desk, then I'll head home and get some sleep. I'm done. I promise."

He nodded and looked at me. "You'll make sure she does? *After* she gets checked out?"

"Of course," I said. As though he needed to ask. My best friend was in pain. If there was anything I could do to help her, I would.

"Then as far as I'm concerned, this can be the end of it. I expect you to get your head on straight and come back to work the captain I trained. You spoke with Dr. Casselman?"

"Yes, sir."

"Right, well, maybe a follow-up appointment wouldn't be a bad idea. Now go on and get out of here. I'll finish up with the crew."

He gave Jet a last worried look, then left us alone in the shadow of the maple tree.

She didn't move, and I followed her absent stare to where Eric leaned against the passenger door of the car holding Gideon. I could just make out the shape of Gideon's head through the rear window and wished I could get closer to dig into those emotions I'd sensed. The fear had struck me as particularly complex. Fear of what they would do to him before sending him home? Fear of what SilverGuard would do when he made his report? Fear for Jet?

A shiver ran through me.

Although I agreed with Jet that he deserved what he got, I couldn't help but suspect there was more to the man's intentions than he claimed.

As soon as Michael walked away, Eric left his place by the car and came forward. I stepped aside, wanting to give them space, but there was only so far I could go. I didn't want to return to the minister's entourage and absorb more of his displeasure, or be in view of the news cameras, and I didn't want to stray too far from Jet in case she needed me.

I sauntered behind the tree so I could at least be out of view.

"You okay?" he asked her.

"Well enough," she said. "I'm sorry I left you out of this. I should have called you."

"Yes, you should have," he said, and I picked up the energy from both of them—concern, love, and the warm vibration of anger. "But I guess we should thank you. After we got Dougall's call, we were ready to barge in to get him out. Whoever set up the bomb must have been watching to start the timer. I doubt we would have made it out before it blew."

"I'm glad I got here first. I can't imagine—" She cut herself off, but I had an easy enough time finishing her thought. If she'd lost Eric and Michael, her foundation would have vanished. Those two were what made it possible for her to take on such a difficult job. A wave of grief came around the tree as Jet fought back her horror of what might have been.

"Hey," Eric said, "it's all right. No one got hurt. It all worked out. But for fuck's sake, Jet, we weren't the ones at risk. You could have killed yourself. To go in there at all, let alone without calling anyone for backup. Turning off your phone? You could have walked into anything with only some foreign agent beside you." He paused. "I know things have been rough, and I know the guilt is eating you up, but that's not the move of the captain I've served for three years."

His concern was almost as great as his frustration, and Jet picked up on it, too, because she said, "I did what I felt I had to do. I don't expect anyone to understand, but I had to do something."

"So do something. Come with me to the memorial service

on Wednesday. Start training the new troops. There's enough to keep you busy."

"It doesn't bother you?" I heard the sharp edge to her words as her own frustration grew. "It doesn't get to you that the syndicate keeps outmanoeuvring us? That information wasn't vetted before orders were given?"

"Of course it does, but it means we can be sure it won't happen again. More precautions will be taken."

"Will they? How do you know? If there's a mole in the department, how can we know they won't slip through the investigation to continue working against us? What if that ghostbomb was a second stab at wiping more of us out, paving the way for something else? Who's going to do something about that?"

Eric's frustration tipped into anger, and I tensed, ready to step in.

"I hate to say it, but you butting your nose in on this might have ruined our chances of finding answers. You talked to the guy yesterday, and now, instead of him, we have another ghostbomb. Maybe if you hadn't gone sniffing around where you shouldn't have—" In a breath, his anger burned out. "I'm sorry, Jet, I can't stand the thought of what might have happened. The minister is on this. They'll track down Dougall. You need to have faith."

Jet said nothing, and he sighed. "Michael's right. Go home and get some rest. We'll take it from here. Let me know if you need a lift to the memorial service."

He headed back to the car, and I came out from behind the tree. I expected her to call after him and smooth things over before he disappeared, but she'd closed herself off again.

For a moment, we stood without speaking. I didn't know where to begin. When it became obvious that Jet was completely lost in her thoughts, I knew I had to give her a nudge.

"You still with me?"

It took a while, but finally she nodded.

"Do you want to talk about it?"

Only after I asked the question did I appreciate how meaningless it was. So much had happened in such a short time. We all needed room to process.

Jet must have felt the same way, because she shook her head. "Michael pretty much said it all, didn't he? He was on it, and we got in his way. I should have kept my phone on and believed him when he said he was looking into things."

In my opinion, Michael held as much responsibility for her actions as I did for encouraging her or as Jet did for following her gut. If he'd given her something to do, she wouldn't have felt the need to go in on her own. I understood his desire to protect her, but he'd had to know she wouldn't let the matter drop. He'd trained her to be relentless. How could he be surprised she'd put that training into practice?

I bit my tongue. Saying it wouldn't make her feel any better—she wouldn't agree with me in any case. In her eyes, when it came to Michael Torrence, he was still the teacher and she the student. No matter how long she was on the job, that dynamic would never change.

There was a lot I was willing to let her sit with for now, but one topic of conversation I couldn't ignore.

"What about Gideon?"

His name was enough to jolt her out of her silent fortress. She turned her head to glare at me. "What about him?"

She could deny it as much as she wanted, but her emotions towards him were incredibly strong, though more negative than positive at the moment. I wished she would actually talk to me about what she was feeling, but if all I got were the vibes pouring off her, I would have to work with it. "You're really going to let them take him in? He's a foreign agent working on Canadian soil without official permission. He'll be sent home. You'll probably never see him again. I doubt he'll ever be allowed to step foot over the border if he was here to spy for SilverGuard."

"What do you want me to say, Madi? That they're wrong? That he has Canadian interests at heart? He used me for information so he could take control of our operation. We would have lost Canadian authority. SilverGuard would have taken what he learned to the American government, and they would have taken away our chance to handle things. He knew what the risks were, and he deserves whatever he gets."

"He deserves to wind up in our detainment centre? Because

you know that's what's going to happen. If they think he got information out of you, they're not going to put him up in a posh hotel and allow him room service until he's ready to go home. They'll see the same risks you do and take measures to keep the intel out of American hands as long as possible."

Jet's jaw worked as she clenched her teeth, and I released a breath, knowing it would be better to drop the issue. If I kept pushing, the result would be Jet digging her heels in deeper. She'd made her choice, just as Gideon had, and would need to accept whatever came.

"So, what do you want to do?" I asked, scanning the increasingly crowded scene. A scene from which we'd been exiled. "Want to go for a drink?"

To my disappointment, Jet declined. "I think I want to be alone right now. Thanks, though."

I tried to read her, but she remained blocked, so I didn't know if her silence, her detachment, stemmed from exhaustion or a dangerous self-pity. I'd give her today, but tomorrow we would have words.

"No thanks required." I searched the street for her car. "You promised Michael you'd go to the clinic to get checked out. I don't suppose I could trouble you for a lift?"

"Sure." She sounded relieved by the excuse to get out of here. "Let's go."

We didn't talk much on the drive downtown. The clinic was quiet when we arrived, and Jet was soon cleared and given strict orders to rest.

After we finished there, I twiddled my thumbs in her office while she wrote up a quick incident report that she left on Michael's desk.

I could have walked home from the office but accepted her offer of a ride, wanting to spend as much time with her as possible. Before I got out of the car, I made sure she was paying attention when I said, "If you need anything, call me. Promise?"

"Promise." She crossed her finger over her chest, but her eyes were empty.

Not happy, but not sure what else to do, I closed the door and watched her pull away from the curb.

I felt like we'd hit a turning point. The syndicate had played their hand and delivered their warning, but they'd pissed off the wrong people in the process. Nan's wisdom circled my thoughts, and I resigned myself to the fact that I'd waited too long to get my affairs in order. Hopefully I had time to make my preparations and be ready to run before another bomb shook the rest of the city off its axis.

Chapter 25

Jet

AFTER I DROPPED Madison off, I drove home, pulled into the parking garage, and dragged myself up the stairs to my apartment. I moved carefully, my muscles and joints in full rebellion now that the adrenaline had worn off, and when I finally closed my door behind me, I threw all the bolts shut.

Only then did I allow my legs to give out.

I sagged against the door, pulled my knees to my chest, and buried my head in my hands.

My conscience warred in my bruised and battered brain, a wild screaming in my skull as my rational and instinctive sides fought to prove themselves right. My rational side gave me shit for fucking things up beyond all reason. I'd set out with the best intentions, wanting to save my friend and find justice for our squad, and instead I'd barrelled my way into a sensitive op. Whether Dougall had been kidnapped or tipped off, our lead was in the wind.

My instinctive side fumed that I'd been left with no option but to go in myself. No one had wanted to loop me in.

Beneath the anger was a screaming terror as the significance of the second ghostbomb became clearer. When the bomb had gone off in the de Lauer building, the cost of the device had been on everyone's tongue. Now we'd learned they could afford to build two. How many more might be out there, waiting to catch someone unaware? Why wasn't the minister putting every available body on this? Although my methods may have lacked finesse, I could still be useful. Why didn't they give me an order? Some way to help? Instead, they were ignoring resources because I'd had the balls to take some initiative and make them look bad on the evening news.

The coat rack beside the door wobbled on its uneven legs, and I forced myself to breathe and calm down.

I rose onto aching feet, my knees screaming, and hobbled towards the sofa. I debated sitting down, but knew if I did, my hips would lock and I would be stuck there all night. Better to keep moving.

I turned on the TV, made my way to the liquor cabinet, and poured myself a healthy glass of red wine. The whiskey beckoned, but I'd drowned enough sorrows in the last couple of days. I needed to hang on to a few to remind myself why I'd done what I had. I refused to feel guilty for taking action. Especially when said action had resulted in saving lives.

The droning news filled my apartment, and I watched as the camera panned the length of Dougall's property. His house was tented, and fumigation notices peppered the lawn. The news anchor stood at the end of the driveway, his face pinched with concern as he updated his viewers about the latest public health scare.

"Sources say the owner of the house arrived in the emergency room in the early hours of the morning complaining of fever and severe muscle aches. Tests confirmed evidence of the hantavirus, an illness spread by infected mice. Exterminators were sent to the house to carry out emergency procedures to prevent the virus—and the mice—from spreading."

I rolled my eyes at the lie but had to give the department credit for coming up with a story no mundane would associate with the de Lauer building. Shame the supernatural community wouldn't be so easily fooled. This was the second incident in a week that had—reportedly—injured one of our own. This attack, no matter how the public perceived it, would stoke the fires that had already been lit.

I hoped the minister was prepared to put them out.

Not wanting to listen to any more media spin, I turned off the TV and took my wine glass into the bathroom. The grey bathmat hugged my toes, and the clawfoot tub in the corner called my name, tempting me with a temporary reprieve from my problems. I set my glass on the tiled windowsill and turned on the tap, fully opening the hot water faucet. Steam filled the room, and I stripped down to nothing, assessing myself in the mirror as my reflection fogged over. I'd expected to be covered in bruises, my skin red with swelling, but as usual there were no visible marks to show the deep discomfort twisting my muscles and soft tissue.

The effort of keeping that powder back, exerting that much strength twice in less than a week—I was tapped out. If my suspicions were right that there were more bombs out there, I didn't have it in me to contain them.

A groan escaped my throat as I manoeuvred my way into the high-sided tub, but as soon as my body sank under the water, I felt an immediate release. Unfortunately, with the release of tension came a loosening of the walls I'd built around my emotions since Michael had reamed me out. My exhaustion, anger, grief, and disappointment rampaged through my skull, and I was stuck replaying the entire afternoon.

I gritted my teeth and pushed through it, accepting the humiliation of being stripped down by my commander, my lieutenant, and the minister of the department. Accepting the remorse of being the possible cause of a ruined lead. Accepting that twice in a week, only my quick reflexes and ruthless stubbornness had stood between me and a brutal death.

None of it felt good, but I'd been trained to let it go. Holding on to grudges, embarrassment, fear, or anger led to poor decision making. I had to reboot, and maybe I would see my way clear tomorrow.

But even after I'd talked myself down from most of today's roller coaster, one looping thought remained.

I reached for my wine and took a gulp, not tasting a thing but hoping the movement, the tartness, the hit of alcohol would make everything slow down.

Gideon had betrayed me again. I'd known it was possible, told myself to brace for it, but even so, I'd started to let my guard down, started to enjoy spending time with him, almost *kissed him*, and all the while he'd been stringing me along. How much of his charm had been an act to get what he wanted— one I'd fallen for again?

Thanks to Madison buzzing in my ear about speaking up on his behalf, I tried to summon a hint of guilt at letting him be taken away, but the thought of him under a security officer's cold stare and pointed questions, stuck in some uncomfortable safe house under constant supervision, filled me with deep satisfaction. At least this time, he wouldn't get to walk away from his lies.

Lies I should have seen through and hadn't.

I wondered what else I had missed as I'd attempted to pry my way into the syndicate's secrets. If I couldn't tell the difference between truth and fiction, there was no way I'd make any headway investigating on my own.

After my bath, I crawled into bed and stayed there for the next fourteen hours. When I woke up to discover it was only seven in the morning, I went down for another four.

My body was mad at me, my mind even more so, and sleep was the best way to avoid both.

Sometime around noon, I rolled out of bed and threw on a pair of scruffy gym clothes. My dreams had been full of death and dying, powder in the air, Gideon's screams in a dark cell, and I felt the need to punch something. Hard and repeatedly.

One of the first changes I'd made to my apartment when I moved in six years ago had been to hang a punching bag in the corner of the living room. It was an old building, with more than one crack in the walls, so every time I used it, I was prepared for the ceiling to cave in, but so far my luck had held. I crossed my fingers my streak would continue, because I was in no mood to go gentle today.

After a warm-up to loosen my muscles and get my heart going, I set into my real workout. A few quick punches of skin to fabric, and as my swings grew stronger, I shifted the air molecules to form pockets around my fists. My blows packed double the punch, the bag shuddering on its hook, the seams loosening. A jab here, a hook there—I threw my entire body into it, never slowing enough to let thoughts sneak in.

I only paused to wipe the sweat out of my eyes. My back and arms were sore and noodly, and my heart was racing. I kept going, losing myself in the rush of endorphins that made me feel like I could accomplish anything—so I nearly threw the bag at the door when a knock interrupted my rhythm.

At first I kept swinging, unable to think of anyone I wanted to see. Then my head filled with thoughts of Gideon, and though I told myself it couldn't be him, I couldn't shake the possibility he'd found a way out. He could have misted under a door or charmed his way to freedom. If that were the case, I wanted to talk to him. Or at least trade my punching bag for his face.

I grabbed the bag to steady it, then went to the door and peered through the peephole. Instead of a lanky, dark-haired man standing on the other side, however, it was a wide, burly blond.

Eric.

I wasn't in a huge rush to continue our conversation from yesterday, but I couldn't ignore him.

"Hey," he said when I opened the door. "I tried calling. How are you doing?"

I tried to get a read on him to predict why he was here, but all I found in his blue eyes was concern. Nothing calculated, nothing unclear. Our years together had given me a chance to understand this man inside and out, but more than that, he trusted me enough to show me the truth. Something Gideon could never bring himself to do.

"Great," I said. "Grateful my face isn't all over the news for being the person to discover the hantavirus in Nepean."

He smirked. "I thought it was a nice touch. At least we know no one will go near the house."

My frustration twitched. "Not good enough, in my opinion. I'll bet the minister's people are so busy scrambling to cover the PR mess, they've forgotten to send anyone after Dougall."

An awkward silence fell between us, and I bit my tongue. My anger scurried back under the rock where I'd buried it.

"Can I come in?" he asked.

I hesitated only a moment before stepping aside, and he passed around me.

"Feel free to put the coffee on if you want a cup," I said, and returned to my punching bag. Obviously I hadn't worked everything out yet.

Eric made himself at home with the mugs and sugar bowl, then stayed well out of reach near the island as I fell into a few easy jabs, finding my tempo.

"I wanted to see how you were feeling about yesterday," he said. "It was a bit of a shitshow."

"A nice way of putting it."

"I'm sorry I wasn't there."

"Would you have come?"

Yesterday morning, I wouldn't have doubted it, but considering his reaction to how things had gone down, I had to wonder.

"We'll never know, will we?" he said. "You trusted a Silver-Guard spy instead."

The jealousy I'd heard on the phone yesterday had resurfaced. I clenched my teeth and swung a little harder. I wouldn't ask about Gideon.

"I was already in the hot seat," I said, focusing on the actual issue lying between us.

"Your choice."

"Yes, it was." I punctuated my words with a one-two strike. A lock of hair fell into my eyes, and I blew it away. "They wanted me to step aside, Eric. You know I couldn't do that. I couldn't look Jane's wife in the eye and tell her everything possible was being done when I was sitting at home watching shit TV."

I couldn't tell him about Madison. While it might change his opinion to know how close the queen was to stepping in, I couldn't mention her without dragging my friend into the spotlight.

Red swam in my vision, but I channelled my resentment into my fists. I'd made up my mind that I was dealing with these twisted emotions, even if it took all day and my wrists were pulp by the end of it.

"I get it, Jet. I do." He released a heavy breath, and the island creaked as he leaned his weight against it. "You're not the only one feeling useless. My nightmares have been—I wake up in a sweat and can't get back to sleep unless I turn on the TV and down half a bottle of scotch. I'm angry. Furious. At everything. And it takes so much effort not to kick the shit out of anyone who looks at me wrong. Michael convinced me to ride with him yesterday because he was worried when he couldn't reach you—otherwise, I'd still be hiding in my apartment trying not to do any damage."

He went quiet, and I thought I heard a choking noise. I grabbed my bag and turned around to find him standing with his head bowed, his shoulders shaking. Sweaty as I was, I went over to him and wrapped my arms around his middle. He squeezed me against his chest in a tight hug and tucked his forehead against my shoulder.

"I hate the feeling that I'm losing you, too," he said. "These missions you're assigning yourself, not telling anyone—it's not like you, Jet. I'm worried. When I saw you outside that house yesterday, the windows fogged with ghost… when I realized you could have died and I hadn't been there with you." He pulled back and brushed my hair behind my ear. His eyes glistened, but no tears fell. "Tell me you won't do that again. Tell me you're going to play this smart and listen to the colonel."

I stiffened in his arms and pulled away under the pretense of pouring myself a glass of water at the kitchen sink.

Why was I hesitating? Hadn't I realized last night that I wasn't capable of pushing any harder? I could end this conversation right now, ease any tension between us by giving him what he wanted. But the words stuck in my throat. I couldn't set myself up to break another promise to him.

I downed a solid half-litre of water and set the glass on

the counter. "Are you here for you, or did Michael send you to make sure I followed orders like a good little soldier and stayed home?"

Hurt flashed in his eyes. "I'm here because I care about you. I can't watch you throw your entire career away because you let your emotions run the show."

My stubborn anger resurfaced, and I realized all my physical exertion hadn't worked out anything. I'd been distracting myself, expelling energy without facing the issues creating it. I don't know how long I would have kept it up, so maybe I had to thank Eric for stopping by and making me see the truth.

"I can't let the deaths in my squad go unanswered for," I said, doing my best to keep my voice level. Eric wasn't the problem. He wanted me to be safe, and I couldn't be angry with him for that. I just had to make him understand my side. "As far as I can see, the department's full resources aren't being tapped here. Did Michael tell you why I went to talk to Dougall a second time? Because I found out the syndicate's been playing our informants, and us along with them, and I wanted to see if he would confirm it. Because when I told the deputy minister what was going on, he treated the news like it was a budget proposal. Is his poker face that good? Maybe, but I wasn't going to take the chance he didn't believe me."

Eric dropped his gaze to the counter and picked at a chip in the wood. "Michael didn't tell me that, no. I can't blame you for being pissed off."

"Pissed off doesn't begin to describe it. Especially now that it's apparently my fault they missed their chance to bring him in. They didn't have to wait for Dougall to call them, but they did. Why? Because they had to wait for the ink to dry on the approval? Don't you feel the execs' priorities are in the wrong order? Process over justice. How is that right?"

"What about the other informants? Did they back up Dougall's statement?"

This was the interest I wanted to see. The curiosity for a puzzle that made no sense. There were too many pieces on the board to know which pawns belonged to which player, but with Eric behind me, I believed we could work it out.

I propped my hip against the island and crossed my arms. "Not to the same level of detail. The closest any of the others came was Rourke, who suspects the conversations he overheard were carried out for his benefit. Someone wanted him to come to us about de Lauer. Now Dougall's gone. He could be one of the plants, but it could also be the same thing happened to him that happened to Weldon, and the syndicate is cleaning house. Either way, that's what we were left with. A bunch of fake details that were never confirmed that led to ten people dead. Maybe more."

"So what do you think—no." Eric cut himself off and waved his hands in front of him. "No, I'm not falling into this trap."

Disappointment hit me like a slap in the face.

He rested a hand on the island, leaning towards me. "They were my guys, too, remember. We trained them together, and it kills me that we lost them. It kills me that we don't know why it happened. Don't you see, Jet? *I get it.* I get how tempting it is to follow these leads. The questions are right there, and we have everything we need to go after them. Everything except the training and—more important—the authority to do it."

"Fuck the authority," I snapped, losing whatever hold I'd had on my contained fury. "Isn't that the attitude you always have whenever you don't like the orders coming down the chain of command? How many times have I had to hold you back, talk you down? Now I'm telling you to go nuts, to cut the leash, and you're telling me to back off?"

Eric blinked, shocked speechless, and it took him a moment to pull himself together. "I don't know what scares me more— that we've switched places, or that you don't see how obsessed you are. What else can I say to make you realize continuing down this path is a stupid idea? It could get you and a lot of other people killed. Go for the psych eval. Talk to a doctor. Talk to Michael. You need help."

"Yes," I said. "I do. I need help finding out why half my team is dead." *And why my friend's future is at risk.*

He said he understood, but he didn't. If he did, we wouldn't be having this conversation. We'd be knocking on doors, asking questions, making the right people uncomfortable.

"Obviously your talk of rebellion and independent thought

was for show," I said. "I follow orders when they make sense. You follow them because you're too afraid of what will happen if you don't."

He jerked his head back, his eyes widening. Then his jaw flexed, and his expression went dark. "You know what? If you want to commit career suicide, fine, but you're not dragging me down with you."

His rejection left a bitter taste in my mouth, joining the acidity of shame I felt over what I'd said. He was watching out for me, but it was clear we wouldn't see eye to eye. Once we both calmed down, we'd go out for a few beers, talk it over, and no doubt wind up in bed, as close as we'd ever been, but right now I wanted nothing more than to get him out of my apartment.

"I think that's a smart move," I said, doing my best not to escalate things further. I didn't want to damage our friendship beyond repair, even if that meant biting my tongue. Because he wasn't wrong. I didn't want him going down with this potentially sinking ship. It wouldn't be fair to him or to the rest of the team. They would need a strong leader to take over if I wound up out of a job—or dead.

But my attempt to diffuse the situation only seemed to infuriate Eric more. He scowled, stormed towards the door, and wrenched it open.

With one foot in the hallway, he stopped and looked over his shoulder. "You haven't asked about your friend," he said, his tone bitter.

The muscles between my shoulder blades tensed. I didn't want to know. "What about him?"

"You might not have bothered to ask him, but we think he knows something about the setup. The deputy's ordered a team to find out everything he's learned since he crossed the border. We can't take the chance he'll hold something back and bring it to SilverGuard. He hasn't said anything yet, but he will. We've been given free rein to get him talking."

It was as though he'd taken out a knife and thrust it into my chest, turning it slowly, creating a piercing, distracting pain that overwhelmed everything else. He couldn't be implying what I thought he was, could he? Gideon wasn't the enemy. Yes, he was a spy and an asshole, and I was in a mood to crack a few comments about applying the thumbscrews, but not seriously. He'd hurt me, but he was only doing his job, the same as the rest of us.

I did my best to keep my expression neutral. "I wish you luck."

It was all I could say. To add anything else would not only challenge my ability to keep my cool but also give away any interest I had in what happened to him. I was already on thin ice for having cooperated with a foreign agent. I didn't need to make things worse by showing personal concern for him.

Eric stared at me, his eyes searching, but I gave him nothing. As long as my partner stood against me, I couldn't trust him. It broke my heart, set my entire world off balance, but I had to follow my gut.

When he didn't find what he was looking for, he turned on his heel and marched out, closing the door behind him.

Gideon knew the risks, I told myself again. He would have prepared for all possibilities, and SMOAC agents weren't cruel. We were a carefully regulated government department, under enough scrutiny by the powers that be that no real harm would come to him.

The logic was sound, and I allowed myself to relax. He would be uncomfortable for a while, but he would be fine. No doubt his ego would be brought down a few notches, and I had no problem with that.

I returned to my punching bag and hit it with so much force it swung into the lamp on the end table. The lamp fell to the floor and shattered, leaving me standing as one more shard in a pool of broken glass.

Chapter 26

Gideon

MY STOMACH GRUMBLED.

I shifted in my uncomfortable plastic chair and ignored my growing hunger. I knew what Jet's lover boy and his rookie partner were trying to do, but I'd been stuck in this situation too many times for them to get the better of me.

They thought if they kept me in this room long enough—the plain white walls, the cold metal table, the cuffs, the irritating rattle of the air-conditioning vent—I would tell them all the deep, dark secrets I'd pried out of my Canadian sources.

Sucked for them I hadn't learned anything useful. That they would consider useful, anyway. Although it hadn't been my primary mission, in working with Jet, I'd learned enough about how SMOAC operated to earn me a solid promotion, and I didn't intend to include these guys in my victory dance.

The first round of questions had gone well enough. Lieutenant Ken Doll, the one who'd wedged his way between me and Jet as though afraid I'd corrupt her with my presence, had left me with a few bruises he could be proud of—some to my face, but most to my pride—while his partner had done his best to lure me into his confidence. All either of them had gained was information they already suspected.

I could have misted out of here at any time, but I wanted to find out how much they knew.

So now I was stuck here waiting for round two. I debated coming up with a good story. A few well-placed lies to keep them chasing their tails. But—and I surprised myself—I didn't want to.

Maybe if fewer lives hung in the balance, maybe if Jet's team hadn't been sacrificed for one man's greed, I might have found a bit more enjoyment in jerking these guys around. As it was, all I wanted was to be left alone until they sent me back to New York. The sooner the better. What reason did I have to stick around? My secret was out, Jet knew the real reason I'd been tagging along with her—or at least, the only reason she needed to know—and by the look in her eyes when she'd learned the truth, there would be no point explaining or apologizing.

The breach of faith hurt. I knew I deserved it, I'd expected it, but it still came as a blow after what had passed between us. She'd risked her life to keep that ghost away from me. I'd watched her flag, falter, and only after she'd realized I was behind her had she thrown everything into keeping the powder back. And afterwards, the way she'd looked at me…

No point dwelling on it. The moment would never be repeated. All I could hope was that she at least pushed for me to be sent home unscathed, but I doubted I'd be that lucky.

Whatever. These guys might make a show of roughing me up a bit, but they were government officials, not some secret underground unit only the prime minister could unleash on the worst maggots of society. With SMOAC, there would be paperwork, and I wasn't worth a lot of it.

Though I was surprised Jet's lieutenant was involved at all. This was a job for the security office, not the task force. Obviously my connection to the captain had made things personal.

The door finally opened, and Sampson walked in, looking even stormier than he had the first time. His partner came in behind him, all goatee and stupid hair and dull brown eyes.

"We brought you something," Carstairs said, and tossed a vending machine sandwich on the table.

I tucked into it, not caring about the stale bread but forcing down the slightly off flavour of the mayo.

"Appreciated," I said, raising the sandwich in thanks. "Next time turkey on rye, if you don't mind."

Sampson dropped into the seat across from me, his blue eyes sharp and penetrating, his jaw working.

"Something bothering you?" I asked. I preferred to stay on the offensive. It was the best way to keep them out of my head.

"You," he said, but from him it didn't sound like a child

trying to push a bully around. He was stating a fact, not trying to get under my skin. "I can't say I like you being here. In this room, or in my country. You come up here without permission, nose around, spin your lies to a SMOAC task force captain, and yet you can sit here like none of that matters."

The faint twitch in the corner of his mouth when he mentioned Jet told me more than anything else. He was worried about her. Likely he thought I *had* corrupted her. The loyal lieutenant determined to blame the American spy for his captain's decision to ignore protocol.

"Don't you care how many people are dead?" His voice was still calm, but the slight strain gave away his anger. "How many more could die?"

I clasped my cuffed hands on the table around the empty sandwich wrapper. "I do, actually. I know you see me as the dark horse, the heartless American who came into your mosquito-infested woods to cause trouble, but the fact is we know what's at stake. We know what ghost can do, especially if it reaches our dealers and our cities in quantity. You think the death toll's been bad so far? Imagine the spike if it crosses the border. So, yes, I care, and that's why I'm here. To prevent that spread from happening."

I'd said more than I'd meant to, but still nothing they didn't already know.

"And you expect us to believe you've been here half the week and have nothing to show for it except the details you picked up with Captain Dawson?"

Another reference to Jet, another tic in his lip. Was he trying to get me to say something about her? If so, it wouldn't happen.

"You don't have to believe me. How long have you guys been tracking O'Malley? Years? You expect me to do in a week what you haven't done in all this time?"

Because you know I could, my tone said.

Sampson's fingers curled. I watched him, enjoying my win.

"In the end," I continued, "all I heard was the same Kingston rumour you've been chasing."

"Who told you about that?" Carstairs asked.

I snorted a laugh. "You expect me to give up my sources? Come on, gents, let's show a little professional courtesy."

Sampson slammed his fist on the table. "Stop wasting our time, Leigh. If you know anything about where O'Malley is or what he's doing—"

My pulse raced with impatience. "*You* stop wasting time. Do you think I would have been following your captain around if I had any solid leads of my own? O'Malley's outsmarting all of us. The closest we came was talking to a few of those informants, and you know how that ended up. So why don't you stop jacking off to impress your superiors and go after the guy who can actually give you the answers you're looking for? Go after Dougall. The fact he's missing tells me there's lots he failed to tell us."

Sampson's jaw clenched as we glared at each other. I was ready for him to reach across the table and grab me.

The moment passed, and a glint leached into his eyes as he sat back in his chair. "I went to see Jet this afternoon."

I swallowed and tried to force my tense shoulders to relax. From references to direct commentary. What was he aiming for?

"And how is the good captain doing after her latest brush with death?" I asked. If he wanted to drag her into this, we would play his game. What did I have to lose? They obviously shared their own complicated relationship, so he would only take it so far.

"She didn't give a shit about you, for one thing."

Ouch. The guy knew how to pack a punch, I'd give him that.

"That must be reassuring for you," I said, lobbing back. Cool, nonchalant, as though it didn't matter to me one way or another.

Carstairs looked between us, obviously trying to read between the lines and, by the confused look on his face, either failing or being tactful enough to pretend.

"As far as she's concerned, you're someone else's problem now."

"A stroke for your ego," I said. "Or is it for somewhere else?"

Sampson's anger returned with a snarl, and he half-rose out of his seat, his finger in my face. "Whatever you hoped to gain by pushing her to disobey orders, you failed. Your mission failed. Now you get to be our guest until we send you home.

No phone call, no room service, and no peace until you agree to help us out by telling us everything you know."

About fucking time, I thought, though I kept it to myself as I raised my cuffed hands so they could escort me to my cushy cell. At least there they would leave me by myself, and the minute their backs were turned, I could mist under the door and vanish from their lives forever. If Jet wasn't going to speak up for me, I would solve my own problems.

Instead of taking hold of me, however, Sampson smirked.

"With such a high-valued guest, we have to take certain precautions in transporting you. We can't take the chance you won't appreciate our hospitality."

His hand curled into a fist, and he banged on the door. It opened, and a grizzled soldier handed him a metal ring about fifteen inches wide and two inches thick. Sampson squeezed it and pulled, and the ring swung open on a heavy-duty hinge. Carstairs grabbed my arm and jerked me forward, and I eyed the ring warily. Was it some kind of tracking device like a leg monitor?

"Ever seen one of these before?" Sampson asked.

"Can't say I have," I said, proud that my voice didn't give away any of the nerves now curdling the questionable mayo in my stomach.

"A recent design. It releases a slight charge that blocks certain supernatural hormones, brain chemicals, that kind of thing." He shrugged. "Can't say I really understand how it works." He snapped the ring around my neck. The metal pinched and weighed down my shoulders, but the discomfort was nothing to the vibration that passed through me, almost taking my legs out from under me. "What I do know is that it blocks all supernatural ability, so you'll be wearing this little necklace every time you leave your cell to take a piss, every time you go for a breath of fresh air. Every time I damn well say so. For as long as you're here, you play by my rules."

His eyes were as cold and hard as diamonds.

It's fine. Once I'm in a cell, any crack in the wall is an exit.

I breathed easier. This discomfort was temporary. As soon as they closed the door on me, the collar would come off, and I was air.

"Carstairs, bring him down to holding. Cell C will do."

"Yes, sir," the soldier barked, and dragged me out of the room.

"Enjoy your stay," Sampson said, and then he was gone, away from my glower and any other quips I might have thrown at him.

Carstairs pulled me down the hallway and shoved me into the elevator. With every step, I tried to prove Sampson wrong, exerting my will to mist my hands, my neck. Trying to find even a fraction of wiggle room I could take advantage of.

"I'd look a little more nervous if I were you," Carstairs rumbled in my ear. "Your ass is ours now."

Something in the way he said it, the rough, sneering laugh

as his words trailed off, raised the hairs on my arms. Where was the dumb oaf who'd thrown me a sandwich? This guy was iron.

He tightened his grip on me, and when I tried to wrench away, he kicked out his leg and tripped me into the wall.

"Give me a reason," he said, and I froze. Not in a million years would I offer an excuse for him to kick my ass.

"That why the lieutenant threw the collar on me?" I asked through clenched teeth as Carstairs hauled me out of the elevator and down an empty hallway lined with thick doors.

"The lieutenant wants to make sure you're still around when it's time to send you home. He thinks you'll be safe enough behind a locked door. He has no idea."

As he pushed me past the door marked C, the already raised alarms in my head started screaming.

What was going on here? Was Sampson in on this? Did Jet know?

The desire to try to fight my way free made me stumble, but Carstairs's grip on my arm kept me on my feet.

"Careful. We wouldn't want you to hurt yourself." He chuckled, and the sound curdled my blood.

By this point, we'd left most of the cells behind us, with only a trio of them around the corner at the far end of the hallway. As far as possible from the security booth near the elevators. My heart was in my throat, bursting to get out. Sweat pooled under my arms and in the small of my back.

Something was wrong. None of this was how it was

supposed to play out.

Carstairs shoved me into the cell marked I, and I fell backwards, my back striking the cold stone floor.

I expected him to close the door and leave me alone in the dark, collared and cuffed, my abilities cut off. Part of me even believed this was a last attempt to intimidate me into telling him whatever I'd been holding back.

But he didn't leave. He stepped into the room with me, his dull brown eyes now filled with cruel excitement, his thin lips spread into a wide smile.

"The syndicate sends their regards," he said.

He closed the door behind him, and I dropped to my knees as an invisible fire consumed me.

Chapter 27

Madison

THE SETTING SUN cast a swath of light through my kitchen, and I drummed my fingers on the table as I waited for my phone to ring.

For the first time in my career, I'd played hooky from work, not yet ready to face Jean-Luc alone. I wanted to make sure my plans were in place in case I wound up without a job.

I understood his disappointment and anger about my working behind his back. Especially considering the way our attempted mission had ended. I'd used my experience and authority to gain access to information I had a full right to see, and passed it along to someone who had, admittedly, less of a right. But my reasons had been sound, and the results were undeniable. We had evidence that SMOAC had been set up for destruction.

What anyone did with that evidence remained to be seen, and at the moment, I didn't know if I would be around to catch the last act.

I'd spent my entire day making phone calls and arranging a few escape routes. From the time I was a child, my grandmother had taught me the importance of keeping my back to the wall. Trust was hard-earned, and to give it away freely was to risk losing everything. Until now, I'd thought she was paranoid and a little ridiculous, but as I stood in my condo, staring out over a city whose seams were fraying, I saw the importance of having a way out.

The syndicate knew too much about the inner workings of SMOAC—that stupid, untraceable, seemingly meaningless note told me that. After so many days of examining the message, the security team had been about to declare it a red herring and nothing more, but now we had a second ghostbomb and were no closer to uncovering the person who'd planted it. How much longer before the next threat on the note was carried out? Before they turned to *anyone connected to the queen*? To me.

I wasn't about to stop doing everything I could to maintain the reputation of the department, but I had to accept that my efforts might not come from the comfort of my office. If I wanted to stay here and play my part, I had to make sure my ass was covered. Disappear into the shadows until the dust settled so I could emerge and find new footing.

"And where do you think you could go that I would not find you?"

The queen's sultry voice made me jump, and when I turned

around, my apartment had been replaced with the familiar vivid meadow. Meril sat where she had before, on the smooth rock I had no option but to see as her throne.

My heart raced, my palms grew sweaty, and it took a great effort not to turn around and run screaming. There was nowhere for me to go.

"I wouldn't think of hiding from you, Your Majesty," I said, as though it weren't my greatest wish.

Her lip twitched, but no amusement touched her eyes. "I am relieved to hear it. I would not be best pleased to know one of my people was attempting to evade my summons."

I squared my shoulders. "Is that why you've brought me here?"

"That remains to be seen," she said. "Sercario provided me with your update and his request that I leave you be, but I'm not satisfied with what I've seen. A second attack, Madison. Rising discontent among my people on this side of the wall. No steps taken to subdue their dissatisfaction. You have heard what's being said? My rule is in question."

I swallowed hard. Nan had said as much, but I'd hoped the talk was quiet enough for the queen's people to have missed it. Wishful thinking. Her growing anger meant our position had become more precarious.

Meril rose to her feet and, faster than should have been possible, stood in front of me. "I cannot allow this dissension, granddaughter. I *will not* allow the questioning of my authority.

Is this clear?"

"Yes, Your Majesty."

"You speak of taking action, of finding the truth, yet here you sit making plans to flee? I will not have it. Tell me why I should not summon you this very moment. At least on the Council, you might achieve something."

Heat burned under my cheeks. "It has only been a few days, Your Majesty, and we've learned much, even if it's not apparent in the reports. The department has a leak. We don't know yet how widespread, but it's there."

"All the more reason to shut things down and reclaim my control."

"To do so would make your people on this side of the wall lose faith, Your Majesty." It was a gamble to say so without rousing her ire, but I had to try. "They see the department as a stronghold. To shut us down would tell them they were never protected. That your side allowed this one to falter. SMOAC has to be saved. I can save it."

Big words, and I said them with a confidence I didn't feel, but it was enough to make Meril pause, her emerald gaze appraising. I held my breath until she nodded.

"Very well. You have one last chance, but I demand progress."

Before I could promise anything, my phone rang. The meadow vanished, and I was in my apartment, the phone vibrating against the table.

"Prince," I said, my voice shaking as hard as my hand.

"That you, Madi?" a familiar voice said, and I let out a slow breath of relief as I settled into my twisted reality.

"Gary, what have you got for me?"

Gary Covent was one of the best-connected gnomes in the city. He was a fixer, and one that had sworn his undying loyalty to my family for once keeping him out of trouble. I never imagined I would be the one putting that loyalty to the test.

"A great place," he said. "Right in the heart of Centretown where no one will think to look for you. It's been empty for a while, so move-in ready. I can get the apartment furnished by tomorrow, and it'll be there whenever you need it."

"What about the car?"

"A plain, boring Dodge. Not fast or flashy, but reliable. I've had her sitting in my garage for a few years but kept her tuned, so she's in good shape. I'll leave her at the apartment building. Just… try not to lose her, yeah? I wouldn't mind getting her back when you're done with her."

"I promise," I said.

"I was going to throw the keys in the mail but don't want to chance them being intercepted. Give me a shout when you need them, and I'll meet you at the apartment along with the paperwork you asked for."

"Thank you, Gary." The gnome tended to be overcautious at the best of times, but right now, I appreciated his suspicious nature.

"I don't know what's going on," he said, "but if it's anything to do with what's on the news lately, I'm proud to be of service. People… they're getting riled."

"What have you heard?" I'd hardly turned off the news in days, but I knew he didn't mean the local broadcast. He picked up information from every group across the city, a hub of gossip and rumour, with enough legitimate intel to make his stories worthwhile.

"Bits and pieces. The department hasn't done a great job putting people at ease about the de Lauer incident, and now this thing in Nepean." He scoffed. "Hantavirus. Did they really think we'd buy that? It was ghost again, wasn't it?"

I didn't bother to ask how he knew. "Yes."

"I'm not the only one who suspects it. These attacks are getting out of control, and people—the regular folk trying to go about their business—are losing patience. They need to trust that their government will keep them safe, or that Meril will help us if the department fails." No, they didn't want that. They really didn't. "None of us wants to be in a position where we need to protect ourselves. That's how shit gets messy. One person—just one—uses magic or some other ability to keep themselves alive, and next thing you know, it's all over the news and the perception filters vanish. But if the department and the queen aren't doing anything, what choice do we have?"

I closed my eyes, and Meril's voice echoed through my head. *One last chance.*

"I know, Gary. I'm doing what I can."

"I believe you are."

I hung up and buried my face in my hands.

He was right. Everything he said echoed the minister's concerns and pinpointed the cause of Meril's wrath. The divide between mundane and supernatural was too wide—a veritable chasm. That was why SMOAC had been created in the first place. If a fight broke out between us, the supernaturals might have the upper hand to start, but how many of us would choose to run rather than fight? How long could those remaining on the battlefield withstand the mundane weapons that rivalled many of our abilities?

And once word got out in Canada, the filters around the world would falter. It would be a global war, and the only choice would be to die or evacuate to the realm, which would struggle to handle the influx. As for the mundanes left behind, they'd have to face whatever supernaturals decided to stay and fight, without any of the protections departments like SMOAC kept in place.

I gave myself a shake as the vision of possibilities reached its bloody conclusion and returned my attention to a city that had no idea of the sword hanging over its skyline.

This investigation was far bigger than drugs and a crime syndicate. And now the people were questioning Meril's leadership as well?

The minister wanted me to sit this out? Fine. But I hoped he knew what he was doing.

Chapter 28

Jet

AFTER TAKING THE broken lamp as a sign the punching bag wasn't helping, I spent a good half-hour in the shower trying to scald my emotions away. That didn't work either. I was still on edge, still an emotional wreck, and my belongings were in mortal peril. I had to get out of the house, go somewhere I was unlikely to get into trouble.

First a coffee to clear my head, and then I would sit down and figure out what to do next.

I grabbed my phone and wallet and headed out, then nearly stepped back in when the humidity of the day wrapped around my throat and squeezed. Within minutes, all the sweat I'd washed off had returned. People on the street shuffled along as though the rising temperature had stolen their motivation. Being trained to move with purpose, I wanted to shove them out of the way, but where did I have to go? I'd been unofficially suspended. Put out to pasture for a rest. I had no orders, no mission. Was this what vacation was like? And people did this voluntarily?

I treated myself to an iced coffee and took it to a park bench, planning to sit for a while and watch the world go by, but with nothing else to hold my attention, my mind was soon racing, trying to put together who might have betrayed us to O'Malley.

And where did Dougall fit in?

The possibility he was another victim made me eager to find him and make sure he was all right, but the thought that he had looked me in the eye and expressed fear and *sympathy*, made me want to heave my over-sweet drink across the park. Had the fucker played me? If that were the case, he'd better hope I never tracked him down.

I wondered if Rourke had heard anything about what had happened to him, or if rumours were flying around The Afterlife about where the skittish snitch might be.

It was too early in the day to swing by the club, but Rourke wasn't my only resource. Michael might have booted me off the task force, might have recruited new soldiers without me, but he couldn't silence my team. I couldn't ask questions that might involve them in my disobedience, but there would be chatter in the group chat.

My hands trembled as I reached for my phone, and I clasped them together until they stilled. I was running on fumes and fury. Exhaustion and grief had worn me out, but rage kept the fire burning. I had to bring this to an end. Gideon believed SMOAC wasn't capable of taking the syndicate down, but I would be damned if I'd let him scurry home to tell his bosses they were right. I'd relied too much on his help, but that was over now. Even if I had to do this by my goddamned self, I was going to prove him wrong, find out the truth about Dougall, and blow the syndicate so wide open they'd be scrambling to put themselves back together for the next decade.

It took me a few tries to unlock my phone, but I finally opened the group chat and scrolled up through the messages to where I'd last checked in. Normally there would have been too many conversation threads to make scrolling beyond the last few hours worthwhile, but as the chat was still quiet, it didn't take me long to reach the flurry of reactions to my message.

HEY, Jason wrote, THE CAPTAIN'S BREATHING!

BREATHING AND GIVING ORDERS. OF COURSE YOU'D MAKE US RUN, PL, said Inez.

YOU COMING TO THE MEMORIAL? Sara asked.

A few hours later, Jason wrote, AND SHE'S GONE AGAIN. ANYONE ELSE GET THEIR 10K TODAY?

I DID, wrote Adam. EASY ENOUGH WHEN YOU'RE MOTIVATED. IF OUTRUNNING GHOST CLOUDS IS PART OF MY JOB DESCRIPTION NOW, FUCKING RIGHT I'M WORKING TO BEAT MY TIME.

My heart ached that he wasn't wrong.

FUCKING HELL, Jason wrote yesterday afternoon. ANOTHER

BOMB? ANYONE HEARD FROM PL? SHE WAS THERE, RIGHT?

SHE WAS THERE, said Eric. SHE'S FINE. SHE CONTAINED THE POWDER, AND THE HOUSE HAS BEEN LOCKED DOWN. NO CASUALTIES.

WHAT THE FUCK IS GOING ON IN THIS CITY? Inez asked. HOW ARE THESE ASSHOLES GETTING THEIR HANDS ON SO MUCH GHOST?

THEY MUST HAVE ACCESS TO THE SOURCE, Sara said. IF O'MALLEY ISN'T JUST DEALING IT BUT PRODUCING IT, THAT WOULD EXPLAIN THE QUANTITY.

AND THE QUALITY, wrote Adam. THE EFFECT IT HAD—HOW HARD IT HIT. BUDDY OF MINE IN THE LAB TOLD ME TEST RESULTS CAME BACK. THAT SHIT WAS PURE.

GREAT, said Jason. JUST WHAT WE NEED. O'MALLEY WITH THE GHOSTMAKER IN HIS POCKET.

Goosebumps bubbled on my arms. The Ghostmaker. The moniker had floated around the department for a while, but never had it hit me like this. Too many phantoms now haunted the basement of the de Lauer building for it not to.

And Sara was right. He had to be here in the city. The speed with which the drug was moving had to mean it was manufactured right here in Ottawa. Even if the Kingston rumour was true, that was only a couple hours away.

What if Gagnon's people were going about this backwards? They were chasing O'Malley, but maybe they should have been hunting the Ghostmaker. Someone had to know who it was, and I was going to find the son of a bitch. I had to. All day I'd tried sitting around, waiting for an update, and the echoes of my screaming squad had nearly pushed me to the brink of madness. Dougall was in the wind, the department was focused on the syndicate. This was something I could do, to hell with the consequences.

A text message from Michael popped up, and I saw it was the third one he'd sent since this morning.

Dawson, report 1300, he'd sent around eight o'clock. At one-fifteen he'd sent, Dawson, not like you to be late. You home? The last message read: Worried about you, kid. Hope you're not doing anything you shouldn't. Call me.

I debated obeying him. How easy it would be to call him and tell him my idea. Let him pass it on to security or Gagnon, go home and crawl into bed. While Madison chased the clock. While Eric did what he felt necessary to get information out of Gideon. While my squad suffered the pain of not knowing why their world had been ripped out from under them.

An asshole was out there whose knowledge of chemistry could kill thousands of people with a well-timed breeze. If there was any chance I could learn where he was hiding, I would do it.

That irritating voice in the back of my mind nagged at me about orders and discipline, but I shrugged it off. I'd been ordered away from O'Malley, but no one had said anything about the Ghostmaker.

I walked home and headed straight for the parking garage. Dougall might have been compromised, but one of the other informants might know something. And if I was lucky, they'd be willing to tell me the whole truth now that one of their fellow snitches had gone missing. Nothing like a bit of fear for one's life to get the lips flapping.

I followed the same pattern Gideon and I had taken the other day, starting in South Keys.

It was strange to make the trip without someone in the passenger seat. Without Gideon. Angry as I was with him, I couldn't deny I'd appreciated his confident presence at my side. Someone to bounce ideas around with. Someone who didn't need me looking over his shoulder all the time. Exactly what I looked for in a partner.

Now, instead of being here, he was buried somewhere in the SMOAC building, being pried for information.

I doubted they'd learn anything. Gideon was a lying ass, but he was a good security officer. While he might want to dick around with them to ruin their day, if he thought he could get what he wanted by cooperating, he would, and since what he wanted was to keep ghost from crossing the border, he had no reason to hold back.

Unless he'd lied about that, too.

I set my prickling anger aside as I pulled into Mitchel Lafontaine's driveway and turned off the car. For a moment, I sat still and stared at the house. The windows were dark, with no sound or movement to draw my attention. I opened my third eye to scan the property, and though I sensed no suffocating energy like I had at Dougall's place, there had definitely been cars and people here recently.

It might mean nothing, but Lafontaine hadn't struck me as the social type.

"Shit."

I reached for my knife beside my seat and hooked the sheath over my belt. The house appeared empty, but I wasn't about to take chances. Especially not when I was on my own.

No motion-sensor lights turned on when I got out of the car, so the driveway remained in shadow as I made my way towards the side of the house.

As I passed the porch, I took in the broken steps and noted that a heavy weight had snapped through another one.

I raised my hands in response, ready to draw the air around me. The muscles in my shoulders and back cursed the anticipation of further strain, but I gritted my teeth and sucked it up. No one was getting the jump on me. I was tired of being hit by the unexpected.

The path to the backyard was open, and my third eye picked up shadows of two people passing through as recently as twenty-four hours ago. If I had to guess, Lafontaine's guests had arrived while the minister was giving me shit for ignoring protocol. I knew I should call it in. I should get back in the car, call Michael, and let him decide how to proceed. I'd come here for information, not for another showdown with whatever waited inside.

I hesitated, glanced at the car, refocused on the vague shadows that moved around me, heading to the back door...

Fuck it. Somehow protocol had led people to our informant's house. Possibly two of our informants' houses, if Dougall was a victim.

If Lafontaine was inside, I couldn't waste time waiting for a team.

I pushed the back door open and immediately turned my head away from the thick reek of blood.

"Mitchel?" I called. There was no answer.

The shadows snuck in ahead of me. Then another shape came in at the other end of the kitchen. Had Lafontaine heard them with his keen ears? Come into the kitchen to see who it was?

I could still leave. If Lafontaine were here and injured, he would have answered my call. There was no reason for me to stay, no rush for the team to arrive.

What about his dog?

It was Mac the Rottweiler that decided me.

With a roll of my shoulders, I allowed my emotions to fall away. Fear, compassion, empathy—none of them mattered right now. My task was to find out what had happened.

The kitchen was dark, so I felt for the light switch, my stomach twisting as my fingers brushed against something sticky.

The sight that greeted me when the ceiling light turned on was worse than anything my imagination had prepared for.

Blood was everywhere. The cracked vinyl on the chairs was spattered, as was the top of the cluttered table. The refrigerator door, the case of beer on top of the fridge, the floor, the walls. Everything.

I breathed through my mouth and followed the drying trail through the room, careful of where I stepped. If anything about this mess could help pin down the people who had created it, I didn't want to disturb it.

"Hello?" I called again, just to be sure.

For Mitchel's sake, I hoped he was dead. I couldn't think of any reason to keep him breathing that wouldn't make for a really bad night.

A bark came from the basement, and I heaved a sigh of relief. At least Mac was alive.

I hit the light and made my way down. The stairs creaked under my weight, and I slowed my pace. If anyone waited for me below, I didn't want them to know my every move. Though when I reached the bottom, my guard relaxed. There was nowhere for anyone to hide. The space was well lit, with a ratty couch in front of a giant flat-screen TV. All the life and person-ality missing from upstairs was down here, where Lafontaine had made a home for himself.

Mac was in the middle of the room, unchained and at full

attention. If anyone with evil intentions had tried to come down here, I suspected the dog would have torn their throat out.

In front of him was a very dead Lafontaine.

Bile threatened to rise at the sight of Mitchel's torn up corpse. Whoever had killed him hadn't been kind, yet somehow he'd dragged himself downstairs so he could die where he felt most comfortable, his canine instincts coming through.

Mac barked as I approached, and I went still. "Remember me?" I asked. "I'm not going to hurt him."

He huffed but didn't move as I knelt by Lafontaine's side and scanned his body, not touching anything. His face was cut up, with a gash that travelled from the base of his chin down his chest. More wounds covered his arms and had slashed through his sweatpants. Bruises had started to form beneath them.

"Come here, love," I said, stretching my hand towards Mac. He growled at me first, but when I didn't move, he let out a whimper and padded closer. Blood matted his fur, but I didn't see any injuries and he appeared to be moving all right.

"Did you see who did this?" I asked.

I wasn't expecting an answer, but when the dog tapped the floor twice, I paid attention.

"Two people?"

Mac nodded. What the hell was I dealing with? Not only the dead adlet on the floor, but an intelligent canine as well?

A suspicion entered my mind. "You weren't his pet, were you? Brother?" The dog barked, and my heart twinged. "I'm sorry."

Adlets themselves were rare, with genetics leaning towards a human shape with varying degrees of canine features. To have a canine born with a human mind was even rarer, and I imagined incredibly frustrating for the lack of easy communication. Lafontaine was probably one of the few people who understood Mac without trouble, and now he was dead.

"Do you have any other family you can stay with?"

The dog barked and whimpered, then nudged Lafontaine's body with his nose.

I didn't know if that meant yes or no.

"You can come home with me if you need a place to crash."

What the hell. It was better than being alone, and he couldn't stay here.

But Mac tossed his head and backed away. His gesture was clear: He would either stay to guard his brother or find somewhere else, but he was no responsibility of mine.

I rose to my feet and stared at the corpse, one more among the too many I'd seen this week. "I'm sorry for what happened. I swore to seek justice for O'Malley's victims, and Mitchel's now on that list. The people who did this won't get away with it."

The dog growled, a deep, sinister sound that raised the hairs on my arms, even though I knew the warning wasn't for me.

I left Mac to his vigil and returned upstairs. Once I got to my car, I called the police, identifying myself as a neighbour out for a walk. The mundane cops would show up first, but it wouldn't be long before the department followed. By the time they did, I would be long gone.

I left Lafontaine's place with my stomach in knots, extra motivated to track down the other informants.

But luck continued to kick my ass.

At my second stop, I found the hobgoblin's apartment door ajar. The place was empty, and all I found was a half-eaten brownie on a plate.

O'Malley's hairstylist was another dead end. When I drove past the salon, the place was roped off and surrounded by cop cars, their lights flashing red and blue through my windshield.

Until that point, I'd kept my fear under control, but as the paramedics rolled a sheet-draped stretcher outside, my heart jumped into my throat.

Rourke.

I sped downtown with full disregard for streetlights and stop signs and arrived at The Afterlife within fifteen minutes.

I expected to find it quiet, but the parking lot was full. Apparently the fact it was a weeknight made no difference to the crowds that frequented the club. I was grateful. It would be a lot easier to disappear in the rush. I couldn't afford to be recognized by O'Malley's people again.

I pushed my way to the bar only to find Rourke's barstool,

the one that had formed the shape of his ass over the years, had been taken over by a slim blonde with an obnoxious laugh and a dress that didn't so much cover as showcase. Either Rourke had undergone a massive change since I'd last seen him or he made number five in the missing column.

Shit.

I scanned the room, hoping to spot him coming back from the can, and my gaze fell on four familiar faces standing against the far wall. Some people might think it was crazy of me to try to get information out of people with whom I had so recently mopped the floor, but I didn't feel crazy. I'd gone well past crazy a few hours ago.

Mike pushed away from the wall and crossed his arms as I approached, glowering down at me.

"You've got balls coming back here," he said.

"That's the best compliment I've gotten all week." I stepped closer. "Where's Rourke?"

His face twisted with disgust. "Who?"

My pulse raced. I wanted to slam this guy's head against the wall to get him to stop fucking with me, but I couldn't cause a scene. The need to go slow, to charm and persuade, tugged at my patience, but for Rourke's sake, I had to try.

"Rourke. You know, the permanent fixture. Your buddy at the bar you were oh-so-worried about last night."

"Oh, that beta. How the fuck would I know? You show up here, talk to him, and he leaves a few minutes after you, never to be seen again."

That stopped me. "He left on his own?"

"Well, he didn't get escorted out by any gorgeous chicks, I'll tell you that much."

If he left right after me and Gideon, he might have made himself scarce without giving the syndicate a chance to do it for him. It could mean he was alive. At this point, any plan I had of getting information had vanished, so the most I could hope was that Rourke, at least, still breathed.

"Thanks," I said vaguely as I walked away.

"Hey, what—" he called after me, but I pushed through the dancing crowd to Rourke's place at the bar and used my hip to shove the blonde out of the way.

"Ex*cuse* me," she said as I nudged her stool a few inches to the left.

I ignored her scoffing and tried to put myself in Rourke's shoes. Working on the assumption he'd left of his own free will, he must have guessed someone would come after him. But he also might have guessed I'd come back.

Had he been so forward-thinking?

I ran my fingers under the bar, crouching down to see if he'd left any kind of message, details he hadn't felt safe saying in person, but I came up empty. Of course I had. He was too smart for that. I wouldn't have been the only one looking.

Pursing my lips, I leaned against the bar and passed one last look around the room. Where else would he have thought to leave me something?

My fingers traced the scarred bartop, most of the engravings worn down by years of spilled drinks, elbows, and cleaning rags. One message was fresh.

Looking closer, I made out a few rough cuttings in the wood, not neat enough to have been done with a knife, but maybe… I cast my mind back to last night, to my fight with Mike and his friends. The bottle one of them had tried to smash over my head. There would have been glass all over the floor. Perfect to carve a few words into the aged wood.

In a misshapen heart, someone had written *M.O. + ?* And beneath it, the words *Think big.*

Really, Rourke? That's all you're giving me?

I set my hand over the scrawl and opened my third eye, hoping some hint of him remained. Flashes of the blonde woman slipping something into her date's drink, a series of other faceless, nameless shadows. They grew hazier as I travelled further back, to the point where I doubted I would see anything useful, but then, finally, there. A mere glimpse of Rourke's face. He was sitting with the shard of glass, looking calm as you like as he drank his beer and carved these shapes into the wood. As though it had nothing to do with why I had been there, just a way for him to pass the time. He looked up, and a flash of fear filled his eyes. He set to work a bit faster, finished, threw the shard down, and grabbed his jacket.

Whether he'd actually made it out before whatever scared

him had gotten him, I couldn't be sure, but I crossed my fingers. The man deserved that much.

I patted the bartop, smacked Blondie's date's drink so it spilled onto the floor, and made my own escape.

As I headed back to the car, I brushed past a dumpster that had been pulled out of the alley for trash disposal and never put back. At the contact, more flashes passed through my open third eye. *Drunks taking a leak. People having sex. Rourke.*

I froze and pressed my palm against the metal, directing my focus. He wore the same jacket he'd grabbed in my last vision of him. *Looking over his shoulder. Grabbed. Slammed against the dumpster. Blood. Bruises. Broken nose. Punching a hulking shadow. Another punch. A move to run. Almost out of reach. A hand grabbing him. A fist to the jaw. Sagging down. Not moving. Body picked up. Thrown into the dumpster.*

Fuck.

Warm tears rolled down my cheeks, and I clenched my fists as I bowed my head. It wasn't fair. Too many people were dead, and I had been leashed. I wanted to march into O'Malley's office, grab him by the collar, and slam my knee into his face. I wanted to gather his lackeys and shut them in a room with the surviving members of my squad. After they'd had their fill, I would close the door, seal the windows, and release enough ghost that O'Malley's thugs would be forced to suffer the same end as my pack.

It was too much. It needed to stop.

I just had to figure out how to stop it, because I'd reached the end of the obvious road. All my leads were dead. What did it mean that the syndicate was wiping out SMOAC sources? Why bother? Each of our informants had told the story O'Malley's people had wanted them to tell. What more could they have told us?

Think big, Rourke had written. How big? How many more people were involved?

My thoughts turned to Madison and Gideon, and my blood chilled. How far would the syndicate go to silence the people chasing them?

Chapter 29

Gideon

UNSEEN FIRE LICKED at my feet, the relentless tongues shooting agony through my blood, up my calves, my thighs, into my groin. A scream burst out of my chest despite my efforts to hold it back, and I jerked at the chains that suspended me from the ceiling.

How many hours had passed since the door had slammed shut? Six? Seven?

The block under my feet shifted, but the sensation of ice biting my toes lingered.

An illusion, I told myself for the hundredth time, but it didn't matter that my eyes saw the plain wooden crate. Not when the man in front of me had climbed into my brain and fucked around with my pain receptors. He could make me feel whatever he wanted, and the twisted son of a bitch was enjoying it.

Twice, the deep cuts of his knife had filled me with a pleasure so deep and unbearable I'd arched deeper into the blade, but the rest of the time he'd stuck with pain. Blinding, nauseating torment from the smallest, gentlest touches.

When the latest wave subsided, I couldn't keep my head up, but when I dropped my chin to my chest, my shoulders screamed at the contorted, weight-bearing stretch.

"Come on, Leigh," Carstairs said. "Play with me. It's no fun if you don't play."

He brushed his belt across my chest. The contact was minimal, barely a scratch, but it may as well have been a thousand nails biting into my flesh, through my ribs, out my back. The warmth of blood from earlier attacks trickled down my stomach and between my legs, though by now I guessed there wasn't much of me that wasn't red.

I coughed and spat out a mouthful of blood, hocking it at his feet. He laughed, his bellowing guffaw filling the tiny stone room.

"I love it when they try," he said, coming close enough for his lips to brush my ear, his breath sending tiny sparks through my head. "They all think they can outlast me. They all think their minds are strong enough to keep me out, but bit by bit, I'm going to eat away at you until you break and all you know is pain."

More blood filled my mouth and spilled down my chin.

He chuckled, the vibration as violent as if I were standing

front row at a heavy metal concert. "You didn't think you were getting out of here alive, did you?"

I clenched my teeth, refusing to let him see my reaction. I'd known the truth the moment he'd stripped me naked and chained me to the ceiling.

How had the syndicate infiltrated SMOAC? Had O'Malley planned this the whole time? Was that why they'd targeted Jet's team—to clear the way for new recruits?

The questions came to me in starts and stops, vague ideas that followed the ebb and flow of nausea.

The thought of Jet did nothing to make my agony more bearable. SilverGuard had ordered me to stay here and learn what she knew. Now she was out there, free and unhurt, while I was left to suffer for the barest tidbits of information.

Bitter rage revived me to my current situation in time to hear the whistle of the belt coming down again. The leather strap struck against my bare ass cheeks, causing my toes to curl, which made them brush against the wooden block, which sent more pain up my calves. I wriggled on my chains, struggling to escape even though I knew there was no way out.

I was trapped here, unable to take a breath, unable to block out the overstimulation of every cell in my body.

The desire to mist away—the inability to follow the instincts that had guided me for thirty-six years—robbed me of coherent thought. The best I could hope for was that consciousness would leave me, but as my mind grew hazy, the pain vanished, replaced by a pleasure that made me gasp.

"You're not leaving me already, are you?" Carstairs pushed the tip of his knife deeper into my side. "We're just getting started."

The sharp edge of ecstasy brought Jet to mind again, and in the brief window of reprieve, my anger stilled. I pictured her face, the depth of her dark eyes, the softness of her skin. I imagined touching her, being anywhere but in this hell that was about to destroy me.

The pleasure faded, and pain returned in a clawing, rasping invasion that made me scream until my voice grew hoarse.

Carstairs laughed. "That's more like it. Scream as much as you need to. It lets me know I'm doing my job."

I clamped down on my tongue so hard more blood pooled in my mouth, and I swallowed the next wave of yells.

He dragged the tip of his knife down my chest, leaving a trail as though I were being branded.

"Suit yourself. I just hate these empty silences." He touched the knife tip to the top of my thigh, and a hiss pierced through my teeth, but nothing more. He shook his head in disappoint-ment, then said, "All right, how about I tell you a story instead? Once upon a time, there was a task force captain who liked to stick her nose where it didn't belong. Her commander tried to protect her from all the big bad wolves, but little did anyone know, the wolves had already found their way in."

His lips were against my ear as his blade pressed into my

gut. My vision flickered, but he adjusted, dropping the pain enough for me to stay conscious.

"The only person who could warn her was caught by the biggest, baddest wolf of them all, leaving the widdle heartbwoken captain to fend for herself." He chuckled again, the sound enough to turn my stomach the way nothing else had. "She still has a chance, you know. We need her to play by the rules. If she does, we stay hidden and she gets to keep breathing. If not…" He shrugged and stepped away. "I'll leave you alone for a little while to think over her odds. Can't wear you out on our first day, can we?"

He reached up and released the chains. I dropped to the floor like a sack of meat, my elbows and knees hitting the stone slabs with a fresh burst of pain. My shoulders and back fell into spasm, and blood rushed through my arms, setting them burning with pins and needles.

"Try to get some sleep. You'll need the energy for later."

He blew me some air kisses before slamming the door shut, and darkness descended around me. No light came in from under the door and there were no windows. All I could focus on were the faint scratching of mice somewhere in the walls and the pain. So much pain. The cold stone under my bare skin, the drying blood that cracked with every movement, the throbbing in my head, my back, my gut.

My thoughts were hazy with exhaustion, but beneath the fog was a terror that made every wound a paper cut in comparison. Not for me—I was stuck here—but for Jet.

There was no way in hell she was going to sit back and let other people take over. For a day or so, maybe, but the questions we'd raised together would nag at her. Eventually she would be driven to hunt down more leads, and when she did, I worried about what she would find. Or what would find her.

The epiphany hit me as the shock wore off, and my body convulsed with shivers.

The reason the syndicate was always so many steps ahead, the reason I'd been given to Carstairs as a squeaky toy instead of being sent home: the mole was someone high enough in the department to give orders.

As soon as that one puzzle piece became clear, so much more fell into place. How the syndicate had known who SMOAC's informants were, how to feed them information, how to use them to spread rumours no one could confirm to waste the department's resources. They knew who to target and how because someone on the inside was directing them.

The adlet's story came back to me, his voice echoing against the bare walls of my cell. Two alphas in the alley. One used to giving orders being put down by someone higher in the ranks. O'Malley had to be one of them, but who was the other?

And how far had the infestation spread? Was it only false information and heavy-handed enforcers, or had someone in the minister's office climbed right into O'Malley's bed? Bastien himself?

As the heat of my pain subsided, a deep cold settled over me. I pulled my knees towards my chest, hissing with every stretch and pull of torn skin, and wrapped my arms around them to try to ease the tremors.

How had I gotten into this mess? I'd come here for information and made the mistake of being honest with SilverGuard about Jet's determination. Now here I was, trapped in the dark with death as my only escape.

Self-pity hovered around me, but I summoned enough anger to chase it away. The fury warmed my blood and cleared some of the fog, growing stronger as I played through every step that had brought me to this point, every bad decision.

Fuck them all.

The collar shifted as I trembled, its effects choking me, suffocating me.

Fuck Jet for saying nothing when they took me away.

Fuck me for not being honest with her from the start about why I was here.

And fuck whoever tried to lay a hand on her.

Another wave of fear passed over me as I thought about what Carstairs had said. She was more than capable of handling herself, but this went beyond a raid or an organized mission. She was buzzing too close to the hornet's nest. How long did she have before she woke the hive and got stung?

Chapter 30

Madison

I LEANED BACK in my office chair and stared at the paperwork scattered across my desk. I'd sat in the same position for so many hours, I was surprised I hadn't left a permanent imprint.

Not that I was seeing much of anything in front of me.

I'd come into the office hoping to find something I could take directly to the minister about Jet's discovery. A leak in the department. We'd been compromised.

I'd promised to stay out of it, but Meril's warning made keeping that promise impossible.

Without knowing how the syndicate was getting its information or how it might be dealing dirty with our negotiations, I was scrambling in the dark for where to start looking, but sorting through files was better than sitting at home waiting for the queen to change her mind about letting me handle this.

I glanced at my watch, and fatigue hit me as I read the

arrows pointing to six o'clock. My day was only starting when it should have been winding down. Just another example of how our world had turned topsy-turvy.

Jean-Luc had left a message for me to join him in his office fifteen minutes ago, but he'd been in a meeting since four, so I wasn't rushing. The odds of him being on time were slim, and I didn't want to be stuck alone with Phyllis longer than I had to.

As it was, his EA wasn't happy to let me wait for him outside his office when I arrived.

"He's not in," she said, her grey eyes steely. Her innocent white hair was pulled into a harsh bun, and her cozy pink sweater belied the hard-ass underneath.

"The minister asked me to meet him here," I said.

"I don't see that there's any point. His meeting will probably run a while yet."

Phyllis and I rarely saw eye to eye at the best of times, but this push to send me away was new. No doubt she'd heard about my role in the Dougall fiasco. Who in the office hadn't by now? She probably thought I'd jeopardized Jean-Luc's standing in the cabinet, which explained her increased disdain. It was almost an election year, and a minister couldn't be too careful about how they and their department were perceived.

I readied a few choice words about what the public would have thought if the second ghostbomb had wiped out a suburban block, but was saved the trouble by Jean-Luc's return.

"Ah, Madison, you're here. Good. Sorry I'm late. Phyllis,

you'll get those complaint files sorted for me, won't you?"

He gestured to the stack of paper on her desk. She didn't spare it a glance, her sour glare fixed firmly on me. "Yes, sir."

"Good, good. Madison, come on in."

I followed him into his office, and he closed the door behind me. The moment he sank into his chair, his upright posture sagged into a slouch. I wished I could read him, but the security measures around his office blocked any kind of telepathic, empathic, or psychic ability. All I had to work with was what he showed me, and what I saw broke my heart.

"Thank you for coming in today," he said. "I understand why you may not have wanted to, but the office isn't as sane when you're not here. We need some grounding. Also, your father called yesterday to ask how you were doing, and I realized I didn't know, which made me very uncomfortable."

I was touched by his concern, but braced for the other shoe to drop.

"I'm well, thank you. Trying to stay busy. Do my part."

"Have you heard from Captain Dawson?" His yellow eyes locked on mine, and I flushed.

"Not since yesterday." Had he hoped to catch me going against his orders? For all that he was worried about me, worry I knew was genuine, he was still the head of the department with rules he expected to be followed.

"I hope she's recovering well," he said, surprising me. "From what I hear, she prevented a catastrophe by containing the powder. The way the bomb was set up, it would have reached the street before anyone else could have stopped it." He sighed and passed a hand over his face. "You've seen the news?"

"Yes, sir," I said, trying to keep up with his rapid subject changes.

"Then you know the public is losing faith in us, in the system we've created. We're facing increasing civil unrest as more provinces react to the attacks. The families of the fallen soldiers are demanding answers and compensation. The one we can and will arrange, but the other…" He shook his head and looked at me. "What do we do?"

I started. "You're asking me? Do about what? The attacks? We work to find the people behind them, just as you're already doing."

He held my stare. "I mean about the queen."

My heart sank. It always came back to her. Even when she wasn't involved, she was involved.

"My sources tell me she hasn't shown any sign of crossing the wall," I said, leaving my personal insight out of it. He didn't need more to worry about. "As long as we keep panic to a minimum and take immediate steps to resolve the matter, it will stay that way."

Jean-Luc relaxed. "That is one concern off my mind. If I can focus on the issue and not divide my attention with worries about her, then perhaps I'll see my way through without losing all my hair."

He rubbed his hand over his thick thatch and leaned forward on his desk. "You'll keep me informed if anything changes?"

I picked up on the dismissal and rose to my feet. "Yes, Minister."

It pained me to have our conversation limited to such formalities. Hopefully, once it became clear what sort of impact my decisions had made on the situation, we could return to our easy camaraderie, but until then, I had to accept where we were.

I reached the door, but before I could open it, he called me back.

"I wanted to say I understand why you passed that information along," he said. "I promise that if you put your faith in me to find out who was behind the de Lauer incident, it won't go unrewarded."

It took a moment to find my words, his request leaving me too stunned to come up with a ready answer. "Thank you. Of course I trust you to do everything you can." I swallowed hard. "If I've ever given you reason to think I've lost faith in you, that wasn't my intention. What you mean to my family—to me… If there's any help I can offer, you only need to ask."

He nodded, and I left, feeling marginally better than I had since yesterday afternoon. At least he and I were on the same page, even if officially he had to pretend otherwise.

Buoyed by hope and Jean-Luc's steady assurances, I approached Phyllis with a more purposeful step than when I'd arrived.

"Jean-Luc mentioned complaint files?" I asked.

Phyllis looked down her nose at me, her nostrils flaring as she adjusted her sweater. Her dislike drifted off her as heavily as her perfume.

With a sniff, she jerked her chin towards the stack sitting on her desk. "The minister asked me to pull every complaint and related file from the past year. As if he isn't busy enough with the coming election, he has to run around putting out fires that should never have been lit."

Thanks to you, her tone said, as though I were the one planting ghostbombs around town.

"Why don't I save him some time and go through them," I said.

Phyllis's eyes narrowed. "I don't think that's necessary."

"It will save you the paperwork. I'll sort them, collate the issues, and draft a summary report of my findings."

Even without reading her, I noted her distrust, her irritation—and the precise moment when it switched to a vindictive satisfaction.

Good. Let her believe I was offering to do penance with tedious paperwork. It would stop her from guessing my true motive: to search for signs of O'Malley's reach within the public's complaints. If the syndicate was trying to destroy SMOAC's reputation, there would be evidence of their leaching darkness. Maybe somewhere in these files, I'd spot a pattern of public discontent that I could narrow down to a specific source.

"Very well." Phyllis cradled the two-foot stack in her arms and dropped it into my waiting grip. The weight of it nearly carried the stack to the floor, but I shifted my hold in time. "You can return them to this filing cabinet once you're done." She gestured to the open double-wide beside her desk, then flitted into Jean-Luc's office and shut the door.

I returned to my office, kicked the door shut, and dumped the files onto my desk, covering the work I'd been staring at uselessly earlier.

Now I had a goal. Surely that would be enough to keep my concentration fixed for a few hours.

But as I read, the complaints and stories of people affected by the recent unrest dragged me back to the thoughts that had haunted me since the first blast. People who had been evacuated from their homes around the de Lauer Estates and Dougall's house. Family of the fallen soldiers looking for closure.

So many problems, and so little being done about them.

Could I have done more to help after the first blast? Yes, I'd passed that information along to Jet, but then I'd stepped back and allowed her to get her hands dirty while I'd done my best to carry on as usual. If I'd pushed harder on my own, maybe I would have stumbled on the leak sooner, maybe the second ghostbomb would never have been planted.

Regrets were futile, but that didn't stop me from worrying

I'd waited too long, given the problem a chance to get bigger. Something about this whole mess didn't sit well with me. The fact that someone had been manipulating our informants. The fact that the syndicate knew Jet was asking questions. The fact that, out of curiosity and concern for my friend, I'd looked into what our security office had done with Gideon only to discover there was no record of him after yesterday's interrogation. It was like he had disappeared.

The department I had fostered and helped structure would never be so careless with its documentation, especially regarding the well-being of a person of interest. We were under too close scrutiny to try to hide anything that big. For decades, the prime minister's advisers had been pushing to cut SMOAC's budget and reduce our resources, and it was only by providing thorough proof of our needs and responsibilities that we clung to what little we had.

This gap, this written silence, around Gideon's status tied my stomach in knots, and I worried what Jet's reaction would be when I told her. Because of course I would tell her. This was something she would want to know. Something she would never forgive me for keeping from her.

I remembered how devastated she'd been when she'd come home from New York. She'd kept me up-to-date on the case as it happened, so I'd known all about the man she was working with. The FBI agent, as she'd believed at the time. They formed a great team, she'd said. The same dedication, the same focus, both of them understanding that the job came before anything else. Then she'd discovered the truth about who he was, and she'd crashed. She'd trusted him with so much, and he'd hidden a crucial piece of information from her just so he could gather what he needed to meet his own ends.

Although she'd never admitted it, he'd broken her heart, and I'd had to help pick up the pieces.

No wonder she'd been so disoriented when he'd shown up here, and now he'd lied to her again.

How could he be such an idiot? Especially when the emotions in both of them ran so deep. Conflicted, yes, but undeniable.

I wanted to kick the man in the shins, but, more than that, I wanted to know where he was.

If Jet never saw him again—never learned what happened to him—I worried she would spend the rest of her life wondering.

I pulled the hair off the back of my neck and twisted it around my hand as I tried once more to focus on the stack of files in front of me. I had to get through these and stop getting distracted. Somewhere in this paperwork could be the revelation we needed, something I could bring to Jean-Luc's attention without getting either Jet or me in trouble.

Not that I should have had to. Considering the manpower on this case, why hadn't any of the investigative teams found anything? It would be so much easier to convince Jet to get some rest and deal with her grief if the people in charge were more transparent with their methods. Yet they'd announced nothing. While it was possible the minister's office was sitting on something they weren't ready to make public, I would have been kept in the loop. Even in disgrace, I was the minister's chief of staff.

Their silence made me wonder if they hadn't found anything yet because the evidence wasn't there to find, or because they were too afraid of the syndicate to push hard enough to uncover it. Or if they'd found exactly what we needed and buried it. None of those possibilities increased my confidence that we would hear something from official channels soon.

I groaned and bowed my head against my desk, letting my forehead drop with a thud. Government wasn't supposed to be like this. There was supposed to be a clear distinction of who did what, every issue to be signed, approved, and moved up the chain of command. The minister's chief of staff wasn't supposed to be involved in criminal investigations, and ministers were supposed to focus on policy. It was the downside of carrying a micro-government. SMOAC had always been the central resource for our community, which meant many hats had to be worn and job descriptions were generic frameworks.

But we'd never dealt with anything like this before.

I waded through another dozen files before my eyes crossed, not finding anything that tied the complaints together except for the blast. I shoved the paperwork aside and pulled my shoes on. Tea. That was what I needed. Not an emotion-regulating one, but a good, strong, caffeinated one. And at this time of night, the line would be short.

I headed down to the lobby expecting to find it empty, so my heart jumped into my throat on seeing Colm sitting at a table outside Tim Hortons.

"What are you doing here at this time of night?" I asked.

He had a dozen forms in front of him, an extra-large coffee beside them, and a deep furrow between his eyebrows. I felt a strong desire to run my fingers over his face to smooth out the stress lines and clasped my hands in front of me to keep them to myself.

He jumped at the sound of my voice, and I felt bad about scaring him, but the apology faded from my lips when his face broke out in its familiar warm smile. "I guess I'm not the only one burning the midnight oil, eh? Things have been so busy I figured I'd rather work late and catch up without any interruptions."

"And then I come along," I said, smiling back.

He chuckled. "I never mind an interruption from you."

My heart pattered, and I excused myself to order my tea. On my way back, he caught my eye and nodded for me to come over.

"You in a rush?" he asked.

The complaint files called to me and the clock on the wall ticked away, but I shook my head. "Nothing that won't keep for a few minutes."

If my time on this side of the wall was limited, there was no one I would rather spend my remaining hours with.

"Care to join me?"

He pushed the chair across from him out with his foot, and I settled into it.

"Give me a minute to finish this one?" he asked, and when I nodded, he went back to his form.

The silence didn't feel uncomfortable or strange, as though we'd been following the same routine for years.

I didn't believe in soulmates. Knew for a certainty, in fact, that the whole concept was ridiculous. But I did believe there were some people whose energy clicked. All the grooves and ridges of their personalities matched, which made knowing and spending time with each other as easy as breathing. Sometimes they were the people you married, or the people who became your truest and longest friends, and sometimes they were the people you met occasionally in a coffee shop who gave you a chance to breathe after a long day.

After the week I'd had, I embraced the opportunity. I watched the way Colm's long, tapered fingers moved from one sheet of paper to another. I watched the furrow on his brow deepen and smooth as he concentrated.

And finally, I watched him tap his paperwork into a neat pile before he set it aside and returned his attention to me.

"Thanks," he said. "I've been putting that off all week."

"Ah, one of those. Always the lowest priority items that get set aside, until all of a sudden they're not as low a priority because you've missed three deadlines."

"This is what I like about you—you get it."

From the desire I sensed emanating from him, he liked more than my understanding, and my blood responded to everything left unsaid, rising under the surface of my skin, sending my pulse racing. The lobby was empty except for us and the cleaning service, and I wanted nothing more than to move closer to him, to feel the softness of his skin under my fingertips, to taste the coffee on his lips.

"What's today's fare?" I asked, gesturing to the pile of papers. I realized the hypocrisy of asking a question that could only ever go one way, but I snatched at any reason to stick around and talk to him. Any reason to stay away from my office for another few minutes.

"Preparing for some transition interviews. So many soldiers coming home needing help, and so many restrictions on who we can help and how far." He rubbed his eyes, and I sensed his frustration, lined with defeat. "You know those days where you see how important your job is because there are so many people who need you, but you *know* you can never do enough?"

I had to hold back a laugh. If he only knew how well that description spoke to me tonight. "You push so hard you think your head—or your heart—is going to explode, and in the end you still disappoint ten people for every one you help."

He met my eye and smiled again, this one full of compassion. "And yet we press on, hoping next week, next month, something will happen that lets us make the real changes we dream about."

"It's certainly what keeps me showing up at the office every day."

As though our chat were a balm on his soul, his tension melted like ice on a warm spring day. Not disappearing, but the harder edges softening, hope and comfort rising beneath his dissatisfaction. I wished I could do more to help.

"I have a hard time sleeping at night," he said, cutting off the rising tide of my longing. "Seven years since my last tour in Afghanistan, five since leaving the army, and I still have trouble getting through the night without waking up in a sweat." He ran his hand over his close-cropped hair and cupped the back of his neck. "It's why I'm glad there's a Tim's here that stays open as long as I need it. It's nice to know someone else is awake when I am."

"You didn't get that kind of company working at the hospital?"

After he'd come home from his final tour, he'd gotten himself a civilian job as a surgeon. He'd stuck with it for two years before turning to government and joining Veteran's Affairs.

"Not in the same way." His dark eyes scanned the empty lobby. "Here, it's a choice. There's something liberating about *choosing* to be up at all hours instead of being scheduled or ordered to do it. It's also quiet. I don't have a million people barking at me for every little thing. It's one of the reasons I left the hospital. That and the emotional and psychological strain. On tour, you see nightmares sure enough, but it's war. You expect it. The shit you see coming through the ER… It left a bad taste in my mouth. I think people are better than their worst days, and I want to be part of the good stuff. Hopefully my work at VAC will do that, even if it takes three times as long and winds up hidden in the archives."

I appreciated so much of what he said. It reflected many of my own reasons for staying with SMOAC instead of joining the Shadow Council. The desire to help the people who needed it, the feeling of doing something tangible and necessary. Of upholding Meril's laws on this side of the wall so she could stay comfortably on hers.

"What about you?" he asked, and the intensity of his gaze matched the open curiosity trickling off him. "Nightmares keeping you awake, too?"

I spun my cup between my fingers. "Not as such. Though they might be chasing me soon enough. Family troubles, mostly—one side wanting me to leave government and join the family business, the other side encouraging me to stay put and help keep things running. Friends going through a difficult time. Just trying to stay afloat. Be the calm in the storm."

It was the best I could do to match his honesty, and it felt like a weak attempt compared to what I wanted to say.

"I don't see that being a challenge for you," he said, the

warmth in his eyes stealing my breath. "What sort of business does your family run?"

"They do charity work, kind of. Helping vulnerable groups of the population get the resources they need to survive. Helping people who need to stay hidden."

"Like women's shelters, that kind of thing?"

"Along that line, yes." It was so difficult to navigate my way around these conversations. I didn't enjoy being cagey. Especially with Colm.

Maybe in another life he could have put his arms around me and held my pieces together until this trouble blew over.

But not yet. Especially not now, when the syndicate had stacked everything against us, leaving us no room to manoeuvre without making sacrifices.

"You've never really told me what you do for the government," he said. "Domestic Trade or something, right?"

My strength broke.

How could I sit here, smiling and pretending everything was all right, when even sharing this table with him might put him in danger? The syndicate was gaining speed, making informants disappear, lurking in every shadow.

"Just a paper-pusher like you," I said, aiming for a teasing tone. "I don't know what the government would do if everything went digital. I think we'd be out of a job."

I rose from my seat and dumped my half-drunk tea into the garbage. "On that note, I should head back upstairs and finish what I need to do if I want to see my bed tonight."

"I'm sorry," he said, standing up and taking my hand to stop me from walking away. The corners of his eyes were down-turned with concern. "I didn't mean to pry."

My heart twinged. How could he read me so well? His fingers were warm against mine. Solid. Steady. I never wanted to let him go. "You didn't. Not at all. But I'd hate to bore you with the details."

I hoped that would be enough to make him understand he hadn't offended me.

"I don't suppose you're in a place to reschedule our date?" He ducked his head, but found his courage and met my eye. "Much as I appreciate my luck in meeting you here at random, I'd love to get you away from the office."

Desire and regret kept me speechless, and again he read me—just not as well as I might have wished.

"Sorry," he said. "I shouldn't push. You'll tell me when—"

"I want to. Believe me, I want nothing more than to schedule something for Friday night. Dinner? A walk along the canal?" *Madison, what are you doing?* I ignored the voice in my head telling me to push him away. "I'm dealing with some sensitive deadlines right now, so I can't write anything in stone, but I'd love if we could make it work."

"Me, too," he said, though I read his disappointment.

"It shouldn't be much longer before my evenings free up. As soon as I can, I would really, really love to pick up where we left off."

I meant it more than anything else I'd said in the last few minutes. I had to believe there was a chance for this to happen, and when that time came, I would grab the opportunity and tell him everything.

His smile blossomed, his eyes brightening, and I sensed his rush of excitement, which stirred mine.

"Perfect," he said. "Sounds good. Great, actually." He shook his head at his awkwardness, then drew me in and bent to kiss my cheek. His soft lips tingled across my skin, contrasting with the roughness of evening beard along his jaw, and I closed my eyes to inhale the subtle hints of fabric softener and soap.

He pulled away, and I forced myself not to follow, not to maintain that brief, fleeting contact.

"Hey, and I'll see you at the Mid-Lister's Conference tomorrow, right?" he asked.

The Managers' and Administrators' Conference. Where he and I had first met and split the last carrot muffin two years ago. An anniversary of sorts.

I nodded. "Wouldn't miss it."

You're a fool, Madison Prince. A prize idiot. Let the man go and keep making your plans to run. There's no room for him where you're going.

I don't care, I told the voice in my head. *I refuse to give up on everything. Not yet.*

I wished him a good night and strode towards the elevators. In the face of the chaos whirling around me, I'd begun to lose hope of ever seeing the end of it. Now, with a vague hint of what might lie beyond disaster, I felt a surge of determination.

The department wasn't lost yet. We would find our answers, tear down O'Malley and his moles, and set everything to rights without the queen needing to take a single step further than she had.

And then, after the dust settled, I would go on my goddamned date… and hopefully not ruin everything by being honest with him.

Chapter 31

Jet

I SPENT THE next few hours driving from one end of the city to the other to avoid going home. The stench of Mitchel Lafontaine's blood lingered in my nose no matter how high I blasted the fan, and I second- and triple-guessed myself about whether I should have urged Mac to leave with me. The thought of him sitting beside Lafontaine's corpse, grieving and waiting, was too heartbreaking.

But he had made his decision, and I had to respect it. For my part, I had to decide what my next move would be. Excluding Dougall, we had six informants missing, presumed dead. Six more people to add to the list of casualties. An increasingly long list the syndicate had to answer for. Had the department ramped up their investigation yet? I glanced at my phone to see if Michael had called, but there was nothing. I debated calling him, but wasn't in the mood for another lecture. Not from him and Eric in a twelve-hour period.

As I turned the corner onto a quiet residential street, my phone rang. I answered the call, and Dr. MacDonald's voice piped through the speakers. "Captain Dawson?"

Without hesitation, I pulled over to the side of the road. If he was calling with bad news, I didn't want to lose focus and form an intimate relationship with a streetlight.

"My apologies for the late hour, but I thought you'd like to know Sergeant Evers is awake."

I jumped in my seat. *Zeke.*

"That's amazing. Thank you so much. How is he? Is he going to pull through?" Mandy's face, first flush with life then grey with death, floated behind my closed eyelids.

"He's made it through the worst of it," he said, and I heard the smile in his voice. "He's a fighter, this one. I don't see any reason he won't make a full recovery."

I glanced at the clock. Well past visiting hours, but there was no way I was going to put off seeing him. "Can I come now?"

"I'll let the night nurse know to expect you."

I ended the call and bowed my head against the steering wheel. Zeke was awake. Just for now, I would enjoy the good news. Reality would punch me in the face again soon enough.

After I gained control over myself and wiped the tears from my eyes, I pulled into the street and headed across town to the Peaview. Getting into the parking garage was too much of a pain in the ass, so I took the risk that bylaw wouldn't hand out tickets in the middle of the night, parked outside the building, and took the elevator down to the hospital.

Zeke's eyes were open, and he wore a lopsided smile when I walked in.

"What the fuck are you doing out at this hour?" he asked, his voice weak and raspy. His hand flailed as he shoved a magazine aside to make room for me on the bed and slapped an invitation for me to take a seat.

I bypassed the chair and made myself comfortable, careful not to nudge any of the tubes attached to him.

"You think I was going to sit around after the doctor called? Someone had to march over here and give you shit for taking your sweet time waking up."

He chuckled, a gruff sound, and his eyelids drooped. He forced them open, and his smile faded. "You going to tell me what happened, PL? I've been trying to piece it together, but my memory's pretty shaky. I asked the doc and the nurses, but no one will fill in the gaps."

I hesitated. Just like with the others, the last thing I wanted to do was slow his recovery by dumping the truth on him. But Zeke had a right to know. He'd helped train our team. He'd taken point and led them into that basement. Beating himself up trying to remember wouldn't make things easier for him.

So I told him the basics, breaking the news in small doses. I started from the moment he'd turned the chair around to Mandy's final moments.

"Fuck," he said, and wiped the tears from his cheeks. "Ten?"

I could only nod. I'd been sitting with the number for days, but it struck me with fresh pain to hear him say it.

"The others are doing great," I said, wanting him to focus on what we still had. "They're waiting for you to let them know you're all right. Some of them are a few doors down, already on their feet and making you look bad."

"I'll make sure to go say hi," he said without inflection, an automatic response. He was still processing, and I gave him a few minutes to sit with the shock. Finally, he raised his eyes to mine, and rage burned in their depths alongside his grief, a look I knew all too well. The same one I caught staring back at me in the mirror. "Do they know who did it?"

"Not yet, but I'm working on it. The colonel's telling me to stand down, but I won't. I can't."

Zeke stared at me a moment longer, then jerked his chin in a nod as he wrapped his fingers around mine. "If anyone can settle the score for the squad, it's you."

I squeezed his hand, and the return pressure was weak. Our conversation, short as it had been, had taken its toll. A moment later, his eyes closed, and his breaths evened into a steady rise and fall. For a while, I stayed where I was, holding on to him and replaying his last words.

Michael was wrong, and so was Eric. I wasn't losing my team. They needed me to keep fighting for them. They needed to believe their captain would go to any lengths to stand up for them and protect them. If I dropped out now, they would forgive me, but I wouldn't be the same packleader that had led them this far.

So where did I go next?

I thought of Rourke's message. *M.O. + ? Think big.* The M.O. had to be Mark O'Malley, but who was the question mark? Had Rourke known but not felt safe writing it down? In his last moments, I bet he wished he had. *Think big.* Bigger than the syndicate? Who else might be in town, hiding in the shadows?

It had to be someone with access to government files. Files that contained the names and locations of our informants and who knew what else. If that were the case, then I was dealing with something way more serious than a drug-smuggling crime organization, something I couldn't see clearly yet, though with every step, I was getting closer.

My thoughts flew to Gideon before I could stop them. Would he have any idea who the question mark was? If he did, would it matter? He wasn't here to ask, and even if he were, how much could I trust him to tell me the truth?

I felt as though I were standing over a chasm—a dark, yawning crack—with no idea how deep it went, and all it would take was one misstep for me to fall headfirst into it.

Chapter 32

Madison

I RETURNED TO the office no more clear-headed than when I'd left. My few sips of tea had woken me up, but my chat with Colm had sent my thoughts spinning in a million directions. I knew it would be smarter for me to call it a night and come back tomorrow with fresh eyes, but fear and my new wave of motivation pushed me to stay until I'd finished at least a first pass on these files.

Silence had settled on the floor. It was closing in on ten o'clock and everyone else had gone home. Smart people.

To try to get my head on straight, I brewed a cup of my grandmother's tea. As it steeped, the floral scent of herbs drifted through the tangled knots in my brain, and my first sip was like a much-needed hug. I wrapped my palms around my mug and turned my attention to the paperwork arranged across the desk.

So far the pattern I was hoping to find amid the complaints hadn't revealed itself, but I'd only made it through half of them, at the same time putting together the summary report I'd promised Phyllis in the hopes that writing out my analysis would help me see something my fatigued eyes missed.

I kicked off my shoes, sipped my tea, and started on the next complaint to be organized, prioritized, and collated. As I flipped through the files to get my bearings, I stumbled across project proposals and permit requests from nine months ago mixed in with the current complaints. I had to assume they were supposed to be here—Phyllis was many obnoxious things, but she was also a loyal and organized EA. She would have pulled everything Jean-Luc had asked her to. Were they attached to one of the complaints? I set them aside and kept reading, figuring I would discover where they fit in eventually.

Some complaints were straightforward enough—citizens angry about the lack of resources, frustrated that their community requests were being ignored. Gradually, however, the project proposals made sense, being plans that would have met those community requests but that had never been completed because of one excuse after another. Insufficient funds. An inability to acquire the necessary permits. All things that could have been overcome with a little effort.

Another batch of complaints had been annexed to a recent assessment of resource gaps in the community. Jean-Luc had tasked the assessment almost a year ago, and it looked like, after a half-dozen delays, we had finally received the report. I pulled the document forward with interest.

Someone had been thorough enough to package everything together in a neat docket, with additional related briefing notes and meeting debriefs included along with the official report. I set the extra material aside and perused the initial findings. If the supernatural media was to be believed, the current community outcry was over a lack of support on both sides of the wall, and this report went some way towards backing up their claims. Drug activity had increased significantly over the past decade with no increased outreach to help with either addiction or prevention. There was a lack of safe housing, and what existed was expensive and poorly maintained. Those who could afford to purchase a home in the current market were few compared to the groups who needed to rent, and rentals that mixed mundane and supernatural could be challenging for families with young children or for people who had a harder time hiding their true natures. The government had promised dedicated supernatural housing, and so far had come up short.

Health issues, discrimination, insufficient programs, lack of community resources… In every category, there were a dozen ways we were failing our people.

Which struck me as odd.

Out of curiosity, I returned to the program funding requests I'd set aside and laid them out beside the report. The assessment flagged a lack of community counselling services in major cities across the country, but the minister had funded a program to fill that gap a year ago. Another flag came from Calgary about challenges to social well-being for supernatural seniors and children, but I found a funding request for a community centre that included before- and after-school care for children, as well as community courses in how to fit into the world, how to use magical abilities safely and unseen, and how to complete the necessary paperwork to qualify for supernatural-only benefits.

Construction of the building had begun six months after the money was received but had been interrupted due to financial shortages. I scanned the funding request again. The millions of dollars requested should have been more than enough to finish construction at the very least. Where the hell had the money gone?

I switched back to the assessment package and skimmed through some of the additional information. The added reports included recommendations to resolve the highlighted issues. Lucien had initialled beside three as his proposed priorities—one to bring more supernatural counsellors into schools and existing community centres; one to create subsidies to help those who were less well off afford housing; and one to enter into conversation with a group called the Federation of Supernatural Affairs, a third-party organization that offered support services for supernatural communities. Based on the decision page, Jean-Luc had approved the first two and declined the third, with a note that such matters were best kept within the department.

At one time I might have agreed with him, but considering the problems we now faced, I debated the wisdom of his choice.

I'd never heard of the group before, and when I searched for them online, I found only a landing page with their mandate and a phone number. According to their small blurb, they'd been founded in 1987 in Switzerland and were committed to the betterment of the global supernatural population, promising benefits packages, international health care, and 24/7 resources to all member-countries.

If the group was legitimate, why had Jean-Luc been so quick to dismiss them? Had he listened to what they offered before he'd declined?

I set the assessment aside to review with him in the morning, then turned to the other flagged issues in the report.

But the longer I read, the more uncomfortable I became. Most of the issues and recommendations were related to matters I was familiar with, having negotiated terms with project leaders. I'd helped create business plans for some of these groups to ensure their projects got off on strong footing.

In earnest now, I went through the pile of cancelled projects and discovered that over two dozen funding requests that had crossed the minister's desk in the past year were for programs or services that would have filled the gaps detected by the assessment.

The requests themselves didn't go into detail about why the projects had failed, focusing only on rising costs and inflation. I tried to read between the lines to see what the real troubles were, but there were too many variables to consider.

The discrepancies nagged at me, refusing to be ignored, so I brought the funding requests over to the filing cabinet where I kept copies of my past negotiations. One by one, I tracked down the original requests and proposals and laid them out on the floor, matching them against the follow-up requests and the assessment.

By the time I finished sometime in the small hours of the morning, my tea was cold, my back was aching, and my nerves were buzzing.

I stood up and stared at the picture I'd created across the carpet. I'd set out looking for a pattern the syndicate might have created, but what I'd found made no sense as far as a crime organization was concerned. For months, I'd heard about the rising dissatisfaction in our community and believed it was nothing more than the natural ebb and flow of politics. Next year was an election year, a time when voices were loud against the government in the hopes that they could get a party leader to promise something that would offer immediate and direct benefits.

Seeing the truth spread across the floor—that the department's standards and accountability had slipped to such a degree—turned my heart to ice.

Over a dozen projects that would have helped boost a vulnerable community had been under-funded, cancelled, or poorly managed. Accidents had happened on work sites; people had lost their jobs over, I realized now, conveniently timed scandals; the proper permits had been denied.

One at a time, it had been easy to miss. Projects often failed. There were so many moving parts, it sometimes took decades and several versions of a proposal to land on something that worked.

For there to be this many, all concentrated around isolating our people, leaving them dependent on whatever scraps were available, suggested a deliberate attempt to create discontent.

No wonder Obscuglas didn't want to do business with us.

The realization hit me like a solid blow. All those failed negotiations. I'd suspected a leak or some kind of smear campaign, but what if the truth was deeper and more terrifying?

That sort of political move didn't fit with O'Malley's business of extending his criminal empire across the country, but who else could be behind it? An opposing party? It was possible, but stupid. If word ever came out that a party had been so desperate to gain power they'd sacrificed the well-being of their people, their political aspirations would be squashed. That's not to say it couldn't be done, but it was a huge risk. Better to offer something more—have programs of their own in the works they could promise to grow if elected. As far as I'd been able to see, nothing like that had happened.

So was it the syndicate? Did O'Malley have his hands so deep in government pockets he was playing with our money? Our decisions? If so, he couldn't have done it on his own. He would have needed someone within the department to make sure his plans went through.

The implications turned my frozen heart to stone, and it dropped into the pit of my stomach.

My department, the primary focus of my life, had been infiltrated by a dark, twisted power. Everything I'd worked for— everything my family had worked for—had been compromised.

How did this tie into the ghostbombs? The attacks? Were they a way to up the ante? Shift the unrest from a lack of community centres to terrorist action? Or was there something more—something I wasn't seeing?

I slammed the assessment report closed, gathered my papers, and laid them out in their organized piles across my desk. The queen couldn't know. Something had to be done to stop whoever was behind this, but it would have to be done carefully. Quietly.

Think, Prince. I paced the length of my office.

What was I supposed to do with my suspicions? My thoughts went instantly to Jet, someone who would tell me if I were seeing patterns where there were none. Although she wouldn't be able to do much more than listen, there was no one else I trusted. As early as this evening, I would have gone to Jean-Luc. We'd spent so many years working together, fighting for the same causes, I never would have doubted his desire to keep his people safe and well.

But how had he not seen this? How had he, of all people, not noticed the problem? After signing off on so many of these funding requests, how had no red flags been raised?

And why had he been so quick to turn down Lucien's suggestion of bringing in a third party?

I was reading too much into it. I had to be. He'd been a member of this department for over thirty years. He and my father had fought hard to build the reputation and integrity of SMOAC from the moment they'd started here, and every decision he'd made since he'd joined the executive ranks had been to strengthen what he'd begun. Everything I knew about my job I'd learned from him, and never once had I caught a whiff of any sort of unethical behaviour.

But what did that mean? I knew all too well the duality of human nature, the secrets we kept hidden. Although I could read his emotions, his thoughts were his own. I couldn't take the chance that after all these years, there was a part of my friend I didn't know.

I dialled Jet's number and tapped my foot impatiently against the carpet as I waited for her to pick up. When her voicemail clicked in, I cursed.

"Jet, I found something. Get over here as soon as you can."

I hung up and dropped my head into my hands to try to

reduce the steady throb that had taken up residence behind my left eye. How was everything going to hell? How was my luck so bad that I'd been caught up in some kind of conspiracy?

And how could Jean-Luc be involved? *Why* would he be involved? I wracked my brain trying to come up with an answer, but the possibility that I was right was too strong a betrayal. My emotional side refused to accept it, even as my rational side demanded that I ask what other explanation there could be.

Before I could come up with one, a loud rumble sounded from the direction of the minister's office down the hall.

I froze.

That was strange. Everyone else was supposed to be gone.

Slowly, careful not to make any noise, I turned towards my door.

Although I could defend myself if I had to, I wasn't about to go out and investigate on my own. I would, however, call security. I wasn't taking chances. Not when the truth was starting to come together.

First, I had to make sure I wouldn't be taken by surprise. I had to get to my door and lock it. Most likely, Jean-Luc had forgotten something and come back to the office. Security would find him, and we could all have a good chuckle at my unfounded paranoia.

I licked my lips to work some moisture into my mouth and padded towards the door. My bare feet pressed into the carpet in silent passage.

The door was ajar, which gave me enough room to peer into the hallway.

A shadow dropped over the gap, the blackness hitting my eyes like a wall. Confusion left me disoriented—had someone turned out the lights?—and my gaze darted around, trying to find something to ground me. But as I scanned upwards, I took in the texture of cloth. Cotton. A black T-shirt. And above that, a twisted smile of someone staring at me from the threshold.

A scream caught in my throat. I threw my mind towards his, tried to claw my way into his brain chemistry, but a pulse like an electric shock shot towards me, throwing me back. The door flew open, and he grabbed me, clamping a hand over my mouth to silence me as he dragged me out of my office.

Chapter 33

Gideon

I^F I'D HOPED to gain a few hours' reprieve from Carstairs's blade, those hopes were soon shattered. It felt like no time at all before he returned for a second round. I'd almost been relieved. Waiting for him to come back had been as exhausting and excruciating as having him here. It had taken me all of thirty seconds to remember what I'd been dreading.

"I wanted to make sure I came back to wish you good night," he'd said. "Send you off with some sweet dreams."

Now, hours later, he was gone again.

Fever raged in my veins as I shivered against the cold stone, and I traced my fingers through the ridges and cracks in the floor to keep myself focused on anything other than the nausea. If I puked all over the place, I'd be stuck with the reek and mess of it until he finally finished me off.

What was taking him so long? Why hadn't Carstairs driven

his blade deeper and been done with it? He would have to explain to Sampson what had happened to me anyway—unless the toy soldier was in on it, which I hadn't ruled out—so why keep me around?

In my long hours alone, I'd narrowed the answer down to two possibilities: Either Carstairs was a sadistic son of a bitch who got off on keeping people chained and bleeding, or the syndicate wanted to keep me on hand in case they could use me against Jet.

My leading theory was a mix of the two.

As soon as I realized it, I turned my thoughts to escaping. There was no way to take off the collar—all my attempts had resulted in nasty electric shocks that numbed my fingers—so I spent the rest of my time trying to bypass its restrictions. I'd used my ability against all kinds of gadgets and gizmos in the past, and so far nothing had stopped me. It was a matter of finding the right weakness, I was sure of it.

I had to believe I could do it, because otherwise it meant I was at Carstairs's mercy, and I refused to feel helpless. If I couldn't find a way out of this collar—out of this room—alive, then I would turn my efforts to alternative solutions. I was not a toy to be chewed and mangled. Better people than him had tried to break me and failed. Either I walked out of here or they carried me out in a body bag, but it would be on my terms.

A door slammed at the end of the hallway, and I cringed, curling further into myself.

Who the fuck was I trying to kid? Either I found a way out of this collar, or I would wait here, hour after hour, day after day, for the next round of torture.

And while I was stuck in here, Jet was out there. Had she gone home as she'd been told? Was she in bed right now cursing my name, hating that she had nothing to do but obey her commanding officer?

Part of me hoped so, for her sake. The other part of me hoped she would keep pushing. That maybe she would push hard enough to learn about Carstairs. To find me in my waking grave.

If so, it had to be soon. I didn't know how much longer I could endure this cycle of anticipation and agony. This nightmare I'd found myself in was crushing me, and if my body didn't break, my mind would.

Heavy footsteps thudded towards the door, and I tensed. The door creaked open, and Carstairs grinned down at me. "Surprise, asshole."

Fear spilled through my belly as he grabbed my arm, and all I could pray for was an end, one way or another.

Chapter 34

Jet

I SAT WITH Zeke for a long while after he fell asleep, taking advantage of the quiet to sift through the thoughts he'd left me with.

In the end, there was only one clear path in front of me—I would have to go against the minister's edict and work with Madison. There had to be another lead buried somewhere in this building, and if anyone could find it, she could. I pulled out my phone to shoot her a text only to see I'd missed a call from her a few minutes ago.

"Jet, I found something. Get over here as soon as you can," her voicemail message said.

Was she still in her office? Knowing her, probably. For once, I was grateful she was such a workaholic.

I put my phone away and patted Zeke's shoulder as I stood up. "I'll check in later, Sergeant," I said softly.

Before I headed upstairs, I popped in to check on the rest of my team, but only Ray was awake.

"Hey, PL," he said, struggling to sit up.

"Stand down," I said. "I can't stay long, so you may as well be comfortable. I was here visiting the rest of the pack. He finally has something to say."

His face lit up. "Zeke's awake?"

"Just, and fresh as a daisy, the lucky bastard." I smoothed out a wrinkle in his blanket. "I told him what happened, and he's going to need you guys. It's rough on all of us, but at least we've had a few days to absorb it."

His smile dried up. "We're on it, Cap. We won't leave him behind."

I hated putting the burden on him and the others, but I knew I could trust them to check in on each other, pull each other out of the depths. That sort of loyalty, that sense of family, was what made the JetPack as strong as it was. As it would be again.

"Any news for us?" Ray asked. "About who did this?"

Wishing I had something better to offer, I gave him a wry smile. "I'm pissing off the wrong people."

"I said any *news*," he returned, and we shared a chuckle.

"Not yet. Nothing useful, anyway." I thought of Lafontaine's corpse, of Rourke's last moments. Nothing my team needed to know. "But the right people are on it, and I'm doing what I can to move things along. I think this is bigger than we thought it was, but—"

The door creaked, and the nurse started when he spotted me. I held up a hand to keep him quiet.

"I'm on my way out. Get some rest," I said to Ray, then left the hospital and took the elevator up to the twenty-fifth floor.

The doors opened, and the hairs on the back of my neck rose to points. My third eye pulsed with shadows coming and going, and I brushed my fingers over the ridges, wishing my screaming apprehension could be a little more specific.

I swiped my pass over the security panel to deactivate the alarm and stepped into the hallway, keeping my hand on the door so it closed silently behind me.

The office was too quiet.

I hadn't expected crowds, but the people who were here— through my third eye, I saw four shadows on this side of the building—revealed no trace of themselves. There should have been a clack of fingers on keyboards or the mumble of co-workers complaining about the long hours, or I should have detected no one at all. This strange in-the-middle hush set my teeth on edge.

With my hand on the wall to help me read my surroundings, I tracked the shadows, not wanting to be caught off guard. All four were on the south side of the building, two of them coming towards me.

I stepped into an empty cubicle to avoid being seen, choosing discretion over curiosity. If they were supposed to be here, they'd know I wasn't, and if they weren't, I was hardly in a place to handle two on my own.

The glass doors to the elevator bay closed, and when I peered into the hallway a minute later, they were gone.

Now there were only two people on the floor. Together, by the feel of it. A late-night office rendezvous? I hoped so, but with the way my luck had gone this week, I couldn't bet on it.

I patted the knife at my hip and, keeping my footfalls soft on the carpeted floor, made my way to Madison's office.

It was empty, but she'd obviously been here recently. There were papers all over her desk—a no-no for a security stickler like her—and a half-finished cup of tea on the table by the window. By the smell, I guessed it was her grandmother's brew. A rough night, then.

Her cellphone sat beside her mug.

None of what I found sat well with me. Forgotten tea, messy papers—something important must have pulled her away. I rested my hand on the stack of files.

Images sped past my third eye. *Madison wild-eyed, shuffling documents, pacing across them, shifting from one stack to another. Reaching for her phone and speaking into it. More paper shuffling. Head jerking up as though she'd heard something. Moving towards the door. Looking up.*

Dougall.

My heart jumped into my throat as I watched him grab her. She reached for the side of his head, probably to use her ability on him, but he smiled and hit her with something I couldn't make out.

I stumbled forward, my mouth filled with the metallic taste of terror.

The scene hadn't played out long ago, which meant she couldn't be far, and she had better be all right.

Regardless, I was going to kill the son of a bitch.

I returned to the hallway. The two shadows I'd sensed earlier hadn't moved, still on the south side of the building.

With quiet, even steps, I navigated a route that kept my back to the wall and away from the windows as much as possible. The minister's office was closed, but I didn't detect anyone in there. No one in the kitchen or in any of the five copy rooms I passed. The cubicles were empty as well. Obviously, the rest of the executive staff was smart enough to be at home by two in the morning.

I finally closed in on the shadows and found myself outside a large boardroom. One door was closed, but the other down the hall was ajar, and a male voice floated towards me through the crack.

"It won't hurt a bit," he said. "A mad rush, and then it's all over. Nothing to be afraid of, and you can be happy you're helping your people. The world will change for the better. Your sacrifice will be noted."

Dougall's voice, so earnest, with only a touch of mockery under the surface.

I peered inside and found him down on one knee, tightening a zip-tie around Madison's wrist to bind her to a conference chair. A white gag was tied around the back of her head, though at the moment she wasn't making any noise. Her head lolled to the side as though she were fighting to regain consciousness.

In her lap was a bomb. Attached to the bomb was a small clear bag of ghost.

Without giving anyone, myself included, time to think, I gathered the air around Dougall and threw him against the wall as I stepped into the room. He was dressed in the same sort of clothes he'd worn when Gideon and I had met him—baggy jeans, black T-shirt, and an oversized black-and-blue plaid shirt rolled to the sleeves. His hair was messy and greasy, and he carried a faint musty odour, as though he'd spent the time since his disappearance in a basement. Considering everything, I couldn't rule out the possibility.

In his hand was a metal clicker, and his thumb was on the button. Even though I had him pinned, this asshole controlled the situation, and he knew it.

"Put me down, or I let go of the switch and take the three of us out in a heartbeat."

"You wouldn't dare," I said. "Do you know who you've got tied up? What would happen if you killed her?" I hoped to bluff him out of his arrogant smirk. He couldn't be so stupid as to murder the queen's great-great granddaughter.

Uncertainty crept into his eyes, and his gaze flicked from Madison to me. "I—I'm only doing what I was told. They said if I killed the negotiator, the queen would be pissed I'd sacrificed her family, the great-granddaughter of SMOAC's founder, and she would tear down the wall and declare war to avenge her fallen kin." His sneer grew wide. "How did I do?"

I tasted blood as my heart rose higher into my throat. Apparently he could be so stupid. What the hell was his plan? Did he *want* to start a war?

"The note. Did you write it?"

Dougall smirked. "Not my style. I was just ordered to play along with it."

I swallowed hard and lowered my hands, releasing him. Scenarios ran through my head of running at him, of stealing the switch and punching a hole through his face. Every option tempted me with action, but I couldn't guarantee Madison's safety if I took a single step.

Dougall knew it, because he didn't hesitate to turn his back on me and crouch down to finish what he'd started.

Completely at home. As though he'd done it a thousand times before.

"You're the Ghostmaker," I said, the picture coming together as more pieces fell into place.

"You caught me." He said it without panic or concern, his concentration entirely on the task at hand. "I'm surprised it took you so long. I thought the bomb at my house would have tipped you off. I heard you were supposed to be smart."

It was like the nervous guy I'd met had never existed. His

hands weren't shaking, and his gaze was steady on the wires and filaments under his fingers.

I caught Madison's eye, and she stared at me with growing terror as her disorientation wore off. My heart thudded against my ribs and my palms grew sweaty. He had my best friend strapped to a ghostbomb. All it would take was for him to push a button and she would be gone.

"Why ghost? Why would you want to kill so many people?"

Anger set off a million other questions: *Why the bombs? Why my team? Why shouldn't I kill you right now to stop you from hurting anyone else, you twisted son of a bitch?*

I held back. Anger might get me an answer or two before he killed us all, but if I got him talking—calmly—maybe we could learn something useful.

Madison was fully awake now, her attention fixed on Dougall. She had to be getting into his head by now, numbing his emotions, making him willing to talk. But when I looked at her again, her eyes were full of desperation and confusion, and Dougall looked even more smug.

"Oh, I don't want to kill people," he said, never losing focus on the bomb's inner workings. "I want them to see the world like I do. I see how everything is made. Its complete chemical breakdown. I can separate things into their component parts and manipulate them. Reform them. Ghost costs me nothing but time to make, and the results—the results are beautiful. The truth of the universe revealed. The veil torn away." He grunted. "If some idiot fucks want to take too much and ruin the experience, they deserve what they get. For the wise, it's a gift. One they're lucky to receive."

I wanted to throttle him. Not only to save Madison's life, but to cut off his pretentious bullshit excuses for melting people's brains inside their skulls.

"You can't honestly tell me you think you're doing the world a service," I said, unable to stop myself.

"Of course I am," he replied, finally looking over his shoulder. "You have no idea what's coming. Change. Change that gives us the power we deserve. No more rules. No more chains. And your friend is going to help make it happen."

Smiling, he sat back on his heels and admired his handiwork, then he flipped a switch on the bomb. Red lights appeared on the display. A ten-second countdown as soon as he released the button.

"Thank you for making this so easy," he said to Madison. He rose to his feet and started towards the other door, the clicker still in his hand. "You'd better get out of here, Captain. Unless you think sacrificing yourself will make a difference."

I braced my feet on the floor, ready to run. He reached the door, and his smile widened, his haggard face lighting up as he tossed the clicker in my direction.

I moved to catch it.

He ran.

I started to follow, but a scream from Madison jerked me

back. The timer had started. Ten seconds to get us out of here. Dougall was already out of sight, and even if I ran my fastest and caught him, there was no way I'd make it back to her before the timer ran out.

The footage from Zeke's body cam played in my head. Friend fighting friend. Soldier fighting himself. Screams. Blood. *Madison.*

I grabbed my knife from its sheath and dove to her side. The blade snicked through the zip-ties, and the bomb tumbled to the floor as I grabbed her arm and yanked her out of the chair. My grip on her remained tight as I launched us through the doorway, and just as I slammed the door behind us, the bomb went off. The floor vibrated, the door trembled, and the clouded glass went white.

I froze, waiting to see if any powder came through the crack along the floor, but the boardroom had been designed for top secret conversations and the seal held.

We'd contained the threat, we were alive, and we knew the identity of the Ghostmaker.

Now I would have to accept that I'd let my team's murderer, the most dangerous man in the city, slip through my fingers for a second time.

Chapter 35

Madison

MY HEAD WAS full of static, and I couldn't stop shaking. I was in the hallway. I was safe. Jet was here. The man with the bomb was gone. I knew all this. Accepted it. But in my mind, I was still bound to that chair, the gag in my mouth and the bomb on my lap. The timer going, slowly ticking down.

As soon as we'd escaped the boardroom, Jet had taken off after the Ghostmaker. Dougall. A man I had encouraged her to talk to.

The moment she'd left my line of sight, my heart had nearly pounded out of my chest. I couldn't stop the tears rolling down my cheeks, and my grip on the wall was all that kept my legs from giving out.

It was only when she returned, her expression a dark thundercloud of frustration, that I realized I still had the gag tied around my head.

I raised my hands to pull it off, but my fingers trembled so badly I couldn't work the knot.

"Here, let me get that," she said, and she was so calm, so gentle, it nearly pushed me over the edge. This wasn't my Jet. I needed her to be strong. Untouchable. If she showed the sympathy I'd wanted to offer her over the last couple days, I would break. And somehow I knew I couldn't. Not yet.

Her deft fingers unwound the rag from my head and pulled it out of my mouth. I ran my tongue over my lips and teeth to regain sensation, then spat on the floor to rid myself of the taste of cotton.

"Fucker," I said, unable to offer anything more eloquent.

Jet rested her hands on my shoulders and looked me in the eye. "Are you all right?"

"I couldn't get into his head. I tried to climb in, but he blocked—no, he *pushed* me out. With this smile on his face like he knew exactly what I was trying to do. I couldn't defend myself."

The memory of my helplessness made my lips wobble, and I pressed them together.

She put her arm around my shoulders and guided me towards my office. "Let's get you home."

I started to go along with her. Her words made sense, and at the moment, all I wanted was some of my grandmother's tea and a place to sit down. I wanted to be somewhere safe where I could curl up and assure myself I was still here. That the bomb hadn't gone off while I'd sat strapped to a chair like some damsel in distress.

More tears threatened to fall, but even as my throat tightened, my earlier anger came to a boil, and I pulled out of Jet's hold.

"No," I said, and straightened my shoulders, forcing myself to stand tall. "We don't have time for coddling. I'm walking, I'm breathing, I'm fine. I need to show you something."

I led the way to my office, allowing my fear to wash away under the strength of my resolve. The revelation that had pushed me to call Jet in the first place had to be a priority over my terror. The only way to tear Dougall apart for what he'd tried to do was to shut down O'Malley, along with his operation and anyone in the department working with him.

Even now, I felt his touch on my arms, and I rubbed at my sleeves to get the pressure of his fingers off me. Forget tea— what I really wanted was bourbon.

To hell with it.

When I reached my office, I headed straight for my overhead bin and pulled down the bottle and two glasses from the shelf. While I poured, Jet leaned over the papers arranged on my desk.

"Is this what you wanted to show me?" she asked. "Is it linked to the idea you said you were working on?"

I handed one healthy glass to her and took a gulp of the other. The alcohol set fire to the back of my throat and burned all the way into my belly, taking some of the ice in my veins with it.

"To start with," I said, and grabbed the pile.

Within a few minutes, I had everything laid out on the floor as I'd had it earlier, organized so the connections were easy to follow.

"I wanted to find proof the syndicate was messing with our negotiations, causing major deals to flop. Thanks to Phyllis, I found my answer and then some. I was going through this satisfaction assessment, the report Jean-Luc requested so we could see where we were losing support in the community. Thanks to that assessment, the evidence is all here in black and white. Every time someone came up with a solution to one of our failings, something prevented it. Look."

I crouched by one of the stacks and showed her the examples I'd put together. "Report says we need more community hubs, like rec centres. This was a funding request a year ago for a rec centre to be built in downtown Calgary. This is the report, dated six months ago, describing the difficulties they were having getting permits, and this is a request for extra funding due to unforeseen delays, denied on advice that the department's financial priorities had shifted. Another instance in Vancouver, another here in Ottawa. Toronto. St. John's. Yellowknife. They're all like this."

The memory of my initial epiphany swung around to hit me on the back of the head, and a shudder ran through me. "I was working through what it all meant when I heard something down the hall. Then Dougall—he was there, at the door. Waiting for me. How did he know I'd be here?"

My vision blurred as more tears welled in my eyes, and I took another gulp of my drink. Jet reached for my hand and gave it a tight squeeze. I thought at first she was showing compassion, but when I looked up to assure her I was fine, her expression was hard. "Where did you say you heard the noise?"

"Down the—" My mouth went dry. "It must have come from Jean-Luc's office." What would the Ghostmaker have been doing in the minister's office? "How did he get into the secure area?" I wondered aloud. "There's at least four layers of security between the lobby and the minister's office, and he got through all of them."

Jet frowned. "Which means he had access."

My gaze dropped to the papers—to Jean-Luc's signature— at my feet, and the bourbon threatened to come back up. I didn't want to believe what was right in front of me. The desire to hide behind a monumental wall of denial was strong.

All those family dinners. All those nights listening to him and my dad exchange stories. That was not a man who would betray his country.

At the same time, all those deals that had fallen through. My failure with Obscuglas. He'd asked me to step in as a personal favour, and we'd still flopped the negotiation. Had it only been because our reputation had tanked without me realizing it, or had something been leaked to Desmond? Why? To make the department look bad?

I couldn't believe it. I didn't want to believe it.

But denial wouldn't solve our problem. I'd called Jet so she could help me piece everything together, see the truth. I couldn't hide from it because I didn't like what we found.

I drew in a deep breath, set aside my raging sense of guilt, and said, "This has nothing to do with drugs or the syndicate." I set my drink down and flipped through one briefing note after another to the decision page at the back. "The syndicate is a smokescreen."

"What do you mean?" Jet asked. She shifted backwards to give me space, her attention following each new memo I touched.

"This is political." I picked up the final briefing note. "All these decisions have held the community back. They've shaken the stability of the supernatural population across the country." I pointed to the scribble at the bottom of the last page. "And they were all signed by the minister."

Chapter 36

Jet

MADISON'S REVELATION LEFT me reeling.

The minister was behind everything? The bombing? The ghost?

"Why?" I asked. "Why would he do this? What could he hope to gain?"

Madison's throat bobbed, and my heart ached for her. This man she had looked up to, worked with, had betrayed her trust, and she had almost died because of it. I was amazed she wasn't screaming or trashing her office.

Instead, though shaken, she looked calm, and her voice was steady as she said, "It's almost election year."

As though she were telling me it was dark at night.

My confusion must have shown, because she added, "What better way to ensure a re-election? You let everything spin out of control and then, at the eleventh hour, piece it back together better than it was. You're the hero. It's the only reason I can come up with."

It made sense. A sick, twisted kind of sense.

But how could he have done it? The head of the department, the man whose job it was to ensure the safety and prosperity of the supernaturals in this country.

Traitor.

My vision flashed red, and the hairs danced on my arms as the glasses and bourbon bottle rattled and rose a few inches into the air. I sucked in a breath, fought to get myself under control, but it took effort. My horror at finding Madison strapped to the ghostbomb, having the truth wind up being so… disgusting.

Rourke, Lafontaine, my team.

My head throbbed, and I found myself on my feet, marching towards the office door before I knew what I was doing.

"Jet, where are you going?" Madison asked.

"To find proof."

"Wait. I'm coming with you."

I paused in the doorway and waited as she gathered all her papers and shoved them into her desk drawer. Once she grabbed her phone, I started down the hallway, and she followed at a quick pace.

"If the minister has taken this many risks for personal gain, there has to be evidence of it somewhere," I said. "What you found is a start, but it might not convince… whoever the fuck we're supposed to tell about this. Who do you go to when your leader is corrupt? Do we take it to the prime minister?"

Madison didn't answer, looking stunned and more than a little lost, so I let it go.

That was a later problem. For now, I planned to tear Bastien's office apart to find something I could use against him.

The door to the secure area around his office was locked, but I grabbed hold of the air molecules inside the security mechanism, shifted them until the latch clicked, and shoved the door open.

At the gore that greeted me, a recreation of Lafontaine's kitchen, I stopped short. Madison stepped on the back of my boot.

I wished I could prevent her from seeing what I saw, but before I could grab her and pull her away, she registered the mess. Her hand flew to her mouth to cover a small cry.

Bastien's executive assistant lay on the floor in the middle of a thick red pool. Her throat had been cut.

I thought I'd grown immune to this sort of brutality. At the very least, I thought Lafontaine's murder had numbed me to what the syndicate was capable of, but this scene hit me just as hard. Mayhem where I should have found peace, chaos where there should have been order. Had everything in my life turned upside-down?

"Jean-Luc?" Madison called, her voice cracking.

She moved deeper into the office, giving the EA's corpse

extra space.

The rest of the secured reception area was empty, but when I directed my third eye beyond the room, all I got was static.

I rubbed the ridges on my forehead to soothe the discomfort. "I can't see anything."

"You wouldn't," Madison said absently. "Security spell."

Well, shit. There went our chance to learn who had done this. I wished now I'd gotten a look at the two people who'd walked out earlier. Hopefully I'd have time to scan the area once we finished here.

Madison stepped towards the minister's office.

"Wait!" I called in a hissed whisper, not wanting her to walk in on anyone who might be inside. When she didn't listen, I rushed to catch up.

The glow of the streetlights poured in through the window, cutting across a room lit only by a small lamp on the corner of the desk.

On the floor, coming out from behind the desk, was an arm.

"No," Madison said, horror and panic filling her voice, her eyes, her entire posture. "No, no, no."

She was across the room before I'd taken a step, and the cry that escaped her, full of fury and grief, made me rush to her side.

The minister was on his back, his dead yellow eyes open and staring at the ceiling. His white dress shirt was soaked with blood, and a knife protruded from the centre of his chest.

"I'm sorry," Madison was saying, repeating it over and over as she tried to find somewhere to rest her hands.

I nudged her aside with my shoulder to distance her from her loss and get a better look myself.

The knife had plunged through flesh and muscle with enough force that the guard had embedded into his skin. Whoever had done it must have been strong. Strong and angry. And though he struck me as a lunatic, Dougall didn't fit either description.

I thought again of those two unknown people I'd hidden from. Had one of them struck the killing blow, then ordered Dougall to set the stage? Had it been a double-cross, or had Madison been mistaken about the minister's involvement? For her sake, I hoped so. It was always a tragedy when we saw our heroes fall.

My walking into that boardroom had ruined Dougall's plan, but even so, everything had changed. The minister was dead, we'd confirmed someone within the department was cooperating with the syndicate, and the boardroom was full of ghost.

My gaze fell on the knife hilt and the imprint near the base. At first, I'd taken it for a regular pocket knife anyone might have brought with them—a basic design with a four-inch blade, titanium handle. But the imprint, a SMOAC armoury imprint, shed a different light on the truth.

"Either we had a security breach in our tactical storage, or someone within the special forces has been supplying the syndicate with weapons as well as information." I didn't want to voice the logical third option: that one of my own had done this.

Madison froze. She raised her wide-eyed gaze to mine, and her mouth fell open.

"What?" I asked, though I wasn't sure I wanted to know.

"Gideon." His name came out as little more than a whisper, but she may as well have shouted it for the way it knocked me off balance.

"What about him?" I braced for the worst. Had Madison heard something since Eric had taken him away? Was he involved? I didn't want to consider it, but couldn't ignore the possibility. What if he hadn't come here to do a risk assessment or to track down the ghost? What if his motives were much darker?

Was that how Bastien had known so much about Silver-Guard being here?

"He's missing," she said. "I was going to tell you, I just—"

"What do you mean *missing?*" I didn't need her apologies.

"I thought you might want to know what happened to him once you calmed down, so I looked into his file. Eric and the recruit interrogated him, but after that, all signs of him disappear. What if—" Her hazel eyes dropped to the minister, and my stomach lurched.

My thoughts rushed down multiple paths as I tried to figure out where hers had gone, and I hoped the truth wasn't nearly as bad as the worst-case scenarios they landed on.

Had he gone from spy to assassin? Was it possible he had escaped and killed Bastien? Why? The reasons escaped me, but how could I rule it out?

There was another possibility: We knew we had a mole in the department. The minister had been killed with a special forces weapon. What if the reason Gideon had disappeared was because he'd gone the way Rourke had?

The idea nearly tipped me into a panic, but I breathed through my fear. I had to keep my head and think this out rationally.

If the syndicate—the minister—whoever was calling the shots—was cleaning house, if they'd killed Gideon, who would be next?

I thought about calling Michael to alert him to the danger, but he would tell me to stay put. He would call security, and I would be stuck here answering questions while Dougall and who knew who else were out there closing loops.

Not to mention we would be found here, alone, after hours, investigating a case we'd been ordered to leave alone, standing over the body of the minister, who had been murdered with a weapon that bore the same imprint as the one at my hip. We had truth on our side, but convincing anyone of the complicated reality when we stood as a much simpler explanation was not a battle I had the energy to fight right now. Especially not if I was busy worrying about Gideon.

Gideon. Every time I thought I'd gotten him out of my life, he came tumbling back into it. Dragging a pile of shit with him.

"I need to get out of here," I said. "I'll go look for him. He has to be here somewhere, and if he had anything to do with this…" I couldn't finish my sentence, the repercussions of what it would mean too huge to consider.

"You think he might be involved?" Madison asked, more shocked by my assumption than I expected.

I narrowed my eyes. "Why? You don't?"

"I would be very surprised," she said, and though I knew she was holding something back, I didn't pry. If she didn't buy my theory, that was a good sign he was in the clear, but I wouldn't believe it until I looked him in the eye and asked him. Or stumbled over his corpse.

My stomach turned, but I did my best to ignore the writhing dread. "While I'm gone, you stay here and call this in."

Madison would know what to say. She'd been attacked. She was the minister's protegée and the queen's representative. She would have a much easier time getting them to listen than a task force captain suspected of temporary insanity.

But she surprised me by grabbing my arm, preventing me from standing up. "Who do we call, Jet? Either Jean-Luc knowingly signed those decision pages because he was working with the syndicate, or he was played by someone else. We have no way of knowing the truth. If we call the wrong people, we won't be able to talk our way free."

I scrambled to come up with an answer. I was too used to

her doing the heavy thinking for me.

"How would they know we figured anything out?" I asked. "Even if Dougall talks, he only knows we've found out about him. We'll play dumb. The people involved will think we don't know any better, and they'll continue on as they were. Meanwhile, we take the time to regroup and go after them."

Madison met my gaze squarely. "If we do that—if we save our asses and pretend to ignore what we've learned—it means turning our backs on Gideon. Leaving him with them."

Her logic pricked my conscience, and I fought against it, impatient with her reasoning and the growing reek of blood and death.

"I don't see why that's true."

"Yes, you do," she said, not letting me hide behind my stubborn stupidity. "If we find him and set him loose, we reveal our hand. They'll know we've been digging, that we uncovered one of their secrets, and from there they'll be quick to guess we're onto the rest."

Fuck. As much as I wanted to argue with her, she was right. Finding Gideon, confronting him or saving him, would give away the truth to any lie we spun. *"It was so strange. First we found the minister dead, and then I just happened to come across the American spy who'd been squirreled away in an undisclosed location. A night for coincidences, I guess."*

I didn't see that story flying.

"All right," I said, my mind racing, trying to keep up as

the floor crumbled beneath me. "I can turn off the cameras. They'll know Gideon disappeared, but they won't be able to trace it back to me."

For a moment, Madison said nothing. She didn't need to. The challenge was right there in her eyes, asking if I would take that risk for him. I said nothing. At this point, I didn't even know if I could track him down. Or what state he'd be in if I did. All I knew was I couldn't let this go without at least trying to find out what had happened to him. I owed him nothing except what my conscience would allow me to live with.

Whatever she read on my face seemed to speak for me. She puffed out a breath and looked once more at the minister.

"I'm going with you." The faint tremor in her voice had returned. "We can make an anonymous call to security once we're away, but the fact is Dougall proved the syndicate has it in for SMOAC. We might have some wiggle room to look into this, but it also puts a target on our backs. I need time to lay out our options before I come forward." Her throat bobbed with a swallow. "Also, I don't want to be alone with him."

I took her hand and squeezed it. She offered a shaky smile, and together we stood up and headed for the door.

The syndicate had infiltrated the department I'd sworn my life to protect. Worse, someone we trusted had opened the door and invited them in. Now that we knew, now that Dougall had given away part of it and escaped, we were in the dangerous position of needing to prove the truth without the fingers of accusation turning in our direction.

But I wouldn't let it rest. Not while I still had breath in my body and the freedom to hunt these fuckers down.

Not while Gideon's fate remained a mystery.

Not while the fate of the entire department remained in jeopardy.

Chapter 37

Madison

I OPERATED ON autopilot as I left Jean-Luc's side and followed Jet through his reception area.

I felt numb. Everything had fallen apart so quickly. I'd gone from digging through paperwork and unveiling a conspiracy to finding my boss dead on the floor.

Guilt. That was one emotion I identified, as useless as it was.

On seeing Jean-Luc's signature on those decision pages, I'd jumped to the conclusion that he'd been responsible for all these disasters. Now he was dead.

I tried to tell myself the timing didn't matter—he would have been dead whether I'd pieced the puzzle together or not—but to have blamed him without him having a chance to explain or clear himself made me feel that *I'd* betrayed *him* somehow.

Even if he had been behind the attacks and the embezzling, the trouble continued after his death. Someone had killed him, and Dougall had escaped. Our best leverage to uncover the truth had been those decision pages, and now they meant nothing.

More people were dead, the queen would find out, and we were one step closer to a full collapse of the wall. Her wrath would overwhelm the mundane world, our secret would be out, and there would be no going back.

Like Jet, I couldn't let this go. Wherever the evidence took me, I would follow, now without the help of my minister and friend.

We headed down the hallway, but before we reached the elevators, Jet grabbed my arm and pulled me back the way we'd come.

"What—"

"Someone's coming," she said in a low voice. "Four, maybe five people. If you want to change your mind about facing this head-on, now might be your last chance."

I looked over my shoulder. There was nothing to give away anyone's approach, but I knew better than to question her third eye.

"We don't know who they are," I said. "For all we know, it's more of the syndicate coming to clean up the mess."

I didn't want to run. If I was wrong about Jean-Luc, then he deserved more than to be left with the people who'd killed him. But if that's who it was, he wouldn't want me to join him.

Unless, of course, he was the one who'd ordered Dougall to kill me.

Conspiracies. They'd always been fun to read about, but now that I was trapped in the middle of one, I understood the metaphor of a fly in a web. I didn't know which way to turn or where the spider might be lurking. The best I could do was watch my back and get out of here alive. After that, I could deal with the problem. I just had to get somewhere safe so I could clear my head.

My grandmother's advice to prepare myself rang in my ear, and, while I'd always believed they were unnecessary, I was never more grateful for the lessons she'd taught me.

We reached the stairwell, and Jet opened the door without a sound. Down the hallway, a door flew open and voices shouted to each other, too far away to hear what they were saying. If they were innocent bystanders, I worried what would happen if they opened the boardroom door, but hoped the clouded-over windows would be enough of a clue to leave it closed.

Jet eased the door shut behind us so it didn't click, and we started down. We didn't speak. In these stairwells, sound bounced like ping-pong balls, and there was always a chance someone might be in here with us.

I was glad I hadn't put my shoes back on. As cool as the concrete steps were through my stockings, we both moved silently, making smooth progress.

My heart was pounding hard enough to distract me from

the pain in my knees and the growing discomfort in my calves. It would look so bad if we were caught. We hadn't done anything wrong, but the fact that we were running away gave the appearance of culpability. If only we knew who'd been coming through those doors—whether they could be trusted.

We reached the tenth floor, and I swallowed a groan that we still had so many more to go. Jet, of course, was barely winded. If anything, she was impatient to move faster. I was slowing her down.

Really, I didn't feel that was a bad thing. She needed time to think. And to prepare herself for what we might find once we reached the detainment centre. I was glad I'd told her about Gideon, but worried what she would do if we couldn't find him. Or if we found him too late.

Bile crept up the back of my throat at the memory of Phyllis's corpse. *All that blood.* At least Jean-Luc had gone quickly. As if he hadn't put up a fight…

I tripped but caught myself before I fell headlong down the stairs. If he'd known his killer, did that make it more or less likely he'd been involved? No matter which way I tried to frame it, I couldn't reach any conclusions. I needed more evidence.

And time and space to sift through it.

On the sixth floor, we had to leave the stairwell and cross over to another. My calves were glad of the break, as brief as it was. Jet remained on high alert, closing her eyes every once in a while to let her third open, the lines on her forehead growing brighter, more pronounced, as she flexed her ability.

We reached the other stairwell and continued down. Fourth floor, third, second, first. I went for the door, but Jet kept going, so I followed her to the basement. Here, she let us out, and we crossed the parking garage. The pavement was rough under the soles of my feet, little shards of gravel stabbing between my toes, but I kept my steps light and only spared a brief thought for my favourite stockings. On my list of priorities, they were pretty close to the bottom.

"The easiest access to the detainment centre is via the elevator," Jet said, keeping her voice low as she scanned her field of view, "but it's also the busiest."

"Are there stairs?"

"One flight. Makes it less likely an open-minded mundane will find the way down. Now for a quick call to the security office." She pulled out her phone, went through her settings to hide her caller ID, and dialled a number. "Someone's attacked the minister," she said when someone answered, pitching her voice to the height of panic. "I think—I think he's dead. In his office. Please, send help! I—" She hung up and slipped her phone back into her pocket. "There. They'll call the detainment centre for backup, so that should clear our way for a while. Hopefully things are quiet enough downstairs they won't leave someone behind."

When a few moments had passed, she nodded her head towards the west side of the garage and led me to the stairwell.

As she opened the door, her brow furrowed, but she didn't respond to my quizzical stare. We were back in the echo chamber, so I couldn't ask what was wrong, but curiosity burned my tongue. Had she sensed something? I opened myself up to any emotional signals nearby and detected nothing. Nothing except Jet's barely controlled dread.

A moment later, she jerked her head forward, and I stayed close as she headed down. The deeper we went, the more uneasy I felt, and when we finally pushed through the door at the bottom, I doubled over at the gust of desperation coming from down the hallway.

"I think I'm going to be sick," I whispered, wrapping my arms around my middle. It felt like food poisoning—the mix of rage, terror, loneliness, grief, all twisted into one angry toxic cloud. I'd never experienced anything like it and prayed I never would again.

Jet couldn't sense what I did, but she'd clearly picked up on something else. Her jaw flexed and her hand shook as she reached for the wall. She closed her eyes, and her posture shifted, hunching in on itself, her expression hardening.

When she pulled her hand away, her body sagged, and her legs wobbled as she took her next step.

"Come on," she said.

Still hugging myself to keep my nausea at bay, I followed her. The shock of the emotional punch faded, letting me breathe again. While I feared what we would find at the end of the hallway, at least it meant someone here was alive. If barely.

I expected Jet to head straight for the line of cells up ahead, but she veered right into the security booth. And froze.

"What's wrong?" I asked.

"No one was here when I called." She brushed her hand over the wall, the desk. "No one's been here for a while. A day at least."

"Is that standard?"

The lines around her eyes hardened. "It really isn't."

The monitors on the desk displayed various sections of the detainment centre. One camera in the stairwell—which meant we'd had our five minutes of fame—one outside the security booth, and one in each of the cells. Of the ten cells, nine were empty. The tenth was impossible to say for certain. Either the lights had burned out or someone had turned them off. The ball that had formed in my stomach gave another spin, and I rubbed my fingers over my middle, wishing the comforting gesture were enough to ease the tightness and slow my heartbeat.

"No point letting everyone know we were here," Jet said, and her voice was strained as she attempted to hide the apprehension that clung to her like a sticky ooze. She sat at the computer and started hitting buttons. I stood by and watched the cameras go dark, one after the other.

Somehow, seeing our tracks vanish so easily made our situation more real than it had been a moment ago. Avoiding whoever had come up the elevator had been a passive manoeuvre. This, though… this was direct and intentional.

Somehow I knew that by shutting off those cameras, wiping the evidence that we'd been here, we had headed down a new path. One that might never lead back.

Chapter 38

Jet

THE LAST CAMERA shut down, and for a moment, I couldn't move. Hiding the proof of our visit was the easy part. A few wipe-downs to remove our fingerprints, a quick sweep to ensure we left nothing else behind, and *ta-da!*

Convincing my legs to take me to the cell at the end of the corridor, however, was a whole other issue.

Madison's reaction when we'd entered the detainment centre had been warning enough of what awaited us there, and the flashes I'd seen when I'd laid my hand on the wall had confirmed it. *One of Michael's recruits dragging a struggling Gideon to his cell.* From the fragments I picked up, Gideon hadn't appeared injured, but the flashes weren't recent, at least twenty-four hours old.

There was also a faint smell in the air. One that shouldn't have been there. The unmistakable, metallic reek of blood.

Or was the stench stuck in my nose from the bloodbath we'd found in the minister's office? Or even earlier at Lafontaine's house?

I was following a trail of grisly deaths, unlucky enough to discover them. To shed light on their awful reality.

But Madison had reacted to *something*. I held on to that above everything else. If it was Gideon, if he was alive and had nothing to do with the minister's death, we would get him out of here.

Once I was sure he was all right, I would kick his ass for not telling me the truth. If he had, maybe we could have worked together. Or I would have put him on a plane back home. Either way, he wouldn't have wound up here.

With that motivation, I pushed myself to my feet. From the corner of my eye, I caught Madison staring at me, concern written all over her face, but I ignored her. If I was going to stay strong enough to open that cell door, I had to detach myself. I was a soldier; this was a mission. There were no personal stakes involved, only strategy.

I also didn't want witnesses to whatever my reaction might be if I found him.

"You stay here," I said. "See if you can get rid of any other security footage."

"Are you sure? You don't want me—"

"If we erase our presence as much as we can, we'll have more time to plan our next move." Keep her focused on the task at hand instead of whatever worries she had about me.

Madison hesitated, but finally nodded and turned to the computer.

I steeled my spine and left the security booth.

The goal: get to the end of the hallway and open the door to Cell I.

It was a straight line and a sharp turn. Not difficult at all.

I drew in a breath and let it out slowly.

The journey down the long, silent hallway felt like an endless gauntlet, the walls lined with heavy cell doors specially designed to withstand the use of supernatural abilities and marked only with a letter and a small, covered strip of window.

Cell I at the end of the hallway and around the corner, squeezed between two others and far removed from the security booth. The door greeted me like a solemn soldier, the thick slab of metal guarding the man within. I entered the room code on the security panel beside it, ordering it to stand down.

The light flashed red. Access denied.

My stomach tightened, a tension that squeezed my chest, my spine, and everything within. The codes were supposed to be on rotation, a new one every month. It should have been changed more often, but the centre had never been busy enough to make it worthwhile.

Had I missed the turnover date?

I ran the schedule through my head three times, but the code wasn't supposed to change until next Sunday. Even if it had been changed earlier, all those with access were given the new codes.

They'd locked me out.

Movement behind me nearly shocked the heart out of my chest, but when I looked over my shoulder, I found Madison standing there. In her grey suit, in the dim light, with her face pinched and pale, she looked more ghost than human. I was more relieved to have her with me than I cared to admit.

Closing my eyes, I rested my hand on the panel. My head ached with the strain of pushing my third eye to its limits. Later, I could deal with the repercussions of today. First, I had to know what was behind this door.

Images rose and fell, and I allowed them to sweep over me. The recruit had been in and out a few times since he'd brought Gideon down, once in the past hour. It was only luck we'd missed him. I focused on the panel and on the fingers hitting the buttons. The vision was blurry through my tense concentration, but after the fourth viewing, I had it.

5-9-8-3-5

I hit the enter key, and the green light was a cry of success. The door slid open, standing at ease, and revealed the scene within. Light from the hallway spilled across the floor, and all my worries, the fears I had tried to suppress, burst to life.

At first, I couldn't believe the man Eric had shoved into the back of his car and the man in the cell were one and the same. Although he'd only been in custody for two days, he looked as though he'd been here for months.

He lay curled on his side, naked. I might have expected him to be shivering, but at the moment he didn't appear to be conscious. Almost every inch of him was covered in blood. At first glance, it didn't look like any of the injuries were severe, so many small cuts at random points on his body. When I stepped behind him, however, his back told another story. The skin was shredded, covered in lashes. Deeper wounds gouged his sides. None were fatal, but enough to take him down.

Around his neck was a collar we were only supposed to use during arrest and transport. A device the department had deemed inhumane for extended use.

"Fuck," I said, and fought down the nausea that threatened to empty my stomach of all the nothing I'd eaten since this morning.

"Meril have mercy," Madison hissed as we both crouched down. She pulled her phone out of her pocket and turned on the flashlight. The brighter light showcased every nick and scratch under the coat of blood and also brought Gideon back to the waking world.

He grunted and turned his head away, his body closing in on itself to hide from whatever new trauma he expected. The light must have turned on whenever the recruit came to him.

"It's all right, Gideon, it's me, it's Jet. I'm here."

I didn't know what else to do. I didn't want to touch him, not knowing what would cause him more pain, but I hated seeing him respond like a scared animal.

Two days.

What the fuck had they done to him?

All I could be happy about was that he couldn't have killed the minister, which meant I wouldn't have to return the favour.

Though, at the moment, I wondered if the soldier already had.

At the sound of my voice, he froze, and Madison tensed beside me. What did she sense? If I had to guess, anger would be part of it. And he had a right to be. I could have asked Eric to go gentle, to keep an eye on him, but I had turned my back. I had allowed this to happen.

Did Eric know? Was he a part of this?

I didn't want to consider it, but after what we'd found upstairs, I couldn't say for sure.

"No one else is here," I said, keeping my voice low and soft. "We're here to get you out."

I turned my attention to the collar, searching for the lock, and when I spotted the little flashing light next to the tiny key slot, my mouth went dry.

"Talk about waiting till the eleventh hour," Gideon rasped through chapped lips, the sound like sandpaper.

"I'll apologize later," I said, but was only half-aware of my answer.

"What is it?" Madison asked.

"The collar."

Gideon's dark eyes filled with terror. "You can't open it?"

My already broken heart shattered. How was he still sane? Two days of that electrical current blocking his abilities… It would be like a mundane caught in a sensory deprivation chamber. We weren't supposed to be stifled like that.

"It's not that. It's—" I reached into my pocket and pulled out the key I kept with my identification. "A month ago it would have been simple, but two weeks ago we upgraded to a whole new system, and now the keys are registered to a specific user. The second I unlock the collar, they'll know we were here. They'll know we know."

Two weeks ago. I couldn't believe it was a coincidence. Someone had known these collars would be used for a darker purpose.

I caught Madison's gaze, and by the worry that crept into her eyes, I knew she understood. All the effort we'd put into hiding ourselves had been pointless. It was as she'd said: If I released Gideon, we'd have the syndicate and the mole on our trail. More than that, the evidence would be right there to hand us over to the security team. The minister dead, the American spy freed. Any hope we had of playing dumb or talking our way out would be gone.

I turned to Gideon and was amazed to find the same understanding in his eyes. The anger was there, but so was the sympathy, the permission.

While they'd tortured him, he must have figured out as

much as—or more than—we had. And he was leaving it up to me to decide what I should do with him. Sacrifice him to save my own skin and maintain my cover as a semi-obedient captain, to either move forward with my investigation under the table or not, or free him and officially mark myself as a rogue soldier. Act against my department to try to save it from whoever was dragging it down from within.

If I stayed in hiding, I would be surrounded by people I couldn't trust, wondering every time I turned a corner if someone would be waiting for me with a knife in their hand.

If I left, I would have people hunting me down, doing their best to clear the way, just as they'd done with Lafontaine, Rourke, and the rest of the informants. Who knew what lies they would spin about me, especially as word spread that I'd walked out with a registered prisoner? To get answers, I would need to disappear and do my best to outmanoeuvre them. For that, I would need some damned good allies.

Fuck.

But from the moment the paths had branched in front of me, I'd known there was only one true option, even if the challenges were greater. I had no idea if I could accomplish my mission, but I stood no chance at all if my hands were tied. At least out there I'd be free.

I grabbed hold of the collar and fitted my key into the lock. A quick turn, a click, and the metal ring came apart in my hands. I threw it to the floor with disgust and handed the key to Gideon.

"Here," I said. "A souvenir of your trip to our nation's capital."

I expected him to drop the key with the collar, but he curled his swollen fingers around it and held it close to his side as he dragged himself first to his knees, and then, with our help, to his feet.

As of now, we had to be ghosts.

It was time to vanish, hunt down the rats, and set a few bombs of our own.

AUTHOR'S NOTE

This series was so wrapped up in my life for so many years and crossed so many influencing factors that I felt it added to Jet, Madison, and Gideon's story to offer a bit of background and context.

The idea for this book was suggested on a whim, almost as a joke, by a friend in the public service while I was working a government contract in 2018.

"You should write a fantasy novel set in government!"

The challenge got me thinking about one of my author influences, Charles de Lint, and how he successfully wrapped magic into our Ottawa home. If he managed to make our government town full of myths and legends, why couldn't I?

Within a week, I had over two dozen cue cards spread out on the kitchen table during my lunch break, each one filled with a character trait or a detail of what my Fantasy Ottawa would look like.

Staring out the windows over the city, watching the cars drive past in the reflection of the building beside ours, gave me the idea of Obscuglas and the need for supernatural-friendly windows. My walks to and from work made me think of the mers in the canal, the gnomes in the garden, the rundown buildings that have never been repaired or torn down. And the sinkholes that keep opening up in the city… well, they were fodder enough for a million ideas.

Year by year, these details built up, forming a world I

wanted to live in and fell in love with.

After many delays in publication, a few close calls at trunking the project for good then persevering, I reached January 2022, when everything aligned to release the book in July.

And then the "Freedom Convoy" happened. For a month our city was under siege by a group protesting Covid lockdowns and mask mandates and democracy. We were left to watch the news while the authorities rubbed elbows with the occupiers harrassing downtown residents with their noise and behaviour. All while a secondary group were blocking routes to the airport and forming pseudo-military barracks in a borrowed parking lot.

At that point, I wondered if it would be wise to release a book filled with terrorist actions, civil unrest, and armed forces. Tensions were high, emotions were raw, and the future was in question.

But then I realized that's the whole theme of this series, isn't it? To persevere under threat. To cling to hope when everything is in doubt. So in the end, I decided to go ahead and release the series this year not in spite of but because of.

We could all use a bit of hope when the world looks dim.

Thank You for Reading

Thank you so much for taking a chance on an independent author. We're living in a wonderful age where it's easy to upload a book to the internet, but that doesn't reflect the blood, sweat, and tears that go into making a book the best version it can be. It takes time, patience, perseverance, and to have the final result end up in a new reader's hands is the best reward. You are the reason we keep writing, so thank you.

If you enjoyed the read, please help support the author by leaving a review at the retailer where you purchased the book. Reviews make a world of difference for an author, helping us reach new audiences and bringing more people into the worlds you've spent time in.

For exclusive character content, announcements, promotions, and special offers, sign up for Krista's mailing list at https://www.kristawalshauthor.com/newsletter

ACKNOWLEDGEMENTS

Considering what a challenge this book has been, there are many, many, many people to thank for helping me get from point A to point Z. If I forget anyone, please know it was not intentional. This book would not be here without your input.

First, my friends in the public service for giving me the idea, for answering brainstorming emails about what superpowers you'd want, for lending your names to my characters, for giving me reasons to laugh and inspiring this supernatural love letter.

Alex Epp, public servant, friend, and first reader, for helping to guide my government structure and offering essential feedback on my memo.

Kate Sparkes, the reader I most trust to smash my work to pieces and help me seal up the cracks with gold, stronger and better.

John Wenzel, photographer extraordinaire, who listened to my proposal, ran with it, and made the experience of using live models for my covers so much fun. The results of his work speak for themselves.

Melysa Parent for being such a wonderful and enthusiastic Jet.

My Writerly author's group (Jean Malone, Angi Black, Mark Benson, Megan Paasch, Jennifer Iacopelli, Jennie Davenport, Christian Berkey, Sarah Blair, Tabitha Martin) for the encouragement, reads, feedback, and laughs.

Diana Gill, my developmental editor, who helped me see

what the book could become with some polish. And who recommended I watch The Old Guard, for which reason alone I'm grateful I reached out.

My earliest beta readers, Adam Brophy-Couturier, Andria Henry, Harvey Thompson, Aighmi J, for helping me figure out rewrite number seventy bajillion and finally nailing the first few chapters.

My incredible editor, Sadie Hall, who was encouraging and supportive and enthusiastic and wonderful, all while very professionally testing every tiny seam in this series to make sure the foundations were strong.

My final beta readers, Traci Otte and Wendy Smith, for assuring me I finally got it right.

Melinda Beck, narrator supreme, who brought my characters to life in a way I never could have imagined.

My family for their support and encouragement.

My wonderful husband who worked with me to sort out a schedule so our toddler had parental supervision—and who made sure I stuck to that schedule. Chris, you are the reason I can still do this job. And am fed. And showered. And clothed. And sane.

My beautiful daughter for being such a bright point in my day regardless of every other stress.

My readers. Thank you for being patient while I worked out all the kinks in this heart project. I hope all the effort that went into it made it worthwhile and you enjoyed the tale and everything coming down the line for our determined heroes.

About the Author

Known for witty, vivid characters, Krista Walsh never has more fun than getting them into trouble and taking her time getting them out.

When not writing, she can be found reading, gaming, or watching a film – anything to get lost in a good story.

She currently lives in Ottawa, Ontario with her husband, toddler, and epileptic blue heeler.

You can find her at www.kristawalshauthor.com or at the local Second Cup coffee shop... but only if you come bearing a Vanilla Bean Latte, half-sweet.

Other Works by Krista Walsh

The Meratis Trilogy

Evensong

Eventide

Evenlight

The Cadis Trilogy

Bloodlore

Blightlore

Bladelore

The Nayis Trilogy

Veilfire

Dreamfire

Cairnfire (coming soon)

The Dark Descendants

The Invisible Entente prequel novella

Death at Peony House

Song of Wishrock Harbor

Shadows in the Garden Hotel

Howl of the Fettered Wolf

Light of the Stygian Orb

Gods of the Stone Oracle